The Dance Band from Deacon Town

Published by Five Points Publishing
A subsidiary of Red Pope Company LLC
8272 East Chino Drive, Scottsdale, AZ 85255
(480) 607-7699 / redpopeco@aol.com

© December 2008

Also published by Five Points Publishing:
TravelSpeak by N.W. "Red" Pope (2007)

This book is a work of fiction based in part on factual incidents and situations. Observations and opinions expressed in this book are those of the author. Many of the names have been changed to protect the privacy of certain individuals. Characterizations of actual persons are not necessarily true representations.

Cover design by N.W. "Red" Pope
Cover illustration by Bobbi Hillman
Book design by Hillman Design Group, Sedona, AZ
Author's cover photo by Bob McBride

Library of Congress Control Number: 2009920768

ISBN: 978-0-9793104-1-6

Printed in the United States of America

www.DeaconTownDanceBand.com

PROLOGUE

Some 20 years after I graduated from Wake Forest College, I began to get a literary itch to write a story, an article, maybe a book, about The Southerners, a college dance band in which I was a founding member and the drummer from fall 1950 through spring 1953.

Periodically I would recall, and chuckle over, an incident, a certain dance job, a place, a person, something that reminded me of some of the best years of my life. Funny things, exciting and outrageous things, some serious and some stupid things, and typical guy things that could happen only to carefree members of a college dance band in those halcyon days.

Usually I would make a note of my recollection and stash it away, to be retrieved one day when I had the time to write it all down in some sensible fashion. For five decades I was too busy working in the corporate environment and being a husband, father and civic worker. Spare time to devote to writing a book was a luxury I didn't have.

From time to time over five decades I'd hear something about one of the guys in the band, or a former college classmate would remind me of a funny or interesting tidbit about the group. It was assumed that sooner or later someone would write *the* story, or at least *a* story about the band. Other than one brief alumni magazine article, no one did.

After 52 years in advertising and bank marketing management and consulting, I retired from the corporate frenzy in 2005.

Now, the one thing I had was time. Instead of a Royal manual typewriter which I had required most of my career, a Dell computer was at my fingertips. It was then I concluded that if anyone was ever going to 'immortalize' The Southerners, in fact or fiction or a little of both, then it might as well be me. I have a passion for writing, so after creating and publishing a humor travel-related book in 2007, Travel*Speak*, I commenced working on The Southerners' odyssey.

Fortunately, I located many of the notes I had made and found several photographs and newspaper articles. Then, in earnest, I began recalling actual incidents, putting a chronology together and remembering the names of players in the band. The more I did to research the times, the places, the people, the music, the nostalgia, the more fun I had with the project.

Over the three years I was in The Southerners, some 28 people played in the group at one time or another. Ten have passed away. But, happily, as

I located and communicated with the other 17 former players, now in their 70s, the challenge to complete the book grew. We all admitted that while the $12 we each made per job was a motivating factor, we really played for the excitement, the fun, and the adventure of it all. And each member of the band I contacted was quick to tell me that my call had revived many long-faded memories of some of the best years of their lives.

The Dance Band from Deacon Town is a documented, reasonably authentic view of reality some 55+ years ago. Although this work is fiction, many of the stories are based on real situations. I have taken creative license here and there to add a touch of spice, generous helpings of humor and nostalgia, and a bit of romance. The names of the actual musicians and several people and places have been changed for obvious reasons.

My descriptions and insinuations about the character and nature of a number of people in these pages are quite exaggerated and not necessarily what their 'real' counterparts were like. The story called for characters, heroes, villains and fall guys and it was easy to provide them.

I truly hope everyone who reads this book enjoys it. I wrote it principally for those of us in the band and our families, for people who attended the "original" Wake Forest College in Wake Forest, NC during the early '50s, and to rekindle my own memories of those special times. It has indeed been a labor of love.

Finally, since the story is told as a narrative in the first person, for perspective and authenticity, I have included a number of very personal stories, observations, memories and asides here and there. This is as close to a memoir as I am likely to get, so just take them in stride.

Now, its dance time. I hope you enjoy the music. We surely did.

N.W. "Red" Pope, Sr.
Scottsdale, Arizona
December 2008

Members of THE SOUTHERNERS Dance Band
(November 1950 – May 1953)

Original Members:

Bill Tomlinson, Thomasville, NC	*Leader and Alto Saxophone*
Roy Fulcher, Rocky Mount, NC*	*Trombone*
Al Dew, Fayetteville, NC	*Trombone*
Hugh Pearson, Pinetops, NC	*Tenor Saxophone, Clarinet*
Elias "Mack" Matthews, Laurinburg, NC*	*Tenor saxophone, Clarinet*
Jack Rogers, Hinton, WVA *	*Trumpet*
G.H. "Bud" Hames, Forest City, NC	*Trumpet*
Phil Cook, West Belmar, NJ	*Alto Saxophone*
Agammenon "Aggie" Hanzas, Asheville, NC	*Piano*
Anthony "Chuck" Lucarella, Trenton, NJ *	*Bass*
N.W. "Red" Pope, Raleigh, NC	*Drums*
Mary Finberg, Wilmington, NC	*Vocalist*

Later Members:

Pat Carter, Raleigh, NC *	*Vocalist*
James "Tiny" Mims, Greensboro, NC	*Alto sax, Clarinet*
Richard "Dick" Beach, Raleigh, NC	*Baritone sax, Clarinet*
Joe Taylor, Lumberton, NC*	*Piano*
Vander Warner, Jr., Wadesboro, NC	*Trumpet*
John Brock, Charlotte, NC	*Alto sax*
Barry Eubanks, New Bern, NC	*Tenor sax*
Fred Hastings, Huntersville, NC	*Bass*
Joe Mims, Raleigh, NC	*Tenor sax*
Kenny Jolls, Raleigh, NC	*Vibes, Sax, Guitar*
Johnny Carr, Goldsboro	*Trumpet*
Jack Upchurch, Raleigh, NC*	*Alto sax, Clarinet*
Joe Neil Ward, Raleigh, NC*	*Trumpet*
Al Boyles, Thomasville, NC*	*Equipment Manager, Drums*
Cary Holliday, Raleigh, NC*	*Tenor sax*
Tommy Huff , Asheville, NC*	*Trombone, Vocalist*

*Deceased

See EPILOGUE for post-Wake Forest biographical information on Finberg, Dew, Warner, Tomlinson, Pearson, Hames, Brock Hanzas, Cook, Jolls, Beach, Eubanks, James Mims, Joe Mims, Matthews, Hastings, Carr and Pope, and brief Obituaries on Fulcher, Rogers, Carter, Lucarella and Matthews.

Pearson entered Duke Med School in the fall of 1952. Warner left WF early in 1953, later received his degree from Virginia Commonwealth University. Rogers and Pope graduated on June 1, 1953, Matthews graduated August, 1953. Fulcher entered the service in summer 1953, returned and graduated in 1958. Hanzas, Lucarella, Beach, Tomlinson and Taylor graduated in 1954. Hames and Cook graduated in 1955. Brock and Tiny Mims transferred to other schools in 1954. Joe Neil Ward transferred to Duke in 1951 and completed Med School. Joe Mims joined the Navy in the summer of 1953, returned to WFU and finished in 1960. Eubanks entered the Army in the fall of 1953, received his degree later at VCU. Pat Carter graduated from Peace Junior College in Raleigh. Jolls spent fall semester '52 at Wake Forest, then transferred to Indiana University. Upchurch went to University of North Carolina Dental School. Carr graduated from East Carolina College with a business major.

Dedication

To Linda, my wife of 23 years,
who puts a song in my heart every day...

...and tolerates my finger drumming on
dining tables, steering wheels, and any flat
surface that will accentuate a driving beat.

In Memoriam

Roy Fulcher
Mack Matthews
Jack Rogers
Chuck Lucarella
Joe Taylor
Pat Carter
Al Boyles
Tommy Huff
Jack Upchurch
Joe Neil Ward
Cary Holiday

Acknowledgements

I am indebted to these many people who provided stories and memories, dates, photos, places and prices, the names of songs and venues, background information, printed materials, and computer technical assistance, all of which have been important contributions to this book.

Monsignor Gerald Lewis, Archivist, Raleigh, NC Diocese of the Catholic Church; Mrs. Joyce Pierce, Wake Forest, NC; Mrs. Mandy Stovall, *OUR STATE* Magazine, Greensboro, NC; Mr. Jim Bowersox, San Diego, CA; Ms. Traci Thompson, Braswell Memorial Library, Rocky Mount, NC; Mrs. Pat Lyon, Carefree, AZ; Mr. Bill Tomlinson, Wilmington, NC; Mr. James E. (Tiny) Mims, High Point, NC; Mr. Dick Beach, Durham, NC; Mr. Elias (Mack) Matthews, Honolulu, Hawaii; Mr. John Brock, Pawley's Island, SC; Claude 'Pat' Caviness, Capt., USNR, Ret., St. Augustine, FL.; Ms. Dina Dudley, Kappa Alpha Order, Lexington,Virginia; Mr. Bud Hames, Lake Lure, NC;, Dr. Edwin G. Wilson, Winston-Salem, NC (Wake Forest University); Wake Forest University Quarterly Magazine (9/06); Mrs. Julie Keiser, Raleigh, NC; Mrs. Clara Ellen Peeler, Charlotte, NC; Ms. Nancy Corbin, Public Affairs Office, Cherry Point Marine Air Station, Cherry Point, NC; M/Sgt. Chris Hansen, 2nd Marine Air Wing Band, Cherry Point Marine Air Station, NC; Ms. Rachel Hedrick, Henderson, NC Chamber of Commerce; Mr. Joe Mims, Raleigh, NC; Dr. Hugh Pearson, Mentor, Ohio; Mrs. Lynne Pearson, Mentor, Ohio; Mr. Ed Morris, Wake Forest Birthplace Museum, Wake Forest, NC; Mrs. Mary Finberg Spencer, Toledo, Ohio; Mr. Aggie Hanzas, Potomac, MD; Mr. Al Dew, Greensboro, NC; Rev. Vander Warner, Chesterfield, VA.; Mr. Phil Cook, Wall Township, NJ; Mrs. Linda Pope, Scottsdale, AZ; Mrs. Anne Henry and Ms. June Cooper, Virginia Beach (VA) Historical Society; J.W. Dunn and Barbara S. Lyle's book "Virginia Beach: Wish You Were Here" ©,Donnelly Co. publishers, 1983; Mr. Bill Batchelor, Rocky Mount, NC;

Hal Leonard Corporation, Milwaukee, WI; Mr. Alex MacFadyen, Raleigh, NC; Ms. Amy Morgan, King's Restaurant, Kinston, NC; Mr. Keith Price, Forest City, NC; Mr. Barry Eubanks, Fresno, CA; Dr. Kenneth Jolls, Ames, Iowa; Mr. John Carr, Raleigh, N.C.; Mr. Fred Hastings, Orlando, FL; Mr. Bob Carter, Rockingham Community College, Wentworth, NC; Mr. Joe Pollet, Radio Station WWL , New Orleans, LA.; Mr. Charles 'Bud' Parker, New Bern, NC; Ms. Ladye Jane Vickers, Raleigh (NC) City Museum; National Offices of Kappa Alpha, Alpha Sigma Phi, Kappa Sigma, Sigma Pi, Sigma Phi Epsilon, Pi Kappa Alpha, Lambda Chi Alpha, Theta Chi and Sigma Chi; Mr. and Mrs. Shane Farina, Scottsdale, AZ ; Mr. Steven Case, State Library of NC, Raleigh; Wikipedia; and The Internet!

Special thanks to my wife, Linda, and to my good friend, Dr. Marty Zais of Scottsdale, AZ, who read and edited the manuscript with professional objectivity and empathetic insight and made numerous positive suggestions.

The Dance Band from Deacon Town

Chapter One

"What the heck is a grand march?" Will asked the 10 of us in something of a panic.

We'd been playing about an hour and a half and just finished *Dancing in the Dark* when this husky, red-faced 40-something guy comes over to where the band was set up at the end of the gymnasium under a basketball rim. He walks up to Will Thompson, alto sax player and bandleader, and says: "We're ready for the grand march now, buddy."

Will didn't have a clue what the man was talking about. He knew there was nothing in the basic dance contract about a grand march, but it was clearly obvious that this guy was in charge and he was expecting us to play the march thing, whatever it was. And *now*.

I'll give Will credit. He nodded enthusiastically and acted as if he knew exactly what a grand march was all about. When the burly gentleman walked away, disappearing in the crowd of folks gathered at the other end of the gym beneath the sagging crepe paper and colored balloons attached to the other backboard, Will turned to us in the band, shrugged his shoulders and asked: "Okay, guys, who knows about grand marches?"

In spite of his seemingly cool demeanor, there was a hint of concern, maybe fear, in his voice. Fear we would blow this job over a stupid march thing, fear we wouldn't get another job to play after tonight, and greater fear we wouldn't get paid tonight.

Most of us just looked at one another with blank stares, but then Mack Mathieson turned from his front row tenor sax position so he was facing the rest of us and spoke loudly enough for all to hear, including Will.

1

"No sweat, guys. A grand march is where everybody in the crowd kind of lines up and then prances around the place in sort of a figure. Starts with one couple, usually the people in charge, and then couples join in and they all parade up and down the floor until everybody is doing it. I played for one at a big wedding reception in Laurinburg once. It's a togetherness thing…a group thing. We just need to play something with a lively march tempo."

Of the 11 of us in the dance band, seven were in the Wake Forest College marching band. They knew marches. I was never in a marching band but had played my street drum for a good many marches for various events in elementary school and Vacation Bible School. So we figured we could fake this grand march thing pretty well if we could find the right piece of music to play.

As it was, all our standard, store-bought arrangements were for dance numbers, not marches, and there was no Sousa score at hand.

Luck was with us. The day before, Will had driven the 17 miles from Wake Forest, NC to Raleigh to get some clip-on lights for the blue cardboard foldout music stands. For no specific reason he had bought five paperback booklets called "Handy Tunes for all Occasions." *Auld Lang Syne, Jingle Bells, Dixie, Turkey in The Straw, God Bless America, White Christmas, Battle Hymn of the Republic, Happy Days Are Here Again, America the Beautiful, The Anniversary Waltz, Happy Birthday…* sort of a just-in-case, potpourri mixture.

Well, it was just-in-case time. Open the potpourri.

Will started thumbing through that little paperback looking for something that could be played in march time and that the band guys could sight-read because we surely hadn't rehearsed any of them. Several of us liked *Happy Days Are Here Again* but Will said people wouldn't think it was `marchy' enough. Instead, he selected *Les Marseilles*, the French national anthem. Like we had ever played that little ditty before!

By this time, the crowd of about 300 alumni of Red Oak High School in Nash County, attending their annual reunion, barbeque and dance, were eagerly lining up at the other end of the gym.

Although we had played two Friday night dances in the Community Building in Wake Forest for the college's Women's Government Association, those had been 'freebies' to get experience. This was actually our first paid dance job; the first contract gig we had landed.

Herb Lupton, who operated Lupton's Music Store on West Martin Street in Raleigh and was head of the musician's union office (American Federation of Musicians - Local 500- James C. Petrillo, President) had called Will and asked if we wanted the job, even though none of us had yet joined the union. The band that originally had the job suddenly folded. Obviously, we were a last minute, last-ditch solution. We were anxious to launch our newly formed group, The Southerners, and figured a great place to start would be for some high school kids in a rural community where they hopefully would be more forgiving if we hit a sour note.

We were mighty surprised, and a little concerned, when we found out upon arrival at the Red Oak High gym that this assumed "little soiree" was, in fact, a huge, well-organized and smoothly-operated event that drew close to 500 adult loyalists, year after year, from this close-knit farming community.

There may have been only one red light in town, but these savvy people knew how to throw a major shindig. And they knew good music from bad music.

Although it was a mild early-April, most of us were sweating profusely — not because there was no air conditioning in the crowded, barn-like gym, but because our collective necks were in a tightening noose called The Grand March. We didn't want this one-night stand to be the *only* night stand of The Southerners.

Will handed a copy of the "Handy Tunes" booklet to Augie Zrakas, pianist, gave another to trumpeters Hank Roberts and Jud Eames, and another to trombonists Hal Dewey and Ray Fulghum. He, fellow alto saxophonist Norm Cookman and tenor sax players Drew Pearsall and Mack Mathieson, would share the other two booklets.

Bassist Anthony"Chick" Corella and I on the drums would keep the beat, no music book necessary.

Pressure. But Will stayed cool, all six feet and slicked-down black hair, as he stepped to the floor mike and boldly proclaimed, "Time for the grand march everybody."

Three hundred folks cheered enthusiastically and began lining up.

With that, he gave me the nod and I pounded out an intro to the basic march beat …dum dum…dum dum…brrrrrrrrr, dum dum… and hit the cymbal. Hank came in dramatically… he actually stood up and pointed his silver Conn trumpet heaven-ward in prayer-like fashion…and lead our cool, calm, collected, well-rehearsed and highly talented, non-union, college guys' band through about 30 verses, over and over again, of *Les Marseilles.*

The Red Oak Alumni marched and laughed, marched and shouted, marched and jigged, marched and clogged, arms entwined, to the steady beat, few having any idea, or caring, what the tune actually was. It looked like a march, it sounded like a march, it probably smelled like a march, so a march it was.

After the loud and appreciative applause ended following the grand march, Will, obviously greatly relieved, stepped to the mike and shouted: "Go Rebels!" To which 300 hot and happy alums, not a few having partaken of some local moonshine, responded: "Go Rebels"! And they clapped, whistled, stomped, and shouted some more.

Will quickly announced an intermission. The band exited a back door of the gym to get some air and a soft drink and find a convenient tree or bush in the darkness. Most of the merry-makers headed toward the punch bowl or the gravel parking lot and their trucks or cars for more locally produced refreshment.

In those days, the union rule was that musicians got two 20-minute breaks during a four-hour dance job. That was it. Whether you were Les Brown, Xavier Cugat, Tommy Dorsey or The Southerners. Just enough time for a Co' cola, a few puffs on a Lucky Strike and some bladder relief.

4

The union pay scale was $3 per musician, per hour. Twelve dollars for four hours. The leader got double. A non-union band at the time, we abided by the practice. Big money.

The remainder of the evening in Red Oak went smoothly although we had to play through our limited repertoire of tunes almost four times. Several of the alums boldly came up to the bandstand as the evening ripened to request songs, poorly concealing the potent clear liquid in Mason jars they smuggled openly into the gym.

"Hey, when y'all gonna' play *Dixie?*" one music lover asked loudly.

Actually, it was one of the handy tunes in the booklet but Will just smiled and gave a little wave with his left hand as we continued with our standard sets until we sent the final notes of *Goodnight Sweetheart* wafting through the rafters, ending the exciting evening.

The Red Oak Alumni honcho came up and handed Will a $150 check and praised the band.

"That grand march piece was terrific!" he gushed.

Will accepted the praise, graciously, and with a look of relief on his face replied, "We always enjoy playing for grand marches. One of our favorites."

It was just past midnight as we peeled out of our Navy blue blazers and maroon knit ties, revealing some very sweat-soaked white dress shirts. We hurriedly began packing instrument cases, drums, and boxes of music, clip-on lights, bandstands, and extension cords.

Cramming all the gear into the rented trailer hooked behind Will's maroon 1939 Pontiac 'Woodie' station wagon, and, with Ray's 1947 four-door black Chevy sedan following, The Southerners were feeling no small amount of pride and enjoying our brief success. We headed back to Wake Forest some 60 miles away.

Our two-car caravan motored down to US 64, north of Rocky Mount, where we pulled into an all-night café-filling station. We needed the still-tasty day-old Krispy Kremes and hours-old coffee to keep us awake for another hour or so until we arrived back among the friendly confines of Deacon Town, or Baptist Hollow as the campus was known in sports jargon.

On that early spring night in 1951, there was a big Carolina moon dominating the starry sky, its bright rays revealing some aggressive kudzu vines inching their way toward the cinder block building. The scent of early alyssum blossoms thriving in wood planters on each side of the screened-door entrance to the café helped offset the gasoline fumes from the nearby pumps.

Once inside the linoleum-floored eatery we grabbed seats at two tables and on three counter stools while calling out our orders to the obviously bored, sleepy and disheveled counterman.

Will patted each of us on the shoulder like a coach congratulating his team after a hard-won victory. He promised he'd cash the check and pay us on Monday, emphasizing we had made enough to cover the $12 for each player, his extra $12 dollars as leader, and have $6 left to go against gas costs and the $7.50 he'd spent on the "Handy Tunes" booklets.

We toasted each other with some very bad coffee in stained, cracked mugs. Champagne in crystal goblets could not have been tastier.

Chapter Two

"**A** dance band at Wake Forest College? Are you crazy?"

That observation was pretty much universal when we talked to friends about starting a dance band on the 25-acre, circular campus located astride U.S. 1, some 17 miles north of Raleigh, in the "forest of Wake County."

And, with good reason.

For most of the 117 years since inception, the North Carolina Baptists had run the school. Its primary focus since 1834 had been to educate young people to become dedicated preachers, lawyers, school teachers, and doctors. Like most typical small private liberal arts colleges, only a handful of various academic majors were available. The bottom line was you could get a bachelor's degree in arts or sciences in four years (passing an average of 16 hours in each of eight semesters) and a sound foundation for making a good living and life-long friends, if you applied yourself.

You'd also likely know the face, if not the name, of every student on campus, and the countless dogs that hung around the tranquil, magnolia-forested campus.

It was often said that if you had $400 in 1950, were Baptist and breathing, you could be enrolled and spend a year at Wake Forest. Being Baptist was not mandatory, but it could help if being admitted was touch-and-go.

The school's crusty, vocal and non-Baptist football coach, Floyd "Pinhead' Walton, was often quoted by the sports press as saying, "The only thing there's more of in North Carolina than Baptists are English sparrows and crab grass."

As for the school's athletic teams' nickname, in 1895 a student designed a logo in colors of old gold and black, featuring a tiger's head over the letters WFC. However, the teams were mostly referred to in the press as The Baptists or the Gold and Black. In 1923, Mayon Parker, editor of the school's paper, referred to the "demon deacons" in recognition of what he called "devilish" play and fighting spirit.

Since a group of elected deacons is the usual official board in Southern Baptist churches, and Wake Forest was a Baptist school, it made sense to the students to adopt the Demon Deacons name. Many were surprised, however, that the word "demon" passed administrative muster.

Until 1941, the Demon Deacon was "alive" in print and art treatments only; however, in that year a spirited student named Jack Baldwin decided the team needed a 'live' mascot to help energize fans. He donned an old black tuxedo and top hat, grabbed a black umbrella, all historic images of an old-timey deacon, and lead the student cheering at athletic events. From that time forward, a fierce, unrepentant-appearing Demon Deacon in top hat and swallowtail coat has been the sports icon for the school.

In addition to the well-known mascot, the little private school had its own unique, delightful character in so many ways. It not only grew on you, it became a part of you.

But, by 1950, Wake Forest College was in the process of significant changes.

The medical school, which relocated to Winston-Salem in 1941and affiliated with the North Carolina Baptist Hospital, was flourishing there. It was renamed the Bowman Gray School of Medicine for its principal benefactor.

In 1946, the Trustees of the College agreed to accept an initial offer of 300 acres of land from the Babcock family of Winston-Salem, NC in order to relocate the college to that Forsyth County, NC community. Mrs. Babcock was R.J. Reynolds' daughter. The family later added an additional 300 acres on which there were several buildings. The school's trustees also accepted a major cash gift from the Z. Smith Reynolds Foundation (Zachary Smith Reynolds was R.J. Reynolds' deceased youngest son) to financially assist the process.

The Baptist State Convention, private donations, additional Reynolds Foundation money, increased contributions by the Babcocks, and considerable funds contributed by the Winston-Salem area businesses and residents enabled the school to move forward on the proposed $27 million undertaking.

An initial, controversial proposal to rename the school Reynolds University following its relocation was discarded. In the 1920s, Washington Duke, head of The American Tobacco Company in Durham, NC, contributed heavily to essentially rebuild what was Trinity College and rename it Duke University.

In truth, from 1946, forward, every student entering school on the original Wake Forest College campus knew that his or her school would no longer exist physically in that forested grove in Wake County after 1955. It was a major decision that would obviously have widespread emotional affect on the school, the town, the students and alumni.

Within a few years the requisite monetary challenge was met and plans went forward to build the new Georgian-style campus, literally from the ground up, 120 miles to the west

As to the fate of the grounds and facilities after the college's future relocation, the newly-formed Southeastern Baptist Theological Seminary agreed to purchase the place, lock, stock, barrel and Groves Stadium. Some administrative officials of SEBT moved into the Music-Religion Building in the early 50s.

But these turns of events, all intended to increase Wake Forest College's financial base, enhance its academic potential, and broaden its scope of opportunity, did not lessen the enthusiasm, the spirit or the sense of belonging that had prevailed in the students for over 100 years. Life on the old campus continued at a lively, focused pace.

The end of World War II brought increased enrollment. More coeds were admitted. There was a new intensity in athletic competitiveness. Life on the campus flourished. Amidst all that was happening to change the future, in the fall of 1950 students lived for the time, for the moment, for the present.

Chapter Three

One thing that wasn't changing was the school's attitude toward social dancing. Many Southern Baptists, those of the so-called "hard shell" variety anyway, were anti-dancing, among other things. The assumption was that dancing, especially the 'slow' kind where people touched and held hands and all, was likely to create acceleration in testosterone/hormone levels, which would lead to sins of the flesh.

While this perception may have had validity on many occasions, and thoughts of sex certainly were entertained by imaginative and inquiring minds from time to time, doing anything about it was seldom an option for the vast majority of Christian-homed Wake Forest students.

Certainly, there were some students, perhaps many, who had the will and found a way. Rumors to that effect were standard fare on any college campus, but they were usually just that, hearsay, conjecture or, in some cases, just wishful thinking. Conquest stories were seldom given much credibility.

For the most part, social dances in high schools, and in many colleges, were held in a gym or an auditorium on campus and were heavily chaperoned by eagle-eyed and highly suspicious faculty and parents. College coeds had curfews to be back in their dorms and high school girls were required to be back home usually within a half hour after the final musical notes of those campus dances faded away.

Unless a couple sneaked out of an event early, and unnoticed, which would be short of miraculous (given the exit door and parking lot 'security forces'), there was little time for fooling around.

Additionally, most couples walked to and from campus dances. That process alone put a real damper on serious hanky-panky.

Paradoxically, the Wake Forest College administration annually condoned several major dances *off* campus, usually in Raleigh's Memorial Auditorium, under the auspices of the Inter-Fraternity Council.

Changing times and post-war attitudes notwithstanding, the school's trustees and administration stuck to their tenets. Other than an annual Sadie Hawkins Day square dance held in tiny Gore Gym each fall, there was no on-campus dancing permitted in 1950 for the 1,377 students, of which 238 were coeds.

Obviously, there was no thought by the college's power structure that a dance band was a useful, necessary, legitimate, or even acceptable activity. The 45 faculty members and dozen or so administration types, with one or two exceptions, were not exactly 'swingers.'

However, as the old adage goes: "Where there's a will, there's a way." Indeed, the neophyte band members known as The Southerners had the will, and were determined to find a way.

Fortunately for the hundreds of dancing-inclined students at Wake Forest, the town's community building was only two blocks off campus and available for rent for Friday evening dances. These events were usually sponsored by one of the college student organizations as a fund-raiser. They drew several hundred students every time. Guys came in coats and ties, and girls dressed in skirts and sweaters. Saddle oxfords and penny loafers were the must-have shoe styles.

Since there was an ordinance banning any alcoholic beverage sales, including beer and wine, within the little town of Wake Forest or a mile and a quarter of its city limits, social affairs at the Wake Forest Community Building were safe, sober and fun. They were perfect for students to meet new people and burn some pent-up energy, and as a test grounds for an emerging student dance band willing to play free.

There were nine national social fraternities at Wake Forest College, each of which held dances periodically in one of the two hotels in Raleigh (the Sir Walter or the Carolina) and the Washington Duke Hotel in Durham, 25 miles west of the campus. They usually booked a local big band for their special formal dances. The major orchestras around at that time were The Duke Ambassadors, comprised of students at Duke University in Durham, and the Burt Massengale Orchestra in Greensboro. These two had the big dance/prom field pretty much to themselves.

With the hundreds of high schools in the area plus the many other university and junior college campuses nearby (NC State, St. Mary's Junior College, The Women's College of UNC, Elon College, Peace Junior College, Salem College and the University of North Carolina, Chapel Hill), there appeared to be plenty of opportunity for another dance band to find week-end playing dates.

While small combo groups were increasingly being booked, principally due to lower costs, we assumed the market for large bands would continue to dominate for several years at least. If our main band was not booked, we could look for combo jobs for some of the players within the band.

As to the availability of musicians among such a small student body populated with Religious Ed majors and pre-Ministerial types, *especially popular dance music musicians,* the challenge was formidable.

The Wake Forest College Marching Band had a total of 50 musicians, excluding the director, the drum major (our own Will!) and six majorettes. The Little Symphony boasted 16 members, many of whom also played in the marching band. The College Choir had 39 voices and The Glee Club boasted 73 members. Most of these groups were more comfortable, and certainly more capable, performing *Onward Christian Soldiers* than *Stardust.*

Such was the setting, in fall 1950, when about a dozen guys, including Will Thompson, Ray Fulghum, Drew Pearsall and I, were in the expansive fourth-floor attic of the Kappa Alpha fraternity house working on decorations for the upcoming homecoming weekend.

"Baldy", "Big Bad Bob", "Uncle" Lynn, and some of the older

brothers who were WWII veterans, had been sipping a few Pabst Blue Ribbon beers, college policy notwithstanding, and giving us underclassmen uncreative direction, when Ray took his trombone from its case and declared he would rather play "some stuff" than paint poorly-drawn figures and rousing slogans on butcher paper banners.

Drew, Will and I had our instruments stored in the attic as well and, without hesitation, we set up and joined the impromptu jam session.

We had all thought about forming a dance band, even discussed it a time or two, but never took the next serious, time-consuming, money-driven steps. Now, in our sophomore year, we agreed there was no time like the present, for if we didn't make the attempt now, we probably never would. We had two saxophonists, Will and Drew, a trombonist, Ray, and a drummer — me. There was a lot of recruiting to do.

However, the first order of business was finding a suitable name.

Kappa Alpha, KA for short, was formed by four young students at Washington College (now Washington and Lee) in 1865 after the War Between the States, or The War of Northern Aggression, as some would describe it. Two were veterans of the conflict. After the war, Robert E. Lee became the college president. Those four men established KA on the strong and genuine moral and spiritual values and ideals of Lee and the preservation of traditional Southern culture. In essence, Lee was the "Spiritual Founder."

Thus, it made sense to the four of us, 86 years later, that the band be named The Southerners in honor of our heritage, and based on the band's territory of opportunity, which was North Carolina and nearby southern states.

There was some concern over the possibility of alienating potential band members in other fraternities with the KA-based label, but that soon passed as we agreed most guys would look beyond petty jealousies if money was involved.

The next priority was to recruit the necessary players to fill out the brass, rhythm and sax/clarinet sections.

Will and Ray, being active in the marching band, began to solicit recruits from that body and immediately hit pay dirt with freshman trumpeter Jud Eames; blond, husky trombone player Hal Dewey; and two bespectacled, dark-haired sax players, Norm Cookman and Mack Mathieson. Hal, Norm and Mack had played in high school dance bands, using stock arrangements, and were enthusiastic about being part of this new venture. The opportunity to earn some much-needed cash added immensely to their enthusiasm.

We were still short a trumpeter, piano player and bass player. And, should the need come up, a vocalist, preferably an attractive female.

Drew was returning to his room from class, walking past the Alpha Sigma Phi frat house when, through an open window, he heard the sounds of a very sweet trumpet. He boldly walked into the `foreign' territory, found Hank Roberts, and sold him on playing with the group. Hank, too, had experience from his days with a high school dance band. He had a powerful, yet smooth style and, importantly, he was tall, dark and handsome. This would not go unnoticed by ladies in our audiences. We understood we needed every advantage.

Hank had come to Wake Forest on a baseball scholarship and roomed in the Colonial Inn, a ramshackle, creaky three-story wooden structure just off the main campus that housed many scholarship athletes, including golfer Arnold Palmer. Hank's roommate was a fellow ballplayer from New Jersey, a short, Phil Rizzuto-type named Anthony "Chick" Corella.

Hank was aware that the outgoing, fun-loving Chick had played some string bass in high school. It took little persuasion to recruit his services.

He and Norm, both from New Jersey, were our only "Yankees," which admittedly didn't concern either one so long as "we aren't paid in Confederate dollars."

One problem arose with Chick however; he played bass but he didn't own one. This shortcoming suggested we either buy, borrow, beg, or rent one as needed. Buying was not a possibility. There were no places around town to rent one. So, borrowing, i.e., temporarily 'lifting' one for rehearsals and replacing it after the fact, was a definite option.

One evening after supper, I ducked into the Music-Religion Building to get out of a rain shower and wandered around the first floor waiting out the downpour. I heard someone playing show tunes on a piano through the open door of a rehearsal room. The songs were from *South Pacific,* featuring Ezio Pinza and Mary Martin, which had opened on Broadway a year earlier.

To be sure, it was not one of the pianist's current curriculum-based musical assignments, which suggested this player had popular music interests and could be our pianist.

Peering into the rehearsal room, I spotted Augustine "Augie" Zrakas at the upright piano playing from memory. Coming from a musical Greek family, he enjoyed playing popular piano arrangements of bandleaders Eddie Duchin and Carmen Cavallaro for his own amusement. Although schooled in the classics, he agreed to come aboard, principally out of curiosity.

Brunette Sara Winberg was in the Wake Forest A Cappella Choir, Glee Club, and Chorus. She had an outgoing stage persona, a smooth "pop" voice, had sung the lead in a number of high school musicals, and performed on local radio. We heard about her from several coeds in her dorm and when approached about singing with the band on a trial basis for our pro bono Community Building gigs, she accepted enthusiastically.

We now had two trumpets, two trombones, four saxophones, piano, bass, drums, and a vocalist. Not one was a music major, although Augie and, perhaps, Norm easily could have been. Only Mack, Hank, Norm and Hal had actually played in dance bands.

When it came to performing in dance orchestras, the rest of us had played along, alone, with the likes of the Dorseys, Artie Shaw, Guy Lombardo, Glenn Miller and Benny Goodman big bands on 78 rpm Okeh, Columbia, Bluebird, Decca or RCA Victor records.

In fact, seven members of the group were hoping to earn Bachelor degrees in business administration. Three were pursuing Bachelor of Science degrees, including one in pre-med and one in chemistry/biology. Two were pursuing Bachelor of Arts degrees, which included Sara, and me, an English major with a journalism bent. Will, Sara, Drew, Ray, Hank and I were sophomores. Augie, Chick, Mack, Norm and Jud all freshmen. Hal was a junior.

Hank was from West Virginia, Chick and Norm were from New Jersey. The rest of us were North Carolinians: Asheville, Rocky Mount, Pinetops, Thomasville, Fayetteville, Forest City, Laurinburg, Wilmington, and Raleigh. None of us had known each other before coming to Wake Forest.

This, then, would be the starting team. Over the next two-and-a-half years some would drop out, others would be added on a permanent or on-call basis, but for openers The Southerners had their players, assuming we would meld as a viable unit, stick together, and by hook and/or crook, find a bass for Chick.

Coincidentally with finding players arose the matter of financing the venture and establishing some organizational ground rules.

There would be music stands and arrangements to buy. We needed promotional flyers to be created, printed, and sent to prospects. How would we generate leads? How would interested prospects contact us? What would we wear? How would we travel and transport instruments and equipment? Who would be the leader? Where would we rehearse? What about a theme song? Would we only play weekend jobs? How much could we make?

Naturally, it was assumed that the band rehearsals and jobs would not interfere with schoolwork — an assumption that proved to be only partially accurate in several cases.

It was obvious no one person was capable of underwriting the band's start-up financial needs. Indeed, few of us had any money to invest even if we had wanted to. Since most of the guys absolutely refused to become shareholders and put any money into a pot to buy the basics, Will and Ray stepped up to the financial plate and "bought" co-ownership. Will's family had an automobile dealership and Ray's dad was in the wholesale grocery business so they borrowed money from their parents to foot the initial costs.

I didn't try to figure out what start-up expenses would total, but I recall Will throwing out a figure of "around $350" would be necessary, a princely sum in 1950 when gasoline was 19 cents a gallon, bread 16 cents a loaf, two Sears tee shirts for 59 cents, six bottles of Nehi grape or orange drink for 37 cents, a basic new Ford could be bought for $1,424, and a new house purchased for $8,450.

Will, six feet tall, slick black hair, tanned with chiseled facial features, and Ray, hefty-built at six one with dark hair and square-jaw, became co-leaders. Since he played sax and sat in the front row, with Ray behind in the brass section, Will got to stand up and front the group.

In a matter of days, the two entrepreneurial band owners contacted Buster Sharpe, a well-known local bandleader from Rocky Mount, NC, Ray's hometown. Buster was disbanding his group since many of his players were going into the military during the Korean Conflict, i.e., War. He was willing to sell his arrangements, most of which were stock, and very reasonably priced. Will and Ray bought the lot of them. There were well over 70 selections, three-quarters of them slow tunes, a quarter of them 'jump' or up-tempo tunes, with some novelty items like *The Mexican Hat Dance* and *The Bunny Hop* thrown in.

Will promptly ordered 12 medium blue fold-up cardboard music stands with a stylized white 'S' on the front and some clip-on stand lights from Lupton.

As to uniforms, that was easy. Each of us had a white dress shirt and a basic dark blue blazer although not the same dark blue color. Two of us had double-breasted versions, but who noticed when we were all sitting down? Will decreed we would all wear grey slacks. Subdued lighting at most of our gigs was a big help since there was a variety of pants shades and materials. Dark shoes, any style. In vogue at the time were knit ties, so seven of us bought matching maroon knit ties at Ben's, the men's clothier in Wake

Forest. The other four opted to use dark red ties they already had, none knit.

So much for 'uniform' uniforms. Fact is, each of us could have bought a complete new wool suit for $28.90!

Will had the Pontiac Woodie station wagon and Ray had the Chevy he had bought with money made over a couple of summers surveying tobacco. The plan was for six of us to ride in the Woodie and five in Ray's car. If we had a vocalist or added another player it was going to be even cozier in the Chevy.

For the first job in Red Oak we managed to put my drums and the fold-up stands in the rear of the Woodie, plus six guys on the two bench seats. Each man was forced to hold his instrument case on his lap or put it on the floor under his feet. Since my drums were loaded in the rear of the car, I was compelled to hold Will's sax case while he drove. The canvas-encased bass fiddle we had rented from Lupton was tied to the luggage rods on top. We carried the box with the sheet music, the stand lights, and a few instrument cases in the trunk of Ray's Chevy.

We found out early that it was no picnic being crammed together like the proverbial sardines, often riding up to two hours or more each way. It was especially bad on return treks since we were usually tired, sleepy, and either hot in the warmer months with no air conditioning in either car or freezing because of a faulty on-again/off-again heater in the Chevy. We drew lots to determine who had to ride in the middle seats. Body odor, halitosis and flatulation activity got old quickly. One benefit was we got to know each other very well.

Ultimately, we resorted to renting a trailer from Claude Taylor's Sound Company in Raleigh and often we needed to rent a PA system with amplifier, speakers, stand mike, and miles of cord from Taylor as well. The trailer helped alleviate space conditions inside the cars but did little to improve the air quality.

The trailer was also the cause of many jokes. The Woodie had what was referred to as a 'spring" rear bumper, meaning it had some 'give,' which apparently would be beneficially protective if it were struck from the rear. But when you attached the loaded trailer to the bumper hitch and started up a hill, or any incline of consequence, the weight of the trailer would "play" the rear bumper. The Woodie had minimum horsepower to start with and there were six bodies inside, so the added weight on the bumper created unpredictable movement.

We would ride about 200 or so yards and then the rear of the station wagon would commence to bouncing. It seemed as if we'd ride a bit, then fall back a foot. We kept expecting the trailer to pull the bumper right off the car, but it never happened. As a precaution, we affixed a chain from the trailer to the rear frame underneath the Woodie, just in case the bumper went. Drew suggested we only book engagements where we did not have to negotiate any hills.

Small challenges aside, our basic concerns were being met. Now all we needed were a lot of rehearsals, a theme song, and some paying gigs.

Chapter Four

You would think finding a place to rehearse, especially in a town of only 3,000 people with a single main business street, would be a snap. We needed only some space, lights, and a piano. Not even a restroom. Heat would be nice (but not a requisite) since this musical mission started in the winter. Maybe just two hours, one or two nights a week.

The search began.

First, we ruled out the Community Building and the local schools since they required hefty rent and were not always available on our schedule. There were several churches around, including Baptist, but we soon learned they were not options. Chick was convinced it was some sort of religious conspiracy against us. We drove every principal street in town searching for space and even talked with the funeral home director about using his chapel on "off nights." I recall Ray suggesting to the somber gentleman that we would play a couple of his 'events' free in exchange for rehearsal rights. The fellow was not amused.

The options were narrowing down to something on campus, which came with major risk since we were a 'sub rosa' organization at best. Nonetheless, we began a piano census.

Of the 15 principal buildings comprising the overall Wake Forest campus, one was a two-story frame house that served as the Infirmary (built in 1906 as the hospital) and another was the crackerbox-sized, 1935-vintage Gore Gymnasium with the basketball court, athletic department and physical education classrooms.

When opened fully, the collapsible stands in the gym came so close to the actual boundaries of the basketball court that players taking the ball out of bounds had to be careful where they stood. It became a ritual for a number of the Deacon football players to sit on the first row and when opposing players stood to throw the ball back inbounds, they would pull the hairs on their legs. Home court advantage.

They especially went after Duke's Dick Groat, Carolina's Vince Grimaldi and State's Dick Dickey. They even good-naturedly pulled hair from our own Boo Corey and Al McCotter. All the complaining by the players to the demonstrative referee Lou Bello or his associate, Jim Mills, was in vain.

A third facility was the ivy-covered, two-story Heck-Williams Building, built in 1878, that served both the library and law school. No piano. There was the handsome brick Georgian-style 2,400-seat chapel, completed in 1949, which also housed the School of Business Administration and ROTC classrooms on the lower level. It had a baby grand on stage, but there was no way we would get to rehearse there. Behind the chapel, to the east, standing over a paved walkway from the campus leading into town, was the revered stone arch, funded by the Class of 1909.

Across from the chapel, to the west, some 200 yards away, stood three-story Wait Hall, location of the administrative offices and classrooms for philosophy, psychology, languages, math and education, plus halls for the two literary societies, the Euzelian and the Philomathesian. It was also the site of the campus bell, which was tolled at a casual tempo for class changes, and vigorously for Wake Forest athletic victories, but no piano.

Four other campus buildings were the Music and Religion Building (completed in 1942), and the piano-less Lea Laboratory or Chemistry Building (built in 1888), the William Amos Johnson Biology Building (built in 1933), and the three-story Alumni Building (1906). It housed the English Department, plus related courses in journalism, public speaking, drama, literature, and art history on the top two floors, with physics courses on the ground floor.

The Alumni Building was widely known for its three flights of creaking wooden stairs, and for the number and variety of dogs that lounged on its front stone steps, under which a cadaver had been secretly placed in new concrete as a prank in 1919 according to my dad (a 1921 WFC grad). No one ever saw, or smelled, any proof to confirm this rumor, however.

Situated centrally in the circular campus was a 1901 two-story edifice, originally used as a gymnasium on the upper level. The lower level had athletic team showers/dressing rooms and a dissecting room for the School of Medicine. Apparently, the famous Alumni Building cadaver had been secretly removed from this area.

In 1935, the School of Medicine and its dissecting room were relocated to the Johnson Building. The old facility was re-named the Social Sciences Building. This relic underwent conversion to classrooms on the upper floor for history and social science courses with the ground floor serving as the site of Snyder's student bookstore, offices for the three student publications (*Old Gold & Black* newspaper, *The Student* literary magazine, and *The Howler* yearbook), and a club room for the Monogram Club which, in a telling gesture, acquired and put into operation the first black-and-white cabinet model TV set on campus.

The 30-foot-wide, dimly-lit corridor between the publication offices, known as Pub Row, and the bookstore/soda fountain had a half dozen wooden booths along one wall which made this a daily hub of activity and *the* place to meet people and hang out. But no piano.

The majestic old First Baptist Church stood its ground on the southern end of the complex inside the four-foot-high rock wall which had been hand-built by students a hundred years earlier. The wall completely encircled the campus and gave it unique charm. For collegiate atmosphere, there was an old well situated between Wait Hall and the chapel. The well was no longer operational, but served as a great backdrop for occasional photo opportunities.

Two of the four dorms, Bostwick and Johnson, were for coeds. Both had pianos in their parlors but we would never be so lucky as to get to rehearse with a 100 or more girls lounging about in PJs and curlers in their hair.

Another dorm, Hunter, was a four-story, all-male facility built in the early 1900s and acclaimed by residents (one of whom was our saxophone player, Mack), as one of America's foremost fire traps. No piano.

Lastly, the brick Simmons Dorm, built in 1937, housed five of the nine fraternities, including the KAs. The original plan was for each dorm section to accommodate 20 men in 10 sleeping rooms. There were three baths, one on each floor (each had one shower, two sinks, one wall-mounted "three-man" urinal and one toilet), plus a sizeable rectangular chapter room. No pianos.

I'm not sure about the other four fraternities in Simmons Dorm, but the KA house housed at least 27 men most of the time. That doesn't include those finding temporary accommodations on a chapter room sofa or a cot in the attic during an emergency or an as-needed basis.

Simmons was across two-lane U.S. 1 from the main campus, a minute-and-a-half mad dash to the farthest classroom buildings, if you could hurdle across the rock wall. All too often, some who attempted to clear the wall wound up in the grass on the other side, bloodied, clothes smudged with dirt, and a late mark in class.

Four other fraternities had their own houses off campus and two had pianos; however, none of our musicians was a member of those Greek organizations and they were not about to permit a dozen non-brothers to blast away on their turf for several hours a week.

It soon became obvious we had to think seriously about the Music and Religion Building.

Certainly, from a purely logical standpoint, it would appear that this would be the sensible, clear and immediate choice since it was home for all the Music Department activities.

However, it was also home for all the departments relating to religious education and pre-ministerial pursuits, and the new seminary. Our brand of music was not found in most, if any, church hymnals nor were the music majors inclined to study the works of Louis Jordan and his Tympany Five.

Most importantly, the Music and Religion Building was where

a no-nonsense fellow named Dr. Duane McDaniel, head of the Music Department, reigned supreme. The two-story brick facility had several large rehearsal rooms. It had many pianos, all tuned. It had lights, toilets, heat and a bass fiddle used by The Little Symphony. It was convenient. Its larger rooms went unused and sat empty most nights.

But, it was the sacrosanct Music and Religion Building and we were (gasp) a *dance* band. An unsanctioned dance band. A rogue group at best.

There were two ways to obtain this potential rehearsal space: Ask permission of Dr. McDaniel or just walk in one night, set up and rehearse, and pray we would not be caught by anyone with authority.

The consensus was that McDaniel would be about as receptive to our rehearsing in *his* facility as Dr. Blackwood, the pastor of First Baptist Church, would be if we asked to use the sanctuary for the purpose. So why ask?

A sin of omission rather than commission.

The night watchman came on duty about 10:00 p.m. and we figured we should be out by then. Even so, we all knew the aging fellow, whom we affectionately called "Sherlock." We were convinced that should we be caught, we could convince him we were preparing for the college drama group's presentation of *Guys and Dolls,* a currently popular Broadway musical.

Basic investigating indicated no regularly planned activity in the building on Thursday nights, thus we scheduled our first rehearsal in early November. Ray found out where the bass was kept, inasmuch as we needed to "borrow" it for the evening.

For that time of the year, darkness came at 5:00 p.m. Thus, the plan was to enter the building singly and from different directions over several minutes' time to avoid suspicion. No one would question people carrying musical instrument cases into a building that housed music activities.

But, covertly getting the stack of arrangements, the stands, and my drums into the building presented something of a challenge.

25

Our solution was to put everything (including my 24-inch-diameter bass drum) into cardboard boxes we had located behind the appliance store downtown, and move in during the supper hour when few people would be around. Observers would assume we were delivering some educational materials.

Five of us loaded the Woodie, drove over to the Wait Hall parking area 35 yards from the Religion Building and, under cover of darkness, calmly walked into a side door with our boxes.

We had been so excited and intent upon having our first rehearsal we never considered what consequences there might be should we be found out. In fact, we were certain our ground-breaking venture would bring fame and glory to the college across North Carolina, and perhaps beyond. We would be a dynamic recruitment tool for the school, and we would be well received, indeed praised, by the administration once the word was out.

Jud suggested we might even be invited to play for the opening festivities of the next North Carolina Baptist State Convention.

Of course, this was only conjecture on our part.

We set up in a choir rehearsal room and for two hours went through 12 to 15 numbers several times, totally undisturbed. While we were not polished and there were more than a few sour notes and timing miscues now and then, the overall opinion was that we had real promise. Many more rehearsals were needed, but on balance, we believed we could make this thing work.

Relieved we had not been found out, we put the bass back in its closet, repacked the cardboard boxes and smugly sneaked out of the building. Our plan worked once so to be sure it would work again.

And, it did, for the next two weeks.

Most of the players had rehearsed the numbers on their own during the interim days, so when we came together for a second and third practice the overall sound was much improved and we moved along much faster. The trusting of one another was evident. The building of camaraderie obvious. It was already great fun. We were excited about the prospects.

On a Monday afternoon after the third Thursday night rehearsal, Will walked into the chapter room where several of us were playing our brand of fraternity house bridge. He looked as if someone had just opened a valve and let all his air out. Sinking into a well-worn, deep red leather chair, he announced with great frustration, "We're screwed!"

He went on to inform us our rehearsal gamble had not gone unnoticed. Or unreported.

He had just come from a one-on-one, closed-door meeting with Dr. McDaniel in *his* Music Building office. It had not been a pleasant encounter.

It seems an ambitious, non-dancing Little Symphony orchestra member who was not identified by name had come to the building to retrieve some personal papers at about the time The Southerners were rehearsing Duke Ellington's *Satin Doll*.

Rather than go about minding his or her business and leaving well enough alone, this orchestra member had discovered an illegitimate musical aggregation desecrating holy ground, i.e., Duane's Domain. Obviously, he or she felt *obliged* to report this sacrilege straightaway. And, the same snitch took the time to write down the names of eight of us he, or she, recognized.

Dr. McD was most displeased that his territory had been invaded. He was especially annoyed, infuriated actually, that the invasion at been by the likes of an unsanctioned, and likely in his mind, unsanitary, dance band.

He reminded Will, after demanding the names of the other members of the band, that we were subject to serious disciplinary action, including suspension from school. For sure Will, Ray, Jud, Hal, Norm, Drew and Mack, all members of the marching band, were subject to expulsion from that organization and both Augie and Mack from the Glee Club as well, as if any of his sparse musical groups could afford to lose seven of their better participants. As for the rest of us, he was confident he could get each of us banned from something.

There was no question that Will got the message. He assured McDaniel that there would be no further rehearsal attempts in his building. Further, he politely emphasized to McDaniel that we had just assumed the Music Building was for playing music and available to anyone interested in playing music to rehearse…otherwise we would have asked permission up front.

Sure!

McDaniel seemed to buy the simplistic explanation or, more likely, concluded that it would be hard to replace seven participants in the marching band. He told Will that he would not inform administration if there were no further occurrences.

Later, Jud heard from a girl he was dating who worked part-time in the Registrar's office that McDaniel did tell Dean Ryan and, likely others, of our sacrilege. Apparently, they all figured the fear had been put in us sufficiently by McDaniel and that we would not repeat our sinful ways, so we never heard from the administration.

Thankfully, Dr. D. was unaware we had "borrowed" *his* string bass on several occasions.

When we got the word to the other members of the band that we had been found out and Will had taken the heat for all of us, we knew we must find another rehearsal space quickly. More critically, we were on a mission to locate the snitch.

Over the rest of that week, we compiled a short list of strong possibilities as to the identity of the 'squealer', but, alas, we never could get enough proof to approach anyone and have a brief, but meaningful interface. Several of our stronger suspects, hearing on the music or ministry grapevines of our having violated the hallowed halls, suggested the entire episode was God's will. Indeed, we had sinned and should receive the wrath.

As to a new rehearsal space, back to the drawing board.

Chapter Five

Indeed, God does work in strange and mysterious ways. Really strange.

Someone had brought a yellow flyer to the KA Chapter Room promoting a traveling carnival that had settled in a large field on the southern edge of downtown. Sponsored by the American Legion, the flyer heralded an exciting midway, several thrill rides, a freak show, some games of skill, food booths and, of course, the "girlie" show.

As a special feature, one carnival entrepreneur was offering $50 to anyone who could stay in the cage with Kong, the Mighty Ape, for three minutes. A king's ransom!

Will, Ray, Drew and I joined a number of the KA brothers on Friday night to take in the carnival. We walked the mile and a half from Simmons Dorm, going under the train overpass, by the College Inn restaurant, along the several blocks of downtown White Street, the cozy, compact, user-friendly retail area.

We passed Morty's short-order café and ever-popular, ever-smoky pool hall; Holding's Drugstore; Dick Frye's and P.D.'s restaurants; Mack's 5-10-25 Store; and Pope's mercantile store. We walked by Mr. Satterwhite's savings and loan; Ben Aycock's men's clothing store; Jones Hardware; Barney Powell's barber shop; the two theatres in town, the Collegiate and The Forest. The Collegiate was showing *A Streetcar Named Desire* with Marlon Brando and Vivian Leigh, while *The African Queen* with Bogart and Hepburn was playing at The Forest.

The major downtown focal point was always the post office, run by the wife of basketball coach Maury Gleason, where each student had a mailbox and visited it daily. Out of habit, we checked our boxes hoping for money from home. Or, from anywhere.

Absent-mindedly entering the one-story brick building to check our mail, Drew and I began to laugh, recalling the time we had sent Darrell Waters, a very naïve classmate, 100 baby chicks we had ordered COD for him through radio station WCKY in Cincinnati. Naturally, we were there when Darrell excitedly took his COD notice from the mailbox to the window to get his presumed gift. Once he had the flat crate with the smelly, chirping chicks in hand, we disappeared.

Making our way to the broomstraw field where the carny tents were set up, we were welcomed by bright, multi-colored lights strung haphazardly across the red clay and sawdust grounds of the midway. Recorded calliope music was competing with the loud engines of power generators. There were squeals of delight and fear from people on the Whip, the Dipsy-Doodle, and the Ferris Wheel. Filling the evening air was the familiar pungent aroma of frying onions and the sweet smell of cotton candy, plus the unmistakable scent of Kong, the Mighty Ape!

It was obvious that a good many Wake Forest students who were not habitués of the Wake Forest Music and Religion Building were pretty much doing as we were. It was a fun, and relatively inexpensive, way to have some cheap laughs. Should you have a date, it was a pleasant walk from the women's residence halls, and for those so fortunate, the brisk air of the season suggested gloveless handholding all the way.

Coeds had to be signed in by 11:00 p.m. on Friday and Saturday nights; however, if the evening was well-planned, one could pick up his date, walk to the carnival, spend no more than a couple of dollars on hamburgers, a couple of soft drinks, some cotton candy, and wander the midway an hour or so. There was even time for a quick game of skill or two to win a stuffed teddy bear for your lady, walk back to the campus, and, hopefully locate an empty bench under a magnolia tree with low-hanging branches for some last-minute smooching.

After devouring a couple of hot dogs with mustard, relish and onions, and a 12-ounce Pepsi-Cola, our entourage ambled aimlessly down the midway. We stopped now and again to wager a dime that we could roll the softball into the angled fruit basket, knock over the leaded milk bottles, toss a hoop over the RC Cola bottles, or burst half-inflated balloons with dull-pointed darts. Needless to say, we came away with less change in our pockets and no prizes won at those canvas-topped booths with the road-worn stuffed animal prizes suspended from tent poles.

On our way to the "girlie" show, we stopped to watch Chuck Leary, one of our more prominent basketball players, shoot free throws in hopes of winning one of those stuffed toys for his date. With a ball less than fully inflated and a loosely connected rim a tad smaller than regulation, Chuck was not having much success, much to his chagrin and embarrassment.

As Drew and I stopped to watch and needle Chuck, Will, Ray, and several others moved on down the dusty midway toward a booth around which there was a building crowd.

There, sitting in a wheeled cage, was Kong, an over-sized chimpanzee rather than some great ape. Nonetheless, he was a smelly, agile, mouthy, lean, mean fighting machine. A sign attached to the cage boldly proclaimed: WIN $50. Stay 3 Minutes With KONG!

Once a challenger agreed to do battle with Kong, the cage was rolled into an adjoining tent where all who wished to watch the excitement could ante up 50 cents for the privilege.

The cage was a box-like structure on automobile wheels, putting it about four feet above the ground. The enclosure was some 10 feet long by about six feet wide and maybe eight feet high with vertical steel bars on two sides. The ends were wood slats nailed closely together with a door in one end, where the challenger was to enter to meet Kong and, usually, exit in far less than the requisite three minutes. The wooden floor was partially covered in hay and broom-straw. Several small floodlights were focused on Kong, sitting on his perch, nonchalantly scratching his privates with one hand while grasping a steel bar with the other. He sat staring and unconcerned

31

into the gathering crowd. He was obviously quite accustomed to such goings-on from past carnivals and was rather blasé about the whole thing. After all, he was the reigning champ.

Drew and I came up to the rear of the crowd, which was now about four rows deep all around the cage. A local, non-student bystander, emboldened by most of a pint of Old Crow, loudly boasted, "That monkey don't look too ornery to me!"

Whereupon his buddy, having had his share of the pint and then some, dared his brave companion to "Git in there and whup that monkey, and git us that $50!"

Naturally, everyone looked at the boastful citizen, whose name was Ernest, and began goading him to put up or shut up.

"Go ahead, boy. Climb in there and whup that ape's ass!"

"That li'l booger don't weigh 40 pounds. Git you some o' that easy money, boy!"

"That monkey ain't big as a biddy. You can beat 'im, fer sure.!"

Emboldened by the chanting crowd, good 'ole boy Ernest, wearing steel-toed brogans and bib overalls stained with mustard, relish and chewing tobacco juice, stepped forward — all six-foot-three inches and 225 pounds --- and took a wobbly giant step towards the cage.

Naturally, the crowd went wild.

Ernest was met by Kong's owner/manager/keeper and corner man, a short, balding guy with a sneer and leer who could just feel the money he was about to make off this local rube. This act had been his bread and butter for years and he knew the likely outcome. People just did not stay with Kong very long. He was too quick, too wily, too constantly in motion for anyone to do anything to him. Once he had a challenger in the cage, he would swing, jump, squeal, and dart here and there. He would bite, pinch, kick, gouge, punch, and create so much confusion that the foolish human competitor would throw in the towel, so to speak, or throw up, which often occurred, or both, and always well under three minutes.

Fortified with alcohol and egged on by the cheering crowd, local favorite Ernest wiped his mouth with the back of his hand and stepped forward.

And promptly fell flat on his face in the sawdust.

No amount of encouragement or tugging or insulting by his pal or the crowd could get a rise out of him. Kong hadn't done him in. Old Crow had.

The crowd was visibly upset that their anticipated entertainment in the adjoining tent was not going to happen. Kong, meanwhile, sensing an opportunity to shine had passed, decided to show off by bouncing around the cage, sticking out his tongue, and doing flips. It was the same routine over and over, from the perch on this end to the vertical bars, toward the door, down to the floor, back up on his perch. Over and over again. And again.

Mightily disappointed, all of us began to disperse when we heard a voice shout out, "I'll do it!"

It was Joe Koker, one of the Wake Forest Demon Deacon football team's linebackers and punter. Although the team had a game at home against Duke the next day, curfew wasn't until 9:30 pm. Many of the players had come to the carnival for some early evening fun. If the coaching staff had *any* idea that one of their players would pull such a stunt as to get into a cage to fight a chimp, there would be hell to pay.

To better understand why Joe volunteered to do battle with Kong, it is important to know Joe and his football teammates.

Koker was no ordinary guy. Or ordinary football player. He was an All-Southern linebacker and punter, and on the number one defensive college football team in America, Wake Forest's Demon Deacons. Word was that he had abundant chest hair and started shaving in the eighth grade. He pumped iron regularly and actually loved the most physical scrimmages.

In fall 1950, the team was on a streak to win six games, including beating the University of North Carolina, tie North Carolina State, and lose only twice, although Wake Forest College had the second smallest enrollment in the top division of the National Collegiate Athletic Association (NCAA). No question: the defense defined this team.

Always competitive, albeit always outnumbered, the Deacons were a nitty-gritty, in-your-face, down-and-dirty, in-the-trenches team.

While Joe was a major reason for the success, he had plenty of kindred company among his fellow defenders, many of whom had been recruited from Pennsylvania, West Virginia, New York, and New Jersey by Coach "Pinhead" Walton, who had a special affinity for rough-and-tough types from "up Nawth," especially defensive players.

Walton came to Wake Forest as head coach in 1937 and was quite successful in recruiting many talented players; however, he concluded early on that most of the Yankee boys he was after were Roman Catholic and reluctant to come to a small Baptist school where they had to pass two religion courses, Old Testament and New Testament history, to graduate. And, the nearest Catholic church was 17 miles away.

The heady and resourceful Walton solved half the problem by convincing the Catholic Diocese in Raleigh to build a small chapel in Wake Forest and to send over a priest each week to hear confessions, which, he assumed, would be numerous.

No one knew how Walton pulled it off, or at what likely expense the building cost some avid Baptist Wake Forest alumni, but St. Catherine's was completed in 1940, some five blocks south of the campus on Main Street, or the Raleigh Road as most students called it.

Thereafter, names like Listopad, Gaona, Barkocy, Paletta, Spoltore, Maravic, Scarpati and Ondilla, were listed on the team roster along with Lewis, Bridges, Blackerby, Beasley, Bartholomew, Bland, Davis and Smith.

It was a superb and highly successful illustration of ecumentalism at its best.

Most of the northern boys blended in quickly, and found a home in Baptist Hollow, but they never lost any of their regional pride or forgot their individual genealogical roots. They stuck together off the field as they succeeded together on the field. Not unlike Alexandre Dumas' *The Three Musketeers*, it was "all for one and one for all."

Now, out for a bit of relaxation, the pride, as in lions, of *very demon* Deacons was gathered about Kong's cage.

Wearing the usual faded jeans and grey WF Athletic Department tee shirt, chilly weather notwithstanding, and loafers with no socks, Joe was a formidable physical specimen. And, now the unshaven, dark-browed, muscular, All-Southern linebacker, former high school football all-star, and state boxing champion, was volunteering to mix it up with Kong!

He had been intently studying the chimp's moves for some time.

The crowd erupted in cheers, drawing even more people to the cage. Everyone knew Joe, and they were sure if anyone could do in the chimp, it would be Koker.

A mini-stampede ensued, spurred by those assembled who were anxious to fork over 50 cents to get a good spot in the tent where the action would be. Even a number of co-eds were pushing their way into the confining arena.

As Joe's entourage of a half-dozen massive football players formed a semi-circle around him, the greaser manager of Kong, chomping on a nasty, unlit cigar butt, made sure Joe understood the rules (principally telling Joe to yell to be let out of the cage). He motioned to two roustabouts lolling nearby to pull the wagon/cage into the center of the tent. Then he went over to a booth to sell tickets to what he felt would be yet another "laugher." He could get at least 80 to 90 people inside the tent, which meant a clear $40-$50, less Kong's meager upkeep.

Now, people were pushing and shoving to get closer or at least a decent view of where the action would occur. Finally, the tent could hold no more and the carny man muscled his way to the back of the cage where the door was. Joe and his gridiron associates were right behind him.

"Now, boy, I'm gonna' throw open this door and you get in there quick 'cause that mean ape is gonna' come bearing down on you fast," announced the greaseball manager. "You better protect yourself, boy," he said, laughing under his breath at Joe's naiveté.

Joe didn't remove his loafers or T-shirt. He just bounded inside the cage the second the door was ajar and stood, motionless, in a semi-crouch, fists clenched, eyes riveted on the chimp.

Kong at first appeared to be in no hurry to vanquish his foe when, suddenly, he squealed a piercing scream and began to come at Joe in that same routine we had watched before. Jumping from the perch in the back, to the bars on the left side toward the door, to the floor, to the bars on the right side, and back to the perch.

"The Mighty Ape" had gone through his practiced maneuver quickly, purposely evading Joe, obviously taunting him, then settled back on his perch. Joe did not move an inch nor flinch a muscle. He stared straight at the mouthy little primate.

Then, after resting momentarily, like a shot Kong came off that perch with a menacing high-pitched squeal and started his usual circular process, with intense energy. It was very evident that this time he was going for Joe.

The crowd, though clearly hoping for the best, was now seriously concerned for Joe, his football career, and our chances of winning the game against Duke, with kick-off just 18 hours away.

Koker still had not moved, keeping his gaze squarely on Kong. When the chimp came off the bars to Joe's right, heading toward the door as usual, Joe drew back his muscular right arm and, as Kong bounded through the air from the bars to the floor, he landed a solid haymaker squarely on the chimp's bony head. Even over the excitement and noise, everyone heard the sound.

Kong fell to the floor, spread eagle, and dazed.

The carny manager could not believe his eyes! But the crowd could. And the cheering that took place was heard all over the carnival grounds and probably reached the campus.

The crowed was delirious, and started chanting, "Joe! Joe! Joe! Joe! But Kong's benefactor, who had bitten through his cigar and now stood motionless, made no effort to open the door and let Joe out, assuming the ape would jump up, outraged, and take out his challenger.

But it was clear Kong did not share his manager's optimism. He wanted no more of whatever it was he just had. He just lay still, blinking off and on.

It was then that Vito Santangelo, a 270-pound defensive tackle, took the scrawny little operator by the shirt, dragged him to the cage door, and said, firmly, "Better open that door little man or we'll tear it open and shove you in there."

There was no smile on Vito's face. The carny guy understood the threat was genuine and quickly opened the door. Joe jumped out to the yells and screams of an adoring public.

Kong slowly rose on his hind legs and tentatively ambled over to a corner of the cage, under his perch, and sat on the floor, staring blankly and rubbing the side of his face that had received Koker's TKO punch. He had gotten Joe's very dramatic message clearly and was of no mind for more.

Vito, once again holding onto the man's grimy shirt in a vice-like grip, and with his face just inches away shouted, "You owe Joe $50!" motioning toward his Wilkes-Barre buddy.

By now, Kong's manager was fully aware of what had happened. He was not happy. And, he had no intention of forking out $50.

"You're crazy. I don't owe him nothing. He didn't fight fair. He was supposed to wrestle Kong. He hit him. That ain't fair. No contest. No money."

The little man was now very angry, very upset, and on the verge of yelling "Hey, Rube!" the carny's distress signal to fellow midway operators and roustabouts. But when he saw ballplayers Vito, Scarpati, Listopad, Gaona, Swatzel, Gregus, and others surrounding him, he thought better of it.

"Okay you guys, the show is over. Not a fair contest. You had your fun. Go on. Move on or I'll call the cops," the vanquished Kong's manager threatened.

Now it was Joe who spoke up.

"Hey, man,...you told me...we all heard it...that if I stayed in the cage with that monkey I'd get $50. Nobody said anything about wrestling.. You owe me $50, mister."

"You didn't stay in there for three minutes," the carny replied. "You knocked Kong down and then got out. Kong was getting up. You violated the rules. You gotta' stay three minutes."

Now Vito stepped back into the fray.

"Buster, you know and I know that monkey wasn't about to do any more fightin'. Either you pay Joe the $50 or we're gonna' wreck that cage, let that little ape loose, and beat the hell out of your slimy tail."

"You do, and I'll see to it you're put in jail, you bunch of guinea thugs!" retorted the carny man.

That did it. Most of the guys didn't mind the 'thugs' comment, but since several were of Italian origin, they and their Slavic-heritage friends took serious umbrage to the racial slur.

Joe and the other six gridiron stalwarts, with enthusiastic assistance from several students in the crowd, commenced to take the cage apart by hand. They ripped the door off its hinges and with an ice pick that appeared out of nowhere punctured all four tires on the cage.

Mr. Carny Man was furious, going into a rage, as he grasped the full meaning of what was happening. Kong was now up and moving and while he was in no mood to get hit again, he was most anxious to get out of that cage. When he saw the open door, he bolted out of it, scrambled over the crowd and out of the tent, seeking solace on top of the SnoCone concession.

As a final gesture, when the last onlooker was out of the tent, some person or persons unknown, knocked the tent poles awry and the whole shebang came fluttering down on top of the dismantled cage.

All the commotion had drawn about everyone in the midway by this time, including the carnival's management, several town policemen, and a handful of Wake County Sheriff's deputies who were feverishly blowing on their whistles and waving their nightsticks in the air.

The crowd quickly dispersed, not wishing to be involved in what was shaping up to be a rather messy situation. The carny guy was shouting at the police, demanding the football players be arrested and he be paid for damages. Students were telling the cops that the man reneged on his offer and he owed money to Joe. Hundreds were witnesses to that effect.

Paying no attention to the loud accusations and counter-accusations, the Wake Forest police, lead by Chief Knuckles, took all the football players, whom they knew personally and liked, the cage operator, the carnival's management people, and 10 eyewitnesses from the crowd to a one-story cinder block building just behind the midway in an open field. Ironically, it was located about 500 hundred yards or so from the City Jail.

It was the American Legion building where the organization held its meetings, had social events and was a gathering place for the many WWI, WWII and now some Korean War veterans in the area.

Currently the Hut, as it was called, was serving as well as the main office for the carnival. Ticket and concession proceeds were counted there, temporary workers checked in there, the Red Cross Aid unit was set up there, and the law enforcement units were stationed there.

It had a rather large main room. It had lights. It had an oil heater. It had an indoor toilet.

And, it had a piano!

One of the 10 witnesses ushered to the Hut was Ray Fulghum of The Southerners, a local college dance band looking for a rehearsal hall.

When the sawdust settled and all was said and done, no one was arrested. Joe's $50 dollars were forfeited to pay for damages to the cage. It was suggested that everyone involved leave the carnival and go home.

The carny guy was livid over this injustice and began spewing rather nasty verbal observations about Wake Forest College, the Town of Wake Forest, the State of North Carolina, and the South, in general. Then he started looking for his sore and disillusioned meal ticket, Kong, whose pugilistic arena was in serious disrepair.

All of the football players and nine of the 10 witnesses took the advice of the cops and headed back to the campus, or found a ride to Forest Heights, precisely a mile and a half out of town to the south, or to Calvin Ray's, located the requisite distance out Highway 98 toward Durham. Both roadhouses served cold beer and had 18-inch black and white television sets for patrons to watch the Blue Ribbon Friday Night Fights.

One person, Ray, stayed back inside the Hut, seeking the person in charge from the American Legion.

The rest of us, on our way back to Simmons Dorm, stopped at Morty's for a fried egg with mayo on a toasted hamburger bun and cup of coffee. We realized we never did get to see the "girlie" show, but we were confident the show we did see was a heck'uva lot more exciting.

Chapter Six

What Duane McDaniel would not permit, the American Legion would. A place for The Southerners dance band to rehearse.

After several conversations with the local Legion's officers, Will received permission for the group to use the cinder block facility on Tuesday and Thursday nights if it was not in their use, and if we would be responsible for any damages, buy oil for the stove, and pay a small stipend to cover the electric bill. I recall we also had to commit to play for one dance for the Legion members, for free.

The pressure was on to find paying jobs that provided sufficient revenue to cover musicians' pay, gas for two cars, regular payments on the stands, lights and new arrangements, and now, rehearsal hall rent and heating oil.

Will immediately set up a rehearsal schedule for two hours minimum on Tuesday nights. We would need to work our academic requirements around it.

The good news was the Hut was isolated so we bothered no one and no one bothered us. The bad news was North Carolina's winter was settling in. The cinder block walls of our rehearsal hall did little to insulate us from the cold weather. Sound ricocheted off the walls. Any conversations held during those winter rehearsals generated white vapors against the frigid air, and even floated out through the bells of the horns when played.

The oil heater, while emitting some warmth, gave off an abundance of noxious fumes to the extent we agreed it would be better to freeze to death than die from inhaling poisonous gasses, and inhaling was a requisite for horn players. So after we took a little chill out of the air early in the rehearsals we usually shut the heater off for the remainder of the night. That also cut down on the fuel oil we had to pay for.

Out of necessity, we became adroit at rehearsing wearing heavy jackets or overcoats and gloves. Several of us wore wool caps pulled down over our ears. Chick had a pair of fluffy, bright red ear muffs with a metal clasp that fit over the head. I wore leather gloves and could still grasp the drumsticks fairly well. The horn, piano, and bass players bought cheap wool mittens and cut off the tips of the fingers so they could play the horn valves, piano keys, and bass strings. Not the ideal situation, but a cold rehearsal hall is better than no rehearsal hall.

Another definite downside was that the Hut sat in a low area of the field and was prone to severe dampness. There was no paved road in, nor a paved parking lot, so when it rained on rehearsal nights, which was often, we had to carry everything from our cars to the Hut through red clay mud.

High humidity and dampness play havoc on pianos and drums and musical instruments generally. Even the cardboard music stands would gather mold if we left them in the Hut storage room for several weeks. The old upright piano had not been properly tuned in months, if not years. Some of the veneer had peeled off, several keys were flat and a few had missing ivory but we could not afford the luxury of repairs and were not about to complain to the Legion, so we made do.

Extremely cold weather tended to coagulate the oil that trombonists put on their slides, and the trumpet valves would stick. Mouthpieces could be freezing cold. As for the drums, that was another story.

My white, mother-of-pearl Gretsch drum set was bought new in 1942 by an 18- year-old kid who earned money working on his family's tobacco farm in Harnett County, NC, some 45 miles from my home in Raleigh. When he went into the U.S. Army shortly after the drums arrived, they were stored in a tin-roofed wood shed behind his house, awaiting his return. He was killed in Europe in

1945, just prior to the end of hostilities. His parents ran a classified ad in the Raleigh News & Observer in hopes of selling them.

On a Sunday afternoon, my Dad and I (I was 14 at the time) drove to the farm and watched the Gold Star mother take the drums from the overhead flooring in the shed with tears in her eyes.

"He only played them a few times," she said, trying to hide her continuing grief.

I almost suggested to my Dad that we just go back home, but it was apparent the lady wanted to get rid of the drums. We bought the like-new ensemble for $125.00, my Dad paying half and I paid half with money earned as a page in the NC State Legislature that spring.

In the 1940s and '50's, drumheads were fabricated from cowhide. I had a bass drum, a snare and two tom-toms. When the drumheads got damp, they sagged a bit. There's less tension, so when they're struck with drumsticks, or the bass drum foot pedal, the sound is like hitting wet cardboard or a soggy towel. Muffled. No crisp beat, and hardly discernable to the other musicians who count on a driving, steady beat, especially in "big" bands.

There were two partial solutions. One was to make the heads more taut with a drum key which is used to screw the metal head rims tighter, thereby stretching the heads. But, you could torque them just so much. The other was by warming and drying the heads. At the Hut I usually put the drums close to the oil heater in cold weather before rehearsals. That worked for about an hour.

The bass drum frame had a half-inch hole placed purposefully near the top, which allowed air to escape during play. Into that hole, I placed an electrical cord and, by removing one drumhead, affixed a light socket for a pale blue light bulb. The light just hung inside the bass about eight inches down from the top. When plugged into an outlet, usually via a very long extension cord, the result was that I could get a modicum of drying heat for the bass heads throughout a rehearsal, or a job, plus the blue tint behind the front of the bass drum presented a rather classy soft visual effect.

The Hut, with its inherent and continuing problems, was far

from the optimum rehearsal hall, but it became home one night a week and we accepted it, 'warts' and all.

There were a few situations where the Hut was put to use by one or more of the band guys for purposes other than rehearsing musical arrangements.

A "town girl" was a female who was not a Wake Forest College student but a local high school student. Lessie Vincent was a "town girl." A very attractive brunette. She waited supper tables during the week and all day on Saturdays at Dick Frye's restaurant, a favorite eating establishment for students, especially males. She developed a mammoth crush on Hank; to the extent she pestered him every time he was having an evening meal at Frye's instead of at the athletes' dining hall, where the cuisine received generally poor reviews. Her behavior bordered on stalking which irritated Hank to no end.

After weeks of this worrisome attention, Hank decided, with considerable expert counseling from others, to ask Lessie for a date and put some moves on her that would scare her off once and for all. Normally college guys did not date local high school girls and when Hank asked her out she was ecstatic.

Lessie's shift at Frye's usually ended about 9:30 p.m. Since she was 17 and had her driver's license, her Dad allowed her to drive an old truck he used in his welding business to work and back home at night. She had long ago convinced him that she and some girl friends often went to a late movie after work. She was usually home by 11:00 p.m., so he assumed that's what she did.

What her Dad did not know, nor Hank, nor any of us, was that Lessie had a very active interest in sexual activity. Most of the local town boys were aware of Lessie's cravings, many with firsthand knowledge, but none of the college guys had an inkling. Instead of going to the movies after work, Lessie was usually engaging in extremely heated physical shenanigans, often in the bed of the welding truck.

Hank asked Lessie to meet him at the Hut after band rehearsal on Tuesday night. All of us in the band knew about the rendezvous

and understood it was his plot to rid himself of this overly aggressive high school girl's infatuation. As we all left, Will handed
Hank the key and told him to turn off the lights and lock up.

According to Hank, when Lessie's truck pulled up to the Hut
on that cold December night she could see lights on inside and no
cars in the lot. Hank saw to it the heater was turned off and he had
opened the front door slightly.

Lessie parked close to the door and noticed that it was ajar. She
walked briskly into the Hut, closing the door behind her. Hank was
sitting at the piano, pecking out a tune and sipping on a RC Cola.

Hank's plan was to ask her if she wanted to go to see *Sunset
Boulevard,* now playing at the Collegiate Theatre, which would
have started 20 minutes earlier. She'd likely agree.

They'd take her truck since he had no car. In the dark and virtually empty theatre, he'd try some moves. Obvious moves. Suave,
college-guy kinds of moves.

The Collegiate Theatre was especially conducive to any non-
movie activities where a sound of any kind might be generated.
Like giggles, gasps, groans, grunts, or low screams. It literally
backed up to the main north-south line of the Seaboard Railroad,
which ran through town, parallel to White Street and to the college campus. When a train came through, the building shook, the
screen shook, and the train's noise drowned out any sound from
the movie, or the audience, for several minutes, depending on the
train's number of cars. Hence, the Collegiate was a wise choice
for Hank's tryst since he was well aware a freight train usually
came through around 10:00 p.m.

Being a young, innocent high school girl, Hank surmised,
Lessie would become properly alarmed, shunning his advances.
He would act upset, be a jerk and sulk through the rest of the picture. She'd walk out, take off in her truck, and leave him to walk
back to his room. Each going their separate ways. He would avoid
Frye's for several weeks, and Lessie would get over her crush on
such an animalistic, uncouth college low-life and all would end as
he planned.

As Hank later recounted his version of the events, his seemingly rational plan was dramatically upset by Lessie's totally irrational plan.

"I swear to you," Hank explained to the several of us at Morty's, surprised by his early return, "she came in, slammed the door shut, and walked over to the piano where I was sitting. I asked her if she'd like to go to the flicks and she said no. So I asked her what she'd like to do."

"What'd she say, man?" Drew asked eagerly, washing an onion-doused hot dog down with a half pint of Pine State Creamery chocolate milk.

"She didn't say a thing…not a word. She walked over to the light switch on the wall and turned it off. By the time I figured out what she was up to, she had thrown off her coat, pulled off her sweater, and was on me like a June bug on a duck. Man, she went crazy!"

Hank caught his breath.

"Yeah…yeah…and…," Drew egged Hank on.

"Well, instead of me coming on to her in the picture show, she was all over me in the Hut," he explained. "Danged near raped me!"

`Then what happened?" Drew asked loudly, totally into the torrid scene.

"I couldn't believe it, "Hank continued, "but then I figured my plan was actually going to work… in reverse! So I jumped up, told her I was absolutely surprised and disgusted at her actions. Here I thought she was a nice girl who just wanted to see a movie or something."

He went on, "I needed to get rid of this girl. So, I figured this way I could act offended. I would get mad and she would get the message. I even told her I was thinking about being a preacher. Then I told her I was not about to take advantage of a high school girl and if she so much as gave me a look at Frye's or anywhere else again I'd be on the phone to her Daddy."

"She bought that line?" I asked, not sure I believed what I was hearing.

"I guess she did, because by the time I walked over to turn on the light she had grabbed her sweater and coat off the floor, wheeled around and slammed the door. She took off like a scalded dog. Last I saw of her she was tearing down the road with metal tools bouncing in the back of her old man's pickup. So, I locked up and got out of there myself. And I'll tell you this, I'm not about to go to Frye's for a while, and have to see that sex fiend," Hank asserted.

"Well, I sure am!" Drew eagerly responded.

Chapter Seven

"C'mon, Will," the bespectacled Mack pleaded, "don't ask us to stand up and play. I'm so near-sighted I can't see the notes when we stand up."

During rehearsal, Will was focusing on when the various sections or individual soloists would stand to play. He particularly liked it when the sax section stood, for that was a visual piece of showmanship on the front line that looked very professional. Obviously, Mack was not a fan. He was among the best music readers we had but, as he readily admitted, he was better at it when he could actually *see* the notes.

Hank, on the other hand, had no problem taking the spotlight, and since he was our resident sex symbol, Will took advantage of his looks and talent and told him to stand and play anytime he felt it appropriate. It was uncanny how he always stood when attractive young ladies came close to the bandstand.

By the Christmas break we had pretty well mastered 30 or 40 arrangements and determined some basic set orders. We determined which numbers would be good solo pieces and who would play them, agreeing that I could take one drum "ride" a night and it would be on *Tuxedo Junction*.

The sound was coming together well, and now we had to sell it.

Although Lupton could refer some business to us now and then, he emphasized we would need a booking agent, or two; people with connections and experience in the business if we wanted to get the better contracts.

Lup, as the musicians called him, also made sure we understood that unless we joined the union he would send no more prospects our way nor could we get any playing dates on military bases or most university campuses since they now booked only union bands. Same with most city facilities like Raleigh's Memorial Auditorium that was the site of many major dances.

We all agreed it was time to become dues-paying members of Local 500, a secret many of us kept from our parents — most of whom were decidedly anti-union at the time. The annual fee was $10. For that, we received a $1,000 accidental death policy, and Lup's support, which was considerably more valuable to us.

The Wake Forest Monogram Club booked the band for its Spring Dance, a relatively small but much-anticipated annual affair held in the Community Building. Although we had played several freebies there before, this was our first local engagement where we were actually being paid. Will cut the cost dramatically, to which we all agreed, so we could gain more exposure and obtain a second notch in our gun, in addition to the Red Oak Alumni endorsement. We were paid five dollars each for a two-and-half-hour job with one break.

Frankly, we would have played for nothing. This was time to "strut our stuff" in front of our classmates and friends and encourage them, as Will did several times on the sound system, to "let your friends back home know about The Southerners." He brought a stack of our promotional flyers to hand out to those who might help promote the band.

Prior to our Red Oak job, we discussed many options for a theme song. We made a list of big band theme songs we liked and which were immediately associated with specific bands by the public: *Moonlight Serenade* (Glenn Miller); *Snowfall* (Claude Thornhill); *Ciribiribin* (Harry James); *Auld Lang Syne* (Guy Lombardo); *I Can't Get Started* (Bunny Berrigan); *Summertime* (Bob Crosby); *Smoke Rings* (Glen Gray); *Sunrise Serenade* (Frankie Carle); *My Sentimental Heart* (Carmen Cavallaro); *Cherokee* (Charlie Barnet); *Sometimes I'm Happy* (Blue Barron); *I'm Getting Sentimental Over You* (Tommy Dorsey); *Harlem Nocturne* (Randy Brooks); *Bubbles in the Wine* (Lawrence Welk); *Racing*

49

With The Moon (Vaughn Monroe);.*Gotta Date With An Angel* (Skinnay Ennis); *Let's Dance* (Benny Goodman); *I'll Love You In My Dreams* (Horace Heidt); *Take the 'A' Train* (Duke Ellington); *One O'clock Jump* (Count Basie); *Flying Home* (Lionel Hampton); *Leap Frog* (Les Brown); *Artistry In Rhythm* (Stan Kenton); *Thinking Of You* (Kay Kyser); *Blue Prelude* (Woody Herman); *Nightmare* (Artie Shaw); *Star Dreams* (Charlie Spivak); *Cocktails For Two* (Spike Jones).

After much discussion and many intense arguments, we all agreed we preferred something "dreamy," a slow number inviting people to dance, instead of a novelty piece or jump tune. Moreover, it needed to be ours, not anything a current mainstream big band was using as its theme song.

A very popular ballad that was first published in 1946 was *Tenderly*. Trumpeters particularly favored the song because it allowed them to show off their range. Charlie Spivak, Ray Anthony and Randy Brooks recorded it early on, and we agreed it had the sound that would be right for The Southerners. Hank, lead trumpeter, thought it was perfect, naturally.

When Rosemary Clooney recorded it in 1952, *Tenderly* became a classic hit. Later Ella Fitzgerald, Nat King Cole, and many others did their versions but we had adopted it as our own in 1951 and opened every dance with it.

We never played the three-bar intro on the stock arrangements, but went straight to the melody. I would start by building a roll on the floor tom tom with mallets, like a tympani, and then Hank would come in, alone, standing, arching his back a bit, and lifting the horn. He exploded the sound, extending the three written sixteenth notes in the first two bars into half notes, "coaxing" the melody from the trumpet bell. Crash cymbal between the third and fourth notes. The rest of the band came in on the third bar. Dramatic. Exciting. Classy. A great song to put people in a dancing mood.

For those who came to know The Southerners, they knew our theme song. And, when they heard it, according to Julie Watkins, a gorgeous popular coed from Georgia, it was "goose bump time." I don't think any of us ever tired of playing *Tenderly*, no matter how many times we did over the two plus years I was in the band.

Lup drove over to Wake Forest to hear the group for himself when we played the Monogram Club affair. Apparently, we passed muster because he told Will about an entrepreneur in Burlington named Lucky Lewis who promoted a number of local festivals and events in Piedmont North Carolina and Southern Virginia. He often booked bands for these affairs and for high school and college dances.

We signed on with Lucky as a client and provided him with 200 promotional flyers, which he immediately began sending to high schools and area colleges.

The good news is that the mailings began to produce a fair number of inquiries. The bad news, or periodic problem, was that our telephone number printed on the flyers happened to be for a pay phone on a second floor landing in the KA House.

If an interested party opted to call us rather than write Will's Wake Forest post office box, or contact Lucky, then any number of guys might answer the phone: "KA House," throwing the caller off base. We likely lost a number of prospects who thought they had the wrong number and hung up rather than ask for Will, whose name was on the flyer.

Our fraternity brothers were instructed to call either Ray, Drew or me to the phone if Will was requested but not in at the time. In effect, we had an answering service of some 25 or more guys, a few of whom actually wrote down who wanted us to return the calls.

Ray decided to sell his piece of the band to Will who was spending an inordinate amount of time getting us jobs and looking after all the financial affairs, rental needs, new music, and other matters totally unrelated to academia. His sole band ownership and necessary related work to make us successful was a practical business course in and of itself. Unfortunately, he received no college credits for all his management and marketing lessons, most of it learned the hard way.

Springtime being the most popular period for high school and college dances, we began to book a number of jobs for April and May through Lucky's initial efforts.

Since the band was charging a minimum of $200 a job for eleven pieces, more if we could get it, we were rarely paid in cash. When we were, the money was never in bills that would enable each man to get his $10 and two ones, or two fives and two ones. Whether the band was paid in cash or by check, it was still Monday when we got our money. But, Will made sure we were paid as quickly as possible.

On reflection, it was most telling that there were never any written contracts between Will and any player. No signed agreements. It was understood who was the leader, who made up the sets, and how much we'd be paid. We did all agree to some basic, albeit unwritten, quasi-rules of conduct, most of which were obvious: no drinking before or during a job, no smoking on the bandstand, no fooling around with women (girls) at intermissions, no complaining about what number was to be played or who he assigned to take a solo. If a player didn't like something, he was to speak to Will privately after a job. If anyone did, I never heard about it.

The only rule I recall being violated periodically was the 'carousing with women' item. A couple of the players asked Will, "How can we ignore good-looking young high school girls when they come up to us at breaks and take us to the punch bowl? After all, it is the polite thing to do. It's good public relations."

Will would reply, "Just stay in the gym, in plain sight, and don't go outside with any of them. Remember, the school chaperones' eyes are on you, for sure." He also added to the rule, "Don't try to fool around with any of the girls you meet after a job because it's bad for our reputation and we need to pack up and get going."

I can recall several times when this additional rule was completely ignored, one instance in particular.

Ray was a quiet guy. Tall, solid build, dark hair, heavy eyebrows. He looked several years older than he was. Quiet. Still water.

Lucky got us a job in late April playing for a high school dance in his hometown, Burlington, about an hour-and-a-half drive from Wake Forest. Unlike most high school jobs where we all sat on the floor level, on this occasion the school had installed risers, which elevated the brass, my drums, and Chick's bass. The sax section and piano were on the floor level. This gave the band a much more professional appearance and none of the players was blocked from view of the dancers. Or vice versa.

About halfway through the third set, as the first intermission neared, a pleasant looking brunette came up to the bandstand and stood, staring. She was not a raving beauty but had a sweet wholesome 'girl next door' look. She appeared older than the other girls at the dance.

"Ray...Ray Fulghum...it's me, Katie Lancaster," she blurted out, as the last notes of *Smoke Gets In Your Eyes* faded away.

Ray recognized Katie right off, for she had, indeed, been the girl who lived next door to him in Rocky Mount. He did a little recognition wave to her, and then indicated through hand signals that he'd be off the stand in about 15 minutes. She backed off a bit, and stood by to the side for the next three numbers that lead to a break.

Stepping down from the riser, Ray went over to Katie, embracing her in a polite hug. As several of us left the stand, heading for an exit and a smoke, Ray introduced us to Katie, who, in addition to having been a neighbor, had also played clarinet in the school marching band. She was obviously several years older than Ray.

"What're you doing here, Katie?" Ray inquired.

"Chaperoning," Katie responded proudly. "I started teaching English here last fall. After I graduated from high school, I went to W.C. in Greensboro year 'round. Finished in three years, got my teaching certificate, and here I am. I found a small apartment near my school, bought a little used Dodge car, and that's pretty much it. "

53

With that, the two headed for the omnipresent punch bowl, engaged in "do you remember-type" conversation for the brief 20 minutes we'd be on break.

Katie did less chaperoning for the rest of the evening than she did hanging around the bandstand. During the final intermission the two of them, talking animatedly, headed back to the punchbowl.

After we finished playing *Goodnight Sweetheart*, the usual closer, Ray quickly removed the mouthpiece and slide from his trombone, placed them in the instrument case, and jumped off the stand. He went over to Katie who was waiting to the side.

"Hey, Ray," Will shouted out, "don't be long. We got to get going."

"You go on back. I'll find a way to school later," Ray answered. With that, he and Katie left the gym through a back door.

"I get the feeling he's not going back to Wake Forest tonight," Norm said to anyone listening.

Indeed, Ray did not return to the campus that night, but was driven there on the following afternoon in a 1947 dark blue, two-door Dodge Deluxe club coupe by the girl who used to live next door.

"I obeyed all the band rules," Ray later told us, "I didn't mess around with a student at intermissions. I didn't go outside with a student after the dance. The rules don't say anything about teachers!"

"So," Norm pushed the issue, "what did you guys do all night?" He was hoping for a lurid, steamy tale. Instead, Ray laughingly answered: "Oh, we mostly just reminisced. You know, about the old neighborhood. Just stuff."

"Must've been a lot of stuff going on in that neighborhood," Norm suggested.

We left it at that.

"By the way, Red," Ray said to me but loudly enough for everyone to hear, "keep in mind teachers are fair game when you're scouting the territory!"

Hal was referring to my 'part-time job' during dances to check out the women in the crowd and relay where the 'winners' were to the other guys during the evening. As a drummer who did not read music, as the others must, I had memorized all the numbers. Thus, I had the freedom to play and stare at the same time.

Another advantage of being on risers from time to time was I had a better sight line over the other guys' heads. While lights were usually subdued at most dances, my 20/20 vision was usually very productive at spotting the better-looking girls in their ever-popular strapless gowns.

Being committed college students and deeply dedicated to academia and higher intellectual pursuits, we rated the girls by A's and B's. Nothing less than a B-minus was acceptable, except now and then an obvious D would get rave scores.

Chapter Eight

"Hey, can y'all play the *Mexican Hat Dance*?" The young couple strode to the bandstand and called out to any of us who might respond.

"Coming right up," Will answered, knowing that sooner or later we would get to it but deciding there's no time like the present to abide by the wishes of the paying customer.

"Okay, Number 43," Will told us, referring to the number assigned to *Mexican Hat Dance*, a lively, sweat-breaking little tune that combined a Latin beat, an Irish jig, a Bavarian polka, and a bit of country square-dancing as well.

We were in the Kinston High School gymnasium, which had been decorated grandly by the kids to resemble a Mexican village street, whatever they perceived it to be or could get from reference books or movie memories. The closest any of them had ever been to a Mexican town most likely was Pedro's South of the Border truck stop/restaurant/gift shop/motel gallimaufry just south of the North Carolina line in South Carolina on U.S. 301.

The industrious students had built multi-colored storefronts out of cardboard tacked to two-inch-wide slat frames, Lots of potted plants including cacti were placed about. A split-rail fence was in the corner, keeping a live donkey munching straw penned in. Another fence had colorful serapes draped over it and clay pots of various sizes stacked around the base. A fake adobe brick well was centrally positioned, serving as part of the decor and doubling as a fund-raising wishing well.

We speculated as to what a lot of those teen age boys were wishing for that night as they dropped their coins into the well,

56

holding their dates' hands in sweaty-palm grips.

The creativity of high school kids always amazed us as they transformed their barren, stark, steel-raftered gyms into tropical Hawaii or mystical China, a romantic cruise ship, or, on this night, exciting, colorful Mexico. Many of us in the band had served on prom committees and done our time hanging crepe paper, strategically placing balloons, hauling sand and furniture, building gondolas and archways, and "planting" vegetation. We appreciated the effort.

The Kinston High dance committee had informed Will in advance what the theme would be, as was often the case. Will made sure we had several numbers that tied into their thematic locale. Understanding the importance of these dances to the teenagers, which many of us still were, we oohed and aahed, making sure we acted as if their events were equally impressive to us college types. Fact is, we were usually fascinated by their ingenuity and originality.

Unbeknownst to the rest of us, Will bought a dozen loosely-woven straw sombreros for us to wear when playing the *Mexican Hat Dance, Frenesi, Vaya Con Dios, Bésame Mucho, Siboney,* and anything else that he thought could be "Latinized." We seldom played a Latin rhythm for this age group more than once a night. The exception was the *Mexican Hat Dance,* always a real crowd pleaser, for it was more jumping around than actually dancing.

Now, some guys like to wear hats, some don't. Some are actually embarrassed to do "shtick," while others really get into it. When Will handed out the sombreros, having kept them boxed until 'the moment of truth,' there was a mixture of comments from "Ay, Caramba!" to "Olé, Amigos" to several Anglo epithets!

The blonde-headed Drew and I, with carrot-orange hair, both about 5 feet 7 inches tall, thin and very WASPy, were into the Mexican hat and shtick as was Chick, whose dark Italian complexion and curly dark hair enabled him to easily pass for Hispanic heritage.

Instead of simply putting the sombreros on as they are normally worn, wide brim up all around, Drew turned the brim down all the way around, virtually hiding his face. Chick pulled the sombrero down as far as it would go, brim up, to just above the bridge of his nose to where it actually engulfed his ears, and I turned the brim up in front and down in back. With the others all playing it straight, the fact that three of us got into character, so to speak, made whatever we were playing more fun for the audience, and certainly for the three of us.

When it came to the sombreros, neither Hank nor the dark haired, suave Jud wanted to hide their faces, Augie didn't want to muss his hair, Hal said the straw scratched his thinning spot, Ray said it made him look too much like a tobacco farmer, Norm complained it made his head itch and Mack said he looked stupid in hats. Complaints aside, we donned the sombreros with every playing of most Latin tunes and the shtick always worked.

Another themed occasion that spring when Will opted to outfit the band to blend with the decor was at the Goldsboro High School Junior-Senior prom. The committee had selected a Gypsy Camp theme. A few years earlier the songs *The Gypsy and Golden Earrings* were highly popular, so in his infinite judgment Will had bought a dozen cheap gold screw-back earrings for us to wear on the stand. One earring per guy.

He also bought some colorful bandanas for us to tie tightly around our heads, expecting them to give us the appearances of his perceived image of a male gypsy's headgear.

To put it mildly, our acceptance was not universal. As a compromise, we agreed to wear the earrings through the first set, showing our participation in the theme. But, no head bandanas. Two or three of the guys tied them around their necks, which looked more like cowboys than nomadic Eastern Europeans.

Following our opening of the dance with *Tenderly*, Will announced the next two songs would be in honor of the GHS prom theme: *The Gypsy and Golden Earrings*. He explained in a joking fashion why the 12 of us were wearing earrings in one ear. It was a good thing he did because I don't think anyone would have gotten it. We ditched the earrings as quickly as the set ended and wondered how women can bear to wear those things all day. Norm kept asking if his ear lobe had turned green from the "gold."

Several days after the Goldsboro High School job, Will was talking on the phone with the high school teacher who had hired us, looking for an endorsement we could use in our promotional materials. She relayed that the evening had been very successful, with one after-the-fact drawback.

It seems the decorations committee for the prom had appointed two boys who had access to pick-up trucks to help obtain a variety of greenery with which to create the gypsy campsite. After borrowing all the potted plants they could from families and neighbors, they persuaded a nursery to loan them some larger potted bushes and a few exotic floral plants. They decided they had all they needed with the exception of some medium-height trees with which to create a realistic backdrop for the canopied gypsy wagon, which was a dominant feature. It also housed a real, very aged fortuneteller who normally did business out near the Seymour Johnson Air Force Base. She had agreed to perform her specialty during the evening for one and all for $50.

Being resourceful, the two eager-to-please boys finally located four 10-to-12 foot-tall pines that they proceeded to cut down and haul to the school gym on Saturday morning before the dance that evening. That night, the Committee received accolades for its decorations and especially the realistic-appearing campsite with the pine trees.

On Monday morning, the school's principal received a call from the Superintendent of Wayne County Schools saying he had received a call from the Goldsboro Mayor's Office who had been called by the head of the Parks and Recreation Department, reporting that four pine trees had been cut down, mysteriously, in a local park quite near the high school.

While no one was certain who did it, or just when, someone had spotted two teenaged boys with trucks in the neighborhood, cruising the park just after dark one night last week. In fact, the mayor said he and his wife had attended a dance at GHS just a few days earlier as specially invited guests and were amazed at how realistic the forested campsite looked. Now he knew why.

Another memorable decorations-gone-awry at one of our prom jobs occurred in the gym at Nashville High School. The Four Aces had made the tune, *Three Coins in the Fountain*, a major hit. The Committee opted to do a Romanesque decor, complete with fake Ionic, Doric and Corinthian columns, the Appian Way, an agora, and a mock Trevi fountain. People could toss coins into the fountain to make wishes.

This wishing well/coins concept seemed to prevail at high school proms, no matter the theme.

One of the male committee members' fathers was a plumber, and he had worked with his dad during the summers and on weekend jobs now and then. He knew the basics of plumbing, and volunteered to install the pipes to bring water to the fountain, which had been constructed of stacked rocks with a plastic liner interior.

No question the fountain was a beauty. On a high pedestal in the center had been placed a statuary borrowed from the monument company outside of town that made cemetery headstones and decorative pieces. This particular statue had David-like features, but unlike the Michelangelo version, wore a loincloth and was holding a jar on his shoulder.

With a couple of colorful jell spotlights on the fountain, and water flowing out of the jar down David's concrete body and into the pool/fountain liner, recycled up again, it was impressive to say the least. All evening the dancers came by, tossed in three coins, principally nickels and pennies we noticed, and made wishes. As usual, we were in agreement as to what the boys were wishing.

Apparently, no one was in charge of monitoring the fountain, that is, the fountain's water level. People came by, tossed their coins, and moved on. About two hours into the evening the unexpected happened. Water began to spill over the liner, over the rocks, and onto the gym floor.

The band was located on the gym floor, not on risers. Since the bandstand was located some 10 feet away from the fountain, we were the first to realize what was going on.

As Augie remarked when the water reached his loafers, "Either the fountain has sprung a leak or that statue is taking a leak on my feet!"

In no time at all a goodly amount of water was making its way in all directions of the dance floor. The band, now in the main path of the mini-flood, quickly picked up bandstands and instrument cases and sought higher ground, which was a stairwell to a balcony overlooking the gym. I picked up the bass drum and high hat cymbals and struggled up the steps. Thankfully, Mack grabbed my equipment case with his free hand and Augie grabbed the floor tom tom and the snare.

It seems someone had tossed a paper cup into the fountain, it had become waterlogged, sunk to the bottom and was partially blocking the small pipe that recycled the water and sent it back to the top of David's jug. Some water got through and oozed out of the jug so no one noticed the stream was not flowing properly. The fountain novelty had pretty much worn off by then and no one was paying attention to it.

The problem was soon fixed. Boys in their Sunday best suits manned mops, girls in party dresses helped 'sop up' with gym towels quickly gathered from the basement shower facilities. Faculty and chaperones gave a variety of panicky directions, usually conflicting.

Not wanting to be a hindrance in the reclamation project, and aware our $12 income did not include janitorial services, the band adjourned to the exterior where we smoked and killed time kibitzing with many of the high school girls who had become "groupies" of a sort. When the partially dried floor appeared to be safe, we continued with our sets for the final hour.

One of the wiser school officials suggested the pump be turned off altogether, which was an added benefit to one and all since we had been forced to turn the volume of the amplifiers up to overpower the pump noise early in the evening.

Arrivederci, Roma.

Chapter Nine

A special opportunity for the fledgling dance band to learn from a master arrived with the February 9-10 Inter-Fraternity Council's MidWinters dance, the major social of the season for the Greeks on campus.

The 16-piece Claude Thornhill orchestra played for an informal Friday evening affair, a Saturday afternoon Tea Dance, and a formal ball on Saturday night, all in Raleigh's Memorial Auditorium.

While several of The Southerners had dates for the triple-event program, many of us opted to stag it on Friday night and Saturday afternoon so we could study the big band performance up close. We donned tuxes for the Saturday night affair and participated in the dancing, but with one ear tuned to the styling, show biz attitude and little tricks of the trade Thornhill's band exhibited. To hear the guys who made *Snowfall* famous was a special treat, and Will vowed to include the number in our library.

Lucky came through on several more dances in May 1951, including a Shriner's event in Durham and a senior prom in Lexington.

The prom was typical, went smoothly and nothing extraordinary or weird took place, which was both refreshing and disappointing since, by now, we expected there to be at least one glitch or unique occurrence at every job. It was becoming the norm.

The theme for the senior prom in Lexington was built around celestial bodies, including stars, the moon, planets, comets, meteors and the like. By playing *Stardust, Moonlight Serenade, Night and Day,* and *I've Got the Sun in the Morning and the Moon at Night*, we took care of musical support for the theme.

We wondered how the kids would come up with a wishing

well, given the heavenly elements, but they managed to create a rainbow that extended from "outer space" down to the earth, as it were and, sure enough, there was a pot at the end of the rainbow into which coins could be dropped and wishes made. We marveled at the creativity.

I was advised by Hank and Jud to keep a keen lookout for attractive, hopefully unattached teachers, now that Ray had set a precedent.

• • • • •

The Shriner's social was something else. The booking was for only eight pieces, so Hal, Norm, and Jud volunteered to drop out, leaving us short a trombone, a trumpet, and a sax. We were still able to get a full sound out of the remaining instruments.

The event was held at Josh Turnage's barbecue lodge out in the country, east of Durham, a favorite party place that could be rented on an exclusive basis. You got the big hall, great barbecue dinner, and the opportunity to purchase from the management a variety of beers and mixers.

Since North Carolina was a dry state and alcohol could be purchased legally only from a state-owned and operated liquor store, people who wanted a libation would "brown bag" it, that is, bring their bottle of choice bought at the ABC (Alcohol Beverage Control) store in a paper sack.

Now, everyone knows that Shriners have big hearts and raise a great deal of money for many worthwhile endeavors, not the least of which is the many children's hospitals across the country.

Most folks also know that most Shriners are fun-loving rascals who wear red fezzes, perform as clowns, and often drive miniature cars in parades. We also are aware that some Shriners are party animals who will, on occasion, take a drink.

Suffice it to say, the Shriners we played for at Turnage's fell in the latter category and ABC store brown bags were much in evidence.

As the night progressed and the dancing became livelier, these fun-loving folk were getting more and more animated, thanks in great part to whatever was in those brown bags. It surely wasn't the ice or the 7-Up. By 10:30 Chick, Ray, Drew, and I were all wearing tasseled hats that genial Shriners had crammed on our heads.

It was shortly thereafter that the Masonic-based group decided this was a good time, and place, to engage in races in their little motor-driven cars.

Normally they do a series of intricate and well-rehearsed routines on city streets at low speeds, but on this night, the idea was to drive the eight 'kiddie cars' as fast as possible, from the dirt parking lot outside, up a wood ramp onto the porch, through the double doors of the building, going round and round and round and round inside.

It didn't take Josh and his staff long to realize they had a quasi-stock car event going on right there *inside* the lodge. Wives and non-drivers were lined up against the walls, climbing on tables and chairs, like pit crews, cheering their favorites to the checkered flag, or checkered tablecloth as it were. As drivers zoomed by, many were doused with a beverage.

As the hall was filling with fumes, and screams of encouragement from the racing fans, Josh and several waiters grabbed brooms and tablecloths and were beating the cars, and occasionally a driver, as they whisked by. Realizing our stands, our instruments and perhaps our bodies were in jeopardy, The Southerners formed something of a human barricade in front of the bandstand in hopes of fending off careening cars.

It took a few minutes to convince them through yelling, threats and towel whippings, but finally the drivers opted to run "off the track and down Pit Road," i.e., out into the parking lot where they cut their engines, bailed out of the cars onto the ground and sat in the dirt, laughing hysterically.

Those Shriners and spouses still inside began to help Josh's crew put things back in order while he surveyed the area for damages. Surprisingly, other than lingering fumes, the only other evidence of the event was some highly visible tire tracks on the wood floor. Josh ordered everyone to leave right then, loudly assuring them the party was over and the Temple would be charged for any damages sustained, assuming he would find some later.

Meanwhile, we were concerned that the perpetrators would leave before we were paid, so Will, Hank, and Ray, the three biggest guys in The Southerners, located the fellow who had booked us as he started to open the door of his car in the parking lot. They confronted him and his wife. He had been one of the racers and was well into his cups.

There was a one-sentence comment made by Ray as to our being owed $200. The Shriner apologetically remembered he had our check in his jacket pocket. In the fun, or melee, he had innocently forgotten we had not been paid. His wife was quick to locate the check in the jacket pocket and hand it to Will. He thanked the couple and the three walked back into the hall. The wife wisely climbed into the driver's seat.

Josh came over to us and asked if everything was okay. After being assured it was and he would not be a party to any legal action, he offered each of us a free beverage. Then, laughing, he said, "Those guys don't mean any harm. They're good fellows out to have a little fun. They do this every year and I raise hell, but I always let 'em know they're welcome back. Some of them are my best regular customers, and one of 'em is my brother-in-law."

We left the fezzes with Josh to be returned. On our way back to Wake Forest we agreed that after college we should look into membership in the Masons and their Shriner offshoot. "That's our kind of civic club."

Chapter Ten

It soon became evident that the band would break up over the summer since all of us needed to work and make some money.

I got a job with the Raleigh Recreation Department driving a truck with a heavy wood and steel "drag," scraping Little League baseball fields by day and taking Coastal Plain and Tobacco State leagues baseball scores at night for the Raleigh *News & Observer*.

Ray worked for his Dad in the wholesale grocery business, delivering produce, canned goods, meats and assorted food items to independent grocery stores in five counties.

Drew, the pre-med student, worked in a funeral home driving the hearse or hauling flowers in a van to cemeteries, erecting gravesite tents and doing a variety of necessary tasks. He never responded when we inquired as to whether funeral home workers secretly removed gold teeth from the deceased, or whether corpses wear underwear under their burial clothing.

Hank surveyed roads for the state of West Virginia, fished, played outfield for cash with some semi-pro baseball team under an assumed name and fished some more.

Chick worked in his Uncle Mario's bakery in Trenton, arriving on the job at 4:30 a.m. and becoming convinced that this was not a career he wished to pursue, family insistence notwithstanding.

Norm worked in an appliance store, selling a wide variety of all the new modern household conveniences, but preferring to repair radios, his passion. He delved into the two-way radio business in a major way and we tried to convince him to secure a pair so the Woodie and the Chevy could stay in contact on band trips. Didn't happen.

Hal got a job with a construction company building houses near Ft. Bragg for military-related families. He learned first hand that quantity and not quality was the driving force behind his particular company's government contract productivity. Nonetheless, the money was very good.

Shy, unassuming Mack had a job with the City of Laurinburg reading water meters where he learned to fend off spiders, small snakes, dogs of various sizes, and the romantic intentions of a few lonely housewives.

Jud worked on the grounds crew and in the pro shop of a golf resort in the NC mountains near his Forest City home and bartended at the 19th Hole of the country club. He offered compassion and understanding to lonely women whose male partners preferred being on the golf course or in the card room to coming home.

Augie found a job working in the lab of the Buncombe County Memorial Hospital, periodically undertaking unassigned chemical experiments on his own, several of which, if gotten out of hand, could have blown up a goodly portion of the psychiatric unit directly above. Not to mention Augie, himself.

Will half-heartedly worked as a salesman in his dad's car dealership but spent most of his time focused on getting band jobs booked for the fall. Naturally, he used the dealership's paper, stamps, envelopes, and mimeograph machine.

It occurred to Will that while Lucky was a "good 'ole boy," and had landed us a few jobs, he had too many little entrepreneurial irons in the fire. The Southerners were not getting his priority attention and we needed to pursue opportunities beyond high schools in Piedmont North Carolina. Bigger fish. With bigger budgets.

Will found out from Lup about the Pumphrey-Allsbrook agency in Richmond, Virginia, which had excellent contacts with the military, many upscale hotels and quite a few colleges in the Carolinas and Virginia. They booked a number of bands very successfully and had actually launched the highly successful big band career of Johnny Long, who had an orchestra at Duke during his college days. We became a client of the agency with high hopes for greater visibility and more aggressive representation. And, more money.

Will's constant marketing efforts included sending promotional pieces to chambers of commerce, merchants associations and groups such as Rotary, Lions, Kiwanis, Jaycees, VFW, American Legion, and any organization he could identify which was involved in fund-raising dances and putting on local festivals. The Azalea Festival in Wilmington was a prime, three-day event that included big dances in The Lumina at Wrightsville Beach. There were many others, including the Blueberry Festival in Burgaw, Sweet Potato Festival in Snow Hill, Peach Festival in Candor, Pumpkin Festival in Yadkin, Peanut Festival in Williamston and the Seafood Festival in Morehead City, to list only a few.

Surely, some of those festivals needed a dance band and not just bluegrass fiddle players, barbershop quartets, or family gospel singers.

• • • • •

Another concern we all had was the military draft. The Korean War was grinding on and many Wake Forest men were being drafted into the Army if they hadn't already volunteered for the Navy, Marines, or Air Force.

One evening, several of us were discussing the real possibility we would be called up. Not being in the ROTC or National Guard where we might be deferred, we decided to go ahead and volunteer, as a group, for the Air Force. They had just come out with handsome new blue uniforms which were a definite plus over boring Army khaki or Navy bell-bottoms with a flap that buttoned up the front on two sides that, we believed, made urgent access difficult.

We were so serious that four of us KAs...Will, Ray, Drew and I...actually drove over to Raleigh and talked with the recruiting officer. He informed us that we would have to take physicals and, assuming we passed, be put on a waiting list before being sworn in and shipped to Lackland Air Force Base near San Antonio, Texas. The delay was because so many men were volunteering for the Air Force they couldn't assimilate them all at once.

It had to be the new blue uniforms.

We put our names on the waiting list and returned to Raleigh a month later to take our physicals. To our great surprise, we all passed!

If I were carrying any kind of disease that was discernable through urinalysis, both Drew and I would have failed the physical since he found it impossible to pee in the little bottle while standing naked and cold at the trough with 50 other guys, even though he had consumed a fair amount of beer the night before.

Being a friend, I accommodated him after I had filled my vial. After all, what are friends for?

Again, we were told it could be several months before we were called but our names would remain on the active list unless we removed them.

The director of the Selective Service System issued a statement on April 12, 1951: "...a student who is registered with a local Selective Service board may be considered for deferment...if he has successfully completed his second year in a college...and had a scholastic standing in his second year class which placed him in the upper two-thirds of the male members of that class..."

Somehow, every member of The Southerners made the grade. As each of us received our marks ending the spring semester 1951, and subsequently got a deferment letter in July from college President Harold Tribble, we quickly called Will, indicating we would report for duty in The Southerners in September, not the military.

The four of us promptly went to Raleigh and had our names taken off the active recruits list. The blue uniforms would have to wait.

Chapter Eleven

Will had wanted to expand the band now that we were getting playing dates for bigger audiences and in venues other than high school gyms. The Southerners' sound had come together well but to fill out the brass section he wanted a third trumpet. The first place to look was in our own back yard.

Randy Warren was already a rising junior, intent on becoming a Baptist minister. A native of Wadesboro, NC, he had played lead trumpet for his high school marching band and was an exceptional sight-reader. The short, handsome, blond pre-ministerial student was president of the WFC marching band and a fine musician. In addition, we could use his positive influence and optimistic attitude.

When Randy was invited to be one of The Southerners, he was hesitant, initially, but finally admitted that his need for money to stay in school somewhat compromised his denomination's outlook on dancing. After all, he rationalized at the time, "I'm not doing the dancing and $12, or more a job will buy lots of sardines and crackers."

The overall sound was dramatically enhanced now, with exceptional harmonies coming from the brass and sax sections. However, unless we wanted to cram six people into each of the two existing cars, we would require a third vehicle. This meant we would likely need to "hire" someone at school with a car just to drive to and from jobs, plus the extra gas.

Will decided for all of us that it was better to cram twelve people into two cars to save the money. His money. Both Chick and I, the shortest members in the band, volunteered to ride in the trailer, assuming we could stretch out somewhat and sleep to and from jobs. Hal reminded us that such activity was against the law.

"Rats!" Chick responded, "I've seen farmers hauling chickens and pigs and cows and horses in trailers all the time. Seems Red and I should get equal treatment with animals."

"As soon as you two are on the same intellectual level as those animals they may grant you an exception," Hal gleefully answered. "Plus we don't want to have to hose out the trailer after every job."

Since Chick couldn't afford a bass and we had to have one for rehearsals as well as jobs, we rented an old 'bull fiddle' from Lupton's for $25 a month. It was now more important that we have an enclosed trailer, one with sides and a roof and a door that could be locked, we arranged to rent one from Claude Taylor when needed for $2.50 a day.

We were having to pay booking agents a 10 percent fee for jobs they secured for us. Scale pay for the twelve of us was $156 for four hours. Gas for two cars to travel 200 miles, roundtrip, at 19 cents a gallon, 15 miles per gallon each car, costs a total of around $5. Payments on the stands and new musical arrangements came to $20 a month. From time to time, we had to rent a PA system, which we included in our pricing, and both the Chevy and the Woodie needed periodic repairs, oil changes, and recapped tires.

Without acing any economics courses, we quickly got the message that in our business model, increased capacity required increased expense, which necessitated increased revenue. We raised our asking price to $300 per job. However, we would take a bit less rather than miss a paying opportunity.

• • • • •

The new fall semester brought four major occurrences to Wake Forest: new students in the form of freshmen and transfers, Southern Conference football, and two special dances.

As active musicians in a dance band, we didn't get to attend dances often as participants, so when one of the major terpsichorean affairs was scheduled by the Inter-Fraternity Council, we opted not to book our band in favor of some personal leisure time. Norm, Hal, Will, Randy, Ray, Drew, Hank, Augie, Bud and I were all in fraternities, so there was no question where our loyalties were on these major social occasions.

The annual homecoming dance was held in Raleigh's Memorial Auditorium on October 27, a Saturday night following the Deacons' afternoon thrashing of the Carolina Tar Heels, 39-7. Charlie Spivak's Orchestra was playing for the dance and since he was one of the top trumpeters of the time, and had a recording of *Tenderly*, we were elated when we heard him do our theme song.

Will and I happened to be standing close to one another, with our dates, when a couple danced by us. The coed was heard to say, "Hey, that's The Southerners' song." Now that was special.

Our dates were rather perturbed, to put it mildly, that we had rather go stand at the foot of the stage and gawk at the Spivak aggregation, listen to their arrangements and take in that big band aura (as we had with Claude Thornhill's orchestra earlier in the year), than to actually dance with them.

Early in the dance, we happily learned that the light green union cards we all carried in our wallets were a ticket backstage. Will was the first to check it out, assuring the off-duty police officer guarding the stage door that musicians were entitled to this amenity and that Spivak would be pleased. Not sure Will's case was valid, the cop checked with Spivak's road manager who allowed that it would be okay for all of the band members to come backstage, meet the maestro and get an autograph at intermission.

Believing that we could dance anytime but hob-nobbing with Charlie Spivak was a once-in-a-lifetime opportunity, Will went one way and I went another, gowned escorts in tow, to locate the other band associates in the crowd amidst their fraternity cliques, and have them join us.

Fortunately, most of our dates were also somewhat in awe of this one-night-stand band whose records they owned, so they agreed we could go backstage if we took them along.

Mr. Spivak, or Charlie as he insisted we call him, was affable and delighted that we were interested in the big band business. While we noted his musicians quickly left the stage and retired briefly to their bus in the parking lot for a pick-me-up, he hung back and drank a Coca Cola, chatting with us and signing whatever we shoved out to him, principally bits of scrap paper we had torn out of an old Ice Capades program we found in the Auditorium lobby.

Hank had seen the 1950 Kirk Douglas movie, *Young Man With a Horn,* and been fascinated by the fact super-trumpeter Bix Beiderbiecke, whose tragic story was featured in the film, carried his cherished instrument in a soft cloth bag with a drawstring.

Naturally, Hank had to have such a carrying 'case' himself, so he found a seamstress working at a Wake Forest laundry who agreed to create a soft bag for his trumpet. It was gold in color, in keeping with the Deacons' old gold and black college colors, with a heavy black drawstring. Although it took some effort, Charlie managed to write his signature on the bag with a blue ink fountain pen.

Charlie never asked Hank why he had the cloth bag, but I imagine he knew.

• • • • •

The next big event was the Christmas Dance in mid-December and although The Southerners had been in contention to play the job, the Bob Lee Orchestra out of Richmond had gotten the work. However, we were under consideration for the IFC's Spring Dance in May.

There were numerous Friday and Saturday nights throughout the fall when The Southerners didn't have a job. Most of us in the band tried to use the time for female interests.

Those of us who were car-less sought every opportunity to find someone with a car where double dating was possible and we could adventure beyond the town's borders. Most coeds were dancing enthusiasts and when one of the brothers with "wheels" suggested an evening at Mann's, I was ready to call Betty Mac, Betty Jo, Molly Dickson or any one of numerous really good dancers on campus for a platonic fun occasion on the other side of the drums.

Mann's was a combination roadhouse and auto auction located about six miles north of Raleigh on the old Wake Forest Road that ran parallel to U.S. 1. It had a sizeable dance floor, booths along two walls plus tables for four around the dance area, and a large, colorful Wurlitzer jukebox that always had the top platters. Ten cents a record, three for a quarter.

For a couple of dollars in the juke box plus the price of burgers and fries, beers and Cokes, two hours at Mann's slow dancing or jitter-bugging to *Nevertheless, My Foolish Heart, Bewitched, Bothered and Bewildered, Mona Lisa, La Vie En Rose, There's No Tomorrow, It Isn't Fair, That's My Desire, You Belong To My Heart, Too Young, Mockingbird Hill, If, My Heart Cries For You, Slow Poke, Because of You, I Get Ideas, Be My Love, Would I Love You* and *How High The Moon* was time and money well-spent.

There were, indeed, many, many very attractive, desirable, dateable coeds at Wake Forest, but of all the band members only Hal and Randy had serious female relationships. What with rehearsals once a week, sometimes twice, playing dance jobs on many Friday and Saturday nights, requisite schoolwork, fraternity demands, and extra-curricular involvements, dating was a most irregular event.

As to those transfers and freshmen coeds, it was a priority for upper-class, social-minded, unattached males anxious for a female relationship, long-standing or casual, to scout out the 'new blood' and, finding a particularly outstanding prospect, stake a claim as quickly as possible. Competition was formidable.

The fact was, not every young lady wanted to have too close a relationship with a musician in a dance band since he would be off playing jobs on the typical date nights most of the fall and spring. Since most of the girls coming to the campus for the first time as transfers or freshmen were unaware of The Southerners, we found it the better part of judgment not to make mention of the M word - musician - early on in a new relationship. If things were looking up, we would casually break the news and hope for the best. If things were not working out, the band was our excuse to break things off — "It wouldn't be fair to you, honey, for us to get something going and I'd be gone on a job and you'd be stuck in the girls' dorm on a Friday or Saturday night. And you wouldn't be able to travel with us 'cause we get back too late. That's just not right. 'Course I'd still like to see you when I can"

Hal had a soul mate in Sandra Johnson, with whom I had gone to high school in Raleigh. Theirs was a quiet, private type of romance, although their studying together night after night in the library, out in front of everyone, made a statement. I tried that approach several times but never could keep my mind on whatever it was I was to be studying, from an academic standpoint that is.

Randy was smitten, to say the least, with Jean Collins, a beauty court member and accomplished organist, whose long-term interests in life were music and devotion to church work. This complemented his desire to be in the ministry. We embarrassed him more than once by asking where they went to make out. In the darkened choir loft after her practice, maybe?

Chick and Norm sought out females from north of the Mason-Dixon line preferably, but they were as scarce as matzo balls at Wake Forest. Periodically, these two would reject their Yankee loyalties and take out a Southern Belle. Norm preferred those with higher intellects; Chick preferred girls with athleticism. There were plenty of both at Baptist Hollow. Now and then, we knew they sneaked over to Duke to find girls from "back home" since New Jersey had the second largest number of students enrolled at the Durham school, next to North Carolina.

Hank had his pick of the ladies and usually attracted more than his rightful share. One in particular, a pert little blonde majorette, was agreeable to romance with him during weekdays as well as weekends, day or night. While he had no car, he knew guys who did and were willing to loan him a ride/private room for an hour or so.

He carefully studied the daily weather reports and when rain was in the offing, washing out baseball practice and marching band field drills involving majorettes, he would make his move. He was the only person we knew who had found deserted places in the countryside for daylight trysts and where the car would not get stuck in mud or sand.

Will knew all the nighttime spots. He had mastered how to approach every one of the 18 holes on the Paschal Golf Course at night, on foot or by car, with no moon. We would joke that all he had to do was get a girl in the front seat and turn on the ignition, whereupon the Woodie would go straight behind some out-of-the way abandoned tobacco barn on a side road off Highway 98 East, on its own. He liked to joke that he was the only guy at Wake Forest who got a discount from that machine hanging on the men's room wall in the Texaco station.

To give him an additional advantage, Will had a "necker knob" attached to the steering wheel which allowed him to turn the car easily, when in motion, with his left hand on the knob while he cuddled his lady friend with the right arm. Will believed in employing whatever technology gave him an advantage.

Most of the more 'aggressive' females in the marching band fully understood why Will always picked the back row of the college band bus on trips.

In his self-professed superior female-related knowledge and experience, Will suggested that our best opportunities for physical encounters with the opposite sex were more likely to be with transfers pursuing a religious education career and whose fathers were Baptist preachers.

"Let's face it," the resident expert on women expounded, "Those girls have been so protected and so deprived of male company and an exciting social life for so long that when they get here, man, its like a caged bird finding the door open!"

How he came upon such a revelation we never really questioned, preferring just to let him run on without paying his claims much heed. We also resigned ourselves to having to listen to his tales of pursuit and conquest since he had the car, and he paid us.

On more than one occasion as The Southerners were on the way to a job, one of us would "discover by accident," down in a crevice of the seat, some piece of unmentionables Will had stashed intentionally for us to find as tangible proof of his conquests. Just to raise his ire we would accuse him of buying the stuff at a local dime store and `faking it,' which was right on the money most of the time.

"Frankly, I believe he's a lot more talk than action," Ray observed about Will's supposed prolific amorous adventures, "but you gotta' give him an 'A' for effort."

• • • • •

Among the arriving crop of feminine prospects in the fall of 1951 were Ellen Roseborough and Ginny Barker. Both transferred in from Mars Hill, a small, two-year Baptist school in the mountains of North Carolina, which annually provided Wake Forest with a dependable stream of students and was noted for its strict social codes.

Of the two new coeds, one's father was, in fact, a Baptist preacher.

But not Ellen's. She was a tall, slender, black-haired, pseudo-sophisticated type from Zebulon, NC, with extremely interesting narrow lips and somewhat exotic eyes. The only child of a very prominent, and prosperous, attorney and gentleman farmer, she was anxious to follow in her Dad's legal footsteps and was ultimately headed for law school. Will, with his superior intuitions and opportunist's eye glommed onto Ellen quickly.

Either she was innocently taken in by smooth-talking musicians, or her two years at Mars Hill had, indeed, deprived her of substantive male interpersonal relationships.

Whatever the reason, Ellen was more than a little man-starved.

It wasn't long before she and Will were studying astrological activities in the heavens while parked in the Woodie behind the chemistry building at night. Will allowed as to how these trysts were "not for credit" lab sessions and he intended on 'acing' the course.

Ginny's dad, however, was, indeed, a Baptist preacher. As pastor of the Grace Baptist Church in New Bern, NC, he was of the literal Bible interpretation persuasion; however, he and his wife allowed their three children to attend dances in high school.

Virginia Elizabeth Barker, known as Ginny but never shortened in the Baptist preacher's household to Gin, was quite slender, about 5 feet 6 inches tall, with light brown hair, a pleasant face, a most engaging smile, and the opposite of buxom. She was on track to become an elementary school teacher. Having grown up singing in her dad's church choirs, she quickly became involved in all the college's vocal groups as a promising soprano.

There was something about Ginny's overall persona that appealed to me. She was attractive but not considered a candidate for the Magnolia Court like coeds Julie, Ann, Jo, Betty, Carol, Patricia, and Virginia. She had a quiet demeanor and a comfortable personality. She seemed sincere, genuine and what other girls would term 'sweet.' She was approachable and, most importantly, she was unattached.

One thing we had in common was that while both of us had dated our share of people through the years, neither had developed a serious long-term relationship.

As the song suggests: "This could be the start of something big."

I did find out, however, that Will's "caged bird" theory about daughters of Baptist preachers who came from Mars Hill did not hold true in every case.

Like mine.

Chapter Twelve

With the fall season also came football, which meant the marching band performed at pep rallies, parades and at game halftimes. These demands on the men who played in the Wake Forest College band meant that The Southerners would have to fit their playing opportunities around the gridiron schedule.

The Demon Deacons were scheduled to play three of their 10 games at home in 1951, and the marching band would travel to four additional games. That's seven Saturdays when no dance dates could be booked.

Nonetheless, rehearsals continued. Randy blended into the band's fabric and jobs were found for those weekends when the football team was in Boston, Waco, and D.C. It was not a crowded schedule for the band but enough work to keep us interested and to provide some spending money.

St. Mary's Junior College in Raleigh was a very exclusive girls' school that had both boarding and day students. It was not far from the NC State campus and prime 'pickin' grounds for college boys. We were booked to play for their fall formal, a major social event in the girls' school year.

About a week before the job, Will was talking with the woman who booked us and learned the event was totally formal which included the band. None of us owned a tuxedo. Now we would have to spend almost as much on a tuxedo rental as we would make to play the job. However, we couldn't back out and we wanted the work and the publicity.

As soon as classes were out on Monday, all 12 of us piled in the Woodie and the Chevy and headed to Honeycutt's in Raleigh, a very fashionable collegiate men's wear store that rented tuxedos. It was across Hillsborough Street from the Bell Tower on the State campus.

I had gone to high school with Susan Honeycutt, one of the three Honeycutt daughters, and had dated her quite a bit. When the 11 of us walked in, I saw Mr. Honeycutt and went over to re-introduce myself. Apparently, I had been a decent suitor because he acknowledged me and inquired what the group was all about. I explained our urgent need and the fact we had been caught unaware. I was careful to explain that we would, in effect, be working for free since all our band pay would have to go for tuxedos. Fortunately, he didn't know how much we made.

He got my poormouth message and although he was a dedicated Wolfpack fan, he thoughtfully opted to cut the cost from $8 dollars each to $5 each, plus another dollar for shirt, cuff links, cummerbund, and studs.

Unfortunately for us, the supply of tuxes was limited since there were several formal affairs that weekend and the State guys had reduced the inventory dramatically. He and three college students/part-time sales clerks went about getting us fitted. It became obvious we were going to have to make do with whatever they could find that came close to our measurements.

The plan was that we would pick up the tuxedos late Saturday afternoon, eat somewhere, then go to St. Mary's, set up, and dress. The dance started at eight o'clock.

Coincidentally, Wake Forest and State were playing football in Riddick Stadium in Raleigh that afternoon, which meant seven members of the band and I (a WF cheerleader) would be involved from noonish to after four. The seven marching band guys went to the game in band busses and Bill Barham, Band Director, permitted me to hitch a ride on the bus with them.

Augie drove the Woodie and Hank drove the Chevy to Raleigh. It was a 15-minute walk from Riddick Stadium on the State campus for me and the marching band members to reach Honeycutt's after the game. Everyone was there just before five. The suits were waiting in Wolfpack Red Huneycutt clothing bags and each had a last-name tag on it. We hung them in the trailer and headed the two miles down Hillsborough Street to the Blue Tower for the burgers, lettuce, tomato, pickles and mayo, very thin fries, coffee, and either lemon or chocolate ice box pie.

Arriving at the gym on St. Mary's campus just before 7:00 p.m. we quickly set up the bandstands and distributed the music before finding the restroom labeled MEN for that evening to change into the tuxes.

As we began to put on the pants and jackets, we all realized that not everything fit well. In fact, almost nothing fit well. It seemed that only a few jackets and a couple of pairs of pants were the correct sizes for the persons on the bag label.

Most of us had waists of 28 or 30, 32 at most. There were only three pairs of pants smaller than 34. Most of us wore jackets that were 34 or 36, maybe a 38. Four jackets were 36, three were 38, three were 40 and one 42!

Quickly we began to try on pair after pair, jacket after jacket to determine if anything fit anyone. There were a few jackets that fit here, some pants there, but I don't believe any of us had the correct sizes altogether. Pants lengths presented some problem as well. Mine were three inches too long while Chicks hit him above the ankle. We would have swapped but the waists didn't jibe.

"No one can see me behind the bass drum so I don't care that the pants are half covering up my shoes. I'll just roll 'em up when I get out there," I said in resignation. And, Chick, you can just stand behind your bass fiddle and no one will notice you're expecting a flood."

"I've got to get some pants with a bigger seat, man," Ray was complaining, "These things are too tight. Makes me feel like I've got on Benny Goodman underwear."

"What're they?" Hal inquired.

"In the groove," Ray answered, laughing.

"Mine are more like Indian underwear," Norm answered, "They keep creeping up on me."

"Lot like a country hotel," I suggested.

"How's that?" Chick asked, bewildered.'

"What does a big city hotel have that a small town hotel doesn't usually have? Think about it."

Several of my associates wrestled with the riddle and I left it unanswered for now.

Tux pants generally don't have belt loops. All had suspender buttons. We had no suspenders. We did have cummerbunds.

With about 30 minutes before dance time we had to make major decisions. We did not have time to go buy suspenders. Huneycutt's was closed, as was Norman's, the other popular men's clothing store close to the State campus.

"Ok, guys," Will instructed, "if your pants are too big, put the belt around the top, on the outside. Put the cummerbund over the belt. Tuck your jacket sleeves under the best you can. Hold your instruments up so your jacket sleeves do not fall down over your hands. Leave your jackets unbuttoned. If the pants are too tight, unbutton the fly button, but be sure the zipper is up. Otherwise, some of you might attract a crowd, especially here at St. Mary's. Drew, you and Chick and Red don't need to be concerned about that matter."

"I knew you'd been peeking," Drew commented.

"Nobody's going to stand up to play anything tonight," Will emphasized. "No solos, no sections. Chances are the place will be fairly dark and no one will pay much attention to us after the first five minutes anyhow."

Will realized that he would have to stand often to front the band and make announcements so he swapped around until he got clothes that fit reasonably well.

The shirts seemed to fit, the pre-tied bow ties hooked properly. Now suited up we walked, slowly, to the bandstand and were delighted only a few people, principally faculty and administration types, were around and the lights were dimmed. This being prim and proper St. Mary's, we knew the lights would not lowered any further.

82

At eight on the nose we hit *Tenderly*, with Hank firmly seated. From that point on, we played well and the dance seemed to be a major success. Nothing out of the ordinary, but we made certain we were as unobtrusive as possible all night.

That afternoon, Wake Forest had stomped State 21-6 in football and I don't recall if any of the Deacon players' uniforms did not fit properly. I remember the game, the highlights, and the final score. Hopefully, the people attending the St. Mary's dance would recall how good the music was, not how poorly the musicians were attired.

Going back to Wake Forest that night we all wondered if Mr. Huneycutt and his student sales help had intentionally given us Demon Deacons the incorrect tuxedo fits. One thing for sure, when we returned the tuxes on Monday there would not be any comment, no sign whatsoever that not one of them had not fit perfectly.

Chapter Thirteen

The last job we played before the holidays was 'at home' in Wake Forest, NC for the local high school's Christmas Dance. Since our expenses were less with no travel and because we wanted to impress many of our professors who would be chaperoning with their kids in attendance, we cut the price to $175.

We had not been playing long when Chick pointed out Rosalie Starling as she and her partner danced by. Rosalie was a cashier at P.D.'s Restaurant in downtown and a local high school senior. We ate at P.D.'s when we were not at Frye's or having a hot dog at Morty's. All of us knew Rosalie because she was pleasant, tall, very athletic, had a gorgeous face, and a flat chest.

The reason Rosalie especially drew our attention this particular time was that all of a sudden, she had developed a "chest." A sizeable one. Now whether it was falsies, facial tissues, socks, or something else, there was no question Rosalie had acquired some temporary cleavage for the dance. We noticed it and evidently a number of her high school guy friends did as well.

Most of the girls were wearing corsages pinned to their dresses on their right shoulders, and all the boys had white carnation boutonnieres. Rosalie was getting a big rush. She was good-looking and a good dancer, but, regretfully, many guys broke in to dance with her for another, and sinister, reason.

It seems before each guy started to dance with her, he had removed the straight pin used to fasten his boutonniere to his jacket lapel. When he began his dance steps with Rosalie and she had her head turned slightly toward her right shoulder, he very carefully "popped" the pin with his right hand into the padded area of her left breast.

Had there been unadorned flesh in that general vicinity a layer or two down, Rosalie would have let out a yell. She didn't. Not once. This meant the pins were going into something between the dress, her bra and her skin, like a pincushion of sorts.

When Will ventured a few feet out into the crowd during Mack's solo performance of *Its All In The Game*, greeting dancers as they floated by, he attempted to determine how many pins were adorning Rosalie's padded bosom.

Best he could tell, there were at least half a dozen pins embedded. It was a mean thing for those boys to do.

Rosalie discovered the pins during the intermission and was very embarrassed. She was also very "frosted", to put it in the teen's vernacular. However, in addition to her looks, personality, smarts, and basketball abilities, Rosalie was devious and vengeful.

She remembered every male who had danced with her in addition to her date who was wise enough not to be involved in such a trick. She had a pretty good idea which ones had done the dastardly deeds.

She left the pins inserted, with her date's knowledge, and told him in no uncertain terms that he make sure all the deviant fellows dance with her again. Being high school boys, and stupid, and encouraged by Rosalie's date to again dance with her, they all assumed that what had worked before intermission would work afterward.

Each one again broke in to dance with Rosalie. Each carried a new pin.

Just as the dance moves began, and before he could insert pins anew, Rosalie removed her right hand from her partner's grasp, deftly removed a pin from her bosom, and whispered ever so sweetly in her partner's ear: "If you make one damned sound I'm going to tell Mr. Lawrence (the school's principal) what you were doing with the pins," she said sweetly, but firmly.

When the boy backed his head off a bit and looked quizzingly at her, not knowing what she meant by him not making a sound, she jammed a pin into his rear end as far as his clothing would permit.

Without exception, there would be a gasp of pain, a hushed cry, after which the wounded partner would quickly thank Rosalie for the brief dance and hustle off the floor. Not wanting to be the only victim of Rosalie's revenge, each dancer never told the others of being "stabbed," making certain the remaining culprits danced with her and received the same token of revenge he had suffered. Then each went to the Boy's Room in the gym to check out his butt.

Within a half hour there were no more pins in Rosalie's bosom, her acquired cleavage remained intact, and her date was very pleased that no one, absolutely no one, broke in on him the rest of the night.

We understood later that Rosalie, having told the complete story to every girl she knew, was being praised by the female population of Wake Forest High School on Monday and that a certain nine boys with sore tails were laughingstocks.

"I should'a stuck every one of 'em in the crotch," she declared later.

Chapter Fourteen

It was well known among those in the music business that the military has specific units concerned with entertainment and social events for the troops. In the Army it was called Special Services.

It was also known that each year's budget is predicated upon the previous year's expenses. If you spent less than your budget, you'd get less next year. If you spent it all, you'd get the same amount, perhaps even a bit more. Therefore, it made sense to those folks in Special Services who book such niceties as off-base bands that they should spend all they had before the end of the year. New Year's Eve was the time to blow whatever remained in the coffers.

In the Marine Corps, the equivalent of Special Services was the MWR (Morale, Welfare & Recreation) unit. They booked The Southerners through the PumphreyAllsbrook Agency to play for the New Year's Eve dance on December 31, 1951 at Cherry Point Marine Air Station. The base was located near Havelock, NC, about a three-hour drive southeast from Wake Forest down U.S. 70, and an hour's drive north from Camp LeJeune, home of the 2nd Marine Division.

Thanks to the MWR's largesse, our pay for the night would be…$750! Fat City!

We'd each get a minimum of $35…not to mention that the band's bank account, usually depleted, would be replenished. The new, handsome professional stands we wanted could be ordered. We could upgrade the rental bass. Get a lube job for the Woodie and the Chevy.

We were told by the booking agency to be at the Main Gate to the base no later than 7 p.m. on December 31. Eat before you arrive. No alcohol. The dance was to begin at 9 p.m. and end at 1 a.m. We'd get two breaks, and there would be snacks available. We would be met at Cherry Point's Main Gate and taken to the dance location.

Most members of the band had gone home for the Christmas holidays. Will suggested that we might as well all come together in Wake Forest no later than one o'clock, December 31st. Obviously, for control purposes, we would make the trip to Cherry Point together. A vocalist was required in the contract, so Sara suggested she have her brother drive her up from Wilmington and meet us there.

We decided that since we could afford it this one time, we'd add a baritone sax and a fourth trumpet. This meant Will had to locate some experienced players who could sight read really well since there would be no rehearsal time on site before the dance. Hopefully he could locate players who were not already booked for the biggest-paying night of the year.

Lupton put Will in touch with Rick Beacham from Raleigh, a North Carolina State mechanical engineering student with whom I had gone to high school. He was a very accomplished musician and had been playing off and on with a local band. He eagerly accepted our offer and would bring both his baritone sax and clarinet.

Neil Warrick, a Raleigh boy as well who had played in the high school band with Rick, was a trumpeter in the Wake Forest band. A pre-med student, he was a steady, competent player who, incidentally, had turned down joining The Southerners during our formative days. He liked the New Year's Eve payout, however, and the go-down-and-back arrangement, so he and Rick got approval from Will to drive from Raleigh and meet us in Cherry Point at the Main Gate no later than 7 p.m.

Other than the fact they were Marines, and this was classified as a Marine Corps Air Station, we weren't sure of the mix of our audience. Naturally, we were all too aware of the Korean War and obviously the Marines were deeply involved, but just what kind of Marine would be at the dance? And with whom would they dance?

There couldn't be that many female Marines at Cherry Point.

During the holiday season, Wake Forest ...the town and the college...were so quiet that on this Monday afternoon you could almost hear the stoplight by the overpass at the intersection of U.S. 1 and Wait Avenue change colors. Any businesses that were open were pretty much deserted since nearly all students were gone for the holiday.

The dorms were closed until Tuesday afternoon, which permitted students to return just before school reopened on Wednesday. The Colonial Inn was open since many of the athletes did not go home for Christmas, and the basketball team played several games during the holidays. Hank and Chick were going to find bunks for several of the band guys at the Colonial Inn for one night or try to con Cecile Fussell, one of the nurses, into letting them sleep in an Infirmary bed. It wouldn't be the first time.

With the instruments, paraphernalia and our uniforms carefully placed in the trailer we piled into the Woodie and Ray's Chevy, wearing heavy jackets against the outside freezing temperature... and in anticipation of hearing more of "the heater's not working in the car."

We had at least three hours to drive if we stayed under the 50 mph speed limit, and we would need to get something to eat on the way.

We enthusiastically agreed to stop at King's Restaurant in Kinston, where we could chow down on chopped pork barbecue, cole slaw, Brunswick stew, potato salad, hush puppies, and ice tea or coffee. No telling when we'd get to eat again.

We pulled into the dirt parking lot at the restaurant just after 4 p.m. and quickly settled down to some of the best Eastern North Carolina barbecue to be found. Our waitress, Amy, informed us there were three plate sizes to choose from: 60 cents, 90 cents or the $1.25 version. A side of Brunswick stew was 25 cents, and a large bowl of banana pudding was 15 cents. For about a dollar or so, each of us got our fill. Pre-sweetened iced tea, indigestion and stomach gas were included at no added cost.

An hour or so later, we were on the road past New Bern, on through Havelock and advancing well ahead of schedule to the Cherry Point Marine Air Station.

Chick, Mack, Hank, Drew and I rode with Will while Jud, Augie, Norm, Al and Randy rode with Ray. To break the scenic monotony of sentinel-like gray barns silently guarding barren and beaten fields, those of us in the Woodie discussed our recent Christmas holidays at home.

Hank's older sister became engaged to a local man her mother couldn't stand. No one else in the family liked him either but he was an Army veteran, owned several Laundromats, and had a cabin and boat on Lake Bluestone outside of Hinton, W.Va. so that counted for something. Jack said he and his brother, Kyle, had done some squirrel hunting a couple of mornings, which triggered the 'inhumane treatment of animals' pacifism in Mack. The vociferous debate was called a tie after the rest of us were fed up with the discourse.

Chick's uncle Mario was extremely upset at President Truman and Senator Joe McCarthy and the fact the New York Giants beat the Brooklyn Dodgers for the National League pennant. Some player named Bobby Thompson had homered to win game three at the Polo Grounds. Uncle Mario was threatening to sell the bakery and move back to Salerno. The family convinced him that was not a good idea and it would be better if he just spent more time drinking homemade wine and playing bocce and less time listening to baseball games on the radio.

Mack's mother insisted, day after day, that he reconsider getting a business degree and become a minister. And, why must he leave the family during the holidays and go back to school just to play at some old dance where there would probably be drinking, and such? Mack unsuccessfully argued with her that he did not drink, which he didn't, but he commented to us that had he stayed home another day he would be giving Demon Rum serious consideration. While none of us was really a big-time drinker, several would imbibe a bit now and then, and we assured him we would be happy to assist and introduce him to the "sport" at any time.

Drew tried to get back together with his former girl friend, Polly, a student at East Carolina College in Greenville. He had given her a powder blue angora sweater for Christmas. However, after politely thanking him for the nice gift, she firmly told him she was not ready to "get serious." Drew lamented that he saw her with some guy in an E C C windbreaker jacket a night or two later in the movie theatre. "She was wearing my angora sweater, and hanging all over the jerk through the whole picture. He had angora fuzz all over him! If she wasn't serious, I'd like to know what serious is!" He mentioned something about carrying out his threat to ask Lessie at Frye's Restaurant for a date as soon as we got back to Wake Forest.

Will admitted that he spent several of his holidays wooing Ellen, or, perhaps more specifically, attempting to seduce her. Her dad apparently didn't fully trust her or surmised Will was something of a slick customer, or both, and went to great lengths to be sure Will had no opportunities in and around Zebulon to add to the lingerie trophies.

As Will emphasized, "Where there's a will, there's a way...and I'm the Will! My birthday is coming up January 17. Guess what she's gonna' give me for a present?" We knew there'd be more to this story.

I had given Ginny a very nice silk scarf, several records, and an engraved compact for Christmas and owned up to calling her a couple of times during Christmas break. I also called Lynne, Elsie, Catherine, Julia, Ann, Juliette, Betty and Sarah to wish them a Merry Christmas and ask for a date. I quickly learned all had been booked by longer-term planners than I, and all were "sincerely sorry" we couldn't get together. Sara had become engaged, obviously by a very long-term planner. So much for old home week.

For two days and nights, I worked as a "jumper" for Moring's Florist, delivering potted plants from the rear of the truck to recipients' front doors all night long. Periodically I'd drive the delivery van since the regular driver, Remus Leathers, liked to ward off the cold with a swig of V.O. now and then.

I had come to know Remus well (he had a twin brother named Romulus) when I worked at the florist on previous Easter and Christmas holidays. He was an aspiring blues singer and the chilly nights were less tedious as I listened to his soulful wailing, which was fair at best. In between songs, there was always his constant, downright funny chatter. Otherwise, I mostly hung out at Five Points in Raleigh with old high school buddies and concluded that Ginny was looking better all the time.

The lack of traffic on the two-lane highway enabled us to reach our destination just before 6:30 p.m., a half hour ahead of the appointed time as we had hoped. Rick and Neil were to meet us, as was Sara, at the Main Gate. We presumed all four vehicles would then be admitted to the base and we'd be taken to our destination. We still had to set up the stands, run the lights, check out the PA system that was to be provided, put on our outfits, and warm up.

Darkness had set in as we pulled up to the high wire gate abutting a one-story brick building. Positioned on the wall was a very large, elaborately painted sign with a variety of military emblems and lettering indicating this was, indeed, the Cherry Point Marine Air Station, home of the 2nd Marine Air Wing, and a dozen related entities. Bright floodlights shone down upon us and we were quick to see a second large sign: STOP.

Two MPs wearing sidearm holsters came out as they saw our lights and motioned us to pull over. Will parked the Woodie off to the side to clear the main entrance, and walked up to the still-closed gate behind which the MPs were standing. Ray pulled up alongside, shutting the engine down as well.

"Looks like the 'greeting committee' has heard about us," smirked Chick," those MPs have guns."

"I thought they called them SPs in the Marines since they're connected to the Navy. You know, Shore Patrol," Drew observed, "but the armbands say different."

Will strode confidently to where the MPs were standing, motionless, serious.

"I'm Will Thompson and we're The Southerners dance band that's booked to play here tonight," he said, showing the Pumphrey-Allsbrook-supplied marching orders to one of the Marines.

The papers were pushed through the fence and briefly studied by one of the MPs. The other had a clipboard with papers on it and was reviewing information indicating who was to be allowed in by previous arrangement.

"Yes Sir, Mr. Thompson," the second MP said officially, "we have your name here. I believe there are 15 of you. Is that correct, sir?"

Somewhat taken aback at being referred to as "sir", Will answered in kind, "Yes, sir, 15, plus the brother of our vocalist. We have 12 here now and are expecting the others any minute. We can wait for them out there since we are early."

Within 10 minutes, Rick and Neil pulled in and drove up to the Woodie. Will got out, greeted the two newcomers and went over to the fence once again to speak to the MPs.

"Okay, these are two of the guys. We have one more to arrive. Our vocalist. Like I said, her brother is driving her."

"What's the lady's name, Sir? We'll bring her in when she arrives," said MP Number Two with the clipboard. "And may I have the name and residence of each person and the make, model and license numbers of each vehicle?"

"Yes, sir," Will responded promptly and went about gathering the requested information.

With the papers now in order and the MPs apparently satisfied we were, indeed, who we said we were, the main gate was opened and we were told to drive in, and stop.

It occurred to us that the two young MPs likely viewed us as unpatriotic types who were using every means possible to avoid the military in a time of war while they were defending our country. If the choice for us was to either go into the military service or stay in college, I think the vote would have been unanimous for the latter, although four of us had come very close to signing up to sleep in tents in the mud in Texas several months earlier.

It also came to our attention that these young men would rather be doing something else on New Year's Eve than pulling this particular guard duty. Candidly, we were proud of them. Not envious, just proud.

Now that the three vehicles were inside the gate, we were anxious to get to the Officers' Club or Recreation Building or Gymnasium or wherever the dance was to be held. We remained stopped, engines off for several more minutes, awaiting orders and directions.

Chapter Fifteen

As we sat waiting in the two cars, we rolled the windows down to ventilate the interiors of our vehicles with some refreshing air and enable us to chat back and forth. Some 10 minutes later, a four-door sedan painted military khaki pulled up. A Marine sergeant got out and came over to Will's window.

"Sir, are you Mr. Thompson?" When Will nodded, the Marine continued. "My name is Sergeant Hansen. I've been assigned by MWR to escort you to the site and to provide you with assistance required throughout the evening. Please follow me."

Before Will could say "Yes Sir" or salute or tell him about Sara's later arrival, Sergeant Hansen was back in his car and motoring out Roosevelt Avenue toward the party place. Our three vehicles fell in behind him, heading into the darkness.

Even though all of us had driven by this base many times on the way to Morehead City or Atlantic Beach, we had no idea how massive an area it was, or what its function was. Now, as we drove slowly along the asphalt road we seemed engulfed in vastness. Lights were on in most of the two-story, dorm-like brick buildings we passed, and we could make out a water tower on the horizon. We passed several wide parade grounds, crossed a number of streets and, periodically, would see some type of military airplane made into a monument.

"Man, this is kinda' spooky," observed Chick. "Don't see many people."

"Probably at supper," Drew suggested, "or getting ready for tonight's party."

"I think the military term is 'chow'," Hank corrected, "and if there are a coupla' thousand guys on this base, where will they all go to party? Where are the women coming from? I guarantee you these guys are not gonna' dance with each other."

Before any speculative answers were forthcoming, Sergeant Hansen's vehicle pulled onto a very wide asphalt tarmac, which turned out to be a runway. In 30 seconds, we saw a massive building in front of us, looming up out of the ground.

The biggest, most humongous building any of us had seen. There were taller buildings in many major cities, but none compared with the width, depth, and expanse of this facility.

At first, we thought it was a hangar…it seemed big enough to handle a dozen major bombers. However, we then noticed small buildings connected to each side and the front was solid except for a sliding door off to the front left that was at least 10 feet wide and 20 feet high. Light poured out from the vertical opening. Hansen drove in and we followed.

Once inside, our eyes widened to behold the cavernous place — our job site for the next several hours.

Slowing to a crawl behind the sedan ahead, we could see scores of people, scurrying like ants, putting colorful paper cloths on hundreds of tables, setting up bars, laying out buffets. People were rolling things, stacking things, hanging things, draping things, lighting things, placing things, adjusting things, cleaning things, doing things methodically, hurriedly, efficiently.

Whatever this facility was, it was taking on the aura of a festive dance hall with more than a few trimmings. MWR was going all out to throw this party, and it was obvious they knew what they were doing and how to do it. Apparently, they had enough left in the annual budget to do it up big.

The metal-skin building had a steel frame with arched structural roof. The floor was a coated concrete, painted gunmetal gray. We guessed it was about 100 yards wide by 150 yards long. Enormous lights encased in wire screening were spotted evenly every few feet in rows across the ceiling, giving a sense of broad daylight. Looking skyward, we could see large net bags holding hundreds of inflated, multi-colored balloons. Crepe paper was flowing in abundance from every rafter. All around the interior walls were more decorations, from military flags and banners to party materials.

A lot of people had been very busy transforming this place for many, many hours.

Whatever equipment was regularly used in this facility was now pushed against the sides of the hangar and covered with tarps.

"I gotta' tell ya'," Drew exclaimed, "this ain't your run-of-the-mill high school gym! This is gonna' be a helluva' prom."

"Yeah," Chick added, "armed escorts add a nice touch."

"Sergeant, what is this building normally used for, and where do we set up?" Will inquired.

"This is the Drill Hall and Field House, Sir," the Sergeant replied. "It is used for a variety of physical exercise purposes, for drills and training, reviews, parades, and a number of athletic events. You can see basketball backboards attached to the walls along the sides there. We've played football in here as well."

Now we saw the backboards, most of which were being used to support military banners with their distinctive and colorful logos. Gym equipment, mats, pommel horses, parallel bars, boxing paraphernalia all stacked against the walls.

"As to where you will be playing…you'll be up there," Hansen said, pointing toward a 20-foot-high "island" rising from the hangar floor, perhaps 20 yards out from the rear wall and centered.

Constructed of steel scaffolding, with a well secured, 50-foot by 30-foot wooden platform as our stage, the tower was draped on all four sides with white parachute material. Risers had been placed properly on the stage, and an upright piano positioned. Chairs were set up and electrical cords were strung here and there.

"Geez…how do we get up there? And how will people hear us if we're playing straight out 20 feet over their heads?" Hank asked.

"We've done this several times before, Sir. We have three stand mikes out front and every music stand will be miked. Our sound technicians will mix and control the sound from a central area and amplify it through the speakers you see placed around the hangar. As for getting up on stage, that's what the rolling steps over there are for."

Hansen gestured toward the high metal steps on wheels that would enable us to walk up, and hopefully, down as necessary. The steps were the same type used by Eastern Airlines, TWA, Pan Am, and other airlines for passengers to board and deplane.

"We'll push the steps up now and you can unload your equipment. These men will assist you," Hansen offered as he pointed to two enlisted men standing nearby. "You can use the rest rooms there at the end of the hangar to change. When you are ready, you will park your cars outside in a fenced area. Keep your car keys on your person, please. We have a table set up over there for you with food, coffee, soft drinks, water, and snacks when you take your breaks. Private Jacoby and Private Gearhardt will be standing by all evening to handle the steps and anything else you might need, as will I."

This guy was so efficient and sure of himself and the preparations that we all admitted the Marine Corps had its act totally buttoned up. Like he said, he had done this before. Given the way things work in the Marine Corps, we didn't think he wanted any "SNAFUs."

One more thing, Sir," Hansen said to Will, looking at all of us gathered around him, "You may notice there's no fence or barrier around the edge of the platform up there. I suggest you don't wander around too much."

"One question, Sergeant," Jud asked, "why are we way up there instead of down here on the floor?"

The sergeant smiled broadly. First time we had seen a break in his military demeanor.

"Well, Sir, in about an hour or so there'll be a thousand or more people in here. Most of the men have just rotated back from Korea. Air crewmen, maintenance and support personnel. Mostly enlisted men, non-commissioned personnel…they have been keeping our aircraft at the ready for combat missions in support of the 2nd Marine Division from Camp LeJeune for almost two years. They all arrived here over the past week. This will be their first New Year's Eve, stateside, in a long time. There could be a rather active party here, Sir. Candidly, for your safety, it is in your best interest that you not be placed in harm's way. This isn't to say anything will get out of hand, but, it is best to be on the safe side."

"What about women?" Norm asked. "Where will you get enough women for them to dance with? Couldn't be that many female Marines around here."

"According to The Windsock, that's our base newspaper, there are over 200 female Marines aboard here now, Sir. That's out of a total of 2800 female Marines on active duty in the Corps. In addition, there'll be several hundred young women from various civic and church organizations and schools in nearby towns…New Bern, Oriental, Morehead City, LaGrange, Kinston, Goldsboro, Beaufort. They're coming in by bus shortly. They volunteer to come here for special social events from time to time."

The sergeant seemed unconcerned that a little hanky-panky just might flare up given the odds of about three or four intimacy-starved men just back from two years at war to each female. Plus all the booze. He sensed our apprehension.

"Every group has a number of chaperones, Sir, and we have a good many of our people here to assure there will be no untoward behavior." He seemed to believe what he was saying. We didn't.

"Where are the pilots?" I asked.

"Most will be at the Officers' Club, I expect, Sir," Sgt. Hansen replied. "That's also where our 2nd Marine Air Wing Party Band will be playing."

"Party Band?" several of us asked in surprise.

"Yes, Sir. We have a large 2nd Marine Air Wing Band, over 40 men and women. From that unit we have an 18-piece dance orchestra and a smaller party band. They are quite good."

Hansen was careful not to cast dispersions upon the college band under his wing for the night, and he was warming somewhat to our youthful naiveté.

"So," Drew asked, "we are playing here because your own dance band got the Officers' Club?"

"We needed two bands in two places, Sir, and we have only one party band on base. But, if you don't mind my saying so, and please don't repeat this, while the Officers' Club is certainly nice, this will be a night you'll never forget. Plus, you'll be paid. They won't."

"Sergeant, we like your attitude," I said, "Thanks for everything you're doing for us.

Privates Jacoby and Gerhardt stepped up and began taking the things we pulled from the trailer up the rolling ladder, now in place and locked down. The rest of us pitched in and within minutes everything was 'aloft' and positioned. Two audio technicians appeared and hooked mikes to each of the blue stands.

"Hello, test. Hello, testing. One, two, three, four…wave back there if you can hear this okay…is it loud enough?"

Someone close to the doors through which we had entered apparently gave the signal that the PA system was working fine.

"Crank it up a notch or two," one of the techs said to the other over by the amplifiers and controls. "With all the people we'll have in here, we'll need more volume for the band to be heard."

Satisfied they knew more about what they were doing than we did, by far, we took our uniforms out of the trailer and headed to the rest room to change.

In a matter of minutes, Sara and her older brother came driving through the gaping Drill Hall doors, following a Marine in a Jeep.

Their wide-eyed facial expressions indicated they were just as impressed with the facility as the rest of us. By now, the many service workers were busily placing party hats, noisemakers, streamers, and plenty of confetti bags on the tables.

It was going to be quite a night.

"Before you ask where we are going to be playing," Hank said to Sara, "it's up there. And be aware there's no railing, so don't wander around too much when you're singing."

After Sara introduced her brother, George, she retrieved her dress and make-up kit from the car and went off to change. George, Ray, Neil and Will followed the Sergeant to the fenced exterior parking area and quickly returned. It was almost 2010 hours — 50 minutes to go until 9 p.m., or 2100 hours.

Within 15 minutes, all of us but Sara had dressed and stopped by the snack table to get a soft drink or coffee.

"Better take a leak now guys 'cause there's no place to go up there," Ray reminded us. We climbed the stairs to our lofty perches and George pulled a metal folding chair over to the snack table knowing it would be his base for many hours.

As Will was thumbing through a stack of music, facing us in our chairs, the horn players were tuning up and adjusting neck straps. I set out the mallets, brushes and an extra pair of sticks. Chick kept playing the scale with Augie. Nervous preparations.

"Before they let people in, let's run through some numbers. Pull up *The Marines' Hymn*. It should be right on top of your arrangements. We'll probably play it several times tonight," Will instructed. He had a separate stand for his music although when he fronted the band he seldom played. Just kept the sax around his neck, for appearances. Like Tex Beneke.

As a brief warm-up, we played several bars of the *Hymn*, which got rave reviews from the people on the floor, plus several bars of four more tunes in the first set. Following the brief rehearsal, we stood, stretched, walked gingerly about our perch, and viewed the proceedings. Sara emerged in her evening gown and carefully negotiated the metal steps. As soon as she was safely onstage, the two young privates rolled the steps away and against a wall. Stranded on our little isle, we were ready for the invasion.

Not a minute too soon.

At 2030 hours, the main door and several side doors were officially opened and the Marines began assaulting their dance hall beachheads. Hundreds of them. Men and women. Dressed smartly in starched uniforms of the day, they quickly took seats, commandeered tables, put on the hats and began attacking the bars set up around the perimeter.

As predicted, after being held back intentionally inside the Main Gate, bus after bus began pulling up to the Drill Hall entrance, each releasing a sea of young women dressed in a wide variety of colorful evening attire partially covered by heavy coats. Corralled neatly by their chaperones in everyday working attire, each group was escorted to an area of tables specifically designated for them. It appeared many of these girls had been here before and knew the process.

In no time, the Drill Hall was filled with talking, laughing, party-ready people. Although they were aircraft mechanics and technicians for the most part, these Marines quickly went into front line recon mode, scouting the field, looking for potential dance partners. All the young ladies were equally observing the advancing troops.

Many of the overhead lights were now cut off, giving more of a party atmosphere to the room. The stage was set.

Will motioned for us all to take our seats and pull up the first arrangements, quickly.

Without waiting for any instructions from Sergeant Hansen or anyone else, Will said, "Okay. It's quarter to nine. Let's get started now. We do *The Marines' Hymn* to warm 'em up, then, Red, go straight to the Tenderly roll intro. Hank, hold those first notes. In fact, make 'em half notes. Let's hear the sections come in strong. Let's give 'em a helluva welcome home!"

I've been overwhelmed by the cheers and yells of thousands of voices at football games. I've been deafened by the cheers and shrill whistles of maniacal basketball fans in enclosed arenas. And, I've gotten blasts of high-pitched screams from lots of thrill-seekers on whipsaw, spinning carnival rides. But, I've never heard anything like the noise from this crowd as soon as they heard the first notes of their *Hymn*.

Bedlam.

Absolute, unbridled, crazy, exuberant, wild, "We're back from Korea, so let's party" bedlam.

As Hank recounted at our first intermission, "Man, I got a lump in my throat so big I didn't believe I was going to get those first notes out."

Norm said he was so overcome by the outburst he looked up from his music and lost his place, momentarily.

Randy informed us that he had an older brother in the service and the emotion of that moment brought tears to his eyes.

Hal reminded us he had spent three years in the Navy before coming to Wake Forest and he knew the feeling these people were experiencing.

Drew said the patriotic outburst almost made him want to enlist. Again. But, the sensation passed.

It was a moving experience to say the least. We all admitted to goose bumps.

As we segued from *The Marines' Hymn* into *Tenderly*, the noise subsided to a dull roar, lines began forming at the bars, and untimid dancers swarmed onto the powdered floor.

The mood of an exciting evening took shape.

We had decided to take breaks at 10:10 p.m., our time, after an hour and 10 minutes of steady playing, then again at 11:40 p.m. for only 15 minutes. That would get us back on the bandstand five minutes before the Midnight hour, and what was likely to be a celebration of major proportions. We would continue without a break until 1:00 a.m. when the dance ended.

At 10:12 p.m. Will announced we would be taking a short break. The crowd moaned, and our assigned Marine assistants wheeled the steps up for our descent. We noted two MPs, with sidearms, had joined them.

After a fast bathroom break, some dip and crackers and a soft drink, we were all back on the stand ready for Round Two. To get the crowd back into a festive mood we opened with *The Bunny Hop*. If the Marines who had been away were not familiar with this particular exercise, the local girls were fully up to speed and in no time virtually everyone in the hall was hopping around, hands on hips (or in the vicinity) and stomping enthusiastically. Intermittent squeals from a number of girls pierced the air, prompting chap-erones to work their way through the melee to make sure their "wards" were not being "bunny-hopped," as it were.

It was becoming obvious that the party was taking on a ma-jor "glow." Now and then a bottle would be heard crashing to the concrete floor and more and more of the Leathernecks began coming to the foot of the bandstand and yelling up to us their song requests.

Deep In The Heart Of Texas was an over-whelming favorite. Many shouted out for us to do The Marines' Hymn again. Will would give them a Thumbs Up sign but we stuck to the pre-de-termined sets. We began to understand why the MPs were in the vicinity.

Will concluded that it would be best if we played mostly slow tempo tunes for the remainder of the set since the fast numbers were further energizing scores of Marines who needed no addi-tional encouragement to loosen up. We stopped again at 11:40 p.m. for our 15-minute breath- catcher. We knew the final hour was going to be a doozie!

As we came down the metal steps, we noticed now there were four of the MPs with 'batons' around the bandstand, and a grow-ing number of party-goers who had gotten closer to the elevated stage. Will suggested we hit the head fast, grab a Coke and get back on the stand quickly.

"Don't take the full 15 minutes," he urged.

We were seated and playing, *There's A Tree in the Meadow,* in nine minutes. The steps had been rolled away; MPs now posi-tioned themselves on the floor at each corner of the bandstand; and Sergeant Hansen, assisted by the two privates stood guard over the steps for fear some ambitious music lovers, anxious to sing with the band or play an instrument, might attempt to join us.

The crowd was now at jet-engine decibel levels, roaring in an-ticipation of the countdown to midnight some four minutes away. Many of the ebullient revelers opted to ignore the appointed hour for celebration and began to throw their streamers, toss the confetti, whirl the metallic noisemakers, and blow as loudly on their horns as their lungs would allow.

Now hundreds of Marines and the brave young women volunteers, true patriots all, were surrounding the bandstand on all sides, assuming this was the designated location for properly bringing in 1952. At two minutes until midnight, we ended *Tree in the Meadow*. Brass players blew the saliva out of their horns, reed players checked their mouthpieces, Sara moved her chair back closer to the piano and I stood a moment before settling back down on the drum throne, as the two-piece padded swivel seat was known.

"*Auld Lang Syne*...number three," Will reminded us. "I'll do a countdown on the mike and exactly at four, all of you, saxes and brass all stand up. Hit it when I yell 'Happy New Year!' We'll probably play it a couple of times."

I can only imagine what the excitement level was in Times Square on VJ-Day, August 14, 1945, but the atmosphere in the CPMAS Drill Hall at this moment had to be comparable.

"Ten...nine...eight...seven...six...five...four (saxes, trumpets and trombones all stood up)...three...two...one...HAPPY NEW YEAR!" Will exclaimed.

I crashed both cymbals as hard as I could and the band played as loudly as we could, straight into the mikes, but I'm not sure anyone heard a note of *Auld Lang Syne*.

A thousand voices screamed "Happy New Year," and all hell broke loose.

The overhead nets with multi-colored balloons were unleashed and the air was filled with little globes descending lazily into outstretched, wildy-waving arms. The sound of thousands of popping balloons surely must have reminded many of the veterans of where they had been. Streamers were flying in every direction, full bags of confetti were tossed like bean bags, paper horns could be heard squaking from every direction, and paper cups, many containing liquids, were sailing through the air, liberally dousing merrymakers. Several made it to the bandstand.

From where I was sitting and getting a very good view of most of the melee, every female was kissed at least once, more likely multiple times, within the next five minutes. Gosh only knows what else was going on in that madhouse of humanity below us.

We played *Auld Lang Syne* only twice. When two of the many parachutes covering our scaffolding were ripped off, we thought the best thing to do was to play something that might break up the semi-riot going on around us. At first, we thought of doing the National Anthem, but that would be a bit too obvious. We settled on *Undecided*, a good tune for jitterbugging and releasing what energy was left in the revelers. It was a tune that Sara and Randy sang as a duet that was a real crowd-pleaser.

Girls fought their way back to their tables and to their distraught chaperones. Marines headed back to the bars, the mob dispersed from around the bandstand, and the noise level died down to a calm roar.

Sara decided no one was listening to anything she sang at this point, so she convinced Will, brother George and Sergeant Hansen that she should be allowed to dance a time or two herself. The stairs were rolled up and she walked down, grabbed the first Marine she encountered and was off tripping the light fantastic. Our Man Hansen ordered one of the two privates to stay close to the vicinity of where she was dancing in order to "keep a protective watch."

At one minute until 1:00 a.m., we went into *Goodnight Sweetheart*. There was the usual groan from the crowd, but a definite calm quickly settled over the revelers. Like most dances, an atmosphere of bliss pervaded the Drill Hall. Not one female was seated. All were on the dance floor, including most of the chaperones.

Precisely at 1:00 a.m., all overhead lights were turned on and as soon as Will had thanked the folks in the audience, the Marine Corps, and the brave young local volunteer women who had fought the Happy Battle of Cherry Point on this momentous evening, our amplifiers were disconnected. There was considerable appreciative applause and some whistles by the weary merrymakers, acknowledging our contribution to this moment in time.

We just sat, motionless, for several minutes. No one even made a move to get up. It had been the damndest experience of our lives. Draining, exhausting, but an exuberant sensation filled each of us.

The gigantic hall began to clear quickly of revelers, as a small army of service people moved in to clean up the debris. Busses were lined up outside the sliding door, exhaust fumes billowing in the cold night air, waiting to take the tired, footsore, but obviously happy young women back to their homes. Many of the visiting female guests went home with the names of Marines written on scraps of paper stuffed in their coat pockets. We agreed a special medal should be struck honoring these women and awarded to each at a full-blown military review here in the Drill Hall.

Within a few minutes we were packed, the cars were brought in, our equipment was loaded into the trailer, we had changed back into our more comfortable, casual clothes, and were gathered around the snack table downing pastries and hot coffee. Sara had danced until the final note, saying she thought she had danced with 27 different Marines in that brief time. It was her contribution to the war effort.

Sergeant Hansen gave Will a MWR check for $750, drawn on the First-Citizens Bank & Trust Co., Cherry Point Branch.

Will tossed the Woodie keys to Hal and Ray gave the Chevy keys to Randy. Several of us might just have a libation on the way back to Wake Forest, this being the New Year and all.

We thanked the audio technicians, shook hands with Privates Jacoby and Gerhardt, and the four-car caravan followed Hansen's sedan back toward the highway.

The Sergeant pulled off to the side as we got to the Main Gate, got out of his car, and stood by the road for us to pass by on our way out. We all stopped our cars and each member of our group, all fifteen, got out, walked over, and shook his hand. Sara hugged him, which he politely, albeit militarily, accepted.

"Sergeant, you told us this would be an evening we would never forget. You were so right. Thanks to all of you for your hospitality. It has been an honor for us to play here…and I'm sure glad your band got the Officers' Club, not us." Will was eloquent in his farewell comments.

"Thank you, Sir," Hansen replied. "You have a terrific band and it was our pleasure to have you aboard tonight. Have a safe trip home."

We returned to our vehicles and drove out onto U.S. 70. Sara and George headed south to Wilmington for a two-hour journey and the rest of us headed north, hoping to get to Raleigh and Wake Forest by 5:30 a.m. Or 4:30 a.m. Or 1530 hours. Whatever.

Semper Fi.

Chapter Sixteen

The Cherry Point job had done several positive things for The Southerners.

First, it gave us a badly needed infusion of cash, individually and collectively.

Secondly, it established the band solidly as a bona fide, 'together' dance orchestra with a professional big band sound. Thirdly, it solidified belief in ourselves and what we had wrought, through commitment, effort, a good deal of personal sacrifice, and a lot of energy over a year.

Most importantly, it was a genuinely unique experience for all of us and we were having fun. Major fun.

Three days later Will put a rush order in with Lup for some very classy new fiberboard music stands, identical to what the traveling big bands were using. A red v-shaped base with a white scroll-type top that fit over it and the words The Southerners imprinted in black script across the white tops. The S was to be a stylized clef. With six stands across the front for the sax section, six on a raised platform in back for the three trumpets, two trombones, and the bass, the striking stands truly gave the band an exciting new and highly professional look.

Unfortunately, a few weeks later both Augie and Norm decided to leave the group to devote more time to their studies and other pursuits on campus. For a year they had been part of the nucleus and there was no question as to their musical contributions, and personal sacrifices, toward making the band work.

Sara, too, left the band, opting to take an academic sabbatical in favor of a job in Raleigh. However, she assured us she'd be maintaining her campus connections and dancing to the band through a very tight relationship with football player Barry Swenson, Number 20.

Again, we needed musicians who could quickly step in and fill the vacant chairs.

A few months earlier in September, Moe Naylor had transferred in from Mars Hill and joined Hank's fraternity, Alpha Sigma Phi. Once Hank heard Moe play the piano, he knew he was right for The Southerners.

Officially named Morris T. Naylor, Moe and two of his grammar school buddies were fascinated by the antics of The Three Stooges of movie fame. Each adopted one of the nicknames. There was a Larry, a Curly and a Moe - Morris. The nickname stayed with him.

With thick, wavy brown hair pulled straight back, horn rim glasses, and an ever-present cigarette dangling from his lips, Moe looked like a brothel piano player right out of Central Casting. And he played like a man possessed. Lean, lanky, walking with a noticeable limp, the Lumberton native was ready for some big band action. He brought us talent, energy, dedication and a definite attitude.

Entering Wake Forest as a freshman from high school in Greensboro, where he played sax in both the marching and concert bands, was Jimmy (Chip, as in "chip off the old block") Mills. A slim, sandy-haired fellow who really grasped the big band concept, he took over Norm's alto sax chair and played as if he'd been a part of the band since the beginning. Many musicians are good at reading the music, and some, not many, are good at solos and a bit of improvisation. Chip brought both abilities to The Southerners, plus his clarinet.

Now, back to full complement. With the exception that we needed to locate a vocalist, the band continued to rehearse one night a week, anticipating an active dance season in the spring.

Meanwhile, the Public Speaking class I was taking had procured a new Webcor Recorder. With the permission of Dr. Shirley

Franklin, who somehow got the impression I was going to practice a speech, I borrowed it to record The Southerners during a rehearsal. We knew the acoustics were lousy in the Hut, but we had
no sound recordings at all and couldn't afford to go into a studio.

In essence, a spool of thin, hair-like wire, made of iron, would
run from a spool on the left of the recording device, through a
magnetic head and be rewound on a spool to the right. The sound
would be picked up by one small mike placed some six to eight
feet away. To hear the recording, the tape would be rewound, right
to left, directly, avoiding the head, and then played back through a
single small speaker plugged into the rear of the equipment. In its
compact state it appeared to be an over-sized portable typewriter
case, with a handle. Made by Webster Chicago, it was a very new
and innovative recording system fancied by private investigators.

Will selected a dozen tunes he felt we had down pat and, one
after another, we played them toward the tiny mike, designed for a
single voice input. We knew the quality would be less than superb,
but we were anxious to hear ourselves as others did. I rewound the
wire and played it back as we sat, huddled around the Webcor.

The good news was we were able to hear the band apart from
when we were playing. The bad news was the sound was tinny
and because there was only one mike, the overall blending did not
come through well. Nonetheless, we accepted the technological
drawbacks and vowed to get into a real studio some day and do
some proper recordings.

After the mid-January recording session in the Hut, we gathered
around to sing *Happy Birthday* to Will. I handed him a wrapped
package, stating it was a special gift from all of us. Will was surprised, and touched. This isn't what college men generally do.

He quickly ripped the colorful paper and ribbon off the small
flat box, threw the lid off and, found, neatly folded inside white
tissue paper, a pair of lacy black panties with a hand-written card:
This is as close as you're going to get, Will! Love, Ellen.

Thanks to Ginny's enthusiastic assistance in the venture, and
Ellen's willingness to be a good sport, she had contributed the un-

mentionables at our request, but not knowing of Will's boast about his potential birthday gift.

Even Will had to laugh over the gag but, quickly recovering, he reminded us that gifts can be given at any time and he remained confident.

• • • • •

Between Lucky, Pumphrey-Allsbrook, and our own contacts, we had an active spring work schedule ahead, taking a couple of nights off to prepare for mid-winter exams, of course. The Inter-Fraternity Council informed us they wanted The Southerners to play both the Spring Dance and the Summer Dance in Raleigh, which was a greatly appreciated vote of confidence by our college peers.

A real shocker occurred soon thereafter when the Inter-Fraternity Council, of which I was a member representing KA, went to the Administration with a very bold request.

Every Monday, Wednesday, and Friday mornings from 10:00 a.m. to10:45 a.m., all students were required to attend programs in the Chapel, with only three allowed 'cuts' per semester. Although there was a typical steeple on top, it was improperly named.

Given the lack of a multi-purpose facility on the campus, the building was used more like an auditorium. The handsome Georgian-style structure was designed to seat as many as 2400 people, so it could easily accommodate the entire faculty, administration and the total spring '52 student body of 1083, including Law School students. It was the scene for all major theatre productions, pre-game football pep rallies on Fridays in the fall and a wide variety of classical music presentations.

It was also the site of graduation ceremonies, band and choir concerts, music recitals, Religion in Life Week events, campus political speeches, and where the campus newspaper was distributed every other Monday. Many of the chapel program speakers were interesting. A good many quite boring. A speaker of less than dynamic delivery might well look out on a sea of newspapers being read by those in the audience instead of attentive faces.

The formal Mid-Winters dance was scheduled for Saturday night, February 9, with the wildly entertaining Louis Prima and his band doing the honors. Prima had a reputation for showmanship, some terrific novelty tunes, and several numbers of double entendre content. The husky, heavy-set Italian had written *"Sing, Sing, Sing,"* which Benny Goodman made famous, and was by no means a shrinking violet on stage. He was purported to be "the original hep cat."

The IFC knew this. Most students who were into big bands knew this. Fortunately, the college's administration had no clue that Prima's aggregation was anything other than a current replica of Glenn Miller, Paul Whiteman, Glen Gray or Guy Lombardo. Nice, sweet sounds.

Our handpicked IFC team of faculty favorites: Football player and Mr. Good Guy Lewis Jackson; great debater Mitchell Wiley; IFC chairman Ed Harrell: and solid citizens-student government officers Gene Royce and Gregg Kendall. All beyond reproach (as opposed to several of us who were likely seen as shameless hucksters), they prepared a solid, sensible case.

Well-rehearsed, they suggested to the powers-that-be that a Prima concert for the Friday chapel program, prior to MidWinters on the next night, would be a great morale builder for the students during a cold and overcast month. It would be a chance for all students, not just fraternity types and their dates who would be at the dance, to hear the popular band.

Surely, it would be a major image-booster for the Wake Forest College administration who fully understood they were not viewed as social pacesetters, and that far too many of the chapel programs they arranged were less than exciting. It was a bold, innovative, tradition-breaking move.

My guess was that all of the more conservative faculty members of the Chapel Programs Committee must have been absent during that meeting, for our group returned with a verdict in our favor. Prima could do a Chapel concert on February 9th !

Previously, through Prima's booking agent, we had learned he was on a tour of colleges throughout the Southeast and was playing a concert at Georgia Tech in Atlanta on Wednesday night, February 6th. Following that, he had no jobs until our event on the 9th. We convinced the agent that Prima should do our Chapel event for an additional $250 above his dance fee, or an additional assessment of just $28 dollars per fraternity, about a buck and a half a head for most of the Greek groups.

Obviously, the 42-year-old Prima bought the idea knowing this added exposure could help sell more of his records like *That Old Black Magic* and *When You're Smilin'*, plus his wildly popular novelty tune, *Civilization*.

When the Old Gold & Black headlines screamed that Prima was to do the Chapel program the following Friday, we were sure there would be few cuts that day, except for those students who had a personal aversion to the music and/or the entertainer.

After everyone was seated in the Chapel and a few requisite announcements had been made, the stage curtains slowly began to open, revealing no brass or reed musicians but only the rhythm section: drummer, pianist, guitarist and bassist.

A murmur of disappointment, of disbelief actually, went through the crowd when, suddenly, from the rear of the Chapel came the rest of the Prima band! Trumpets, trombones and saxes, came marching down the right aisle toward the stage, with Louis leading the way playing *When The Saints Go Marching In* on his trumpet. Sensational!

The students stood and went wild with applause. I was sure the Infirmary would have to take in several faculty members.

Although every student had a specifically assigned chapel seat assignment, all The Southerners were on the very first row for this chapel program, having skipped our previous classes to make sure we got the best seats in the house.

The New Orleans native did not disappoint. In his gruff, gravely voice he sang *Robin Hood, Angelina,* the hilarious *Please No*

Squeeza Da' Banana, and *Felicia No Capicia.*

He and his vocalist, the stunning Keeley Smith (actually Doro-thy Keeley, a part-Cherokee native of Norfolk, Virginia) did duets on *Be Mine* and *Enjoy Yourself,* and she soloed on *Autumn Leaves* and *I've Got You Under My Skin.*

Playing the trumpet in one hand while dancing and hopping all about the stage, the man who coined the phrases "Solid, Jack" and "Crazy, Man" was a major hit.

When he concluded the 40 minutes, everyone rose in applause, demanding an encore. Aware that classes were to begin in about 20 minutes, Prima wisely walked off the stage down to the Chapel floor, retracing his entrance steps and playing *Way Down Yonder In New Orleans* with Keeley following and singing sans mike. His band stayed on stage.

It was a boffo piece of showmanship. Like the Pied Piper, he lead the crowd out of the Chapel, shook hands, and signed auto-graphs in what had turned into a bright and sunshiny day for all the students who had clapped their hands and kept the beat with their feet the entire concert. To say it was a successful Chapel pro-gram would be a major understatement.

More importantly, it had set a precedent of sorts, one The Southerners were hoping to capitalize on at some future time. The word afterward was that none of the faculty and administration in attendance appeared to have had the urge to get up and jitterbug. It was noted that a handful smiled periodically.

As the Prima band was packing up following the concert, Louis and Keeley came back in the Chapel and walked onstage, joining the others. All our band people were gathered around, classes not-withstanding, when Will invited the two to come over to the KA House for a few minutes.

To our surprise, and delight, Prima agreed and while the band bus took the musicians into downtown to P.D.'s for coffee, he and Keeley walked over to Simmons Dorm, into the KA House, where they spent a spellbinding hour telling funny stories to an enthralled crowd of brothers and non-brothers, most cutting classes, jammed into the Chapter Room.

Adult refreshments were served.

This was a milestone event at Wake Forest. For The Southerners, it was a lesson in crowd-pleasing by a master of the art.

Chapter Seventeen

"I'll tell you one daggone thing...in my next life I'm coming back as a piano player!"

I was going through the usual time-consuming and boring routine of dismantling and packing up all my drum equipment now that the dance was over, and complaining out loud to anyone within earshot in the emptying gym. Not surprising, none of the band appeared to be anywhere in the vicinity.

Then out of nowhere, Moe yelled out sarcastically, "Man, what are you *doing* in here?" He and Mack had come back in to needle me. The two, and the others, had finished taking the stands and their instruments to the trailer. "You're slower than molasses."

Mack smiled, knowing what I had to go through before and after every job and every rehearsal. He had heard me complain often enough.

"Yeah, we've been waiting out in the cold for half an hour while you screwed around in here." Mack enjoyed getting his jabs in. Usually, he and Moe were the only ones who helped me carry my equipment in and out of the dance halls, so they understood my routine frustrations.

"You got any idea how many things I have to set up and take down on every job? Twenty-eight! Twenty-eight! You piano players walk in, sit down, play, get up, and walk out. Sax players open the instrument cases, take out a horn, slip in a mouthpiece, wet the reed, put a strap around your neck and that's it. Trumpet players shove in a mouthpiece and they're ready. Even Chick ...he just hauls in the bass, uncovers it, plays and, zippo, he's done. My mother tried to get me to stick with piano but, oh no, I just had to play drums!"

I was venting, again, over the process I had to go through twice a night, plus the fact I had to do it alone!

"Twenty-eight things, huh?" Moe asked, "Have you really counted them?"

"What else I got to do while you are out having a smoke and I'm packing up? You don't believe me...I've got the bass drum, the foot pedal, two side braces on the bass, and the front gripper. There's the tom tom I have to connect to the bass, and the floor tom tom with the chrome stand I have to unfold. I have to screw on the cowbells and wood block. Put on the two cymbal stands and then screw both Zildjians on right. There's the high hat I have to unfold and set up and then put the two cymbals on it. I have the snare drum and its two-piece stand. I have to set up the throne, two pieces, and connect the bass light. Half the time I have to untangle the durned extension cord. Then I have to find an outlet to plug it into. I get out two pairs of sticks, a pair of mallets, a pair of brushes, and a drum key. On top of all that, I have to take off the canvas covers for three of the drums and haul around the heavy fiber equipment case. How many is that?" I demanded.

"I counted 143," Moe quipped. "This is what you get for not reading music and wanting to look at women during a job."

"And not listening to my mother! What we need is an equipment manager," I suggested.

"Fat chance of Will buying that. C'mon, there is just enough room in the trailer for all this junk. Let's go." Moe was ready to roll. He grabbed the heavy equipment box, Mack picked up the two canvas-encased tom-toms, and I grabbed the bass drum with both hands. We headed out of the now-empty gymnasium to the trailer.

This had been a major event tonight, in several ways.

A major coup was our being booked through Pumphrey-Allsbrook to play a dance at the Women's College of the University of North Carolina in Greensboro. "W C," as it was better known, was totally female and most of us who had gone to North Carolina high schools knew many girls there from "back home." To be invited to a dance by one of the girls at WC meant a serious relationship was working.

The event was sponsored by the WC Junior Class and held in Rosenthal Gymnasium, which the girls had expertly decorated. Overhead, amidst the entwined requisite multi-colored crepe paper, were several suspended revolving crystal balls off which strobe lights were producing exciting patterns throughout the 'ballroom.'

The norm was that these were card dances, requiring that the girls switch partners often, much to their dates' chagrin. The girls' wrists were adorned with both the hanging dance cards and corsages to complement their formal gowns. If the event didn't call for tuxedos, the males were always dressed in suits or jackets with ties.

One of the drawbacks in playing in a dance band was that you did not get to do much dancing yourself. One of the advantages was showing off, as a musician, sometimes for former classmates. It was one thing to play in a high school marching band, which I never did, but to be in a college dance band, one of a dozen musicians sitting up there in the limelight, perhaps playing a solo once in a while, now that was something else!

Throughout the evening, all of the North Carolina-raised boys in the band would spot girls we had known in high school, some of whom we had dated. Now and then they would recognize us and come up to the bandstand to say "hello," their dates in tow but obviously not keen on the idea.

Given our self-elevated unique musician status, we graciously, but oh so suavely, acknowledged their greetings. Of the dozen or so that I knew in the WC crowd that night, I waved a drumstick at Sarah Martha, did a kind of salute to Alice and two Ann's, nodded knowingly to Mary Scott and mouthed a raised-eyebrow "remember me?" to Roselle. It was fun spotting the girls from Broughton High, and recognizing Roselle whom I had not seen since the 10th grade. I had come to know her during a two-week visit to my grandmother's hometown of Clinton, NC and had developed a very brief crush on the brunette beauty. She looked even better than I remembered.

I gave my biggest smile and a loudly voiced "hello" to Lynne Foreman, a petite, pert, pretty blond on whom I had an incredibly serious, deep and true, multi-year, one-sided love affair in high school. I had dated her as often as possible, along with Dusty, Buddy, John Nick and no telling how many others, but without any measurable success. She had graciously been my date in 1950 for The Old South Ball, a special springtime 1860s-era themed gala held in Raleigh in which the KA chapters of Duke, UNC, NC State, and Wake Forest all participated.

While women may, indeed, go for men in uniform, the rented gray wool Confederate Private's outfit I wore for the Ball sadly did not enhance the unrequited relationship with the lovely Lynne. I don't think a General's outfit would have helped either.

Apparently, Will had an especially active social life in high school across several counties for he won the "former dates recognition contest" at WC, hands down! An undocumented fact he proudly brought up, repeatedly.

Curfew for the girls was midnight on Saturday, so the dances usually ended at 11:30 p.m. We stopped at The Toddle House and had scrambled eggs, hash browns, bacon, buttered toast, sliced tomatoes and coffee before heading through town on West Market Street, out to U.S. 70 and back to Wake Forest through Durham.

Standing on the street in front of the King Cotton Hotel and several blocks beyond, in their suits, ties removed, holding their Dopp kits, would be a couple dozen guys who had been to the dance, having thumbed rides to Greensboro from Duke, UNC, NC State, or Wake Forest.

Now, it is after midnight, and there is no car to get them back home. No money to stay in a hotel unless four or five shared a room. The last bus was usually gone before midnight, so they stood alongside the road and hoped for the best. Often, it would be dawn before they would get a ride, likely as not with one of the morning newspaper distribution trucks or a tractor-trailer from a dairy. However, to get a chance to spend a few hours with the girl friend was worth the inconvenience.

Earlier in the evening, as The Southerners were taking a break outside the gym, wandering about and wondering why a statue of the goddess Minerva was given so much prominence on the campus, I saw Billy Gibson, a Kappa Sig at Wake Forest, and his date. A few weeks earlier he had asked me if we had any room in one of our vehicles because he had been asked to go to the dance at WC and was looking for a ride. Unfortunately we didn't, so when I saw him at the dance I asked how he got to Greensboro.

It seems a Kappa Sig pledge, Jody Winston, had a convertible at school. However, he seldom allowed anyone to ride with him, saying his Dad absolutely forbade him to haul "a bunch of rowdy guys around." Obviously, this did not set well with his potential frat brothers, so when they learned he was going to the big dance at WC, but wouldn't take anyone with him, they went to his room on Saturday morning, demanded his car keys, fed him an ample dose of ExLax, took him to the bus station in Raleigh, and put him aboard a non-stop Greyhound to Greensboro.

They called his girl friend, telling her they were calling at Jody's request and that his car had developed some engine trouble. He was taking a bus to Greensboro and wanted her to meet him at the station when it arrived about 3:25 p.m. Then the four of them took the convertible to Greensboro and the bus station.

"Well", giggled Billy, "we had just driven up when the bus pulled in. When the door opened, Jody came tearing off that thing like a shot out of a Roman candle. He didn't even slow down to say hello to his girl. He headed for the men's room and stayed there a very long time. We waited for him, gave him his car keys, and asked if we might have a ride back to Wake Forest later that night. He said he'd be delighted to give us a ride. In fact, he was more than anxious to offer us a ride.

Last time we saw him that afternoon he was heading to Belk's to buy some new underwear. We saw him at the dance and he was as nice as nice can be. A little pale, but real friendly. He got the message."

Chapter Eighteen

Thanks to the popularity of Keely Smith, Helen Forrest, Martha Hilton, Rosemary Clooney, Ella Fitzgerald, Jo Stafford, Perry Como, Frank Sinatra, Don Cornell, Dick Haymes, Connie Haines and Kitty Kallen, among many other male and female vocalists who were singing with the better-known big bands, many dance contracts were now requiring that The Southerners have a vocalist.

Now that Mary had left, our first choice was to get another Wake Forest coed; however, the rules governing female students, especially their sign-out and sign-in stipulations, ruled out that option. It would be fine if a job were in The Community Building at Wake Forest and the coed could be back in the dorm by 11 p.m. or so, but for one to travel with "the boys" and not get back from a dance until the wee hours of the morning was out of the question., even if we finagled a bed for her in the Infirmary.

It was here that Rick Beacham, our NC State baritone player, suggested to Will that we go listen to Patsy Carson, a very attractive former student at Broughton High in Raleigh and now at Peace Junior College in the Capital City. She was singing in a student talent show at the college several weekends later, so Will, Rick, Hank, and I drove over to hear her "audition."

Not only did she have the looks and a terrific voice that would work extremely well within a big band sound, she possessed poise and showed exceptional stage presence. Will caught up with her after the show (she came in second...a classical pianist took first place...three faculty members were the judges) and told her about The Southerners. He offered her union scale and said he would arrange her transportation to and from Raleigh as necessary.

At her insistence, he also agreed to meet her parents and convinced them that he (of all people) would personally be responsible for her safety. They agreed to give it a try. She required that no one ever call her Patsy, preferring to be billed as Pat. All the rest of the band members assured her we would protect her from Will. She thought we were joking.

With the addition of Pat, and Will getting Rick to agree to play baritone sax at every opportunity, the band had grown to 14 pieces. Now a third vehicle was a necessity.

That problem was resolved when very tall, very skinny Paul Avery Broyles, aka Pab, (Will's freshman first cousin from Thomasville) who had a powder-blue Pontiac convertible, readily agreed to drive for gas money and $5 per job. He played French horn in The Little Symphony and knew music, but was anxious to play drums. He agreed to undertake the duties of equipment manager, hoping to give me some relief now and then, and I counted on his set-up/break down help.

When the deal was struck, I quickly informed Moe and Mack that my wish to get an equipment manager was coming true, and deservedly so. They insisted I must be giving half of my band pay to Pab.

• • • • •

Two big jobs in spring 1952 held special meaning for all of us, and a third job broke us into the festivals arena where we had hoped to make inroads.

In addition to playing for the annual Leaksville Cotton Festival on May 8, a major ongoing event that drew thousands of folks from central and Piedmont North Carolina, we were booked to play twice in Raleigh's Memorial Auditorium, the scene of those traveling big band concerts and dances all of us had been to so many times.

When I was in high school and getting into big band and jazz music, I had attended many concerts in this venue. As bona fide musicians in The Southerners and college students attending a dance or concert, we had stood at the base of that stage, ogling whatever aggregation was performing and dreaming that some day, one day, we would be up there ourselves.

Now, thanks to the Junior-Senior Prom of my old high school, Needham Broughton in Raleigh, and our own Wake Forest Inter-Fraternity Council, The Southerners would, indeed, take to that stage.

Usually, the Broughton dances were held in the gym; however, due to remodeling and new construction at the school, that was not an option, so the auditorium was selected as the site. Since Rick, Pat and I were former Broughton High School students and had actually received our high school diplomas on that very stage, we were especially delighted to play this job.

Because the auditorium was so large, with a balcony, and no rafters, there was an absence of crepe paper and some of the usual prom decorations.

Regretfully, there was no wishing well or fountain.

We decided to keep the curtains closed until the dance began rather than just walking out from the wings and starting the job as most big bands did. We were hoping for a dramatic opening.

Arriving earlier in the afternoon, we set up our stands and lights and walked four blocks up Fayetteville Street to the Mecca Café for supper, returning at 7 p.m. Instead of putting our uniforms on in a small men's toilet, a team locker room or out in the open in a parking lot as we often were obliged to do, there were several dressing rooms assigned to us. Pat had her own. Her parents had come to hear her debut with The Southerners.

At 7:30, Will had us all come onstage to make sure the arrangements were in order on each stand, check the click-on stand lights and tune up briefly, before we headed back to the wings to wait for his set call.

The faculty chaperones had all arrived. As I peeked through the small "check out the house" peephole in the heavy, burgundy velvet proscenium curtain, I could make out several familiar faces of former teachers amidst the dozen gathered: Coach Holloway and

Miss Barnett (were they or were they not?), Mrs. Ruth (whose legs, unfortunately, were so afflicted with varicose veins that some mean-spirited students nicknamed her "Map Legs;" Florence Starks, the male-starved drama teacher whom we were positive was giving Harley Sutter private lessons of some sort in the prop room after school, and Mr. Ira Dee Raker, the ultimate pipsqueak.

At 7:55 p.m., we all took our places on stage. The sole stage-hand, Horace, knew that in addition to dimming the house lights, he was to draw the curtains, which were to open outwardly from the middle to reveal the band as soon as Will gave him the sign.

It was at this precise moment that Pab (our new equipment manager, driver, and hopeful drummer) was moving farther from the stage sightlines, into the wings near the electrical control panel. He was still looking at us on stage, when he, literally, backed into a large galvanized metal trashcan, sending it and the lid crashing to the floor. It sounded like multiple Chinese gongs had been struck.

Will, hearing the crash, took advantage of the screw-up by immediately signaling Harold to start pulling the curtain ropes, and for me to hit the tympani-like roll on the floor tom tom leading into *Tenderly*. By the time, I had completed the intro drum roll, Hank was on his feet with the first trumpet notes, and the curtain was fully open.

We wanted a dramatic opening. We got a dramatic opening!

Apparently, the gathered crowd thought the crash was, indeed, some sort of unusual musical sound made on purpose to get their attention, for as the curtains parted and the theme song came forth through the microphones and over the house sound system, their focus was totally on us.

Pab left the over-turned garbage can on the floor and, wisely, took to a straight-back chair out of the way.

Rick and I decided against seeking out any of our former teachers at intermission. Leave well enough alone.

Chapter Nineteen

B efore the forthcoming Inter-Fraternity Council Spring Dance, we played a small high school event in Roxboro, NC, about 60 miles northwest of Wake Forest. As usual, we delved into conversations about a variety of things to kill the hour-plus we had to drive through less-than-exciting countryside.

However, on this particular Friday afternoon the small talk was a bit more serious when Randy asked us what we thought of the upcoming national elections in November of '52.

"I know the Democrat and Republican conventions haven't been held yet, but it looks like Eisenhower is going to be the Republicans' guy. You know he's asked President Truman to release him from his Supreme Allied Commander job. He'll retire from the Army for sure."

"No question "Ike" is a good leader." Mack said, "He proved that in the war, but he's no politician. And to get anything passed through Congress you have to negotiate. Give and take.

"But," he continued, "with all the saber-rattling Russia is doing, and China saying we're using germ warfare in North Korea and the Mau Maus killing folks right and left in Kenya, I'd rather have someone with a military background running the show."

Will added, "For my money, he's a sight better than Stevenson. Adlai just doesn't do it for me. He's a great orator, that's for sure. Makes the most flowery speeches I've ever heard. Lots of promises. What's his background? Governor of Illinois one term? Some Federal bureaucratic job?"

"Yep, that's about it. The Democrats don't seem to have a strong candidate in the wings. Stevenson will probably get it by default.

Maybe they'll do a straw vote at school before the elections but I don't think it will be close... You know, I think Hal is the only one of us who's old enough to vote," I reminded them.

"Hey," Drew spoke up, "did you guys see where some doctor named Salk has come up with a vaccine that might cure polio? I hope it works. You know, we had a KA brother to die suddenly from polio just last summer. Burt Britton. He was from Enfield. Really good guy. Just a sophomore."

"Maybe you can come up with some kind of miracle drug one of these days, Dr. Pearsall," Mack suggested.

"Naw," I broke in, "he's more likely to invent something dumb like that new cereal Kellogg's just introduced. You know, the Frosted Flakes stuff? That'll never catch on."

"Pay me enough and I'll invent whatever type cereal you guys want." Drew was practical, to say the least. "But I think y'all would benefit most from bran flakes and prunes."

"You're really more suited to inventing something like that Mr. Potato Head toy that just came out. Talk about a dumb idea that won't last," Will added.

The radio was tuned to WDNC in Durham and there was too much talk about farm subsidies, hog futures, pest spraying, and weather predictions according to the Farmers' Almanac. No music. With all of us voicing complaints, we asked Randy, who was sitting in the middle of the front seat, to find some music we could all enjoy.

"Have y'all heard that piano player, Dave Brubeck?" Mack asked. "He is way out there. They call it 'progressive jazz' but I don't get it. Can't follow any melody."

"I tell you what's a great new tune," I threw out, "talking about piano players. George Shearing just came out with a thing called *Lullaby of Birdland*. Got a terrific beat. We ought to get it, Will."

"Speaking of wild stuff, "Drew broke in, "The other day I saw that new morning TV program that just started on NBC-TV called "The Today Show." Some weird guy with horn-rimmed glasses named Dave Garroway runs it. The funny thing is, he's got this chimpanzee on there and he's a riot. Named J. Fred Muggs. That monkey is really talented!"

"Hey, does he read music? Maybe he can take your place on tenor," Will joked, provoking similar comments from the others.

"There's another new TV program with a 22-year-old guy named Dick Clark who does a record-spinning teenage dance show. He plays all the top tunes. Good stuff." I offered, "If you've got nothing else to do on Saturday mornings but watch more teenagers dance, as if we don't see enough of that on jobs like tonight."

"I sleep on Saturday mornings, and that includes when I've got early Saturday morning classes." Drew responded matter-of-factly. "I did hear somewhere that there are 17 million TV sets in America. Seventeen million! Still, I wouldn't watch a dance show. I guarantee you that Clark guy will be off the air in six months."

"Let's change the subject," I suggested." Rather talk about women."

"Okay, you first Drew," Will said. He snickered at the thought of what Drew's 'women discussion' would be.

"Sure. Okay." said Drew, "I've given it considerable thought and decided I'm going to romance Elizabeth, the new Queen of England. She's just right for me. Not too tall. Twenty-five years old. Not bad looking. Got her own house. And rich. What'd I be? A Duke? An Earl? A Prince?"

"You'd be the little guy that stood two feet behind your wife and kept his mouth shut," I responded, "but you'd have snappy uniforms. Epaulets. Maybe a sword."

"I'm sure you'd have a great chance with Elizabeth under normal conditions, "Randy commented, "but she probably doesn't go for younger men. Or commoners."

"Drew's about as common a guy as you'll find, so maybe you'd better pass on the royalty possibilities, my friend." Will continued to jibe Drew who always seemed to bear the brunt of our jokes. "Okay, we've already discussed politics. We can't really talk about women or religion with Brother Randy here, and you all don't know anything about women or sex anyhow, so whatta' you want to talk about?"

"Whatever the subject," I said, "you know my motto: Often wrong, but never in doubt. Anyway, I'm going to sleep." I answered. "Wake me up in Roxboro." The others agreed a nap was better than small talk.

Amazingly, the entire evening at Roxboro High went without a glitch, or any bizarre occurrences. The gym was decorated like a carnival midway, which brought back some vivid memories but Kong, the chimp, was nowhere to be seen.

To our delight, there was a wishing well, of sorts. This time, however, coins were tossed from a booth counter onto a board with varying sizes of colorful painted circles. If a coin landed in one of the several smallest circles, perhaps three inches in diameter, it would mean the dream would come true. If the coin ended up in a middle-sized circle, maybe six inches in diameter, there was a 50-50 chance of realizing the dream. If the coin went into a large circle, a foot in diameter, or between circles, forget the dream. An interesting twist on the wishing well approach, but, again, we agreed the boys' dreams were probably pretty much the same regardless of the method of wishing.

On our way back down Highway 501 from Roxboro to Durham, then over to Wake Forest on NC 98, Hank, Hal and Mack were riding with Ray while Chip, Moe and Jud were with Pab. Chick, Drew, Will and I were in the Woodie, with Randy driving. To help us stay awake and kill the hour and a half it would take to get to Wake Forest, we began describing different types of couples we'd spot on the dance floor at just about every dance.

Often during a job, Chick and I, positioned next to each other on the bandstand and not having to read the sheet music, would scan the crowd, pointing out to each other special "finds" of one sort or another. Invariably, there were several couples whose terpsichorean "attitudes" grabbed our attention, so we began to label them.

"It's easy to spot the 'huggers.'" Chick declared. "They are so in love they wrap their arms around each other and just sway. Don't even move their feet. I swear you can't see where one of 'em's head stops and the other starts. Frankly, I think it looks obscene.

"And they never do the fast stuff, just the slow numbers so they can blow in each other's ears and sniff shampoo," I added, having watched many 'hugger couples' from my perch behind the drums.

Will added, "They'd never get away with that at St. Mary's. If you can't see daylight between the two dancers, some faculty chaperone with a grey bun and nose specs comes over and separates them. Remember?"

Randy was driving, keeping his attention focused on the dark, two-lane highway, but spoke out: "I get a kick out of the 'well pumpers.' When I have a pause and look out I can usually see some dancers moving their clasped hands up and down, up and down, like they're pumping water from a well. Or an oil rig. Their arms must be tired when the dance ends.

"You know what a well is, don't you Chick?" he jokingly asked the big city boy from New Jersey.

"Sure I do. I saw one once in *Gone With The Wind*...just before Sherman torched Atlanta," Chick, our token Yankee, retorted.

"Ouch," reacted Randy, faking a hurt expression." You probably applauded when Rhett rejected Scarlett."

"No, only when he told her he didn't give a damn."

Drew chimed in. "I love the "acrobats"...especially the jitterbuggers who throw their arms and legs out and do bizarre moves. Jump up, squat down, spin and do crazy things with their feet. No rhythm, just wild antics. No need for them to take P.E...just put on a jitterbug record."

"And then there's always the 'show offs, "I added. "They've got all the fancy moves. Or think they do. They dip, they turn. Arms stretched out stiff in front like an Argentine tango couple. I break up when they try to do those Latin dances and don't have a clue how dumb they look. Must have gone to some dance school to learn all that stuff in one easy, short lesson."

"Or watched that Arthur Murray Show on television," Will inserted. "How 'bout the mad bull types? You know, they just barrel around the floor, bumping into people, charging ahead, paying no attention to anyone else, like the floor is all theirs. You can see other people get teed off. I keep hoping a fight will break out."

"My favorites are the ones that can't dance worth a crap to start with, but they don't know it. They think they can, though," he added

Drew was describing what we all saw a lot of, especially at high school dances, where many of the students gave it the old college try, or as my mother would say," their dead level best."

"Got to give 'em credit for trying," Randy remarked with his usual positive outlook on everything. "A lot of those young people don't have the chance to take lessons or go to many social events. Too busy working on farms to watch that teen dance show on Channel 2 in Greensboro. This may be the only dance they go to in a year. I think they are pretty brave to get out there. Not sure I could."

"Good point." I answered, "You're right, as usual. You know, back home, it seemed like all the high school girls had their little cliques. They would gather at one of the girls' houses and have slumber parties. They'd dance with each other to learn all the latest steps. Especially the fast stuff."

"Yeah," Drew broke in, "and most guys didn't know one step from the other. Or care. Especially the jocks. To most guys, it either came naturally or girl friends taught us just enough to get through it."

"Man, we had some guys in high school who could really dance, especially the jitterbug." Will was saying," As a matter of fact, I was a pretty good dancer myself. Not too big on the fast stuff though."

Before he could go from dancing to romancing, which was a given if he had the time, I broke in.

"I loved the jitterbug. Loved the fast stuff. Most guys didn't like to jitterbug but girls were really into it, so I got a lot of dancing action." "

"Must have been the dancing 'cause it ain't your looks, "Drew suggested.

"Or the intelligence...or...." Chick went on.

131

" It was the red head and fast feet they dug. That'll do it every time," I quickly added before someone could take another verbal jab at me. "But, you know, every time we play a high school job or a college dance, whatever it is, and see those folks all dressed up for their big night, and watch the looks on their faces as they dance with their favorite girlfriend or boyfriend, to *their* song, I see a lot of happy people. And it makes me think what we do really does make a difference. It gives a lot of pleasure and good memories to a lot of people."

"No question, we are in the 'memory-making' business," Randy observed very philosophically. "These kids will have memories of the prom all their lives. They may have a scrapbook with photos and a pressed corsage, maybe a program or some other memorabilia they can actually see, but they'll also remember their favorite song, their special song, the person they went to the prom with and the live big band that played. That's us, and we need to keep that in mind on every job."

"Yep, we're truly in the satisfaction business. Theirs and ours," I added seriously.

Will ended the conversation with, "You're right. We don't just make music. We create a little bit of magic, too."

Chapter Twenty

We were making exceptionally good time with Randy behind the wheel when, suddenly, he exclaimed in a startling voice: "Uh oh! Oh no!"

Will sat up quickly in the front passenger seat. "What's wrong?" We all feared some sort of car trouble.

"I just remembered, "Randy responded, "I'm preaching tomorrow, outside Franklinton at Turlington's Crossroads Church. And I don't have a choir."

As he drove around the outskirts of Durham, Randy related that one of his pre-ministerial courses was about sermon preparation and delivery. As part of that course, the students were not only to observe various pulpit preachers, but they had to actually do some pulpit work to get "the feel of it." The faculty selected those students they thought would do the better jobs in the "intern" stage. Randy was a natural.

Just as some public schools allowed college education majors to do requisite practice teaching there, some small rural churches without fulltime preachers allowed future ministers to fill their pulpits from time to time, like at Wednesday night prayer meetings and Sunday morning services. Turlington's Crossroads Baptist Church was among them.

Although he was not yet out of college, much less graduated from the seminary and ordained, Randy had that aura about him, the requisite pulpit charisma .He looked the part, he lived the part. He knew his Bible. And he was an exceptional public speaker with an outstanding vocabulary. Best of all, he had a very realistic, down-to-earth approach to living by The Good Book. We teased him that he'd probably hit it big as a TV evangelist someday.

"What do you mean you have no choir?" Will asked.

"I just remembered that tomorrow there's a big Gospel Sing and Choir Festival down in Benson and the Turlington's Crossroads choir is going to be there. I don't even have a piano player. I mean, I can lead the congregation in singing a capella alright, but it won't be the same without a piano. Or a choir."

"Pull over at the next place you can, "Will said somewhat sternly, "and make sure Ray and Pab see you and have room to pull over, too."

Fifteen seconds later, Randy eased the Woodie into the lot of a closed Sinclair station. Sensing trouble when they saw the Woodie's taillights move off the highway, Ray pulled off and stopped.

Hank leaned out of the Chevy window and yelled out, "What's the matter?"

Will cut the engine, and all of us got out and walked over to Ray's car. By this time, Pab had pulled in and all his car windows were rolled down.

"Well, it seems like we have an opportunity...or as many as want to," Will announced.

"Want to do what?" Moe asked from the back seat of Pab's car, being careful not to spill any libation from the Dixie cup.

"Go to church in the morning."

"Are you nuts?" Moe responded. "What brought this on?"

"Okay," Will explained, "here's the deal. Randy's preaching in about eight hours or so. Near Franklinton. He just remembered his choir is at some Gospel singing thing, so he needs a piano player and a choir. How many of you sinners are in?"

No question this 'opportunity,' as Will put it, had caught everyone by surprise. Had the thought come from Mack or Hal, two of our straighter types, it would've been understandable—but from Will?

"I'm going to drive Randy up there. He can lead the singing but he needs back up and a piano for sure. Lord knows we could all use a bit of religion about now. Moe, what about you?"

"Uhhhhhh....well, I've done some church playin' and could probably bang out a few of the older hymns. Can't let old Randy down, so, okay, I'm in. The Mars Hill folks would be proud."

Randy was obviously moved by this gesture to help him out.

"Hey, if you guys can't make it, I'll understand. Don't worry about it."

One by one every guy agreed to go to Turlington's Crossroads and support Brother Warner, except Drew who had to go home to Pinetops for some family thing.

"Tell you the truth," Drew remarked, "I'd rather be with you in the choir than going to my grandmother's 85th birthday party. I love the old gal, but she doesn't have a clue who I am."

Pab spoke up, "I'm writing my Mother about this, that's for sure, but she'll swear I made it up just to impress her that I'm going to church down here."

"Hey, wait a minute. I'm Catholic," Chick confessed. "I can't do this. And I sure don't know the process, certainly not the songs."

"Well you can run the Bingo game after the service, "Moe told him, "and getting some Southern Baptist sawdust on you won't hurt a bit. Just move your lips when we sing and nobody'll know the difference. And don't flinch when I hand you the snake."

"When you do what?" Chick's eyes got as big as two 45-rpm records before he realized he was being had.

"Okay, "Will announced, "we'll leave the KA House at nine in the morning. We can be in Franklinton by 9:30. Church starts at ten, right?" He looked at Randy.

"Ten is right. I probably need to be there by nine though. Better leave at 8:30. And we can pick out some hymns tonight so you'll know what we're going to sing."

"Let's do the good old timey stuff," I suggested. "Choir directors these days don't seem to want to sing the old hymns much anymore in the city churches, but I'll bet the folks tomorrow know all the good old-fashion numbers. You know, our choir director back home is also an organist and it's like he has to do a Bach or

Wagner concert every Sunday and blow everyone out of the pews with the pipes at full steam. You can't hear yourself or anybody else sing when those prima donnas are blasting away. Old Johann Sebastian Bach played the organ in a massive cathedral, not a church that seats 500 people. I'm not a pipe organ fan."

Hal piped in, "I got that message loud and clear. You know, the other day I heard about a church that was having a capital funds drive and the preacher did the entire sermon on how badly money was needed to build this addition to the Sunday School, how important it was for education, family unity, missions, and whatever. The assistant organist was filling in for the main guy that day and when the preacher turned to the congregation and asked for anyone who'd pledge $500 to the drive right then to stand, the fill-in organist played The National Anthem. I heard the regular organist was fired and they promoted the assistant to the job fulltime."

"Works for me," voiced Randy, with a major grin. "I'm going to file that for future reference!"

"Jud popped up, "I agree, these modern hymns just don't have the feeling, the rhythm, or that old time religion beat. The spirit, if you know what I mean"

Hank broke in and suggested he could do a solo on *Old Rugged Cross* when they took up collection.

"Man, you'll do anything to attract women, even in church," Chip joked.

"Let's do *Rock of Ages* and *Amazing Grace*," said Mack.

"Have to sing *Holy. Holy, Holy*. That's the first song in the Baptist hymnal." I was showing off my Hayes Barton Baptist Church upbringing.

"Okay, we leave at 8:30, then. Everybody wear the blue blazers and a white shirt, if you have a clean one, "Will suggested. "No ties. Gray pants. Now let's go get four or five hours' sleep. And. Chick, we promise we won't tell Monsignor Gerald."

Chapter Twenty-One

Somehow, the 11 of us managed to get a bit of shut-eye, find a clean shirt, and show up on time on Sunday morning. We let Ray's Chevy get a breather, putting six in the Woodie and five in Pab's convertible, with the top up.

"We got to stop somewhere and get some coffee, and a sweet roll," I suggested.

"And some aspirin," added Moe.

Since Morty's was about the only place open at that time on a Sunday morning that had take-out coffee, we quickly swung into town, got our paper cups to go, and a few packaged Honey Buns and were soon out on U.S. 1 north to Franklinton.

In 40 minutes we had passed Youngsville, swung left at Franklinton on N.C. 56, made it to Turlington's Crossroads, and the church.

If Norman Rockwell had wanted to paint a typical, wood frame, one-story, white rural church with a steeple, forget New England. This was the place for his subject. High pitched tin roof. Over-sized windows down each side. Mammoth old white oak trees shading the dirt parking lot, with lots of pines and several maples and magnolias spotted around. Even one weeping willow. There were several wood picnic benches off to one side in a shady, grassy area, and a 'working' well, complete with tin dipper.

A small side building was attached at a right angle to the rear of the church building. Gray cinder block supports elevated both buildings off the sand by about 18 inches with azalea bushes spotted here and there on pine straw beds. Two dogs, a beagle and a "Heinz 57," dozed nonchalantly just under the front of the building.

Three dozen or so cars and pick up trucks were already parked in the lot.

"Sunday school," Randy said pointing to the vehicles. "All the classes but the adults are in the little building in the back. The adults meet in the sanctuary. And no smoking, chewing or dipping allowed in church."

He was looking at Hank and Chick, knowing that a number of baseball players liked their 'chew' of Red Man, often mixed with a stick of Juicy Fruit chewing gum to keep the wad together. He knew as well that neither was a tobacco man but many of us were smokers.

We grabbed our blue blazers, throwing them over our arms or shoulders for the time being, and followed Randy up two steps to the little porch that jutted out in front of the building. We entered the small church through double doors and stepped into a vestibule which ran the full width of the building and was perhaps 15 feet deep. On each end was a small rest room, one marked MEN and one WOMEN. Hinged, floor-to-ceiling double doors with narrow vertical windows lead to the sanctuary.

The main room appeared to be about 75 feet wide by 200 feet long. The floor was wood and a deep red-carpeted aisle ran down the center, separating 12 rows of pews on each side. A narrow aisle ran down each outer side, under the windows. Perhaps 250 people could be seated in the room comfortably. Sun rays were streaming brightly into the room through the undraped windows on the east side of the building.

Down front was a red-carpeted platform, some two feet high by about 20 feet wide and ten feet deep with steps on each side. Positioned on the left up front was an upright piano and off to the right was a table with the Sacrament utensils. Mechanically carved into the side of the thick tabletop were the words "In Remembrance of Me." A heavy wood pulpit with a cross carved into the front stood centered on the platform.

A low wooden wall separated the raised platform from a two-row elevated choir loft to the rear. A baptistery with a stained glass

138

background of John baptizing Jesus was behind the choir loft. A door on each side of the platform on the floor level lead to the rear of the building and to the loft doors. The entire room appeared to have been freshly painted.

Looking inside his first non-Catholic church Chick asked, "Where're the candles?"

As soon as the adult class had its closing prayer and the older folks went outside before re-entering for the church service, Moe walked down to the piano, pulled up the bench and began to thumb through the hymnal index so he could mark the songs he was to play. Hank joined him, carefully removing his trumpet from the cloth bag and quickly fingering the valves. Randy went over to shake hands and greet the adults, whom he appeared to know well. The rest of us hung back awaiting Randy's direction.

Excusing himself from his temporary parishioners, who were curious as to who we were and what we were there for, Randy came over to where we had seated ourselves on the front row by the piano.

"Here're a few orders of service I mimeographed this morning. We'll open with *Holy, Holy, Holy*," he said. "Then a short prayer. Some announcements by the chairman of the Deacons. I'll introduce who you are. That may be a challenge, of course. Then y'all sing *Rock of Ages*. And, I hope you can carry a tune. Be heavy on the piano if you need to, Moe, so you can sort of drown the choir out."

Randy continued the instruction, "I'll read the scripture for today, Philippians 4:19, and there's a prayer. I usually ask all the younger boys and girls to come down front and I do a five-minute special little story with a moral. The congregation sings *Amazing Grace* and then we'll have the collection. Hank and Moe do *Old Rugged Cross*. When the ushers bring the collection plates to the front we all stand and sing the Doxology, that's *Praise God From Whom All Blessings Flow*.

"Then I'll preach the sermon for about 20 minutes. After that, we all say The Lord's Prayer and then everyone sings, *Standing*

On The Promises. I'll do a Benediction and that's it.

"Moe, will you play something for about three or four minutes after the Benediction while people go out? Thanks."

"Hey," Jud asked, "maybe in that first prayer you ask the Lord to bless our singing."

"Or bless the crowd for having to listen to us. By the way, could I do a solo?" Chick asked, jokingly, "Maybe something in Latin."

Mack had promised Chick he would sit next to him and help him through the service, especially the part where you put folding money in the plate.

"Before people come in, Randy, let's run through a verse of *Rock of Ages*," Will suggested.

We made it through with Mack and Chip actually singing tenor parts and Hal doing a mean bass. Chick lip-synched.

Believing we were as good as we were going to get, Randy started for the front of the church when Chick wanted to know what he was going to preach about.

"Sin," Randy answered.

"Are we for it or against it?" Chick asked.

Randy smiled, threw his arms up in the air and said aloud, "Lord, this is the man I was telling you about. Well, one of 'em." Then he went out to the front to greet people coming in while "the choir" went through the left rear door and up to our seats in the choir loft.

Mack, Chick, me, Chip and Jud on the first row with Hal, Will, Pab and Hank in the second. Moe stayed at the piano, earmarking pages of the hymnal of songs to be played.

When people entered the sanctuary, their eyes went straight to the nine of us in our blue blazers, looking very saintly. Fortunately they were not close enough to see our reddened, sleep-deprived eyes or get a whiff of a coupla' guys' breaths. The low wood wall kept them from closely examining our wrinkled grey pants.

At the appropriate time, Randy gave us the nod and we all stood, almost in unison, hymnals properly poised. Chick was a second late but got to his feet and Mack showed him how to hold the hymnal out in front. Then Randy gave Moe the high sign. It was obvious from the start that the spirit had gotten through to him big time.

Moe went into his zone and started playing as heavy a gospel piano as you would have heard backing Sister Rosetta Tharpe or Mahalia Jackson. His left hand was driving home the chords with his right giving the melody "what for." I don't know what the regular pianist sounded like, but Moe got the crowd in the right frame of mind right off with an up-tempo, down home *Holy, Holy, Holy.*

Most of us had grown up Southern Baptists or Protestants of some sort, and knew the words to many old hymns by heart. When time came for us to do our thing on *Rock of Ages*, we were primed and ready. Hal, Mack, Chip and Jud had good singing voices and were able to overcome the flat notes the rest of us offered up. Now and then Chick would slip and actually sing a few words, reading from the hymnal, prompting Mack standing next to him, to poke him in the side and stifle a laugh.

The announcements focused on the need for folks to come to the Wednesday night prayer meeting and to keep up their financial pledges. Brother Lawrence also reminded everyone that next Sunday there was to be a big "dinner on the grounds" after the service and people should call Sister Bertha Godwin to coordinate what covered dishes they planned to bring.

I made a mental note to return to church here next Sunday and get some real home cooking. I could taste the fried chicken, deviled eggs, cornbread, candied yams, turnip greens, field peas and black-eyed peas, and fresh butterbeans cooked with a streak o' lean and a streak o' fat, mounds of potato salad, homemade sweet pickles and pickled beets, homemade chunky apple sauce and chow-chow relish, country-ham biscuits, juicy blackberry cobbler, pecan pie, fresh-baked pound cake, and gallon jars of sweetened tea.

I wasn't sure what I could contribute to the big spread other than an appetite. Maybe get my Aunt Pearl to send me a jar of her pickled peaches and some Nahunta-style liver pudding and sweet potato praline and a couple of her incredible thin-crust chocolate pies with slightly browned meringue piled on top.

Shaking off the daydream, I heard Randy introduce us simply as fellow students at Wake Forest College who kindly volunteered to fill in for the absent choir. He left it at that. I imagine the membership in attendance thought we were fellow ministerial students.

A soulful, stirring *Amazing Grace* by the entire congregation, plus the dynamic choir, filled the building and there were numerous "Amens" heard as people sat after the hymn.

Time came for Randy to call for the offering. Four deacons came to the front with their silver plates, stopped and bowed their heads for the prayer. Hank stood up, looking around as if to ask, "Where's a spotlight when you need it?

The prayer ended and when people realized Hank was standing, trumpet to his lips, there was an audible gasp.

Moe gave him a very slow four bar vamp-like lead-in and Hank went into *Old Rugged Cross* with his eyes closed, playing totally from memory, surprising us all.

Then, Randy took his trumpet from behind the pulpit and, following some sheet music he had placed there earlier, played harmony to Hank's lead. Totally unrehearsed. Totally dramatic.

There wasn't a dry eye in the house when they finished. As the final notes drifted away there were still more serious, heartfelt "Amens." Then, right there, the 127 people (I had counted them from the loft) stood up and applauded! In church. A Baptist church, no less.

Those of us in the loft applauded. Chick even applauded, after crossing himself for safety's sake. It was, indeed, a moving experience.

The crowd settled down. The deacons brought the money down, Randy thanked the Lord for what had been given to His glory, the deacons departed, and Randy settled down behind the pulpit.

It was a grand sermon. Had to do more with God providing

what man needs than about sin, per se, which relieved our minds knowing his text had not focused on sin with us as the subjects. But he never mentioned any of us, thank you, Jesus. He did manage somehow to work Gabriel blowing his horn into the sermon. The guy was good.

Not wanting to be outdone by Hank, Moe pulled out all the stops on the closing number, *Standing On The Promises*. On his own volition, he upped the tempo considerably from the hymnal version. His hands were moving up and down the keys, head bobbing (sans cigarette) and both feet, first one and then the other, pounding out the rhythm on the wood floor. From rural Robeson County, Moe knew what 'camp meeting' music was all about.

The audience fell right into the spirit and started clapping to the beat as they sang. If Randy had hollered out that he was getting up a crowd to go to the Promised Land right then and there, I do believe he'd 'a gotten a busload.

After the last verse, Moe segued reverently into the traditional *Blest Be The Tie That Binds* as Randy walked up the aisle toward the front door. As soon as he gave the benediction from the back of the sanctuary, Moe swung into a Dixieland version of *Closer Walk With Thee*, three-quarter time.

Unbeknownst to the rest of us, Chip had smuggled his two-piece clarinet in, hidden in his folded blazer, and slipped it down under his choir seat. He eased it out during the benediction, and when Moe got to about the second bar, Chip came in wailing. The two of them did a hyped tempo duet that sounded like a New Orleans 'Second Line' coming down Rampart Street heading for the cemetery. All we lacked were the umbrellas.

Folks were caught dead in their tracks, in no hurry to leave. The high-energy music was exhilarating and they wanted more, like an encore or two. Finally, realizing this was their exit number, people began to strut down the aisles and out the door, smiling broadly. Hallelujah!

As we filed back into the sanctuary from the loft, we were greeted by people coming over to show their appreciation.

"You boys were real good. You know ya'll gonna' have to come back now, you heah?"

"That was real nice horn playing, son," one fella' said to Hank.

"You sure do play a mighty fine piano, too, boy," another commented to Moe. "Had my toes tappin' on every song."

"Young man, that *Closer Walk With Thee* made me think of my old home church outside Moultrie, Georgia when I was a girl. Don't believe I ever heard it played so beautifully," she gushed to Chip.

We accepted the plaudits and walked out of the church into a bright sun where Randy was getting due praise for his sermon, his trumpeting and for arranging the exciting musical program.

"Wish our choir could'a heard you boys," one older gentleman allowed. "It might spark 'em up a bit. You sure have made Wake Forest proud."

We had hoped to be musical ambassadors for the college alright, but just hadn't figured it would be in this particular way. Not in a million years! Where was Dr. McDaniel when we needed him?

Randy said he'd been invited to have Sunday dinner with some of his church people and they would bring him back to Wake Forest.

"I can't tell y'all how much I appreciate what you did for me today. You saw how everyone enjoyed it. You truly brought a blessing, and I thank you. Moe, you and Hank and Chip generated a great spirit in there. Never saw people so excited. In fact, Chick, I believe I even heard you singing. Why, there's even a chance for you...'"

"Easy, Rev," Chick said, "I'm still in shock. I've got to go straight to confession."

We shook Randy's hand, told him it had been an unusual and most gratifying experience. Moe admitted it was the most fun he'd had playing the piano in a long time.

We shed the jackets, got into the two cars and headed south to Wake Forest, very pleased we had answered the call, so to speak.

"What's with you knowing that hymn by heart, Hank?" Ray asked, still surprised at the trumpeter's stellar performance. "And, Chip, you flat had that clarinet smokin'."

Leaning back in the seat with a very smug grin on his face, Hank confessed: "My Mother's been the music director at First Baptist in Hinton as long as I can remember. She had all us kids performing in church early on, 'specially during revivals. Heck, I coulda' played a dozen hymns from memory. And, by the way, Randy told me earlier that he was going to join in on *Old Rugged Cross*, but we never rehearsed it."

Chip broke in. "Moe and I decided to one up Hank so we figured we'd just wing that last number. Pretty good, huh?"

"And you guys thoughts I was just some heathen type," the hip piano player remarked snidely.

"You know," I said," if anybody ever writes a book about our band, this is one story that has to be told, but I'm not sure anybody'd believe it."

"Amen, brother," said Randy.

Chapter Twenty-Two

Springtime at Wake Forest was to most of us a taste of what Heaven could be like. Warm, lazy days. Hundreds of trees leafed out with the many magnolias in full bloom, giving off a campus-wide sweet scent that even the perfume counter at Hudson-Belk department store in Raleigh couldn't equal. Birds. Lots of birds. The omnipresent campus dogs ambling aimlessly from building to building, searching for preferred spaces to sprawl out, purposely daring students to step over them.

Coeds beginning to seek out-of-the-way places to get tans on their winter-white legs. Guys in short-sleeves and tee shirts looking for girls getting tans. Sitting in the bleachers to watch a college baseball game, with the memory of our Wake Forest team representing the United States at the Pan-American games in Argentina the year before.

A time to stake out the better bench locations on campus for evening romancing. Walking into town. Thumbing to Raleigh. The Azalea Festival in Wilmington. The Greater Greensboro Open. Magnolia Festival events on campus.

There were times when I, and surely others, felt we were living in a very special place, in a very special time, surrounded by a rare genuineness, and quietude, almost insulated from the "real world." The Wake Forest campus was so small and compact, it wasn't unusual for every student to see most every other student day after day. And it was commonplace for everyone, routinely, to speak to each other. We were so few in numbers compared to our academic peers at larger campuses, there was an inherent sense of togetherness and belonging that was indeed rare.

Whether you were a football player from Pennsylvania, a peanut farmer's son from Potecasi, or the daughter of a prominent
Charlotte attorney, the campus was everyone's hometown neighborhood. It felt comfortable to be there. You belonged; you could
be what you wanted to be.

• • • • •

From open coed dorm windows early each evening, DJ's Gus
Brierson or Mitchell Wiley could be heard on "Deaconlight Ser-
enade," spinning sentimental music over the airways of WFDD.
At precisely 10:00 p.m., virtually every radio then was tuned in
for two hours to Jimmy Capps' "Our Best To You" on 50,000-watt
WPTF, 680 on the dial.

Mixing romantic lines of poetry and passionate prose in his
soft seductive voice while filling requests from college students
within 150 miles or more of Raleigh, Capps was a captivating
"love guru" to the college crowd.

Whether you were hoping to hear the dedication you mailed in,
were lucky to have a song dedicated to you, or just interested in
knowing who was getting attention, it was vitally important to re-
ligiously listen to the bespectacled, 40-something Jimmy Capps.

"LJ in the KA house at Wake Forest wants Sara Helen in Johnson Dorm to know he's thinking of her tonight, and every night."
Then he'd spin *The Very Thought of You* by Ray Noble.

"How do I love thee? Let me count the ways. Elsie at Salem
hopes you're listening there at Duke, Brad." The sound of Perry
Como and *No Other Love* would fill the airwaves.

"This is for Pat, a Durham sophomore at WC, from the Lyon
Man at Carolina, who says he can't wait until this weekend." *The
More I See You* by Dick Haymes.

"If you're listening there in Slay Dorm at East Carolina, Scotty,
Alice at Meredith wants you to know she's sorry about last Satur-
day night and is anxious to hear from you." Billy Eckstine sings
I Apologize.

"From Bill, The Bachelor Pike at State, to Genevieve at Wake Forest on their fifth anniversary together, he wants her to know the best is yet to come." *Our Love Is Here To Stay* by Nat King Cole.

In between every third or fourth dedication, Jimmy would read portions of selected poems or romantic sonnets, maybe a bit of Shelley, Keats, Browning, or Lord Byron in his quiet, soulful heart-touching manner.

Few commercials. Never a fast or raucous tune. The perfect record being selected in support of the sincere dedication. Short, tantalizing, 'dreamy' words to all those college "guys and gals out there in Radioland." There were definitely a lot of gals out there in Radioland, and all of them knew every word to Jimmy's theme song, *Our Best To You*, by Eddy Howard.

• • • • •

Springtime intensified the Will-Ellen togetherness and the Red-Ginny relationship, although Will's seemed to be progressing at a decidedly higher level.

The Drew-Lessie escapade never happened, for he was now looking for new campus coed company rather than a high school girl, physical interests notwithstanding.

Hank and his groupies activities continued. Hal and Sandra maintained their low profile but obviously sincere romance. Randy continued to be enamored of Jean and we suspected they were doing some serious handholding on the way back to the dorm from her organ rehearsals at First Baptist Church.

Spring was baseball season. If Hank and Chick made the traveling squad, we would have to find substitutes or do without our seasoned lead trumpeter and a bass player on some engagements. While we hoped their diamond activities were successful for their sakes, we quietly preferred they didn't do well for our sakes.

The biggest thing to happen to the band that spring came in the form of a special delivery letter to Will from the Carolina Cotillion Club in Rocky Mount, inviting us to play for the June Germans on

Chapter Twenty-Two

Friday night, June 11, 1952.

In North Carolina social circles and dance band parlance this was the jackpot, the Mother Lode, the Mt. Everest of opportunities.

We would have to be at our very best for this one.

While it was exciting to look ahead to the June Germans, we had other major events to focus on, including the IFC's Spring Dance on Saturday, May 10, in the Raleigh Memorial Auditorium and the Tri-City Cotton Ball in Leaksville, on Friday, May 16.

Ginny and Ellen both evidenced an interest in going to the IFC dance, knowing Will and I would be playing most of the evening. Their pitch was they could enjoy the music, critique the girls' gowns, chat with dorm friends, window shop up and down Fayetteville Street before the dance, and get us to buy their supper in Raleigh before the job.

Ellen informed us she was getting written permission from her mother to go home to Zebulon, 25 miles east of Raleigh, for the night. Will was ecstatic over that turn of events and his mind began to shift into high gear, considering all the possibilities. Ginny, however, would need to get back to the dorm by special curfew, 1:00 a.m.

Through a variety of strategic and tactical maneuvers, Will arranged to swap cars with cousin Pab. He and Ellen would take the convertible and bring Ginny and me with them. Pab would drive the Woodie and trailer over with four others, and Ray would have three with him. Rick would drive to the Auditorium from his home in Raleigh. Pat's parents would bring her to the site, stay the evening, and take her home after the dance. Logistics 101.

Will's plan was to leave the Auditorium as quickly as he could after the job and take Ellen to her home in Zebulon. We were certain the half-hour trip would likely take several hours and instead of a straight shot down N.C. 64 it would be by some very circuitous route he had carefully devised. In fact, we figured he had likely spent most of the previous afternoon driving the countryside of eastern Wake County scouting for "opportunity spaces."

Fortunately, Ginny and I were offered a ride back to the campus by Sam Turner, a fraternity brother, and his date, Shug Torrance.

For supper our choices were either the Canton Chinese Restaurant on Hillsborough Street, a 15-minute drive from the Auditorium, Clyde Cooper's Barbecue on East Davie Street, the S&W Cafeteria on the ground floor of the Insurance Building downtown, or the Hotel Sir Walter Coffee Shop across the street. Hardly a tough decision for the ladies who preferred silverware over chopsticks, waiter service to handling a tray, warm Parker House rolls to hush puppies.

When these IFC events took place, two-feet high by 18-inch wide by six-inch deep, neon- lighted metal signs of each of the nine fraternities' official emblems were brought to the scene and all positioned in a row across the front of the elevated stage. In most cases, these emblems were the actual signs that were usually suspended over their fraternity house entrances in Wake Forest. Positioning on the front of the four-foot-high stage was determined on a first-come, first-served basis. Long nails on which the signs were placed had been pounded in the front of the four-foot –high stage wall years before, ostensibly just for this purpose.

At intermissions, each of the fraternity groups would assemble in a circle on the dance floor, brothers and dates, hold hands, and sing various songs of their particular Greek organization. We decided it would be very impressive if we obtained the music to at least one song from each fraternity and play it during the evening, endearing us to the very people who made it possible for us to play the IFC dances.

Anxious to have their song showcased, each fraternity gladly gave us the sheet music to their favorite number, most of which could be categorized as "sweetheart" songs. We realized that the melodies were different but the meanings predictably similar. Gorgeous, faithful, sweet, caring, tender, young, loving women, all.

We wondered how the men would act when they realized another fraternity's song was being featured, so Will announced when the dance began what we intended to do. Happily, there was applause and although each fraternity cheered loudly upon hearing its own song, they were polite when others were showcased.

Will spaced the songs out, one every 25 minutes or so during the evening, and he announced each as we hit the first few notes. We started with The Sweetheart of Sigma Chi, followed by A Sweetheart of Lambda Chi, The Sweetheart Song of Alpha Sigma Phi, then The Sigma Pi Sweetheart and the Kappa Sigmas' Sweetheart.

Next came the Dream Girl of Theta Chi, The Dream Girl of Pika, and The Wonderful Sig Ep Girl. Lastly, to avoid favoritism, My Kappa Alpha Rose.

At the first intermission, Chip suggested it would be more fun playing lustier numbers, those most likely sung at beer parties, of which each fraternity had several. For our purposes, the musical tributes to gorgeous, faithful, sweet, caring, tender, young, loving women, all with incredible eyes, incredible hair, incredible lips and other incredible attributes, were best achieved with dreamier, mood-setting songs.

"I still think we should play *Dixie* for the KAs," the newly initiated Pab said. "Would've been more fun."

"Did you know that four of the nine fraternities here were all started in Virginia?" I responded. "In addition to the KAs, so were the Sig Eps, the Kappa Sigs and the Pikes. So they could all sing *Dixie* legitimately."

" Where'd you dig up that trivia?" he wanted to know.

"Research, man…for a term paper I wrote for Colonel Heatherby's Education class. Hey, anything about the South will get a good grade from him. I wrote a term paper on Robert E. Lee for Frank Gaona in that class and he got an A."

"Gaona…the tackle from Aliquippa, Pennsylvania?" Bud inquired. "Man, he doesn't even know who Robert E. Lee was."

"Don't tell Heatherby that," I answered, "or Frank and I'll both be in trouble."

"By the way," Will injected, "did you see who's here as the faculty advisor for the Sigma Chi's? With his wife. Our good ol' dance-lovin' buddy, Dr. Duane McDaniel."

"You've gotta' be kidding, right?" Hank couldn't grasp that thought.

"Nope, I saw him talking to Harry Nickerson and Virginia Deyton at the break."

Will continued, "…thought I'd dedicate a song to him. Got any ideas?"

"How 'bout Tony Bennett's *Cold, Cold Heart*" Hank offered. "Or Artie Shaw's *All The Things You Are*. I got a coupla' suggestions."

"Fats Domino's *Ain't That A Shame*, maybe?" Jud added. "It's a shame we can't rehearse in the Music Building."

"I've got it," Drew chimed in, "*I Hear You Knocking*. You know, Gale Storm. I hear you knocking, but you can't come in…. like, into the Music Building."

Not to be left out, I suggested *Crying in The Chapel*. Or, better, "Crying Outside The Music Building."

"Maybe we'll just leave it alone." Will ended the game but all of us continued thinking of the possibilities.

As the evening moved on toward the midnight closing dance, many of the folks were leaving early, proclaiming interest in having a snack at the Blue Tower, then driving the 30 minutes back to Wake Forest to the dorms by 1:00 a.m., the expanded witching hour. More likely, to park for a half hour or so, perhaps at Gresham's Lake on U.S. 1, and then return the date to the dorm.

Forget the Blue Tower.

Since Pab was always anxious to play the drums, Will agreed to let him sit in for me on a few numbers during the evening so I could dance with Ginny. Will took off several times later in the evening to dance with Ellen, simply abandoning his alto sax part.

By midnight, the place was virtually empty except for the crew of fraternity advisors/chaperones who had to gut it up until midnight. Before we could finish breaking down and packing the trailer, Will had corralled Ellen and the two of them were taking off for parts unknown, or known only to Will.

As they went through the stage door Moe yelled out, "We'll

see you guys at the Blue Tower or the Toddle House in a few minutes."

Will never looked back but threw his arm up in the air in an 'Adios amigos salute,' and shouted: "Yeah, sure, we'll save you a seat," and began whistling *Happy Birthday.*

Pab graciously said he would finish packing up my drum paraphernalia since Ginny and I were riding with Sam and Shug and had to make tracks back to school. Sam's deal with me was, however, that I had to drive with Ginny riding shotgun while they enjoyed the amenities of the backseat.

Another golden opportunity lost.

• • • • •

Once again, Lucky Lewis came through for us, this time with a booking to play the 14th annual Tri-City Cotton Festival, the "cities" being Leaksville, Spray, and Draper. They were all cotton textiles manufacturing towns within five miles of each other, about 40 miles north of Greensboro.

A fund-raiser, co-sponsored by the Junior Service League and the Tri-City Merchants Association, the 9:00 p.m. to 1:00 a.m. affair was held in the Leaksville Armory with several hundred patrons enjoying the festivities. A week prior, the *Leaksville News* ran a 16-column-inch story on the band with a three-line, two –column headline and a one-column photo of Ray with his trombone. We had seen blurbs about the band, before and after a performance, but nothing on the scale of this publicity.

The day before the event, a major story appeared in *The Leaksville News* with a paragraph on the band, stating, "The planning committee felt very fortunate in securing the popular college musicians." An ad promoting the dance appeared on the same page, featuring in large bold type that attendees would "dance to the music of Ray Fulghum and The Southerners."

A smaller ad on the same page was promoting a prize drawing at the Eden Drive-In theatre outside Leaksville. The prize was a

17-inch, black and white television set. This was an opportunity we hoped wouldn't reduce the number of people coming to the Cotton Ball.

Given the publicity Ray was receiving, we figured he had relatives in the area, on the planning committee or working for the newspaper. He flatly denied any kinship thereabout. We later learned that Lucky had a first cousin on the newspaper staff and the photo of Ray with his trombone was the only single-column picture he had of us. Hank suggested we arrange for campus photographer Irving Grigg to shoot photos of us for potential publicity purposes going forward. He was quick to state he would get his sitting arranged on Monday.

All ladies wearing cotton evening dresses to the Cotton Ball were invited to participate in a competition to be selected as the 1952 Cotton Queen. In addition to the honor, the queen received a silver loving cup, a bouquet of flowers, and a kiss from Mayor John Smith. A sizeable number of contestants entered, likely more for the honor than Mayor Smith's buss. Following the selection and appropriate coronation, there was a Grand Promenade.

Will had purchased the "Handy Tunes for All Occasions" booklets for every member of the band, but I don't think we had rehearsed or played *Les Marseilles* since our first job in Red Oak.

Memories of that initial Grand March came to those of us who had sweated out the challenge. It went much more smoothly this time.

Chip remarked that since each of us was wearing a cotton shirt perhaps we could enter some sort of competition as well. Had there been a judging based on white cotton shirts drenched in sweat we would have had at least a half-dozen fully qualified entrants.

Chapter Twenty-Three

Over the past several months it was becoming obvious to us all that a hard decision needed to be made as to whether the band would break up over the coming summer of '52 or somehow stay intact. The June Germans event was to be two weeks after the semester ended and we all agreed to stick around or make some sort of arrangements to be in Wake Forest for rehearsals and then the big Rocky Mount job.

To lighten the academic load and give us more time for extra-curricular interests, love interests, music interests, more sleep and just less work our two final semesters, Will, Ray, Hank, Drew, Moe, Mack and I decided in April to go to summer school. We would be losing Hal to graduation in June but he was going to play the Germans with us before he went out into the real world. The others said they would stick around the two weeks through the June 13 job, or commute from their homes, knowing we would do a lot of rehearsing.

With the seven of us available as a nucleus to keep the band going, but needing to add a sax player, a bass player and a trumpeter depending upon how many pieces we could book, we encouraged Will to push to get summer gigs. We figured we could each take three courses, nine hours, and that would give us plenty of time to recreate.

The challenge for us all was to find courses we wanted, courses we needed and courses we could hopefully ease through. In my case, I had more than enough quality points but needed 32 hours to finish. My personal plan was to knock off nine in the summer and only have 23 more, minimum, to get my bachelor's degree.

That's only 12 hours in the fall semester and eleven my final semester. Of course, I could go over the 128 hours required, but why overdo it?

A couple of the guys needed the summer classes to stay on course. One or two needed to get back where they should be academically. Or to stay out of the Army.

Instead of going to classes on Monday, Wednesday and Friday or Tuesday, Thursday and Saturday, as was the usual procedure during fall and spring semesters, summer school involved the same course six days a week over a five-week period. Six days meant Saturdays, unfortunately. The good news was that all the courses I wanted were taught in the mornings by professors I especially liked, Dr. Ed Wilson, Dr. Dwight Gentry and Dr. 'Cap'n Eddie' Folk. The bad news was that Gentry's Business 66 (Advertising) was an 8 a.m. call - T, T and S.

Although there were two summer sessions, all of us signed up for the first only, hoping we could line up dance jobs from mid-July until school started again in early September.

Now we were facing final exams as well as playing one more high school prom and preparing for the 79th Annual June Germans.

The prom was to be on a Friday night in Greenville, some two hours east of Wake Forest and 50 miles from New Bern, Ginny's hometown. Settled in 1710 by Swiss and Germans, the town was named after Bern, Switzerland and, ultimately, became the first capital of colonial Carolina under Governor William Tryon. Authentic historical markers were to be seen in about every block, including one that pointed out where Pepsi-Cola had been invented in the late 1880s.

I suggested to her that we borrow my Dad's 1950 Nash Ambassador, drive from Wake Forest on Friday afternoon to the dance job and, after we finished, motor on down to her home for the weekend. She liked the idea and received the requisite written permission from her mother to be away for the weekend.

Coincidentally, her sister, Jeanette, was having her junior prom on Saturday night and we could take that in as spectators, and afterward, watch the midnight submarine races by moonlight on the Trent River. We'd do the family church thing on Sunday and drive back to Raleigh that afternoon. My folks would cook up an early pancake supper and then take us both back to Wake Forest before Ginny's 10 p.m. curfew.

A white collar, one-car family, my parents lived in a two-story, white wood frame house with a slate roof at 1817 White Oak Road, just five houses from the well-known Five Points area. They could walk to church, the grocery store, the drug store, dry cleaners, and about anywhere they needed to go on a weekend, so they consented to let me have the car as planned. I thumbed a ride to Raleigh after classes on Thursday afternoon and brought the gray Easter egg-shaped V-6 to the campus that evening. I parked it behind Simmons Dorm, not out in front.

My Dad had a very good friend, and fellow church deacon, who was the local Nash dealer. He cut my father a very special deal on the car, and price was much more important to my father than what a car looked like. Or, what *I looked* like driving it. Noted as having less-than-handsome styling, the four-door Ambassador Airflyte's most outstanding feature was the fully reclining seats, which, according to the four-color ads in *LIFE, LOOK* and *The Saturday Evening Post*, could provide enough room for three adults to sleep.

Or, whatever.

Although the car was a particular favorite of young people, for obvious reasons, it was either 'before its time' or plain ugly and never took off. My guess is, it was the latter. However, for my purposes — basic transportation — it would do. To be sure, I would never mention in the company of the Reverend Barker and his family what its special feature was.

Sensing a rare feeling of freedom, what with Ginny's weekend pass, a car of my own with no other passengers, and two days with Ginny, we talked the entire way to Greenville, arriving in time for an eastern-style barbecue dinner at Parker's Restaurant. We then found our way to the high school gym by 7 p.m.

My first cousin, Jimmy Kerr, was a student at East Carolina College in Greenville and possessed superb musical credentials, having played trumpet in the U.S. Air Force Far East Band. Now that Jimmy was out of service and in school at ECC, I asked him to come by, bring his horn, and check out The Southerners in case he might want to sit in with us now and then. He showed up shortly after Ginny and I pulled in. We visited until the rest of the band began arriving. He stuck around for the entire evening and, at Will's invitation, sat in on several numbers. He was very good, and obviously loved being part of the big band scene.

East Carolina College was known athletically as the Pirates. The high school decorating committee, in a rare show of tradition breaking, had chosen to do a pirate theme for their prom since they could get exceptional help from the college Theatre Department and borrow a number of their props.

On one end of the gym, built of stage flats and covered in heavy, creatively painted muslin, was the side of a 16th century galleon. Rising some 20 feet off the floor out of a simulated ocean, it had portholes, gun holes, a mast rising toward the gym ceiling, canvas sail, lanterns in the windows and rigging. It was a beautiful piece of work.

Here and there, hanging from the gym rafters, were period flags of Spain, England, France and Portugal, rulers of the oceans, and the prey.

Across the gym was a second galleon, the predator. This was a sleek pirate's ship, with the Jolly Roger flying aloft, fluttering in a breeze created by a hidden electric fan. It was equally detailed, with guns (fashioned from painted tin pipes) sticking through the lower deck gun holes, ready for action.

As imagined in the days when Blackbeard roamed the Atlantic Coast not more than 75 miles to the east of this site, the creative decorators had installed a lengthy plank on the rogue ship's deck, and extended it out over the make-believe sea. We assumed no one would be made to walk the plank; however, given this decorating extravaganza, who knew what was planned?

Instinctively, as we entered the incredibly festooned scene we looked for the wishing well. Instead of the well there was a wooden treasure chest, half buried in sand, with a slit at the top for coins, and folding money. A hand-painted sign was attached:

Aye, yer dreams will come true, 'ave no fear
If ye drop yer pieces of eight in 'ere!

Given the theme, we wondered if Will had brought the head bandanas and earrings so we could get into "costume" and fit in.

To add a real touch of ingenuity, the bandstand was situated on a deserted island. Two small, tiered platforms had been set up for us, surrounded by tons of white sand hauled in from Minnesot Beach where the Neuse River ran into Pamlico Sound. On each side of us were very realistic-looking palm trees.

After we had set up and warmed up, taken a break, and returned to the bandstand, the teenagers began to arrive. They were dressed in costumes of the Pirate era instead of the usual formal wear, an innovative approach that added dramatically to the occasion.

It was then that Will revealed his latest "let's fit in" idea: black eye patches for each of us.

"Hey, you'll look like The Hathaway Man...you know the shirt guy in the ads," Will commented.

Immediate and mixed reaction set in as expected.

Hal, Randy, and Jud spoke out, almost in unison, saying that it was tough enough to see the music as it was but with these "horse blinders" it would be a disaster.

Mack, who with Moe wore glasses, reminded Will of his near-sightedness and suggested a one-eye approach would only add to the problem.

Chick borrowed Mack's patch and put one over each of his eyes, to which Moe remarked that his bass playing would be no worse if he couldn't see what he was doing.

Drew put his patch over his nose.

Hank suggested his patch obviously made him look very suave and debonair.

Someone asked if we were going "trick or treating."

Chip remarked we'd look better with live parrots on our shoulders. "They could sing, too."

Ray allowed as to how we should've gotten fake facial scars.

Finally, we each slipped on our eye patch, with the promise we'd do *Tenderly* in costume but that was it. We had been unable to come up with any meaningful songs about piracy to support the theme, shunning *The Pirate King* from Gilbert and Sullivan's *Pirates of Penzance*, *Fifteen Men On A Dead Man's Chest* and *Yo, Ho, Ho, The Pirate's Life for Me.*

Will, patch firmly in place, welcomed the dancers after our opener with the inane greeting in a very fake English accent, "Ahoy, mateys!"

Of all the proms we had done, this one was perhaps the most spectacular, due to the elaborate decorations and the fact everyone was in costume instead of rented tuxedos and gowns. It was truly a unique concept, with fair maidens in distress and lecherous, teen-aged pirates at every hand.

An hour into the dance, the faculty lady who had booked us came to the bandstand and asked when the vocalist was going to sing. The only female we had in our entourage was Ginny who was sitting with Jimmy off to the side.

Will was completely unaware a vocalist was required. In fact, he recalled, vividly, there was no stipulation for a singer in the contract. Nevertheless, there was no question the folks who were paying us were expecting one.

Now in a real quandary, Will came over to me and asked, "Do you think Ginny can sing a couple of songs?"

Ginny had a very nice soprano voice. She knew how to sing. But she was no soloist and she certainly was no pop singer. I assumed she had done some shower singing, and I knew she was very experienced in choir and chorale singing, but certainly not accustomed to vocalizing in front of hundreds of people with a dance band.

"Go ask her," I responded, certain that if I said anything she'd think I was crazy.

Will called for a short intermission and, with me at his side, walked over to Ginny.

"We have a little crisis, Ginny, and we need your help....bad." It wasn't exactly smooth talk but he got to the point quickly.

"We just found out that these people are expecting us to have a vocalist. Pat's not with us. And you can sing. I've heard you and you're good. How about doing a couple of numbers to satisfy them?"

Before Ginny could react, Will continued.

"What are some tunes you know by heart that we can play? You know our stuff. What do you want to sing?"

If Ginny had been the profane sort, Will would have gotten an earful. She turned a deep red, stuttered, blurted out that she didn't know the lyrics to what we played, or didn't recall any, and there was no way she was going to stand up in front of these people and make a fool of herself. Besides, she added, she wasn't dressed the part, as if Will cared a whit at this point about her outfit.

Now Will was desperate. I had walked up, so Will poked me, saying, "C'mon, Red, how 'bout getting Ginny to help us out here. Man, we are in a bind."

I knew I had better not get too involved in this discussion or Ginny would be on a Trailways bus to New Bern, and I'd be driving back to Raleigh, alone.

In what I hoped would be in defense of Ginny and a point for dropping the idea, I said, "I think the only song she knows by heart that's not religious or classical is *Summertime*. But she's never sung with a band or done stage performances. Not her thing."

Will was not buying any excuses or rejections. He just kept pleading. Now Hank had come over, and Mack, and Randy, and they were encouraging her to give it a shot.

In desperation, I looked over at Jimmy and asked, "Can you sing?"

He quickly answered that he could not carry a tune except with a trumpet.

Finally, Randy, who knew Ginny's choral work, firsthand, assured her she could do this

And, if it would help, he and Hank would bring their music down to the front and play while standing beside her.

Maybe Randy prayed silently for a miracle, or it was the pressure of everyone begging her to help out, but something pushed Ginny into agreeing to do *Summertime*.

Now it was my turn to pray. For Ginny. And, the band. Maybe even the audience.

The Woman's Government Association

of

Wake Forest College

requests the honor of your presence

at the

Magnolia Ball

from eight until twelve p. m.

May 18   Community House

The Interfraternity Council

of

Wake Forest College

requests the honor of your presence

at the

Christmas Dance

featuring

The Southerners

Raleigh Memorial Auditorium

December 13, 1952

Formal   8:00 'til 12:00

Finals Dance

featuring

Harry James and his Orchestra

May 13, 1953

Formal   9:00 'til 1:00

The Interfraternity Council

of

Wake Forest College

requests the honor of your presence

at the

Finals Dance

featuring

Tex Beneke and his Orchestra

Raleigh Memorial Auditorium

May 16, 1953

Formal   8:00 'til 12:00

The Original Southerners, 1951. From left, front row, Chuck Lucarella, (bass), Red Pope (drums), Drew Pearson, Mack Matthews, Bill Tomlinson, Phil Cook (saxes), Mary Finberg (vocals). Back row, from left, Aggie Hanzas (piano), Al Dew and Roy Fulcher (trombones), Jack Rogers and Bud Hames (trumpets).

The Southerners, 1952, front row, l to r; Al Boyles, standing in for Joe Taylor; Tiny Mims, Bill Tomlinson, Mack Matthews, Drew Pearson, Al Dew, Roy Fulcher. Back row, Chuck Lucarella, Red Pope, Bud Hames, Jack Rogers, substitute for Vander Warner.

Raleigh Memorial Auditorium
Image courtesy of the Raleigh City Museum.

Wake Forest Community Building
Image courtesy of Mr. Ed Morris, Wake Forest Birthplace Museum.

Combo group Red Pope (drums), Jack Rogers (trumpet), Bill Tomlinson (sax), Tiny Mims (clarinet) and Joe Taylor (piano) in front.

Tiny Mims (clarinet), Joe Taylor (piano), Jack Rogers (trumpet) Bill Tomlinson (leader), Red Pope (with drum sticks).

2

Tenderly

Lyric by
JACK LAWRENCE

Music by
WALTER GROSS

Valse moderato

The eve-ning breeze ca-ressed the trees TEN-DER-LY; _____ The tremb-ling

trees em-braced the breeze TEN-DER-LY. _____ Then you and

I came wand-er-ing by And lost in a sigh were

Tenderly - 2

Frat Song Circles

Cherry Point
Marine Air Station
Drill Hall

The Surf Club

Combo from The Southerners, 1952. L to R: Kenny Jolls, Joe Taylor (at piano), Jack Rogers, Red Pope; vocalist Pat Curren. Joe Terrell.

Cotton Ball Orchestra Has Unusual Beginning; Gains Popularity Quickly

Wake Forest Student-Musicians Get 'A Lot Of Fun' And Payment Too For Engagements

A little more than a year ago four Wake Forest students, with musical talents decided to spend a Saturday night on the campus doing something different—something other than sitting through the "horse opera" at one of the downtown theatres.

Music instruments were brought out, dusted off and put into use and some of the most unusual music in years was floating around the attic of a fraternity house. It was the smoothest rehearsal ever heard, and it was the start of things to come.

Early Trials

The out-of-the-ordinary diversion proved highly successful, and since that time last March an organization known as "The Southerners" has made its appearance in eastern North Carolina, emerging from the small "combo" without music into a 12-piece orchestra with more than 75 arrangements in its repertoire.

The name of the group was chosen through the process of elimination, and since the four boys were members of a fraternity, the present name was chosen. Of the dozen men now playing with the organization, only one is not a native of some state below the Mason-Dixon line.

The early trials and tribulations of a dance band were quite numerous, but with the advance of time came an advance in technique and managerial ability. Now with their first birthday almost here, the road to future success seems much less rocky for the musical aspirants who have a yearning to make money while they make music.

Bill Tomlinson and Roy Fulcher, two juniors with musical background and a keen foresight into

ROY FULCHER

one of the needs of Wake Forest college, were among the four who opened their instrument cases that Saturday night and began what was to enlarge into an ever-growing, ever-improving dance and concert orchestra. With Tomlinson playing the lead saxophone and Fulcher utilizing the trombone, fraternity brothers "Red" Pope on the drums and Hugh Pearson playing another sax, The Southerners were born. The attic of the KA House may never have a plaque commemorating the birth of a band, but to the original members it was Carnegie Hall without the finery.

Few Qualified Musicians

Word soon got around the campus that the two leaders were looking for musicians who wished to join the group, and many answered the call. Music was purchased from a down-and-out band leader with whom Fulcher had played in high school and practice sessions were begun. Jack Rogers teamed with Joe Ward in the trumpet section, Dave Dickie lugged the bass fiddle, Aggie Hanzas played the piano, and Al Dew and Mack Matthews were added to the trombone and sax units respectively.

The idea of a larger band could not be dispelled, and further recruiting was carried on for some time in order to bring the crew up to the strength and potency of a full-size orchestra. There were no tryouts, for this campus certainly had no abundant supply of musicians who were willing and capable of playing dance music. At long last 12 men were brought to-

Midway

(Below) Announcement article in THE WINDSOCK, Cherry Point Marine Air Station newspaper, referring to New Year's Eve, 1951 event.

Drill Hall Site Of New Year's Dance

Bill Tomlinson and his Southerners will provide the music for the Enlisted Men's Dance at the Drill Hall New Year's Eve.

Dancing to the ten-piece band will run from 9 p.m. to 1 a.m. Free noisemakers will be provided at the admission-free affair, and refreshment stands will be set up at various spots in the hall.

Uniform of the day will be worn.

Officers CLUB NEWS

TONIGHT
1630-1800—Happy Hour
SATURDAY
1300-1800—Open Bowling
1630-0045—Club Hours

WINDSOCK and Fulcher—Leaksville News

Louis Prima leads his band into the Wake Forest Chapel for a concert on February 9, 1952. The band played for Mid-Winters the following night.

Johnny Long Plays For Rocky Mount's June German Held

Several Thousand Attend And Dance 'Till 5 A.M.; Many Parties Are Held

BY FRANCES J. LYON

Blinking lights; the shuffle of dancing feet to swelled music; gaiety at its peak; thousands of beautifully gowned pretty damsels and formal dressed young men, could only add up to one thing — Eastern Carolina's top social event of the year — ROCKY MOUNT'S ANNUAL JUNE GERMAN!

For years now, in fact, for over a half century, June in Rocky Mount has brought to the minds of many, both far and wide, this annual affair. The German, which has been staged by the Carolina Cotillion Club since 1900, even dates back to the 1890's when it was called the Ring Tournament, later to be given the name "Queen City Cotillion Club". For 52 years now the organization has been known by its present name.

Living up to tradition in all its [illegible] Rocky Mount was [illegible] from all over the [illegible]

played by the orchestra at 5 a. m. Then, the trek home, no doubt!

Johnny Long Plays

Johnny Long won the hearts of the thousand dancers and spectators, that packed Planters Warehouse to an overflowing capacity. He ran the gamut from jazz and swing to novelties and sweet ballads for a well -balanced program of music that pleased all who heard him and his talented musicians.

A native of Newell, North Carolina, the orchestra leader received his early education in the Charlotte schools and was graduated from Duke University where he organized his band and is now rated as the Number 1 College Band in the country and called "America's Favorite".

Johnny is a musician in his own rights. A left - handed fiddle player, he wields a magic bow over his strings, to charm all of his listeners. The orchestra is composed of 17 pieces and has two vocalists, Rod Kinder and Dick Perry.

Johnny and his group of musicians have played at Hollywood Palladium, Oregon Ballroom, Chicago, Illinois; Cafe Rouge, New York; Frank Daley's Meadow Brook, Cedar Grove, New Jersey and at Universities and Colleges throughout the state and out of the state.

Prior to the ceremony, the Southerners' thrilled the spectators with their "Southern" style of music. They presented a concert of music [for] the first two hours after which Johnny Long and his orchestra played [illegible]

[illegible] converted from a huge structure — golden weed" is auc- [illegible] place of breath- [illegible]ing — of Wake Forest. [illegible] of warehouse

[illegible] from supper [illegible]ties were [illegible] house affairs beginning [illegible] afternoon and continuing through [illegible] evening's three intermission periods with many breakfast tables spread following the last number played by the orchestra at 5 a. m.

ACTIVE FIGURE. Shown in the above picture are a few of the lovely lassies which participated in the active member figure Friday night of the annual June German. Members and their dates formed the three C's of the Carolina Cotillion Club to the delight of the audience.

THANKSGIVING
DANCE
——CABARET STYLE——

FRIDAY, NOV. 27th

MONK'S WAREHOUSE # FARMVILLE, N. C.

Music By North Carolina's Finest Band

★

SPONSORED BY
FARMVILLE
POST 9081
V. F. W.

★

★

INFORMAL
ADMISSION
$1.00 EACH
9:00 Til 1:00 O'clock

★

THE SOUTHERNERS

Under The Direction of Bill Tomlinson and Featuring Patsy Carter

Band Recently Featured at 1953 Rocky Mount June German and Thomasville Sesqui-Centennial, Sept. 1952

FREE!　FREE!　FREE!

New 1953
Belair Chevrolet

Given To Holder of Lucky Ticket To Be
Drawn At Intermission

11:30 — 12:00

YOU DON'T HAVE TO BE PRESENT TO WIN

Chapter Twenty-Four

We all returned to the bandstand and Ginny walked up to the mike. She had on a nice dress, not a ball gown or cocktail outfit, but an okay frock considering the situation.

As a rule, we did not play *Summertime* although we had the music and had performed it a time or two. Will quickly dug through the arrangements, found it, called out the number and all the guys started digging for it. It was going to be a sight-reading exercise, like it or not.

"Okay," Will whispered to Ginny off mike, showing her his sheet music, "we'll do an intro of three bars, here, and then you come in and we'll follow you. Let's drag the tempo a bit. Earthy, like Ella Fitzgerald or Lena Horne. You'll do great. Just pretend you're singing in the choir."

Ginny was shaking, with a death grip on the mike stand, staring blankly at the crowd which was now aware of the "vocalist."

When the time came for her to come in, she was right on it. At first, the notes sounded a bit warbly, tentative, but as she went through the familiar lyrics she actually got into the number and sang a most acceptable rendition. In fact, once she hit her stride she appeared to be enjoying herself. She had a fine voice and she used it well.

When she finished the dancers applauded enthusiastically. Ginny turned beet-red, gave a little half- wave 'thank you' to the dancers, turned to the band and mouthed a big 'whew!' and walked over to where Jimmy was waiting, and clapping.

"Good job!" he exclaimed. "You'll have to do an encore."

Ginny answered quickly, "That is not a good idea," and sat

down, emotionally exhausted from the ordeal.

At the break Will and I were quick to come over to where she was seated.

"Great, Ginny, really great! I owe you."

"That you do and I'll remind you of it, believe me."

"Proud of you, gal," I said. "You were terrific. Thanks for all of us,"

"Let's just say I have a greater appreciation for band vocalists now," she replied.

All the others offered their thanks as they made their way to the rest room. Ginny, Jimmy and I went outside into the warm May night air where I lit up a Lucky Strike and we indulged in 7 Ups. Ginny's color had returned.

As we got back on the bandstand in twenty minutes Will said to me, aside, "Red, we got to get her to do one more number."

"What's the 'we' crap? Are you crazy? No way she's gonna' do that again. Besides, she only knows that one song, believe me." I felt that should end the matter.

"These folks aren't about to let us off the hook with one vocal all night. I'm gonna' ask her to sing something else. She can pick what she wants and use my music. It's got the lyrics." Will was getting back into the desperate mode.

We played a dozen more numbers and, as we were pulling up the next tune, Will walked over to Ginny. I could see he had put the repeat performance to her. There was considerable head shaking and apparent heated discussion when, suddenly, Ginny got up, walked to the mike, turned to me and just shrugged.

Will turned to us and called out, "*Summertime.*"

Every guy in the band blinked in wonder. Didn't she just sing that an hour ago? Is he nuts?

"Okay, got the music up? On four.... two, three..."

Again, we went into *Summertime*. She sang it well enough, not great, but certainly passable, did her little wave and walked off.

Before we could get up the next number the faculty lady in charge walked up to Will and asked, "Mr. Thompson, is that the only song she knows?"

Quickly Will shot back, "Of course not, but we had a request from somebody to do it again, so she did it again. Apparently someone out there really likes the song. Maybe it's some couple's special number."

She appeared to buy Will's response, turned and walked away. What seemed apparent to us was that more vocals were expected by the woman in charge if not by the dancers, One thing for sure, Ginny was finished with her singing for this night, given the limited repertoire. *Summertime* once was nice. Twice borderline. Three times, no way.

At the next break, I made a suggestion to Will.

"Listen, these folks are expecting someone to sing several times. Now, we have over an hour to go. What about Randy doing a number? We know he can sing. He and Sara did that *Undecided* duet at Cherry Point. And I think we ought to try out one of the novelty numbers we've been talking about doing."

The nationally known big bands were doing more and more specialty, or novelty tunes, and using all the musicians like a chorus. Prima did it. Glenn Miller's band all sang, or shouted out, the theme line on *Pennsylvania 6-5000*. Tex Beneke, one of Miller's sax players, had sung a solo on *Kalamazoo* and even done several songs with The Modernaires.

Kay Kyser had a trumpeter whose real name was Merwyn Bogue but went by the stage name of Ish Kabibble. When translated from the Yiddish *Isch ka bibble*, it means "I should worry?" He, and the band, did a fun version of *Three Little Fishes*. Boop, boop, dittum dattum, whattum, chew….and they swam and they swam all over the dam."

Jimmie Lunceford's swing band put on a show when it played dances, and they featured several novelty numbers. Of course, Spike Jones was famous for his musically challenging and nutty tunes, and several of his musicians doubled as novelty singers.

And there was Ziggy Talent, a sax player in the Vaughn Monroe orchestra who sang a novelty number that absolutely fascinated me, *The Maharajah of Magador*. I had memorized all three verses, we had rehearsed it a time or two and the band knew the wild chorus, so, why not take a shot?

Hey, if Ginny could do it, I could do it. The only difference was she could sing. I could carry a tune but could not possibly be classified as a vocalist. Then again, I reminded Will, *Maharajah* was not exactly an operatic aria.

"I like your Randy suggestion. A lot," Will admitted, "but I'm not sure about that *Maharajah* thing. Not sure this crowd is ready for that, or us either for that matter. I'll think about it."

A few minutes later Will asked Randy to do a vocal on *Dream* and he asked cousin Jimmy to take Randy's horn chair.

He didn't indicate whether my moment in the sun, or overhead gym lights, was coming.

When Randy, the "cute little blond guy," stood confidently at the mike, a dozen piratesses, or wenches, or whatever female pirates are called, immediately came up to the 'island' we were stranded on and in Sinatra-like devotion stared at him as he sang. No swooning, but close enough. He played to them like he was working up a collection in a revival tent.

As he walked past me to sit out another number with Ginny and let Jimmy continue, I said loudly, "I can't wait to get back and tell Jean about your fan club, Romeo. You might as well give up the trumpet and the pulpit and head to Hollywood."

He gave a little bow towards me, wearing a major smile, and I knew he was already thinking of ways to get me back somehow, sometime.

At 11:40 p.m., twenty minutes from the end of the dance, Will motioned me to come on down and for Pab to take over the drums. Assuming my time for stardom had arrived, I stepped down from the upper tier and headed to the stand mike in front of the band.

Show time. The *Maharajah of Magador's* moment had come.

When Will asked everyone to pull up the music, they broke up. Every last man.

Mack said to Will so everyone in the band, especially me, could hear, "You must have already been paid to pull this stunt."

"I hope his singing will make them want to listen to instrumentals only for the rest of the evening," Chip added. "Or maybe they'll all just go home in fear he might do another number."

Hank was quick to add, "Stand off to the side when you sing, Red, so we don't get hit with the tomatoes."

Even normally subdued Rick Beacham quipped, "I assume we don't want to come back here again."

"Hey," Chick suggested, "let's ask Ginny to sing *Summertime* again instead."

Pab quickly settled onto the drum throne with tympani mallets in hand, knowing the intro and most of the verses had a steady underlying floor tom tom beat: bom, bompa ba bom, bompa ba bom, ad infinitum. He was grinning broadly. No, snickering aloud would be more precise.

At the last intermission, Moe had found a gym towel and had been using it off and on to mop his brow. He had casually draped it over the piano, so before I made my "entrance" to the mike I wrapped the towel around my head, turban-style, hopefully giving a passable 'maharajah' appearance.

Drew bellowed out loud, followed by boisterous jeers from all the other guys, drawing total attention to the stage. Obviously, the foolishness on the bandstand sent a signal that whatever was coming was likely to be out of the ordinary. People came to the stage to see what was happening.

After the drum and snake-charming clarinet intro, I jumped in with a nasal singsong monotone style:

"There's a rich Maharajah of Magador
Who had ten thousand camels, and maybe more
He had rubies and pearls and the loveliest girls
But he didn't know how to do-oo the rumba.
He could afford…a big reward
So to his people one day he said:
Ah ah ahahahahahahaha…
Ah ah ahahahahahaheha…which means…

Chapter Twenty-Four

> Take my rubies and take my pearls
> Take my camels and take my girls
> Rumba lessons are wanted for
> The rich Maharajah of Magador.
> Ah ah ah ahahahahaha"…

The "ah ah ahahahahaha" part could best be described as a falsetto bag-pipe-like sound done with strained vocal chords. The band all joined in on the second and last "ah ah ahahahahaha ha…."

Now the band was really loose and into the number with the downtown New Delhi flavor. The three trumpets and two trombones were moving their horns side to side and the five saxes were moving their horns up and down, none of which had been pre-planned or rehearsed. Chick was thumping the bass in time with Pab's driving beat and periodically whirling it around 360 degrees. Moe was moving his head side-to-side, belly dancer style, as he vamped.

At this point the obvious theory was, if we're this close to the precipice we might as well jump into the abyss all the way, so I went to the second verse and the band kept bopping behind me.

In the middle of the verse I glanced over to see Ginny with her head buried in her hands. It occurred to me this act was not likely making many points for me with her. Jimmy was breaking up.

Not sure whether to laugh at me, with me or feel great pity for me, the gathered audience got the drift quickly that this was a gag tune, a novelty number, being performed by a non-singer who had more chutzpah than sense. Or talent. They began to clap with the rhythm and joined in on the chorus with a wild array of improvised sounds.

The last verse relates how a lovely young lady accepted the Maharajah's offer, taught him to do the rumba, and then took his rubies and all his pearls, took his camels and all his girls and left the *rich* Maharajah the *poor* Maharajah of Maaa--gaaaa---dooooor.

We ended with a flourish and on a high note, literally. I bowed, somewhat majestically, to my subjects bunched at the bandstand, who graciously had decided to applaud vigorously for this weak-minded soul. It may have been a sympathy vote, but it was obvious the crowd got a kick out of it, the band had a ball and I satisfied a great yearning to do the thing.

Good-naturedly, Will walked up to me, put his arm around my shoulders, looked at the crowd and just shook his head side to side. Shtick! Good stuff. Vaughn Monroe and Ziggy Talent would have approved. Louis Prima, too.

Coming back down to earth, we ended the dance with *Stardust, Too Young* and *Goodnight Sweetheart,* slow numbers that enabled the dancers to conclude their evening in a romantic mood.

Apparently the vocal by Randy and my comic presentation offset the fact Ginny sang only twice, and *Summertime* both times, for the lady in charge thanked us, paid us and even commented on the opening act eye patches as a nice touch.

Jimmy told Will he thoroughly enjoyed listening to the band, and playing with us, and he'd be happy to play an entire job if needed.

Then he came over to where I was starting to pack up and said, "Stick to the drums, cuz." He told me about his volunteering to Will to play with the band periodically, we shook hands and he was off.

By this time Ginny had come to the bandstand. I wasn't sure just what she'd say but she knew my right-brain persona well enough and she had heard me sing *Maharajah* for fun often enough to know that one day, Will agreeing, I would just have to sing it in front of God and everyone.

"You were terrific," she said, tongue in cheek, "and I'm glad you finally got to show off your incredible vocal talent publicly. However, I don't think Perry Como or Bing Crosby have a lot to worry about. But I am going to tell Dr. McDaniel he should get you to sing with the Glee Club."

"Now that's an idea I know he'll go for. Hey, how 'bout if I do it in church Sunday morning?"

"I have enough trouble explaining you to my parents as it is. Let's don't make it any harder."

Pab came over and helped me unscrew, fold, encase, collapse, remove and generally toss everything into the box and drum covers. "I'll get all this stuff loaded. Y'all head on down to New Bern," he suggested.

I thanked him and started for the restroom to wash up before the drive when Hal, Hank, Randy and Moe came up, grabbed me by the arms and legs, lifted me up and started walking to the pirate's galleon across the gym floor. Now I knew who was going to have to walk that plank!

Had there been real water there instead of a hard floor I'm confident I would have been blindfolded and prodded with a rusty saber in the butt until I jumped headlong to meet my destiny. Ginny did not protest one iota.

The four musketeers released me, and jokingly threatened to go through with a similar, but real, injurious act if I ever sang that number again.

Hank looked me in the eye: "It was lucky for us that Ginny and Randy could sing. They got us off the hook. And you almost got us back on it."

"You didn't go for my singing?" I asked bravely.

"You almost got us hanged from the yardarm," he replied, pointing to the pirate ship spar and rigging, "and without the grog."

Shortly, Ginny and I were on the road out of Greenville, heading to Craven County. We hoped to arrive by 2:30 a.m., unless we could find some place for coffee, which was highly doubtful on that lonely stretch of NC 43 through Vanceboro.

In the midst of small talk, we listened to station WWL broadcasting the "dance music of Leon Kellner and his orchestra from the Blue Room in the Hotel Roosevelt in downtown New Orleans." Most radio stations signed off at midnight with the National Anthem, but WWL was an all-nighter and one of the few very powerful stations we could get clearly on the car radio in that rural area at that wee hour of the morning, and the live big band music was outstanding.

I remarked to Ginny, "You gotta' admit, this band business is a lot of fun. And we're pretty good."

"No question its fun, I can see that", she readily agreed, "but if you're referring to your singing being in the 'pretty good' category, it was certainly in a class by itself. I don't think anything we do for the rest of the week-end will quite measure up."

Frankly, I was sorry to hear that. Not surprised, but sorry.

Chapter Twenty-Five

In several more weeks, the spring semester was done and the campus population, and activity, diminished dramatically. Ginny had signed up to wait tables for the summer at the Carswell Baptist Assembly, an Atlantic seaside campus below Southport where members of the Baptist faith in North Carolina churches went to retreats and to recreate.

If absence makes the heart grow fonder then this separation should give our romance a major boost.

The summer session began on June ninth, so every morning of that week the seven of us went to classes while Hal, who now had his sheepskin, Chip, Jud and Chick hung around the campus for the week, knowing we would be rehearsing most afternoons at the Hut through Thursday. Rick drove over from Raleigh each day for rehearsals and Pab came down from Thomasville on Thursday to drive several of us the following night.

In addition to playing for dancing for three hours, we also were to play for the official presentations and figure, which was not unlike a Grand March. In the event we needed music for the latter, Will made sure we would be prepared with the "Handy Tunes For All Occasions" booklets, but wasn't sure *Les Marseilles* would be appropriate in this instance. Just in case, we had it on the back burner.

It was required that we wear tuxedos for the big event and in anticipation of the rush for rentals by a great many guys who would go to the Germans, Will had gotten our sizes and reserved everything through Ben Aycock who owned the fashionable men's store in downtown Wake Forest. Ben had access to several lines of tuxes such as After Six and Rudofker which he would order as needed. Once they were returned he had them cleaned and shipped back. Now just a convenient fifteen minutes' walk for each of us, we dropped by Ben's several days before the event to be sure of the fit.

One ill-fitting tuxedo fiasco was sufficient.

The drive to Rocky Mount would take no more than an hour and a half at most, taking 98 east through Bunn, Spring Hope and Nashville. Pat was coming down with her parents.

We decided to arrive by 6:00 p.m., take advantage of some outstanding barbecue at Melton's Restaurant and get to Planters Warehouse on northeast Main Street about a mile away by 7:30 at the latest. We would have plenty of time to change into the tuxedos, warm up and settle down before our 9:00 p.m. start. We doubted many people would arrive before 10 p.m.

While the big traveling name bands looked upon this event as just another job, except for the unusual 1:00 a.m. to 5:00 a.m. hours they would play, our view was entirely different. This was a major audition on a very large 'stage' before many people who booked bands for all types of parties and dances. Will remembered to print a large quantity of promotional flyers, just in case.

Leaving Wake Forest in our three-cars-and-a-trailer caravan at 4:30 p.m., we heard the weather report for Eastern North Carolina: clear, sunny, high 88, humidity 80 percent. No rain, high humidity and no air-conditioning in the warehouse equals much sweat in the 100% wool tuxes.

On September 29, 1870, the citizens of Rocky Mount, a small but socially prominent tobacco center in the eastern part of the state, decided to throw a major party and dance for their friends in surrounding counties. They called it the Grand Celebration Ball. A major success, the event became an annual affair and was moved to the spring.

In 1903, the Carolina Cotillion Club renamed the event the June German in honor of the month in which it was held and the term, German, which was a popular intricate group dance, involving the forming of figures on the floor as arranged by the dancers. The dance was held annually from that time forward.

Although it was staged in a mammoth tobacco warehouse, appropriately decorated and adorned by the Cotillion's Women's Committee, dress was strictly formal and attendance was by invitation only, as determined by the Cotillion's membership. Many hundreds attended the party each year, making it the premier social gathering in the state, if not in the South. It was *the* place for college kids to gather a week or so after schools ended for the summer.

Parties were held in people's homes, in rented restaurants and halls and, literally, in the streets. Reserved tables were set up on the warehouse floor with fine linen, candelabra, fresh flowers and a variety of snacks, and drinks, until replaced by breakfast spreads as dawn approached.

Aware of the economic and public relations value of the annual affair, the Rocky Mount Police were understanding and lenient in enforcing a number of local ordinances, public display of alcohol being prominent among them.

The basic format was for a 'noteworthy area band' to play for dancing from 9:00 p.m. until midnight. After a formal presentation of officers, which ends with a figure created by some 200 participants, a national 'name' band plays from 1:00 a.m. until 5:00 a.m.

The Southerners had been selected as that 'noteworthy band' to play on the front end of the Germans, and for the formal intermission presentation, a major coup.

Johnny Long, the left-hand fiddle-playing Newell, NC native and Duke grad, had one of the most popular, nationally known big bands of the day and it was to be the featured group for all night dancing and entertainment.

Home to Kay Kyser, the well-known bandleader of the Forties and radio host of the Kollege of Musical Knowledge, and to Theolonious Monk, who was getting rave reviews in New York for his unique jazz piano-playing and break-through arrangements;

Rocky Mount's population was just about 28,000. However, on Germans night it played host to more than a thousand guests. All stops were pulled for the much-anticipated event.

The town of Rocky Mount was literally divided in half by the main line of the Atlantic Coastline Railroad. On the eastern side of the tracks, the town was in Edgecombe County, to the west it was in Nash County. Sober or otherwise you had to look both ways when you crossed either east Main Street or west Main Street to be sure no train was barreling down on you.

Many communities across Eastern North Carolina had tobacco markets where farmers brought their crop of bright leaf tobacco in late summer to sell at auction to American Tobacco, Liggett & Myers, R.J. Reynolds, Brown & Williamson, P. Lorillard and other major tobacco products manufacturers. Rocky Mount had one of the largest and most active markets, and Planters Warehouse, located just a block from downtown, with its 50,000 square feet of sales space, and was among the largest of the several sales warehouses.

The rectangular one-story structure sat empty most of the year but was a major hub of activity for several weeks when the market opened in September. And for the Germans.

It had a weathered red brick front and sides, and featured large wooden doors on three sides which enabled the unloading of leafed tobacco, usually from farmers' pick-up trucks, or horse-drawn wagons, onto large baskets for the auction line. In the rear, its doors opened for tractor-trailer trucks to take the sold tobacco to the purchasing tobacco company's storage facilities, usually in mammoth wood hogsheads, or barrels.

As our entourage was permitted inside the roped-off area around the warehouse and we began to unload the trailer, we spotted Johnny Long's band bus parked just ahead. They had come in early to get some sleep in a local hotel before making their way to the dance site around midnight.

"That's what we need. One 'a them busses to take us to jobs. No more cramming our butts into three cars."

Moe knew his comment was for levity only but the idea was appealing to us all.

"Yeah, we could get Pab to drive the bus and we could sleep, get up and stretch our legs..." Chip added.

"Store all our stuff in the baggage area instead of that rickety trailer...which, by the way, leaks...in case anybody cares." Drew was heard from.

"Right now I think we had better get our minds on why we're here and not on busses we aren't gonna' have." Will had a 'cut-to-the-chase' way about him.

Ray had been to a June Germans event before since this was his home town, and Drew had dropped in to hear some big band one night from his home in Pinetops sixteen miles down the road. The rest of us had just heard and read about the extravaganza and never actually attended.

Just as we were overwhelmed by the sheer size of the Cherry Point Marine Air Station Drill Hall six months before, the warehouse was awe-inspiring in its own rustic way.

It was big. Real big. The dance area could easily accommodate three-four hundred people at a time. Speakers were positioned on many of the wood columns throughout the spacious area to carry the music to every corner.

The building inside was of heavy wood post and beam construction with wide wooden plank flooring. Square wood columns ran the length of the building in even rows from the floor to the expansive tin roof, which covered the facility. A few skylights had been added to augment the several overhead lights during daylight, but at night the entire place was bathed in a romantic glow of temporary lighting and any moonlight that could ease through the skylights.

There were only four small restrooms in the building which would present a variety of challenges to attendees throughout the night, especially the women. There was no air conditioning, no fans and even with the doors thrown wide open on three sides there was not much in the way of stirring air. If the temperature was below

80 degrees and the humidity was low, conditions were not too bad, even in tuxedos and ball gowns. Sadly, that combination was seldom in effect in mid-June. And certainly not on this night. It would be well over 100 degrees inside the warehouse, for sure.

Quickly we unloaded the cars and trailer, carrying our instruments and the stands to the stage inside.

Built of four by fours and heavy wood planking, the stage was tiered with two levels above the floor. Around the exterior on three sides a fabric 'skirt' had been attached and behind the stage, rising perhaps eight feet above the back level and the width of the entire stage was a blue cloth backdrop.

Decorating Committee members had placed several potted palms on either side of the stage and a couple in front. The sound system with multiple floor mike stands was in place and obviously had been tested.

"Just another high school dance," Jud remarked, gazing at the expansive dance floor in front and the row upon row of tables and chairs beyond. Off to the right a section had been roped off for spectators with perhaps a hundred folding chairs.

"Yeah," Chip responded, "but where's the wishing well?"

Having acclimated to the facility we set up promptly and then took to our places for a fast run-through of several pieces. Satisfied we were in tune and in sync, we left the stage to put on the tuxes, make a last trip to the john and wait an hour until show time.

At 8:50 p.m., one of the Cotillion officials found us lolling about in folding chairs behind the stage.

"You guys ready to go?" he inquired.

"All set," Will answered, and gestured for us to go ahead and take our places.

"Who'll be handling the Presentation business and the Figure after midnight?"

The young official, not yet outfitted in his tails, indicated he would be the emcee and would tell us when to play the figure background music, sometime around 12:15 or so.

"At midnight you can wrap up the dance, take a break, and then we'll kick off the formalities."

"Got it." Will joined us onstage, running down the numbers that would take us to 10:15. We'd take ten minutes and then come back on from 10:25 straight through until midnight.

Precisely at 9:00 p.m., we hit *Tenderly* for the fifty or so people who had arrived early, more in a mood to drink and talk than to dance. No one took to the floor through our first three numbers, but we knew things would be lively soon.

Jitters and butterflies had long since gone and we settled in to do what we did best, play the tunes whether people danced or not. After all, the pay would be the same.

By the break an hour later there were a large number of dancers, principally the older folks who did not intend to tough it out all night. Will had correctly calculated what music would be preferred and we stuck to the slower standards with a few '40's jitterbugging numbers here and there. This was not the *Bunny Hop* or *Mexican Hat Dance* crowd but they did their thing to *In The Mood, String of Pearls* and a toned-down *One O'clock Jump.*

At the break, as I was getting down off the stand, I heard someone call out my name. Turning towards the spectator section, I saw my first cousin, George Bailey, from Raleigh. He had driven my parents, and his, down to hear the band. They had been there since we started at nine o'clock. It was the first, and only, time my parents ever heard me play with the band.

My mother had borne the agony of listening to a teen-aged boy banging away on drums for four years to big band music played very loudly on a RCA 78-rpm record player. While she was generous in her plaudits on this night, to the extent the very reserved lady she was could be, I'm sure she would much rather I had been playing the piano. I was certain as well that my practicing the drums all those years had something to do with her early-diminished hearing.

My dad and relatives were lavish in their praise of the band, and of my performance specifically, of course. We visited briefly, I made a fast trip to the dark parking lot outside and the rear tire of the Woodie, grabbed an RC Cola and was back on the stand in the requisite twenty minutes.

Will asked if I had been with my parents and when I said 'Yes', he told the band to do *September Song* first and then my solo number, *Tuxedo Junction*.

"Might as well show off for the home folks," he suggested.

"Then maybe I should do The *Maharajah of Magador?*"

"You gotta' be kidding! This crowd would run us out of town. Stick to *Tuxedo Junction*."

Sensing my cheering section was about to depart for Raleigh, I motioned to George to keep everyone around for two more tunes. He did, and they got to witness what the money they had been paying to Wake Forest College for some three years was paying for, at least in one sense.

When Will learned that family supporters of both Ray and Drew were among the spectators, he made sure each was featured on a tune as well.

Our final sets enticed more and people to the floor as the warehouse began to fill with the black-and-white bedecked revelers. The noise level was reaching new heights, as was the interior temperature. The party was truly coming on strong.

Instead of ending with *Goodnight Sweetheart* as per usual, given the fact the evening was really just beginning in earnest, we concluded with *Tenderly*. Will took the mike on the last bars and thanked the Cotillion for booking us and the dancers for their participation. By this time, the emcee had arrived and announced a fifteen-minute intermission to be followed by the Presentation and Formal Figure.

At the all-too-quick break, we mingled with the white-jacketed members of the Johnny Long Orchestra who were gathering behind the bandstand. They commented most favorably on our band. Johnny came over to Will, shook his hand and remarked that he had gotten his big band start at Duke, taking over what had been a band lead by Les Brown. He, too, was most generous in his praise of our sound and said if any of us wanted to sit in at anytime with his band during the night, just let him know. As if!!!!

We returned to play, repetitively, a medley of five numbers Will had selected as background for the formalities. No *Les Marseilles*. A half hour later The Southerners were done and, as instructed, we removed all our stands and equipment so the Johnny Long Orchestra could set up and kick off at 1:00 a.m.

After listening to the Long aggregation do their *Shanty In Old Shanty Town* number, Randy drove the Woodie back to Wake Forest with Mack, Chick, Jud and Hal. Drew went home to Pinetops a few miles away. Ray went home several blocks away. Pat's folks drove her and Rick back to Raleigh.

Will, Jack, Chip, Moe and I stayed back, with Pab, to hear more. Pab was commissioned to drive us back in his car, making sure we made our eight a.m. class on time. He was not to take a libation stronger than 7-Up or Nehi grape all night. That edict did not pertain to the rest of us.

Since we knew a good many of the people in the crowd from Wake Forest, we wandered from table to table, "flitting", and graciously accepting a libation now and then.

Somewhere around 2:30 a.m., Hank got up the nerve to ask Johnny if he could sit in on *Time Waits For No One*. Then about an hour later Chip asked if he could sit in on *My Dreams Are Getting Better All The Time*. Both distinguished themselves by playing the correct notes in the correct keys and to the correct tempo.

Moe, Will and I decided we were not ready for our major big band debuts just yet.

As the very early morning light was creeping over the buildings in downtown Rocky Mount and the dazed throng was slowly, blindly dispersing before the 5:00 a.m. conclusion, we realized we had classes in a few hours and Wake Forest was an hour's drive, or more, away. We found Pab asleep in his convertible, top down, in the lot next to the warehouse. We jostled him awake with orders to take off but insisting he had to stop somewhere for coffee.

The morning was cool and there was a light coating of dew on the car. People were milling around in the streets, still dressed in formal wear. Far too many people were stretched out on car hoods, fenders and any area of grass along the streets they could find. Some never made it off the sidewalk. There was much unpleasant evidence that many of the revelers couldn't hold whatever they'd been drinking. It was going to be a very long day for all these victims.

Chip sighted a fellow opening his café as we drove through town so we pulled over and went in, knowing we had to wait for the coffee to brew. We had some buttered toast, ultimately poured our coffee from mugs into paper cups, and were back on the road. It was our first food since Melton's barbecue fourteen hours earlier.

As we crammed our six tired bodies into the car, we began to realize just how hot it had been in that warehouse all night long, how dusty it became, and how sweaty we all were. Pab had the good sense to keep the top down so we could air out.

There was little traffic on the two-lane road on a Saturday morning so we made good time, arriving in Wake Forest about 7:00 a.m. Growling stomachs superseded changing clothes or any attempt at showering so we stopped for a quick fried egg sandwich and more coffee at Morty's. It was now 7:15.

Sitting on the counter stools, Hank, Will and I realized we all had Dr. Dwight Gentry's Business 66 / Advertising class at 8:00 a.m. and we might as well go as we were. Although we were about to fall asleep standing up and our aroma was probably less than seductive, going to class in any condition was better than taking a cut.

Without books, notepaper, pencils, or any accoutrements of academia, we strolled into class in our wrinkled, smelly tuxes, eager to learn.

Our classmates, unaware of where we had been but knowing we all played in The Southerners and had obviously been on a job all night, cheered as we entered and took our seats. At eight, Dr. Gentry entered the classroom, looked up and saw the three of us without bright eyes or bushy tails. He, too, knew of our band affiliation and, being the good guy he was, said:

"Gentlemen, I seriously doubt if the three of you are receptive to learning anything this morning…and I am convinced you will make no positive contributions to the class. So, in the name of all that is holy, healthy and hygienic, why don't you just go on home?"

The class cheered, Gentry smiled, the three of us gave a grateful nod of appreciation to our beloved professor and we departed.

It had truly been a night to remember.

Chapter Twenty-Six

To play for the Interfraternity Council's Summer Dance in the Virginia Dare Ballroom of the Sir Walter Hotel in Raleigh on Saturday night, June 28, we would require several personnel changes.

Chick had returned to New Jersey and a summer baseball league, and avoiding employment in Uncle Mario's bakery.

Hal had graduated and accepted a job with an insurance company in Greensboro. One of the mainstays since The Southerners began, he served three years in the Navy and attended Guilford College for a year prior to entering Wake Forest. Hal was a solid trombone player, totally dependable and a quiet, somewhat introspective man of strong character. He had been a positive influence on all of us and would be deeply missed.

Randy needed to make tuition money and some living expenses for the fall semester so he returned home to Wadesboro and hoped he could find a decent paying job until September.

Mack also was hard-pressed for money so he returned home to Laurinburg, his meter-reading job and avoiding lonely housewives, plus hoping to play some combo gigs now and then.

Usually new students in the fall resulted in a number of potential players, but that didn't help fill the roster in mid-summer. Rick, who had decided to leave NC State and enroll at Wake Forest, changing his major from Engineering to Mathematics, knew of several musicians in Raleigh who might be available for the one-night job.

Frank Umstead was a stellar sax player, fresh out of high school, but with several years' experience with a local dance combo. Jack

Terrell and Ronnie Steen, bass fiddle and trombone players respectively, were college seniors and had played in a number of combo bands for a half dozen years.

To take the open trumpet spot we called my cousin, Jimmy Kerr, who had sat in with us a month or so back in Greenville and was spending time at home in Goldsboro, fifty-two miles away.

The good news was all of these men were available for that particular Saturday night, and all agreed to play the job. The bad news was we would not have an opportunity to do a major rehearsal with the new people but only a brief run-through an hour or so before the job. The other good news was all these players were very good readers, very experienced and had done a lot of fill-in work.

Since the number of students enrolled in summer school was less than a third of the normal number during fall and spring, the crowd at the hotel event was relatively small but no less enthusiastic or appreciative of this break in their six-day study routine.

Jack, Ronnie, Frank and Jimmy joined the nucleus of the band at 6:00 p.m. for a half-hour rehearsal in the ballroom, and then we broke for supper until re-grouping at 7:45 p.m., fifteen minutes before dance time. The fill-in musicians brought their versions of blue blazers and Will provided dark red knit ties for each from a supply he now maintained.

The informal affair was easy to play. We stuck to the pre-arranged sets, the dance floor was always filled and the fraternity groups got in their sweetheart singing at intermissions. Plus the hotel was air-conditioned.

Will paid the four substitutes in cash then and there and each enthusiastically offered to join us again if an opportunity arose. The three Raleigh boys headed home while my cousin Jimmy informed me he had made arrangements to stay overnight with a friend in town. He never volunteered the name, gender or location of the friend but I had a gut feeling it was a 'she' with an apartment.

After the job, we considered dropping in at a place called Fat

Daddy's Danceland in south Raleigh. One of the hotel's service staff, a young black trumpet player, had invited us, suggesting we would hear some great music by some fantastic local players. He also assured us there would be no safety challenges, color notwithstanding, since we were fellow musicians. We could sit in with the house band and that would automatically make us welcome, according to our potential host.

As enticing as the offer was, and as much fun as a jam session in those surroundings would be, the lateness of the hour prompted us to take a rain check.

After dropping Pat off at her home out on the Durham highway just outside Raleigh, Will pointed the Woodie towards Wake Forest with Moe in the front seat and Hank, me and Drew in the back.

As soon as summer school ended, Hank would be going back to West Virginia for the remainder of the summer.

Drew would complete his pre-med requirements in the summer session and had been accepted to Duke Med School in the fall. A KA brother, he had been one of our four original founders, from the "what if" days to the band's creation. He was a veteran of the Hut rehearsals, the non-fit tuxedo affair, the many "where's the wishing well?" proms, the Shiner's midget car races, the June Germans near his home and New Year's Eve with the Marines.

In addition to playing a fine sax, always eager, always agreeable, he was a fun guy whose sense of humor and willingness to be the butt of many jokes kept us all loose. A big loss in musical and human terms.

Between sips of some stimulating refreshment, obviously known more for its low cost than its high quality, out of paper Dixie cups and with a splash of 7-Up, our conversation turned nostalgic, even melancholy.

We knew the band would continue without Drew and Hal, and it would be a good band, but it would never be the same. Just as we had continued successfully when Augie, Norm and Sara had left, we would find qualified and energetic replacements, they would

200

quickly blend in and the sound would come together night after night. New talent would bring new excitement, as Moe and Chip, Pat and Rick had energized the group when they came aboard.

The "do you remember the time?" stories came out, one by one, all the way back to school and we laughed at each well-remembered tale.

"Somebody ought to write all this stuff down," Hank suggested.

I responded, "yeah, maybe in fifty years when we have nothing else to do."

Chapter Twenty-Seven

Several weeks earlier Will had told us he was going to try to find some combo jobs during July and August. He would put the groups together based on what the opportunities were. While most of the guys indicated they would not be available for one reason or the other, Ray, Moe and I decided to join Will if he could get some 'paying' bookings in fun places.

Theoretically, at least, Ray, Will and I were slated to graduate from Wake Forest in a year, June of 1953, and Moe a year later. Assuming the draft didn't get any of us.

I had worked in the 8th grade as a page for three months in the State Legislature in 1945 and again in 1947. After school for seven months and on Saturdays I worked in the mailroom at WPTF radio during my junior year in high school.

Every summer since getting my worker's permit in the 10th Grade I was employed at something. During my junior year in college I assisted in the college News Bureau in the afternoons. For two weeks following my junior year at Wake Forest I was a press correspondent for the *News & Observer* covering the 30th Division National Guard encampment at Ft. McClelland, Alabama, and for three months that summer I pulled those phone-answering night shifts in the sports department. By day over two summers working on Little League fields for the City kept me busy and on holidays I continued to "jump flowers".

Now heading into my senior year, I realized that 12 months from now, hopefully, I would be into a fulltime career somewhere, with only two weeks off a year. So, I figured once summer school had ended, this would be a good time to take some time off for fun.

• • • • •

Thanks to the Pumphrey-Allsbrook agency, we had two bookings lined up, each for seven musicians, and at above union scale.

The first was for four nights at The Heart of the Beach Club at Atlantic Beach, NC, July 23-26, and the other was for three nights, July 31-August 2, at The Surf Club at Virginia Beach.

We couldn't ask for any more fun spots than these. The Atlantic Beach job paid $500 for the four nights, or seventy-one dollars per player, and the Surf Club was paying $400 for three nights or fifty-seven dollars per. That would give each of us $128 for the seven nights, enough to pay our expenses and then some.

Will managed to get the booking agency to cut its fee almost in half, to fifty dollars for both jobs, and we agreed to pay seven dollars each towards the agency fee. Those of us who were to ride with Will agreed to pay him three dollars each in gas money for the Virginia Beach trip. With a net of $118.00, that would be a bit over $16 dollars a day for room , board and miscellaneous, more than sufficient if we doubled up or found free lodging, ate two meals a day and did not spend unwisely on wine, women or song.

The point was, we were not doing this for the money, but for the fun of it.

Immediately, Will got on the phone to find a trumpeter, a sax player and a bass player since he, Moe, Ray and I would be bringing a sax, trombone, piano and drums.

Trumpeter cousin Jimmy was quick to agree and young Frank Umstead, now intently devoted to playing more with The Southerners, signed on as second sax. Additionally, Frank had developed into a premier Dixieland clarinet player. Finding a bass player was a major challenge however, and even Lupton at the union was not having any luck helping us.

Rick, who had been a fount for finding players when we needed them, had checked out a number of players he knew fairly well, but all were working and couldn't take the time off. Finally he suggested we talk to a young man from Raleigh he had heard play in a three-piece group at a wedding reception. Rick had introduced himself, related his involvement with The Southerners and they had exchanged phone numbers in case playing opportunities arose.

This 18-year-old Broughton High School grad, Lenny Boles, did not play bass; however, he did play guitar…and saxophone… some piano…and the vibraphone!

Will jumped on the phone, talked to Lenny, promised to pay his union dues for a year and no telling what else and got the young-ster's agreement to play both the Atlantic Beach and the Virginia Beach jobs. Finding Lenny turned out to be a real coup since in addition to being a sensational player of several instruments, he could arrange music as well. It was his love, his passion, and he was excited about an opportunity just to play music.

Ray still had his Chevy, albeit its best days were long past, and he opted to drive from Rocky Mount to Atlantic Beach. Moe had access to his brother's car for a few days and he was driving over from Lumberton. I prevailed upon my parents to let me have the Nash for four or five days and they consented, knowing I was go-ing to pick up cousin Jimmy in Goldsboro.

Will drove from Thomasville to Raleigh for a few days prior to going on to Atlantic Beach. While there, he managed to con-vince the Taylor Sound Company people to sell him the tired, but still serviceable, trailer we had been leasing on an ongoing basis. Taylor asked, and got, fifty-five dollars for the unit, and threw in a slick, no-tread spare. Will's intention was to have the rust-ing, rattling trailer repainted, including the band's name on both sides, but that opportunity would have to wait for another finan-cial windfall.

He was staying with an aunt and uncle at night in Raleigh, or some of it, but spending the greater part of the time with Ellen. In addition to whatever else they were doing, they were aggressively trying to figure out a way for her to get to the beach while he was there. He came by my house on Tuesday afternoon and I loaded the drums into the trailer. He would bring Lenny and Frank with him. It was the first time either had been away from home to play a dance job.

We planned for everyone to meet at The Heart of the Beach at 2:00 p.m. on Wednesday, the 23rd, rehearse for a couple of hours and then be prepared to play from 8:00 p.m. until 1:00 a.m. from Wednesday through Friday nights and until midnight on Saturday. Our 'uniform' would be long white cotton pants and dark blue, collared golf-type shirts. Shoes optional.

No one at this point had any idea where he would sleep. Will had the back of the Woodie as an option and I had the celebrated, but never used, fold-down seat/bed in the before-its-time Ambassador. Ray and Moe could surely sleep in their cars if necessary but Johnny, Frank and Kenny would need some sort of accommodations.

Toilet facilities were always available in some restaurant, service station or in the Heart of the Beach club and, as several of us had learned first hand during our high school days, it was easy to locate empty beach cottages and use their outside showers. Or sleep on their porches. Or under their porches. Or on the strand wrapped in a blanket.

Lots of options, but if we were going to clear any money from the job we couldn't be spending it on such niceties as motel rooms, even if we put three or four in a room. I suggested we all bring several blankets in case use of some of the more adventuresome lodging locales became necessary.

It was an hour and a half drive from Raleigh to 714 East Ash Street in Goldsboro where Jimmy lived and another two and a half hours to the beach. I arrived at 10:30 a.m., picked up Jimmy and a generous lunch packed by Aunt Margaret in some plastic-type containers called Tupperware that had been recently introduced and we were on our way.

We were not two blocks from his house when he informed me he would not be needing any sleeping arrangements nor would he be coming back with me. He had been made aware of a major house party of East Carolina students and was confident he could work something out regarding a bunk. As to his return, several of the beach party folks (meaning females) were from Goldsboro and he would hitch a ride with them. If that didn't work out, he'd thumb home.

The Heart of the Beach Club was, indeed, in the heart of Atlantic Beach, straight east off Highway 70 south of Morehead City, over the Bogue Sound causeway.

It was a one-story, unpainted, wood board and batten building with a tin roof. It was supported by pilings three feet out of the ground and had wood shutters that propped open for ventilation. More than a few neon signs advertising various beers adorned the exterior walls. Rusted metal Coca-Cola, Pepsi Cola, 7 Up, Nehi, RC Cola and Dr. Pepper signs were tacked to the exterior. A failed attempt had been made to maintain screening over the windows.

Since all the beach traffic came and left on roads that passed by the building, it was a well known and a popular hangout for the college crowd. Close to an entertainment mecca with miniature golf, a few games-of-skill under colorful tent tops, several hot dog stands, an ice cream and cotton candy wagon and a bowling alley, it was a short two blocks from the water's edge and within easy reach of most of the better-known motels and hotels.

It looked like a honky-tonk, beachy, no shoes required sort of place. It faced kitty-cornered to the northeast, and a twenty-foot wide covered porch welcomed one and all. Over the double-doored entrance was a large, somewhat garish professionally painted sign, front lighted, announcing broadly that this was, indeed, the heart of the beach. A rather sizeable packed sand and crushed shells parking lot was to one side, and in back was the delivery and service entrance. An expansive fenced-in area for employee parking, trashcans, stacked empty bottle cases and a tarp-covered pile of lumber was out back.

Extending off to the side was a railed, open-air patio or deck, equipped with an outdoor beer bar, spacious dance floor, tables, and benches. Several strings of colored lights cris-crossed overhead. Four speakers piped out the music from inside. Great place to enjoy a suds while listening and looking for romance under the stars.

Upon sighting our 'home away from home' for the next four days my first thought was this is not the Sir Walter Hotel or even a high school gym. My next, and more positive thought, was, "this looks like a great place to really let it all hang out."

Jimmy was familiar with the spot, having been to Atlantic Beach often in recent months, and he allowed as to how this place would be packed and swinging at night, especially over the weekend.

I parked the Nash in the lot, locked it ("Who in the hell would want to steal this car?" Moe often suggested), and walked in, looking for the others. Neither the Woodie nor Ray's car was in the lot with the several we saw.

Moe was sitting at the bar, which smelled of stale cigarette smoke, stale beer, an abundance of Coppertone and grilling onions. He greeted us immediately, holding a cold one, and indicated the black Ford coupe outside was his brother's. He would never be able to sleep in that two-seater.

The three of us took a table alongside the dance floor and lunched on burgers with grilled onions while waiting for the others to arrive. I looked for the NC Department of Sanitation restaurant rating card normally posted in sight, but didn't see it, which in and of itself was rather telling.

Looking around we agreed this was typical of the 'juke joints' that were so popular during summer months at beaches everywhere. Open, well-worn booths along the walls, tables fronting the dance floor, large Wurlitzer jukebox in one corner. Speakers positioned here and there on wood columns.

Stuck, nailed, pinned, glued, stapled and adhered in many fashions to the columns, and to many of the inside wood walls, was a wide variety of college paraphernalia. Logo T shirts, colorful pom poms, chenille college and frat letters, all sorts of caps and hats in dark blue/white, red/white, light blue/white, purple/orange, gold/black, pennants, banners and window decals of schools and fraternities. It was an eclectic montage but gave the shack a lively collegiate, colorful, fun atmosphere.

In one corner was what served as the bandstand. It did have a riser large enough for the drums and two other players. An upright piano was positioned on the floor off to the left a bit and seven straight back wood chairs were stacked in front of the riser. Suspended over the area was a large and very dusty green fishing net with corks stuck here and there, lending a definite, albeit timeworn, nautical motif to the stand. A single mike stand was positioned off to the side.

A variety of small spotlights with colored gels were strung around and a low-hanging rotating 'crystal' ball was suspended from the ceiling with a white spot focused on it. No question this place had the atmosphere young folks were comfortable in.

Jimmy spoke up. "I was here about a month ago with some guys from school, and this place was wild. Wall to wall. There was a decent band playing, people were dancing and having a ball. Lots of women. This can be fun!"

Shortly, Ray pulled in and joined us, followed soon thereafter by Will with Lenny and Frank.

And Ellen.

As soon as I spotted her out of the open window, I spoke out, "Well, there's no surprise there. The master has managed another major coup. Can't wait to hear how they pulled this off."

Before the four walked in, Moe and I pushed two tables together for the seven of us to work out the game plan. Ellen spoke to each of us while Will went off looking for the proprietor, or manager, or the person we were working for. Moe went over and got Cokes for Ellen, Frank and Lenny.

Mr. "just call me Cap'n" Abernathy was the man in charge. It was his place and in a few short words he spelled out what he expected of us. Show up shaved and sober and be ready to play at 8:00 p.m. Play until 1:00 a.m. every night but Saturday when we quit at midnight since no beer could be sold after twelve. He would give us free soft drinks during the night, up to a point, and one free beer after each night's job. He didn't care if we drank a bit, but it better not be openly and it better not affect our playing.

Chapter Twenty-Seven

He expected us to take some breaks but "don't overdo it."

"Most places down here don't have live music, so I'm paying a ton for you guys hoping we'll draw big crowds. Your job is to make damned sure they're dancing 'cause that means they'll be drinking and eating. I ain't heard y'all play myself but they said you're pretty good, so you play what folks want to hear and dance to. Understood?"

We understood. Pretty simple, straightforward rules. We also got the subliminal message that if we didn't play what people wanted to hear and dance to, eat and drink to, then our contract might be shortened.

Although there were a half dozen guys lolling about at the bar, Will got approval from the Cap'n for us to cut power to the juke-box and rehearse for an hour or so. We still had to figure out where we would all sleep.

That is, all of us but Ellen and Will. They had made arrangements. Not Will's preference, but an arrangement of convenience. And Ellen's safety.

Chapter Twenty-Eight

Playing for college and high school dances is one thing. Playing at a beach joint is something else. The former require lots of slow tunes with a few jitterbug numbers and an occasional novelty piece thrown in.

Beach places demand lots of fast stuff, loud tunes, with a 'raunchy' piece here and there. As the surf and sand evenings mature and one-night-stand romances flare, slow tunes were more in order.

The 'shag' was the hot dance craze and every jump joint with a slick hardwood dance floor was witness to this revived phenomenon.

A form of swing dancing, the Carolina Shag, as it was named when reintroduced along the coastal Carolina beaches in the Forties, required an up-tempo beat, but it was slower than the faster-beat jitterbug. At 115-130 beats a minute, four-four time, solid R&B-type numbers were preferred by the dancers. Emphasis was on the foot movements, slow easy shuffle at the bottom, and southern soul at the top. Not a lot of bounce.

Some people called it the "lazy man's jitterbug", but the real aficionados made it a dance form of its own and it was the rage at Atlantic Beach.

We had discussed this music differential over the past week and Will had spent considerable time, and some money, getting stock arrangements for most of the currently popular hits and many oldies that young beach-goers expected and we did not have in our current Southerners library.

He had told each of us by phone what the new numbers were so we could familiarize ourselves with them and there would be no surprises. *House of Blue Lights, 60 Minute Man, Caldonia, Let The Good Times Roll, Is You Is Or Is You Ain't My Baby?, Choo Choo Ch'Boogie, Lady Be Good, Rag Mop, Opus One, Ain't Nobody Here But Us Chickens, Lullaby of Broadway* and *Open The Door Richard* were among the new jump tunes.

Since we now had a genuine vibes player in Lenny, Will added Lionel Hampton's *Flying Home*, and with Frank's exciting Dixieland talent, *Muskrat Ramble, South Rampart Street Parade, Sweet Georgia Brown* and *Down By The Riverside*. We already had the music to *When The Saints Go Marching In*.

After an hour or so unloading the trailer and rehearsing, it was late afternoon and time for us, with two notable exceptions, to find adequate sleeping digs.

Will informed us that Ellen had an aunt and uncle who were currently renting a cottage on the south end of the beach and they had an empty bedroom. For Ellen. However, they consented to let Will sleep on an Army cot on their screened-in front porch. Now Will would put his mind to work to make the most of that arrangement.

With the Woodie free, Moe decided to sleep there. I could easily sack out in the Nash and Ray decided the backseat of his Chevy would be adequate. That left the two youngsters, Lenny and Frank, to take care of.

Neither was accustomed to this type of 'roughing it,' informing us their previous camping experiences had been limited to overnights that included Boy Scout tents, sleeping bags and nearby latrines. At first Frank suggested he could sleep in the trailer. It was certainly long enough and with the rear door, left open there would be plenty of ventilation. Lenny simply was not the type to rough it on the beach, under a boardwalk or on the open deck of a vacant beach house, yet to be located.

I sought out the Cap'n, asking if he knew of any inexpensive, i.e., cheap, places where two guys could sleep. He thought a moment, then replied, "I got an ex-wife who runs a place about a mile from here down on the sound. The Wheelhouse Motel. It ain't fancy but it's clean. I'll call her."

211

Ten minutes later he was back. "She's got one room with a connecting bath. Two beds. Says she'll let 'em have it for four nights for ten dollars a night. It is high season, you know."

"We'll take it," Lenny quickly spoke out. "That's twenty bucks for me and twenty for Frank off our pay, but I'd rather pay it than take a chance. We can afford it out of what we're making, and if we get some tips while we're here we might cover the cost."

"Makes sense," Frank agreed, but we all knew the college crowd we were going to attract did not tip the band.

"If we get any tips it will all go to you two guys...up to the forty bucks, "Will suggested, "If that's okay with you other guys."

We agreed it was a good idea and asked Cap'n to call his ex-wife and tell her Frank and Lenny would be checking in shortly. Cap'n also agreed to let us park the Woodie, Ray's Chevy and my Nash in his fenced-in back storage area overnight for our security, while we slept. He was accustomed to bands having to be innovative in their lodgings.

After un-hooking the trailer from the Woodie, Will and Ellen left to find her relatives' cottage. I took Jimmy, Lenny and Frank with me to locate their residences. Moe and Ray moved their cars into the lot to await our getting back together somewhere for supper around six-thirty. They told us they'd be inside having a libation when we returned. No surprise there.

We realized before we ever left home that we would not be paid until after the job on Saturday night or Sunday, so each of us had to have some living cash for four days. We could eat for about six dollars a day each. Other than Lenny and Frank, our bedding, as such, was free. That left incidentals, entertainment and for four of us, gas money.

If we spent over $35 each for the four days we just hadn't worked the system very well, i.e., accepting free refreshments from 'fans', figuring out where there were house parties where we might finagle invitations to meals, and not getting carried away with after-job dates that cost anything beyond a beer or two. Or three if that was what was necessary.

The Wheelhouse Motel was everything we expected it would be. One-story cinder block painted a sea foam blue-green. Flashing ship's wheel neon sign over the entrance. Twelve units in a row, all facing the busy road. Window in the front, mini- window in the rear of each room. No air conditioning. A small office was centered between rooms six and seven.

Pearl, the Cap'n's ex, was a sizeable lady with predictable bleached blond hair but a very unpredictable frizzy hairdo. She was attired in a faded gray XL-size tee shirt with the U.S. Coast Guard logo and Semper Paratus silk-screened on it, ragged cut off denim shorts from which enormous thighs were struggling to escape, and barefooted. A lit, unfiltered cigarette dangled from the corner of her over-lipsticked mouth and she could well benefit from a trip to the dentist.

"How could the Cap'n ever let this bra-less beauty get away?" Jimmy whispered to me as we went inside, Lenny and Frank behind us.

"C'mon in, sweeties," Pearl invited, leaning over the wooden counter in a most revealing, unlady-like manner," been waiting for you. Which two are staying with me?"

Jimmy quickly pointed to the two younger guys. Pearl had them sign in, grabbed a key ring off a hook on the wall behind the counter, and then lead us out the front door, down two doors, to number eight.

"My lucky number, "I said for no reason.

The room was small, but it appeared clean enough. Linoleum floor, wall to wall. The décor was WWII Navy gray, including walls and the obviously military surplus furniture. Single beds, more like a metal cots with springs, were on either side of the room, the heads backed up to the rear wall. A metal nightstand was under the tiny window in the rear, between the two beds with a lamp and a shade that featured palm trees and a Hawaiian motif. A metal dresser was against one wall at the foot of the bed on the left, and a grey metal chair was at the foot the bed on the right. No pictures.

The window that opened on the front, with the main road a scant thirty feet or so away, had a screen but several holes large enough for the least ambitious mosquito to fly through easily. On the right, before the bed, was a door that lead to the small, narrow shared bath. It had a tiny shower, a small sink and a toilet. A large and well-used bath towel with embroidered ship's wheel in blue and a small bar of high-scent Lifebuoy soap were placed on the lightweight chenille spreads on each bed. All the comforts of home.

"You boys paying in advance, right? That's how come you got the good rate."

Both Lenny and Frank dug down and found twenty dollars each, for which they got a single key to the room. They brought their bags in, checked out the bath, made sure their door to the john was locked from their side, closed the front window and locked it, remembered to take their white pants and blue shirts and we left Pearl's place to locate some house party of girls from East Carolina.

The directions Jimmy had gotten from one of the girls were simple and accurate, and we soon pulled up to a two-story house on the beach that seemed to be overrun with females. As soon as he got out of the Nash, which drew questionable and condescending looks from the girls, Jimmy was recognized by several bikini-clad coeds. Obviously, his good looks, military background, and more-maturity-than-these-college-guys demeanor had put him in good stead with the fairer sex on the ECC campus.

Several of the reception committee squealed "Jim-meeee" and ran out to greet him. A couple of shirtless males now appeared on the second story porch, recognized their arriving classmate and waved, beers in hand. This place had all the trappings of a very dangerous operation but I figured if Jimmy could survive two years in the Air Force in the Far East, he could manage whatever challenges arose in this volatile setting.

He grabbed his gear and trumpet case and told me he'd be at the job by seven-thirty. I drove back to the Heart of the Beach and pulled into the gated lot behind the place, otherwise known as home for four days.

Deciding against another dose of Heart of the Beach food, we were directed by one of the bartenders to check out The Conch House down on the sound. A pylon-supported shack sitting over the water, it had better food than décor and both the price and the quantity of food were right. There was a varied selection of seafood and all the trimmings for two-fifty and we took advantage of the free second helpings of hush puppies and iced tea.

We pleasantly concluded the fish we ate was absolutely fresh and not one of those new frozen food sensations by someone named Mrs. Paul. "Another flash-in-the-pan gimmick," I predicted. "Or fast fish in a pan." No laughter.

Properly outfitted, fed, and ready to play at eight o'clock, with the Cap'n standing off to the side to make sure we were playing by his rules, we kicked off the first number, *60 Minute Man*, in the shag tempo, just to set the stage. Not many people were expected on a Wednesday night, which gave us a chance to play under 'simulated battle conditions' and test the waters. Will had produced a series of sets that focused on shag and jitterbug in the early hours and the slow stuff would be featured the last hour or so.

We also had decided that Lenny would play only the guitar on the first night and break out the vibes the following three nights, which would give us a chance to rehearse his specialty numbers, and some of Frank's Dixieland tunes, on Thursday afternoon.

The evening went well. Ellen came down about ten to hang out, there was a good house from ten to midnight, a good many dancers inside, and a few on the deck, but at one a.m. there was only a scattering of folks when we stopped. After a brief post-job libation, Moe drove Lenny and Frank to their digs in the Woodie, dropped Will and Ellen off at the cottage, and returned to the 'compound' he was sharing with Ray and me and our mobile bedrooms. Jimmy had already arranged a ride, and most likely a bunk of sorts, with a most comely young ECC coed.

Ray discovered an outside shower, indicating the nightclub had likely been someone's beach house before urban in-fill took it. The water was cold only, but in the July heat, even at that hour, it was warm enough to allow each of us to get the job done. I had a large bar of 99.44% pure Ivory that we shared.

Earlier, I had actually pre-tested the collapsible seat on the Nash so I positioned it quickly into the reclined position, wadded up the blankets I had brought from home, rolled all four windows down half way, and went down for the count. Moe wasted no time spreading blankets into the back of the Woodie and crashing, leaving the tailgate down. Ray was having a bit of a problem fitting his six-foot frame comfortably in the back seat of the Chevy but finally managed.

The outside security light high on a pole attached to the back of the nightclub was shining brightly, illuminating the entire yard area, including the interiors of our cars, but it had no negative effect on the three of us. It had been a long, long day.

• • • • •

Far too early the next morning there was considerable activity going on in the yard as vendors brought in the day's foodstuffs, soft drinks and beer, passing our makeshift boudoirs as we slept until eight. I finally gave in to the hubbub, grabbed my toilet kit, and, wearing well-worn moccasins, swim trunks and a KA-escutcheoned burgundy tee shirt, strolled to the Heart's men's room.

The counter man-bartender had made a fresh pot of coffee so I indulged myself with a 'freebie' until Ray and Moe wandered in. The consensus was that Moe and I had slept rather well but the Chevy's backseat never allowed Ray the same privilege and he complained of a major backache.

"Tonight I'm sleeping in the trailer," he avowed. "Can't be worse that the car."

Before we could decide on where to eat one of our two main meals for the day Lenny and Frank strode in. They had walked the mile or so from the homey Wheelhouse Motel.

"So, how'd it go out at pretty Pearl's palace? I inquired, playing the alliteration card.

216

"Well," Lenny spoke up quickly, "it was okay for about the first hour or so and then all sorts of loud noises and sounds came from the next room for about an hour."

"Best we could tell, it sounded like a man and a woman," Frank added, "and from all the carrying on and groaning and yelling out and all that she was doing, I'd say she was pretty daggone upset, or really sick. That guy should have taken her to a hospital."

"It's just a wild hunch on my part," Moe said, laughing and looking at me and Ray, "but I doubt she was sick."

Chapter Twenty-Nine

B y the time Jimmy and Will showed up at the HotBed, as in a "hot-bed of activity" (our nickname for Heart of the Beach using its initials HOTB) at 12:30 p.m., we had had a hearty breakfast at Miss Lucy's Café, a mom and pop place catering to young folks wanting lots of filling food at a minimal price. For one-fifty you could get all the pancakes or eggs, and sides, you wanted.

Knowing we were to rehearse with the vibes, Lenny had unpacked the long, stout case, set the instrument up near the piano and was getting in some practice with four mallets.

Will was reasonably spry and apparently had gotten some sleep on the porch cot, likely under the occasional gaze of his wary hosts. Whatever romantic activity transpired was apparently short and not on the premises.

On the other hand, Jimmy looked as if he had been "rode hard and put away wet", as the old rural saying went.

"Hate to say it, Jimbo, but you look like the devil," Ray pointed out to the hung-over associate.

"Feel the same way. Just need a little 'hair of the dog' and I'll be as good as new. Gonna' be here four nights…got to remember to pace myself."

"Where'd you wind up staying?" I inquired.

"Well, from about three-thirty until about eleven this morning I slept on the porch at that beach house where you dropped me off yesterday afternoon. But from about two until three or so I was in some room at the Wheelhouse Motel."

Ray, Moe and I broke out laughing. "I'll bet it was room number seven," Ray said.

"You know, "Jimmy replied, "I think it was."

Lenny and Frank, somewhat left out of the picture until now, finally got it.

"Next time, Jim, do the honorable thing. Take that poor girl to a hospital," I said, glancing at my two young friends who were getting an unexpected education.

"Huh?" Jimmy asked, wondering what he said to cause the laughter.

"I'll explain later."

Having the vibes made a world of difference to the sound, and the swinging Dixieland tunes, although not great dance numbers, gave the combo a new energy. Even Cap'n came over after rehearsal and indicated the vibes gave a 'class' look to our group and the Dixieland sound would surely hype beer sales, which was obviously more important than the sound.

We all spent the rest of the afternoon napping and lazing about. Jimmy hung out with his house party crowd, Will and Ellen opted to do the sunning thing in front of her relatives' cottage. Ray tested the Woodie's napping capacity.

I had found a number of February and March issues of *The State* magazine in the car, apparently left there by my mother. For several hours I read about canoeing down the Cape Fear River in thirteen days, how Piedmont Airlines continued to fight for survival, about orchid growing in Moore County, the Azalea Festival and the Battle of Bentonville.

In between reading about North Carolinian of the Year Gordon Gray and Judge Susie Sharp and Appalachian State's music department, I poured salted Planters Peanuts from the bag into a bottle of RC Cola, shook it up and "fired" the carbonated-driven morsels into my mouth. Went through three nickel bags. Good stuff.

Lenny had developed an obsession as to just where we were, geographically, topographically and historically, He had picked up a free area map and several tourist promotion pieces at the Esso station and was studying them diligently on the HOTBed's front porch.. Frank borrowed several old copies of Modern Screen and

Photoplay from the motel's lobby, probably Pearl's heavier reading, and joined Lenny.

"Everybody needs to know what Maureen O'Hara and Ava Gardner are up to these days," he said by way of an excuse. "And since Ava is from Johnston County, NC I feel obliged to stay current."

After a sumptuous mid-afternoon hot dog lunch during which Lenny informed us that he had read where Americans eat an average of 42 hot dogs each a year, he, Frank and I strolled two blocks to the beach to wade in the low surf and keep an eye out for meaningful feminine sights.

Redheaded, white-skinned with freckles, I was not a good candidate for the tanning business. Wearing a long-sleeved light blue Dickies work shirt I acquired for just such a purpose, and long khaki pants, moccasins and a baseball cap, I was not winning any style accolades. But I also wasn't a candidate for layers of Noxzema or other sunburn ointments. I had learned that lesson the hard way too many times in the past.

Thin, lean, and 'tannable', Frank and Lenny were both without shirts or caps and wore bathing trunks and sandals. At only two or three years their senior, I felt like their dad.

Thursday night's crowd was somewhat larger and when a light shower shut down the deck around ten, the dancers all crowded into the main room. Many were attracted to the vibes and stood, drinks and Lucky Strikes in hand, close to Lenny, fascinated by the swift, true mallet movements striking the keys, especially when he played with two mallets in each hand.

The remainder of the night went well and at one a.m. we packed it in, thinking more about sleep than any after-job activity. Everyone returned to his room, porch, car, trailer, or whatever, knowing that the coming weekend crowd would be large, loud, and demanding.

Ray had pushed things to one side in the trailer and made his pallet bed there in lieu of another cramped night in the Chevy. He decided to sleep with his head towards the open door, feet pointing towards the front. Somewhere around three a.m., a rather heavy downpour, much of which was coming in through the rolled-down windows of the Nash, awakened me.

In the light of the HotBed's security spotlight, I could see Ray, soaking wet in his shorts, standing outside the trailer. Apparently, the cloudburst was coming down with strong winds out of the northeast. By happenstance the trailer's open door, and his head, were facing the northeast. In a word, half of Ray and half his new bedroom were soaked before he could get up and close the door. What with the strong winds, it was not an easy task, but he finally managed to back into the trailer and pull the door after him, securing it from flying open with every gust. There was still water in the trailer but apparently he ignored it or found some dry space to bed down.

Will had decided to forego any additional rehearsals so it was every man for himself during the day on Friday. After what appeared to be an uneventful Thursday evening for all of us but perhaps Ray, and Will, who was allowed to move the cot into a living room off the open porch in the storm, I decided to drive over to Beaufort and knock around. Then I'd come back to Morehead City and get a lavish early seafood dinner at the Sanitary Fish Market, one of the more popular dining places on the Carolina coast. Lenny, Frank and Moe had never been to those parts and they joined me.

Ray got the key to room number eight in the Wheelhouse Motel from Lenny and crashed for some daytime sleep in dry surroundings. Jimmy did the beach thing with his ECC friends and Will, with Ellen, had decided to investigate the sea oats surrounding a deep indentation in a dune far down the beach. Apparently such searching required a blanket and a stocked Styrofoam cooler.

By the time we arrived at 7:45 to settle in on the bandstand the HotBed was chocked full of partygoers. College kids were butt-to-belly button in their various forms of colorful stylish wear, most with sorority, fraternity or some college name splashed prominently across the chest. Using the highly visible logo as an introductory talking point to engage conversation with a potential date was a tried and true method of getting down to business.

We ramped up the volume on the speaker system and began with a shag number right off the bat. Feet were shuffling and torsos moving as fully half the crowd started dancing. The main room was three-quarters filled and the deck had a good crowd as well. The date selection process was in full swing and it was easy to spot the pleased male winners and the dejected losers: the former danced closer and held on tighter to their newfound property for the night, while the latter kept wandering around, in, through and about the crowd looking for new possibilities.

By eleven or so the place was packed. The deck was over-flowing. The speakers were blaring out to the world to come on in and join the party. The Cap'n was elated with the size of the house and the purchasing activity. We were earning our keep.

By midnight the action was slowing, people were moving out and on to other adventures and we had gone into the slow dance numbers mode for those who had "hooked up." There is no place where the girls are prettier or better put together than at a North Carolina beach in the summer, and I had watched some of the finest glide by the bandstand for the past five hours.

How good it would be if Ginny were here, I thought, and not cleaning up after folks at some massive dinner-on-the-grounds. I decided to try to reach her by telephone the next day to see how she was doing.

We packed it in at one as planned, had our usual after-the-job bite to eat and those without feminine projects opted to get ten hours sleep, minimum.

I had adjusted to the built-in crevices and humps in the Nash wonder seat, Moe had figured out it was better sleeping at an angle than straight ahead in the Woodie and Ray was grateful the trailer and his blankets were now dry. Whatever late night activity there was at the Wheelhouse Motel took place away from room number eight allowing Lenny and Frank to rest in peace.

Jimmy was in love, for the weekend anyhow, and spending all non-musical waking, and apparently some sleeping, hours with his new lady. Will was working on logical reason he should continue to sleep inside the house, close to Ellen's bedroom, as opposed to outside on the porch.

As soon as I walked into the HotBed on Saturday morning I knew today was going to bring a different crowd.

Already, at eleven, dozens of Marines from Camp LeJeune Marine Base, forty-five miles south of Atlantic Beach, were lined up at the bar. They had overnight passes and would be around until late the next afternoon.

Most musicians leave their horns on their chairs during breaks, and drummers normally leave their sets intact since there's so much to disassemble. We needed to rethink that practice.

Musicians know as well that aggressive males who drink excessive amounts of booze tend to think they can (a) sing, (b) dance and (c) play a musical instrument, or perhaps all three. Given the time these Marines had to drink, my guess was many of them would unashamedly and aggressively attempt to play a horn, the piano, vibes or my drums that night.

I immediately began to take my drum set apart and Ray began to disassemble Lenny's vibes As soon as we had everything in cases we made three trips to the trailer, put the drums and vibes inside, locked it and went to find the Cap'n.

Bending over some invoices foisted on him by the Budweiser deliveryman at the bar, the Cap'n was not in a good mood. Anytime he had to pay out any money for anything he was not in a good mood.

When he was free, we approached him with a suggestion that some temporary railing or barrier be placed in front of our band because we had a rough idea what the possibilities might be late in the evening.

"We don't want to spend half the night fighting off drunks who want to play with the band, or sing," I appealed to Cap'n, "and if they screw us up then that's going to mess up the dancing."

"And the college crowd sticking around," Ray added. "And the beer buying."

The Cap'n was most knowledgeable about such possibilities, having been in the dance hall business for many years. He loved the money the military guys brought in, but he also knew their temperament when they were drinking.

"I don't have any railings to put up," he said matter-of-factly, "and I don't know who does."

"There's a landscaping nursery in Morehead City, "I countered," and they usually have some picket fence type of railings we might use. I can drive over there and get some if you'll pay for them. Then you could have them on hand all the time. Good investment." I was trying to show him that a little money spent now might save him a goodly amount later.

"I got a better idea," the Cap'n responded out of the blue, "and it won't cost me any money. You boys wait here."

In ten minutes the Cap'n was back, smiling.

"Got it all settled," he reported. "You know those wood slat fences that the county puts up to hold the sea oats and sand in place so the wind don't blow 'em away...you see 'em all up and down the dunes...well, I called a buddy what works for the county and he's gonna' go git a load 'a them fences and bring 'em over here. He says we can prop 'em up with cinder blocks and he'll bring some 'a them, too. Now I'm counting on you boys to put 'em up."

"You got it, Cap'n. Good thinking. No wonder you're rich and famous." Moe was laying it on a bit thick but we did agree the old guy had come up with a practical plan.

While awaiting the county truck with its makeshift fortifications I found a pay phone and began the challenge of finding Ginny. She had not known the phone number before she went to her summer job so I began with Information in Brunswick County. Once I got the Carswell Assembly main number I asked to be connected to the Jordan House, the place where she was staying. A young girl ultimately answered, and when I asked for Ginny Barker there was a pause and I was told she would look for her.

I had a handful of change, but was now wondering if I would be able to pay for the time it was taking. Shortly the young lady came back on and reported that Ginny was probably working or out somewhere because she was nowhere around.

Disappointed, I asked her name and she replied 'Lucille." I asked Lucille if she would take a message. She agreed but had to leave the phone again to get paper and pencil. The Operator came on to suggest I drop in some more coins. I was running low but covered the fee. When Lucille finally returned with pencil and paper I dictated an obvious 'miss you, love you' message, reminded her how to spell Red, thanked her, and hung up.

Two hours later all the band but Will and Jimmy were constructing a rickety four-foot high fence of thin wood slats held together with rusted wire. Along the base we placed two lines of cinder blocks and worked to get the fence pieces to stay in place, upright. In some cases it took four stacked blocks to hold the fence up. The entire thing ran about thirty feet in a semi-circle, enclosing the piano and all the musicians' chairs, including those of us on the riser in back.

"Well, it ain't pretty, and it sure ain't too steady, but maybe the sight of it will keep any ambitious types from getting to us." Moe was positive, but wary. "Then again, if some of those guys really want to get to us, it won't slow 'em down."

When Lenny showed up and saw the porous barricade, and heard what the possibilities were, he quickly decided he was not going to set up the vibes.

"No way I'm going to put the vibes out there for some drunk to bang on with a beer bottle," he stated forcefully. "I'll play guitar."

When Will arrived just after seven and saw the set up he agreed with what we had done but was disappointed the vibes were staying in the trailer.

"I understand," he said to Lenny, "and I hope the Cap'n will. He sure does like those vibes."

I had no choice but to haul in my drums and set them up.

By seven-thirty, the place was already crowded and fully a third of the throng was Marines. We had managed to put everything in place behind the fence, realizing that the Camp LeJeune inhabitants had been spending weeks learning how to go under, over, around and through a lot tougher obstacles than we presented. Our hope was the visual presence would be a deterrent.

"Where's them vibes?" Cap'n asked as he came over to review our defensive battle positions, He was obviously irritated.

Lenny shot back, very boldly: "Locked up and safe. I'm not risking getting them banged up, and I don't think you want to pay what it would cost to replace them."

Obviously not pleased, but understanding he would be liable for damages should they occur, he muttered 'okay' and sauntered off, unhappy.

College girls spending a week or so at the beach for the most part prefer college boys to military men they don't know and who have been drinking beer for several hours. College boys do not wish to frequent places that cater to the military because in any case of confrontation, college boys lose. And yet, lonely, away-from-home, youthful military men like to dance as much as the college boys, and many are probably better at it, something college girls who like to dance understand.

It can make for an interesting evening when there are one-third college girls, one-third college boys and one third Marines, a dance floor, music and beer.

Now settled in our thinly protected environment, the jukebox was unplugged and we kicked off the music at eight. There was a good Saturday night crowd, anxious to enjoy the evening. Soon the dance floor was crowded with college boys and college girls, the Marines hanging back as if scouting the objectives before moving in. Reconnoitering as it were.

Unbeknownst to us, a number of soldiers, perhaps thirty, began to filter in. They were from the 82nd Airborne Division at Fort Bragg, NC, some two hours to the west. They, like the young Marines, were also on an overnight pass. Most of the afternoon they had been down on the beach, drinking, tanning, drinking, swimming, ogling girls, and drinking. Soon they were at the bar.

Our first break came at 9:30. The Heart of the Beach was now a genuine hotbed of young people hell-bent on partying. We eased out from behind the sand dune fencing and elbowed our way through the crowd to grab a Coke and get a smoke in the night air. Standing out back near our cars, away from the mounting throng, we commented that things were under control and perhaps our fears were in vain.

"It's early," Moe observed. "Keep your fingers crossed…and your eyes wide open."

For the next half- hour, the shaggers and jitterbuggers were in command and we pushed all the slow tunes to the bottom of the stack.

Around eleven several Marines who had been in the place for hours and were well in their cups, tried to break on some college men. The shoulder-tapping approach was somewhat forceful and when it was evident the girls involved did not want to dance with the Marines, a bit of mouthing-off occurred. In seconds, Cap'n was in the middle of the 'discussion', calming everyone down and suggesting the Marines might want to wait until a girl asked them to dance, which was highly unlikely of course.

When Cap'n was gone, the military youngsters decided they were not going to be denied in their quest for social engagement. As they began to approach dancers on the floor once again, many of the college types wisely began to exit the place, taking their dates and/or acquaintances with them. In several minutes, literally a fourth of the crowd had left, leaving the Marines, the Airborne types and perhaps a hundred non-military male and female dancing enthusiasts who had paid more attention to their footwork than the growing tension.

At this point, two of the Airborne jump-boys approached the bandstand and, leaning over the fencing, suggested strongly that they wanted to play the drums and guitar. Will nicely, albeit incorrectly, told them the union didn't permit such and while he appreciated their offer, we had to say 'No'. The two were not happy.

All of us got the gist of the conversation and were hoping Will's explanation would suffice. It didn't. They continued to get louder and more demanding so Will called an intermission and suggested that everyone take their instruments with them as we vacated the bandstand. Obviously, I couldn't take all my drums but I did grab the snare, sticks, and tympani mallets.

As soon as we were outside Will sought out Cap'n and informed him of the growing storm. A seasoned old Navy veteran of WWII and many a saloon encounter, Cap'n shrugged it off and said he'd talk to the guys. We were not convinced that approach would work and Ray suggested that Cap'n ring up the local cops and get some MPs as well, just in case.

"No need for that," he responded, "I'll take care of it."

Settling back down on the bandstand, but definitely feeling unsettled, we began the set with a slow tune thinking that might cool the performing ambitions of our would-be musicians, but no such luck. In no time they were back at the fence, with two comrades who insisted they should sing. It was getting difficult for any of us to pay attention to the music for being wary of the mounting confrontation.

Will told Lenny to take his guitar and go find Cap'n. Lenny eased out between numbers, very aware the four plane jumpers were staring at him and literally hanging over the poorly set fencing. I decided to move the floor tom tom back out of the way but there wasn't much else I could do to protect my drum set.

At that point, a handful of Marines who had been standing off to the side of the bandstand fondling Pabst Blue Ribbons saw there was trouble brewing and decided it was their duty to take over the situation. They walked up to their Airborne counterparts and one boldly suggested, "Hey, men, why don't we let these guys play and not bother them?"

"Mind your own business, boy," the shaved-head would-be drummer from the 82nd answered.

"Who you calling 'boy'?" The crew-cut Marine hunk shot back.

Now the ranks were closing, Marines inching towards Airborne, two opposing forces of tanned, hardened eighteen and nineteen-year-olds, all physically fit and certainly psychologically imbued with the idea they were superior to all men, anywhere, anytime.

It was shaping up to be a "My daddy can whip your daddy" event, a proving ground as to whether the Marines are tougher than Airborne or the Airborne tougher than Marines.

Hearing this mounting vocal clashing of opposing forces, Moe made the wise decision to quit playing the piano, rose carefully and eased out of the area. Will, Frank and Ray concluded this would be a good time for them to leave as well so they stood together and started to file out carrying their instruments. This did not please the Airborne lads and when they started yelling at our departing musicians, someone threw a fist at someone else.

Before I, or Jimmy, both still on the bandstand, could depart or anyone could yell "FIGHT!" there was one.

Jimmy, having experienced this sort of military reasoning before while with the Air Force, smartly bailed out the open window behind the bandstand, dropping six or seven feet to the ground, holding his trumpet close to his chest.

Alone on the bandstand I had to figure out where I'd go, and how. I couldn't go to my left because an onrushing squad of Marines was storming the bandstand beachhead from that direction. I might try to escape off to the right side past the piano as Moe had done or perhaps go out the window behind Johnny. As I was giving thought to these options, none good, I crouched down behind the bass drum, almost prone, as the melee became a full-scale battle ten feet in front of me.

Suddenly there was a loud, distinct "tha-whomp" sound and I felt my bass drum wobble. Moving my head slightly from behind the bass, I saw that a beer bottle had been thrown with a mighty force and sailed right through the blue shield logo with my initials, RP, painted on the bass's cowhide head. The bottle, with beer foam oozing out the neck, lay motionless in the bottom of my drum. For some reason I fleetingly recalled the term "dead soldier."

Fearing more missiles to come, I followed Jimmy's heroic lead and put my 130-pound frame through the same window. Without yelling "Geronimo" or pulling any kind of ripcord, I soared awkwardly the seven feet, landing with a thud. Fortunately, the sand was reasonably soft.

People were pouring out of the HotBed like mad wasps from a disturbed hive. I decided to run out back where our cars were, assuming the action would occur inside. Of all the things I was not, pugilist was high, very high on the list.

All six of the others had gathered outside by the Woodie, waiting out the storm inside. Shortly we heard the sirens and knew the sheriff, the local cops and Military Police were on their way. Meanwhile the battle between the Marines and the Airborne raged on the dance floor. How they could tell one another apart escaped me since they all looked exactly alike in size, shape, dress, builds and haircuts.

In ten minutes the action was ended, participants rounded up and hauled off and the HotBed totally emptied, save for some valiant bartenders, two shaky short-order cooks and the Cap'n himself.

When we ultimately walked in through the rear service entrance we saw the sheriff talking to Cap'n amidst a sea of beer and what appeared to be little boats of bottles and cigarette butts bobbing about. Our rickety defensive wall was totally destroyed, the band chairs tossed on the dance floor and several cinder blocks, likely weapons during the fight, were lying about. One was actually on the piano keys.

Other than the head of my bass being ripped open, none of my other equipment was damaged. Frank and Ray's music stands had been knocked over and sheets of music scattered around. It was not a pretty sight.

We assumed the bar, which had been undisturbed, was the place to gather and figure out Plan B. Now the only patrons in the place, we walked over and casually ordered something to calm the nerves, as it were. Shortly we saw Cap'n walk the last of the law out, close the front doors and lock them. It was twelve o'clock and the entertainment was done.

Cap'n came over to us as he returned to assess the damage, which, amazingly, was principally in broken bottles, a dismantled sand dunes fence, and a severely banged-up piano.

"Well, I guess you guys were right," he admitted. "Shoulda' gone ahead and called the police like you said. It got ugly, but don't look like too much damage was done. What about you guys, you okay?"

"Looks like the only thing is Red's bass drum," Will reported, as he pointed to the wide gap in the Gretsch. "And we got a job to play in Virginia Beach next week so he's gonna' need to be paid for that. We can clean up the rest of the stuff. Guess this job's over, huh?"

"How much is that drum thing?" Cap'n asked. "If it ain't too much I'd rather pay you for it than file insurance. Takes forever and they'll screw me anyhow. Don't need for my rates to get any higher."

"Thirty-six bucks," I stated quickly, not completely certain but it was close enough. If it was too much I figured I could find a place for the remainder.

"Whew! That's a lot of money, but okay." He reached in his pocket, withdrew a wad of bills, and peeled three tens, a five and a single, which he handed to me.

"Might as well go ahead and pay you guys off for the week right now," the Cap'n suggested. He located larger bills in the cache, counted off $520 and thrust it all out to Will. "I throwed an extra twenty in 'cause you boys done real good. Folks liked your playing, 'specially them vibes. I'll have to git you back here one 'a these days. Too bad the fight broke out but you was 'bout done anyhow I reckon."

We thanked him for the job, and the libations we were enjoying on the house. While Will went off to the side to figure out the payments and getting change from a bartender to pay each of us, we returned to the scene of the recent crime to gather the music and pick up the stands. The horn guys found their instrument cases and packed them carefully while I commenced to take the drums apart and pack them. I left the damaged head intact to show to Lupton on Monday when I hoped I could get a replacement. I didn't leave the empty beer bottle that had done the damage.

Will handed each one of us the hard-earned $64, $71 less $7 for our share to the booking agency. After getting our permission, he gave Cap'n's generous twenty bucks extra to Lenny and Frank to offset their motel costs. As we surmised at the outset, there were no tips. We had put an empty beer mug on Moe's piano with a sign suggesting Tips Here. But if there was ever any money in it we never saw it.

Ellen had come down to pick up Will in her uncle's car and was just as glad she had not been around for the activity. Jimmy's love, a pert little blond sophomore from Williamston, appeared in her daddy's-gift white 1951 custom Ford V8 stick shift with overdrive, rag top convertible to fetch him back to the lair. After loading the trailer carefully so as to keep a space open for Ray to sleep, and agreeing on arrangements for the coming week, we bade farewell to the HotBed.

"Can't say it wasn't fun," I remarked casually as we broke ranks.

Moe headed to the solace of the Woodie, Ray wormed his way into the trailer and I ran Lenny and Frank down for a final night at the Wheelhouse Motel before returning to the enclosure and bedding down, Nash-style. I considered writing the auto company with an endorsement if I thought there was any money in it. Since Will was going to drive Ellen back to Zebulon the next day, I volunteered to take Lenny and Frank back to Raleigh.

By nine-thirty Sunday morning we had vacated our premises, had our eggs with country ham and red-eye gravy grits, biscuits and coffee at Miss Lucy's café and were on the causeway heading home. To a real bed.

Chapter Thirty

L eaving at 8:00 a.m., it took over five hours for us to get from Raleigh to Virginia Beach on Friday. Will was behind the wheel of the Woodie, trailer attached, with me, Moe, Lenny and Frank switching seats every hour or so when we stopped for a break. I had called Lup as soon as his store opened on Monday morning and was grateful he was willing to take a new cowhide bass drum head off an existing set and let me have it for $22.50. The original head with the custom logo was now a keepsake, a rather stark reminder of a most unusual night.

The extra $13.50 from Cap'n went as a down payment on a new 16-inch Zildjian cymbal.

Moe had thumbed from Lumberton to Raleigh the day before and slept at the YMCA on Jones Street behind the State Capitol, where Will picked him up on Friday morning. Jimmy drove his 1948 Plymouth Club Coupe the forty-five miles from Goldsboro to Rocky Mount, where he picked up Ray, giving the worn-out Chevy a rest, and they proceeded northeast to rendezvous with us. Their trip from Rocky Mount was an hour or so shorter than ours from Raleigh.

We were to play at the Surf Club on Friday, Saturday and Sunday nights, August 1-3. Music was to begin at 8:00 p.m. and continue until midnight. Requiring appropriate dress for the sophisticated, upscale clientele, Will decreed we wear white pants with our blue blazers and open- collared white long-sleeve dress shirts. Just in case, he had a supply of the red knit ties.

By calling the Chamber of Commerce, Will had identified a service station on the south side of the highway leading into Virginia Beach where we were to meet at 2:00 p.m. That would give us time to find lodging, eat dinner, get to the Surf Club, unpack and set up, change and be ready to play at 8:00 p.m. We hoped we could find supper of some sort at the Club that evening.

By the time we had passed through the business and residential areas of the town of Virginia Beach and arrived at the designated Esso station at the beach itself, Ray and Jimmy were there.

None of us knew this area as we did the North Carolina beaches and we figured we should take no chances finding a house party or an empty beach cottage or risk sleeping in cars or on the beach. We had to play this one much closer to the vest.

Ray and Jimmy had gotten some suggestions from the service station manager where we might stay. His first choice was the Pink Pelican Motel, a mom and pop establishment on Pacific Avenue at 14th Street near Lake Holly. Mr. and Mrs. Goodman operated the Virginia Beach motel during the summer months, shut it down after Labor Day and went to Ft. Lauderdale, Florida where they operated their other Pink Pelican Motel for the winter.

Luckily, they had some cancellations and we were able to get two rooms for three nights at their place for fifteen dollars a night. They arranged for us to book one room at the adjoining Fun 'n Sun Motel at the same price.

Lenny and Frank, Moe and Ray took the two Pelican rooms with Will, Jimmy and I opting for the solo room next door. The manager obligingly put a folding cot in with the two single beds. I quickly yelled out "dibs" on a bed but by flips of the coin I got the cot.

After a fast wash-up and putting our basic belongings in the rooms, we asked the motel manager where we might get a good meal, reasonably. We assumed that out of 351 orange-roofed Howard Johnson's nationwide there must be one around this area somewhere.

She suggested we drive over to Grumpy's on Atlantic Avenue, a popular local spot. The owner, a former professional wrestler who apparently acted like Disney's dwarf 'Grumpy', was holding down the cash register. We made the most of his highly acclaimed fish sandwich on a toasted bun with cole slaw and pickles. Fries and sweet ice tea, followed by a slice of homemade lemon meringue pie, ended the stomach gurglings.

By four-fifteen, we had driven past the prestigious Cavalier Club and were in sight of The Surf Club on 57th Street, sitting conspicuously alone in an area where there were very few beach houses and no retail establishments whatsoever.

Contrary to the very informal, barn-like ambience of the Heart of the Beach facility, the Surf Club was strictly uptown. Located on unspoiled, undeveloped beachfront property on north Atlantic Avenue near Marshall's high-end motel, the sole lodging facility in the area, it was designed and built as a private club and opened on Memorial Day, 1936. Weathered shingle siding. White lattice work. Expansive parking area fronting 57th Street.

An extremely popular spot after Prohibition, the Club was said to have had a very private back room in those days. The sign on the door warned: FOR EMPLOYEES ONLY. In actuality, it was a gambling den, very popular with high rollers and the Norfolk expatriots who had relocated to less-expensive Virginia Beach after the Depression.

The Surf Club itself was a long, narrow, one-story building with a bar, dining room, men's grill , ladies parlor, card room, men's and women's changing facilities and rest rooms, and a bounty of cabanas, umbrellas and chairs beachside. It was something of a Mecca for outdoor enthusiasts, offering volleyball, badminton, calisthenics, paddleball, and ocean swimming.

Across half of the building's front, along the ocean, was a very large outdoor dance floor, a popular spot for afternoon tea dances and musical nights under the stars. A semi-circular bandstand jutted out a bit onto the dance floor. To each side were tables, chairs and benches for dancers and spectators. Understated lighting was placed in the ceilings of the two side breezeways and in the bandstand.

Overhead, on the reinforced roof of much of the structure, was a railed deck terrace for casual dining, sunbathing, card-playing, reading, cocktailing, salt-air breathing, napping and gazing at the ocean or down on the slick dance floor beneath. A sizeable striped awning was positioned on each of the two upper decks that ran parallel to the dance floor, shading clubbers from the sun. White-jacketed waiters moved about energetically. They appeared to be college students working summer jobs.

The sixteen-year-old club was the exclusive playground of the well heeled who had danced on this very site to the music of some of America's top big bands over the years, including Jimmy Dorsey, Carmen Cavallaro, Guy Lombardo and Sammy Kaye. Louis Prima was an annual favorite and drew packed crowds. Surf Club audiences knew good music, they were accustomed to good music and our seven-piece combo was going to have to rise to the occasion. As to the ages of the dancers, we had no idea what to expect.

There was easy access from a parking area to a rear door of the bandstand, which made unloading simple and fast. I set up my drums and plugged in the blue light, knowing the damp ocean air would muffle the drumheads somewhat.

By five o'clock, the afternoon beach crowd had given up on swimming and tanning and left. The pre-dinner cocktail crowd had yet to arrive. Since there were few members about, Will sought out the Manager and asked if we might shower and change at the club, and hinted a bite to eat would be in order and "we will certainly pay for it." Graciously, Mr. LeCoste, or more precisely, Monsieur Pierre LeCoste, consented to let us use the Men's Dressing Area and agreed to provide, gratis, burgers all around at the Grill. He indicated we should not expect such generosity for the next two evenings, however.

When we took to the bandstand at 7:50 p.m. to tune up, there were at least a hundred people hanging about on the dance floor awaiting our music. For the most part, they were in their 'mature' years, the women impressively bedecked in tea-length dresses and modest heels, the men in summer suits or slacks and jackets, and ties. The overall seersucker and linen scene reminded me of a page out of F. Scott Fitzgerald's The Great Gatsby.

For the first hour we played standard sets, dominated by big band classic ballads and a few of the slower beat jitterbug numbers requested by the silver-temple and blue hair patrons. As the evening progressed the older folks retired and younger faces, mostly couples in their mid to late thirties, took over the dance floor, asking for more upbeat tunes.

One of the waiters told us that Saturday night would bring a majority of twenty-something's and college kids, children and grand-children of the members, who liked to hit the less-pretentious joints on Friday night and then dine and dance off Daddy, or Granddaddy as the case might be, on Saturday nights. Sunday night would be back to the older folks who were spending the summer in their private homes.

After each number the dancers would stop and applaud politely, something we were unaccustomed to but pleased to hear, and quite often they came up to the bandstand with a brief plaudit or request. This was as pleasant a way to play a dance job as we'd ever had.

A few minutes after midnight I had packed my drums in their cases, leaving them on the covered and secure bandstand for the night. Lenny carefully placed his vibes in the heavy-duty case and shoved them into the back of the Woodie while the others had taken their instruments and the music sheets to the cars. Tired after a very long day, we passed on any post-job libations and even the usual late-night breakfast routine and made our way down Atlantic Avenue to the comfort of the Pink Pelican and Fun 'n Sun motels.

Saturday was a day to work hard at doing nothing. Massive late breakfast, followed by a casual stroll by several of us in the main part of town while the others took to the strand for sun and she-seeing. Then a brief afternoon nap, a treat to which we were most unaccustomed. We took advantage of the ocean offerings and had an early seafood supper at The Colony Restaurant on Atlantic Avenue near 19th Street. We were informed it was the only restaurant in Virginia Beach to be approved by the American Restaurant Association, a differential and distinction that did not appear to bother Grumpy.

"This is the way to play jobs," Ray said, "sleep all morning, get some beach time, eat decent meals, play in a swanky club where folks appreciate you. Let's see if we can get more gigs here."

"I'll check," Will replied, "but they only have live bands once or twice a month and the season's about over."

"I'll play for room and board until school starts," Ray continued.

"Good idea," I added, "how 'bout checking it out, Will?"

"Will do," Will responded, "but now let's go hit it. This ought to be a big night."

Arriving at the Club at 7:30 we noticed there were a good many cars in the lot already, suggesting a major dinner-dance evening was underway. There was almost no breeze, and the humidity had to be in the nineties at least. The moon was inching its way up into the sky, casting wide bands of light on the sea and making the phosphorous in the water even more electric. A few couples were walking barefoot on the wide strand between the dance floor pavilion and the breaking waves of the incoming tide, holding their wing tips and pumps as they strolled. It was a gorgeous night.

As the knowledgeable young waiter had predicted, Saturday night's crowd was considerably younger and in more of a party mood. Dressed to the nines as benefited the location, and their parentage, this crowd had more of a college feel, a mixture of the Hollins, Mary Baldwin, Sweetbriar scene with UVA, William & Mary, Washington & Lee and VPI lads.

It became evident that the Carolina shag had invaded Virginia Beach as well, for time and again we were asked to do a 'shag' number.

By eleven o'clock the party was in full swing. The dance floor was crowded and no one was leaving. When we took a break before the final hour Johnny, Moe and I wandered to the edge of the dance floor and, looking out, counted quite a few young people, likely non-member teenagers, who had gathered outside the Club perimeter on the dunes closest to the bandstand and were soaking in the music. Apparently, this was a common occurrence as the next dancing generation, albeit kids of the non-well-to-do in this case, listened and learned from the current one.

As we came back to the bandstand Will called us to gather around for he had an idea he wanted to run by us. He outlined his plan and got total buy-in from all of us. The execution would require some alterations in our process, but we were prepared to make them.

At 11:45, Will called for *Stompin' At The Savoy* where Lenny took the Lionel Hampton role and really put on a show. He had spent most of that day arranging the tune for the seven-member group, giving a fresh approach to the usual stock arrangement the big band used.

Vibes were not often used in most bands and in addition to offering a unique sound, they provided the player, the good players like Lenny, a major opportunity for showmanship. As soon as we started the tune, a sizeable number of the dancers came to the bandstand to watch Lenny perform and clap to the upbeat tempo.

When we finished we got a rousing ovation, or at least Lenny did. Then, quickly, before the crowd could disperse and by pre-arrangement, I counted out loudly…"One, two, three, four"…and immediately went into a march beat. Dum dum, dum dum, brrrrrrrrrrr dum dum.

While I kept the beat going the others stood, took off their jackets, then their shoes and socks, and rolled up their pants legs above the knees. Moe took my floor tom tom off its pedestal, picked up an extra drumstick I had on the bass and began beating on the tom tom as if it were a marching bass drum. Lenny picked up his guitar and Johnny hit the universally known first notes of *When The Saints Go Marching In.*

Knowing what was coming I had already done the jacket, socks and shoes removal thing and had taken a length of venetian blind cord I had found in a storage room off the bandstand, and fashioned something of a shoulder strap for my snare drum.

As the other six formed a single file, all now playing *Saints* from memory, I fell in behind them, continuing the march beat as best I could with the snare bouncing side to side. Moving across the dance floor in a New Orleans struttin' style, the crowd immediately sensed what was going on and fell in behind me, clapping their hands and singing. A snake line was now at least forty people long, and growing.

Will lead the band and our enthusiastic marching entourage across the dance floor, down the steps to the sand, across the hard-packed strand and into the small waves that were rolling in to the shore. By the time the water was up to his knees almost, he stopped and turned towards the shoreline. We lined up beside him, still playing and doing our best to keep our instruments out of the salt spray and the incoming tide.

Undaunted, most of the dancers, now probably sixty or more, marched straight into the ocean with us, many not bothering to remove any clothing at all, with one notable exception. One winsome lass quickly shed shoes, dress, and slip and splashed about in her unmentionables to the delight of all the males and the feigned shock of her female friends.

After two or three minutes of playing in the surf, literally, Will gave us the sign to end the tune and we all sloshed back to the dance floor laughing and yelling. Many of the young folks had not rolled up their pants legs, and in some cases had not taken off their shoes. They quickly made their way to the outdoor bars, sloshing about and showing high water marks on their trousers.

We made our way back to the bandstand, followed by a handful of delighted dancers who raved about the wild act. After putting our instruments down, we joined our young friends at the bar and were feted handsomely.

I thought, Louis Prima would have loved this.

After lazing about all day on Sunday we returned to the Surf Club for our final night but having no compulsion to top the previous evening's performance. As expected, the crowd was sparse and the dancing predictable and sedate. When he paid us by check after the job, Monsieur LeCoste was generous in his praise of the combo and admitted he was sorry he did not witness the "unusual spectacle of last evening" about which he had heard a good deal.

"Well," Will suggested, "ask us back and we'll give you plenty of warning next time."

It was a great way to end our summer playing season.

Chapter Thirty-One

The 1952 fall semester at Wake Forest was to commence on Tuesday, September 2nd. Students began arriving three and four days early to get settled, renew acquaintances and acclimate to the fact they were going to get Dick Frye's and Morty's cooking instead of mom's.

I had called Ginny every week during summer school and the several weeks after the Atlantic Beach job. I made one week-end trip in the Nash to New Bern to see her after the Carswell Assembly duties were over, staying at her home in the old two-story manse. I was very careful to make up my bed, display proper manners, help clear the table and attend both Sunday School and church with the family on Sunday.

Fortunately, she and I picked up where we had left off in June, or perhaps even a pace or two ahead, and the midnight Trent River submarine races were every bit as exciting as I had imagined them to be.

On the down side, Ginny's teen-age brother, Charlie, was into cars and well aware of the Nash's distinctive feature, a matter he brought up at the supper table on Saturday night. While I preferred not to lie about it, and certainly not under the preacher's roof, I quickly stated I had not known of such and perhaps we could check it out the next day. The Reverend didn't look up from his pork chops. Ginny knew I had slept in the car at Atlantic Beach but kept silent, for which I was most grateful.

· · · · ·

242

As my senior year began I was looking forward to a lighter academic load, continued involvement in several extra-curricular areas that would help me in my journalistic career, considerably more time with Ginny and the final months with The Southerners. The other seniors, Hank and Ray, had similar aspirations. Will had opted to take the five-year route to graduation, knowing that Ellen would be in law school right there at Wake Forest for another three years.

He had begun to seek replacements for Drew on sax and Hal on trombone among existing marching band members but that supply was limited and the interest level low. Hopefully the fall influx of frosh and transfers would bring some options.

Rick Beacham had decided to transfer to Wake Forest from NC State which would give us a fulltime baritone and clarinet player, and Lenny Joles was coming in as a freshman who would provide us with a guitarist, vibraphonist and arranger.

A junior transfer from Mars Hill and three incoming freshmen resolved our remaining concerns.

When Moe learned that Don Block, a solid alto sax player from Charlotte he had known at Mars Hill, had come to Wake Forest he tracked him down and enlisted his talents in the band straight-away.

We didn't know if it was his 'big city' Charlotte upbringing or the fact he had played in a band at Mars Hill with Moe and something rubbed off on him, but when Don showed up, sax in hand, he looked the part, he acted the part, and he fit the part perfectly. Will had wanted to stop playing in addition to fronting the band, preferring the latter, so when Don came on board Will focused on leading the group and kibitzing with dancers. Don settled in immediately.

Ginny was informed by her sister that Harry Banks, a handsome dark-haired tenor sax player from New Bern with considerable local combo experience, was entering Wake Forest so Will located and signed him up quickly. Young, but very talented, Harry was an exceptional player with terrific phrasing and immediately became a solid addition in the sax section.

Ronnie Hough, a dynamic blond trombonist and vocalist from Asheville who had played, and sung, in a local dance band, had heard about us from his sister at WC, and he actually sought Will out at the first marching band meeting. He took Hal's trombone position and added the male vocal dimension.

In addition, Frank Upchurch, who had played sax with the combo at the two beach gigs, was now a freshman at State and let us know he wanted to play at every opportunity.

This now gave us a front man/leader, three trumpets, two trombones, five saxophones, piano, bass, drums and guitar/vibes. And we still had Pat Carter as vocalist with the addition of Ronnie as a singer.

Ted Hastings, a KA brother from Huntersville had a blue jacket, a car and great aspirations as a guitarist. Thus far he had not mastered much beyond four or five basic chords, nonetheless, Will added him to the band when Lenny focused on vibes. Will suggested to Ted that he stay partially hidden behind the music stand and unless he knew what he was doing, not to actually strum any strings. Ted's part-time addition now enabled us to promote a 17-piece band including two vocalists. It was thought to be the largest dance band in the Carolinas at the time and the only one with a vibraphone...and a five-chord guitarist.

As always, our Saturday nights and some Friday night bookings had to be worked around the football schedule since so many of our players were in the marching band.

September, which was a bit early for the dance season, was totally available. On October 19 the Deacons played Boston College in Bowman Gray Stadium in Winston-Salem and on the twenty-fifth the team played in Chapel Hill, both close enough for marching band trips. November 1 was Homecoming with NC State coming to Wake Forest, on the 15th Duke was scheduled for Groves Stadium and on the 29th Wake Forest played South Carolina, again in Winston-Salem, which left only the 8th and the 22nd as possible Saturday night playing dates. Fortunately, most high school proms were on Friday nights and Will had secured a number of easy jobs to keep us going.

• • • • •

On Thursday afternoon three days after classes began, Billy Moore answered the KA House phone on the landing between the first and second floors and yelled out, "Red? Telephone!"

This was the standard procedure for letting someone within earshot know he had a call. If the person was in the house, he yelled back, "Okay" or "Yeah" and came to the phone. If he wasn't in and someone knew he was away, he would call out, "Not here!" If no one responded at all within approximately ten seconds, the caller was informed so-and-so was out. On rare occasions, a name and number would be taken. Very rare occasions. Even then, the number was often written in pencil on the brick wall and lost in the maze of other numbers and doodles.

Fortunately, I was in my first floor room and responded.

Herb Lupton was on the phone from his union office in Raleigh. It seems a traveling show, known publicly as the New York Stars Revue, was booked to play two days, Friday and Saturday, in the Princess Theatre in Henderson and the show's drummer had taken ill in Danville, Virginia and been hospitalized. They needed a union drummer to play the job. Was I available?

It was common practice for live shows, often billed as 'revues' and featuring an emcee- comedian who likely doubled as a magician or juggler, a song and dance act, a "pit band" and a chorus line of "beautiful New York showgirls" to play tobacco markets in small towns during the sales season. It was, in effect, an itinerant low-budget burlesque show. Farmers had money from their tobacco sales and the local movie theatre would book the nomadic shows to take advantage of the temporarily cash-heavy locals. Usually the show would play one town for a couple of days, then move 50 miles or so to another tobacco market town, and do several days there.

245

Henderson was the county seat of Vance County, just 34 miles north of Wake Forest, up U.S. 1 It's tobacco market had been in existence since 1872, and was usually among the first in North Carolina to open on the bright leaf sales circuit each season. It was a popular market for area farmers with early crops.

Although people knew full well that the *New York Stars Revue* offered something less than Broadway-quality material, the show was a welcome break in their demanding agricultural pursuits. For a buck fifty, the mostly male audience could see a picture show and then, for a half hour or so, laugh at the latest corny and ribald jokes, be amazed at the prestidigitation of a magician, and, sans their spouses, ogle 15 beautiful showgirls who, in fact, were usually five, well-traveled ladies who appeared on stage three times each in three different costumes.

From a distance, scantily clad, wearing wigs and make-up applied by a trowel, the ladies did, indeed, appear to be quite lovely. The costumes, or lack thereof, had much to do with the active box office.

Hoots and hollers, whistles, catcalls and loud ungentlemanly comments, were commonplace during the shows. Just good 'ol boys with cash burning a hole in their bib overalls, letting off a little steam.

Throughout the half-hour show, there was constant musical support from the pit band, which consisted of a pianist, trumpeter, sax, and drums.

I was to be the drummer.

Prior to a feature movie, there was a *Fox Movietone* or *RKO Pathe* newsreel, a short feature or documentary and one or two cartoons. The first movie began at 11 a.m., with the *Revue* following about 12.30 p.m.

Every two hours, from 12:30 p.m. until 11 p.m., six shows were presented on both Fridays and Saturdays. Twelve shows in two days at union scale. How tough could it be?

I told Lup I'd take the job, knowing I would probably have to miss a couple of classes to get to Henderson in plenty of time to find out what I was to do. Will, who was as curious as I was about the job, agreed to drive me up on Friday and stick around just for the fun of it. He'd see the first show and then go back to Wake Forest, to return on Saturday night at midnight to take me back to school. Not having the multi-purpose Nash, I'd need a place to sleep on Friday night.

We found the Princess Theatre, which fronted Garnett Street, the town's main drag. The building appeared to have been built in the mid-'20s with its marquee over the sidewalk promoting the *New York Stars Revue: 15 Beautiful Girls. Fri & Sat Only!*

Will parked the Woodie in a rear lot and we entered through a side stage door about 10 a.m. I soon located the man Lup told me to see, Angelo, the revue manager, emcee, comedian and magician, aka "The Amazing Angelo."

Introducing myself, I was quick to admit I had never played a show before nor could I read music. I also indicated that I was sorry his drummer was ill.

"Aw, Leo'll be okay. He just forgot he was on the second floor of the hotel in Danville and fell down a flight of stairs. Broke his collarbone, sprained his arm, got some bad bruises on his legs, but he'll be back in a few days, by the time we get to Wilson next week. I 'preciate you coming up here to help out, son.

"Now, about the music, can you keep a beat?" the fiftyish, balding impresario asked.

"Yes sir, I can do that alright."

'Well, here's what you do. You face the stage and follow the action. The piano will pretty much drive what's happening. When the girls bump, you hit the bass drum heavy, followed by a cymbal crash. When they prance around, work a tom tom beat. When they wiggle, you play the cymbals. When they grind, roll the snare. In short, you work the drums and cymbals and just follow what the girls are doing on stage. Heavy, driving rhythm. Lots of boom-booms. Got that? After one show, it'll come easy."

"Yes sir. What's the music?"

Angelo yelled out, "Eddie!"

247

A short, swarthy, pudgy fellow in his late-40s, with very long hair falling to his shoulders but with a bald spot in the back, ambled out of the darkened wings.

"Eddie, play some show music for our drummer, Red, after he gets set up."

Eddie nodded and disappeared back into the wings, apparently waiting for me to assemble the drums and call him. He acted as if he were extremely bored with his job.

"Eddie's sort of quiet. A loner. But he's real good at the piano. Been with me for years. He'll run through some of the numbers so you can get a feel for it. Just bring your gear in and set up down there," Angelo instructed, pointing to an empty area down front in the theatre where two rows of seats had been removed to create an "orchestra pit." "And, one more thing, don't fool around with the girls. Got it?"

"Yessir, I got it. No problem, Angelo."

"Good. I'll see you later." He disappeared into the theatre blackness.

Chapter Thirty-Two

Will helped me haul the drums in and set up two feet back from, and facing, the stage, which was about four feet high. The piano was on my right and two chairs for the sax and trumpet players were on my left. They had music stands, but I figured they had played the tunes so much they had everything memorized. Or they improvised. No one would care.

As soon as I had everything in place, I called out for Eddie who reappeared, mumbled 'hello' and sat on the revolving piano stool ready to lead me through some of the show scores. He was sucking hard on a cigarette.

"This is the opening," Eddie said as he proceeded to run through the number on the upright. He moved through the repertoire rapidly. I concluded it was a bit of Barnum & Bailey with a pinch of honky tonk and a slight hint of ragtime. Definitely had a jazzy beat. There was a Latin tempo to one of the two numbers "The Dazzling Danzigers Dance Duo would do; the other piece was a waltz tempo. The female Dazzling Danziger was one of the chorus girls; the male, Daryl, was her husband, prop man, stagehand, and all-round gofer.

Tight little group. Sort of like the Von Trapps .

I rehearsed with Eddie on several numbers, stopping when he pointed to his watch, indicating the movie would begin shortly. He motioned for me and Will, whom I had introduced, to follow him backstage where we would apparently hang out until showtime at 12.30 p.m.

"I'm going to run over to the Vance Hotel and get a room for tonight," I told him, "and grab a sandwich. Do you want anything?"

"Nope, thanks. Had a late breakfast. Make sure you're back here in about 45 minutes."

The Vance had a single room available for $7. I put my gym bag containing the Dopp kit, clean tee shirt, extra white shirt and change of shorts on the bed, then Will and I went to the café next door where we got tube steaks and chocolate shakes. That would hold me until supper.

"You sure you want to hang around?" I questioned Will.

"Man, this is getting more interesting all the time. Yeah, I'll stick around and at least see one show." What he meant was he wanted to see the girls.

In a half hour we were backstage, looking for Eddie and a place to sit until the live show started. People, mostly men, were drifting into the theatre. I was getting nervous.

We found a couple of straight-back chairs against a side wall and noticed, for the first time, that there were two very small dressing rooms and a single bathroom built against the back wall. The two dressing rooms had been commandeered by the five females while Angelo and Daryl Danziger were making do with a folding table, stand-up mirror, and naked light bulb dangling from overhead for their theatrical make-up needs. Costumes for all the performers were hung with some semblance of order on three steel-rod racks off-stage.

About 12:15, Eddie showed up with the trumpeter, Horst, a very red-faced, over-weight German in his 60s whose extremely large pants were being held up by wide galluses. Behind him was Reggie, the sax and clarinet player, a slender, pale young man whose dirty blonde hair was brushed straight back. He wore large, black horn-rimmed glasses which gave him a most intellectual appearance. Their attire indicated that fashion was not required to play with this ensemble. I fit right in.

After quick introductions, Will nudged me with an elbow. His head was angled to the right and he was nodding toward the dressing rooms. He had spotted the showgirls emerging from their powder-room bunkers. No surprise, his interest was piqued.

"Before you go getting into trouble," I said, knowing Will well," remember I'm here to play a job and don't need any screwups. One of 'em is married to that dancer guy. Probably others are married, too, so just take it easy. I've already been warned." He grinned slightly.

Eddie motioned for me to follow him down the side steps to the theatre floor and into our pit seats since the movie, *The Red Badge of Courage* with Audie Murphy, was about to end. Horst and Reggie showed up seconds later, horns in hand. They placed some music sheets on the stands and looked to Eddie for a downbeat.

Within seconds of the credits ending on screen, Eddie counted out loud, "two, three, four" and the three went vigorously into the overture, a two-minute abbreviated medley of the numbers to be played over the next half hour. Being more concerned with keeping a steady beat than doing anything of consequence with the sticks, I joined in as basic, not fancy, support.

The curtains parted, revealing a well-lit stage with a dark red velvet curtain across the entire rear. No scenery or props. In anticipation of the exciting show to come, the audience, perhaps a third of the house, broke out in applause and whistles.

Ending the overture, as it were, Eddie modulated into the opening number which was a rousing introduction of the five beauties dancing in sync onto the stage. Dressed, somewhat, as blooming flowers, large multi-colored petals behind their heads and carefully-arranged bits of shiny floral foil elsewhere, the beauties stopped in a semi-circle mid-stage. Eddie eased into a raunchy, heavy left-handed tune as each girl did her bumps, grinds and whatevers. The loosely choreographed sensual action would make most men, and likely a wide variety of flora and fauna, wilt, which, of course, was the intention. The energized patrons went berserk.

I got the message quickly and focused my attention on the girls as they did their semi-gymnastic interpretations in sequence. Never had the bass drum and my right ankle gotten such a workout or the cymbals been struck so much. I worked up a sweat keeping up with the incredibly physical activity onstage which went on for about four minutes.

As quickly as they came out, they were off. Angelo bounded onstage dressed in a tuxedo, and positioned himself center stage. No mike, no house sound system.

After he calmed the hollerin' hordes, he welcomed one and all, praised the town of Henderson, lauded the farmers' many contributions to America, and went into a series of jokes for four minutes that would have bombed with bored, long-incarcerated inmates in solitary confinement, but went over great with the Princess Theatre crowd.

Angelo next introduced the "Dazzling Danzigers Dance Duo —straight from The Latin Quarter Supper Club in New York City," who waltzed and skipped and, otherwise, filled the stage for three minutes with their terpsichorean showmanship. Polite applause.

Now wearing a top hat with his tux, Angelo reappeared with his magician's stand and several visual props. If there's one thing (other than semi-nude women) that most sodbusters like, it is magic. And, Angelo was pretty good at it. He made some items appear and more items disappear. He did some shtick with a rope and scissors, poured water into a funneled newspaper and it evaporated before their very eyes. He kept their attention for almost six minutes and they gave him very generous applause.

Again, it was time for the second line-up of five beauties, out of the 15 ladies promoted on the marquee. Each came out singly to strut her stuff and do her specialty. The overall motif was sports, with Roxie in a baseball cap and a very modified, down-sized umpire's chest protector (as if!); Ginger in football shoulder pads and helmet; and, Honey dressed in an almost-below–the-bosoms version of a sleeveless basketball shirt with #1 and striped high socks; Roxie wore a Ben Hogan-style golf cap with two well-placed tees and a head cover for a small three-wood; and, Carmen was attired in garb of the sport of kings, wearing colorful jockey silks without the jodhpurs or boots, but spurs and a whip.

As each did her themed act, we played appropriate but dramatically rearranged and bastardized support music, in suitable tempos, from *Take Me Out To The Ball Game*, the Globetrotter's theme song *Sweet Georgia Brown*, to the Notre Dame fight song. We did The Kentucky Derby's *My Old Kentucky Home* with the trumpeter's call to the post and something I didn't recognize but was told later by Eddie it had to do with golf. Songs for the ages. I worked the cymbals overtime, heated up the two tom toms, and did enough rolls and paradiddles on the snare to make my wrists ache. My ankles were already throbbing from pounding the bass pedal with my right foot and working the two-cymbal high hat with my left. This act took over five minutes.

Back came the Danzigers for another three minutes of Latin-type dances and paraphernalia that included a long, flowing boa, conga drum and castanets.

Quickly, Angelo and Daryl Danziger, who had changed out of the ruffle-sleeve shirt and into an oversized orange sweatshirt, very large glasses, and pork pie hat in record time, ran onto center stage and began to do a fast series of earthy jokes as if they were two end men in a minstrel show without Mr. Interlocutor. Most of the stories were rude and crude and appealed to the audience, which had gotten well into the spirit of the show. After four-and-a-half minutes of one-liners, mother-in-law jokes and some barnyard humor, the two departed to make way for the big finale.

And big it was — A Salute to America. A massive flag of the Good Ol' US of A with all 48 stars unfolded at the rear of the stage. Our final five beauties, true patriots all, marched smartly onstage in tasseled boots with three small gold stars strategically placed. Each was adorned as well with red, white, and blue streamers coming from some sort of headdress that emulated the Statue of Liberty. Long legs in high heel shoes supporting ample anatomical assets, strutting about, bumping and grinding, moving their tri-colored hand scarves around, over, between and under, making you proud to be an American. I got goose bumps just watching the spectacle.

No question the concept reached our audience, many of whom were veterans. They were now on their feet, whistling, shouting and aggressively making a number of suggestions as to moves the dancers might undertake as a really big finish and fitting salute to this great land, from sea to shining sea.

It was a moving experience in more ways than one. I was exhausted, and realized I had five more of these barnburners today and six tomorrow. But now I knew the drill, and could really get into the music. Plus I could pace myself, accordingly.

When I came backstage, sweating, Will was laughing out loud.

"Now that was a helluva' show!" he exclaimed. "We need to work some of that into our dance jobs." He was having trouble containing himself.

"Great idea! What do we all wear...pasties?" I shot back.

"The sports number was terrific. Now, if we could all dress in various Demon Deacon athletic gear, but no shirts and just jock straps, would that not get some attention?" Will suggested.

"Sure would. We'd be thrown out of some prom, barred from the union, and the cops would haul us in for indecent exposure," I responded cooly.

By this time I was ready for a major break. As Will and I walked behind the heavy red backdrop, the newsreel was on and a second audience had come into the theatre. Will's attention, however, was focused on the two dressing rooms where the doors were wide open and the five showgirls were peeling out of their reds, whites, and blues. It occurred to me he had been backstage throughout the entire show and obviously transfixed on and mesmerized by the several costume changes.

We had not met the ladies and didn't know one from the other except from what we could remember when Angelo introduced them individually to the audience during the first extravaganza. From the pit, it was difficult to really focus on their faces, especially since it was their body moves I was to follow, and they changed wigs as well as costumes for every routine.

Will sort of hung back, waiting to see what transpired now that the revue was done for an hour and a half. In a couple of minutes, three of the dancers appeared, each partially swaddled in a well-worn robe, and bare-footed. All were smoking and all were poorly bleached blondes. Surprisingly, they had rather attractive faces and their extensive physical attributes were beyond rational definition, especially for sheltered Wake Forest men.

"Outstanding show, ladies," Will exclaimed in semi-hushed tones so as not to overpower the newsreel announcer talking about the *S.S. United States* having recently set a trans-Atlantic record on her maiden voyage.

The three nodded but kept walking toward the stage door where the old man who guarded the entrance was waiting to take their midday meal order. Will and I fell in behind them.

"Leave it, Will," I suggested. "Let's go get a big orange or a root beer."

As much as he wanted to remain and take on the challenge, he followed me out and we crossed the street to the café.

"When are you heading back to school?" I asked.

"Well, I've already missed all my Friday classes. I might as well stick around here."

"I'll bet you have a date with Ellen tonight," I reminded him, "and you'd better get back and rest up for that." I was determined to get his mind off the obvious, and back onto Ellen.

After a couple of sips, Will agreed it would be prudent for him to get back to Wake Forest, but he reminded me he would come back for me the next night and, perhaps, he might find a way to come early. No big surprise there.

"Ginny knows I'm playing some sort of job up here but you don't need to go into details if you see her," I remarked, hoping he would avoid her altogether but knowing he couldn't wait to give her a grind-by-bump-by-grind description.

The second show was more crowded and no less raucous and aggressive, but it was far easier for me to play, a matter to which Eddie concurred. Between the third and fourth shows, I went to my hotel room and washed up, got a burger and shake for supper, and walked around a block or two to get some air.

The fourth and fifth shows both had full houses and for a while during the 8:30 p.m. *America Salute* show, I thought the crowd would storm the stage. The theatre manager was prepared and had a couple of the Vance County Sheriff's men on standby. Common sense prevailed when Eddie, knowing his audiences, ended the act with a playing of *The National Anthem* with Horst, Reggie and I following along. The crowd stopped their shouting and abruptly stood at attention with proper respect. They assumed this was the normal ending.

After the fifth show of the day, I was physically drained but had fallen into the routine. I wondered how these people did this day after day, week after week, and how much they made working such a demanding schedule. How did they keep their health, such as it was?

While I was half-snoozing in a cane-bottomed straight chair before the last show of the day, Ginger (I had figured out who was who during the backstage breaks) came over and asked where I was from.

My take was these people were together so much every day they had run out of conversation and any new face was an opportunity to break the monotony.

For the next few minutes, I gave her a brief synopsis of my comparatively mundane college life. The five-foot-ten, brown-eyed, one-time-brunette pulled a chair up and was sitting astraddle it, facing the rear of the chair with her arms folded over the back. Deeply inhaling cigarette smoke from a Viceroy, she was totally unconcerned that the pale yellow robe with purple and white chenille pansies was draped around her body ever so casually, and revealingly, as she listened attentively to my unexciting discourse. It was a challenge to keep my mind on the subject.

Then, as if a spigot were turned on, Ginger told of abruptly leaving an abusive father and an unconcerned mother in western Pennsylvania when she was just 15, traveling to New York, working as a waitress, staying in cheap hotels, fighting off drunks, would-be rapists and dope peddlers, and finally putting the dancing lessons she had taken in school to use in a burlesque show in a seedy section of Newark.

"It was a living," she stated matter-of-factly, "and I made enough to take more lessons to where I got pretty good. I auditioned for this show and have been on the road for almost 18 months now. Angelo is good to us and he's honest, so I get paid regularly and have even saved some money."

"Where do you go from here?" I asked.

"You mean the show?"

"No, your life. What do you want to do down the road, whenever that is."

"Well, I want to marry a farmer and live on a farm and raise vegetables and have chickens and cows and stuff. And kids. Live close enough to a town so we can see a movie and do some shopping once in a while."

"What about school? How far did you get?"

"I finished the 10th grade. Left right after that…in June. Yeah, I'm almost 20 and I'd like to finish school but I can't do that until I'm off the road, settled down someplace."

"How do you expect to meet your Prince Charming farmer?" I wanted to know.

"Oh, I meet lots of guys in these little towns. It's easy, if you want to go out between shows, sit in a café, and wander around a car lot. I guess I could meet men at a tobacco warehouse."

"Yep, but most of 'em would be married already. Your best bet might be to leave the show in a college town, a college that offers courses in agriculture for people who want to be farmers. Probably take over their dad's farm. Schools like NC State in Raleigh. Or, Clemson in South Carolina. Auburn in Alabama. They have a veterinarian school. Get a waitressing job in a restaurant near the school, or even find work at the school. Never know what might happen."

"What about Wake Forest where you go?"

"Town's too small and they don't teach any Ag courses there. Now if you want to snag a preacher, or maybe a would-be lawyer, or a school teacher, that's as good a place as any."

Ginger was obviously into this serious conversation when she realized it was time to get into her floral petals for the last show of the day.

"Maybe we can keep talking later," she suggested.

"Sure. Absolutely."

The audience at the final show of the day was by far the most vocal, likely prompted by a variety of alcoholic contributors. It was a younger crowd, given to whooping and hollering, and their continuing talking, shouting, jibing and laughing throughout the show made it difficult to concentrate on the performers. With my back to the audience, I was constantly uneasy about what might be happening behind me, or coming at me.

Just after 11 p.m., we played the finale with tempered gusto, but as usual the *Salute to America* brought the house down. Everyone standing and applauding for some sort of encore by the lovelies in the stars and stripes, and little else. This would have been a great place for an Army recruiter.

I quickly removed the cymbals and put them, the snare, sticks and mallets into the carryall fiber case, closed it, and went backstage to find a secure spot to store the equipment until tomorrow. As I looked around, Ginger saw me and came out of a dressing room clad only in pasties and a G-string.

"What're you doing?" she wanted to know.

"Looking for a safe place to put this drum stuff until tomorrow"

"Here. You can shove them under the counter in the dressing room. Nobody'll bother them."

"You sure that's okay?" I asked.

"Oh yeah. Only us girls come in here anyhow. C'mon."

I followed her into the well-lit room that smelled of familiar powder and make-up and theatrical aromas I recognized from the many stage plays I had been in during high school and at Wake Forest. Roxie and Honey were deep into the cold cream process, also clad in only the bare essentials, and totally unconcerned with my presence. I quickly, nervously, shoved the drum case under the makeup counter, told the ladies 'good night' and backed out.

I was very thankful Will was not with me and made a mental note to try to avoid this activity tomorrow night when he was around.

Ginger had stayed close by and as I started to leave she asked, "Would you want to talk some more tomorrow? You know, about stuff?"

"Sure," I responded. "Maybe you want to get a cup of coffee tonight, after you dress, if there's anything open. Where're you staying?"

"In a motor court out on U.S. 1. Me and Honey share a room."

"I'm down the street at the Vance Hotel, and don't have a car. My friend, Will, brought me up ...so I wouldn't be able to take you out to the motel later. We'll have to pass on the coffee, I guess."

"Yeah, too bad. We usually ride back with Angelo or Daryl. I'll see you tomorrow."

"You got it," I replied, both relieved but sorry the conversation ended.

By the time the Princess Theatre marquee lights were dark I had showered and crashed, totally beat.

Chapter Thirty-Three

After sleeping soundly until 9:00 a.m. on Saturday morning, I dressed, gathered my items together and put them in the gym bag, remembering I had to check out by 10:00. I paid for the room and went to the café for waffles, sausage and coffee. I decided to walk a bit in the fresh morning air, going down several retail blocks until I reached a tobacco warehouse, which was bustling with activity. I watched the auctioneer intently as he wandered up and down the rows of pungent and dusty dried tobacco leaves stacked in large baskets, selling it to the buyers from major companies who followed along across the rows. I was intrigued and mystified by their code utterances and hand signals.

Sufficiently exercised and mentally prepared for what was going to be another long, demanding day, I returned to the Princess and entered backstage before noon to set up for the 12:30 p.m. first show. Ever so cautiously I knocked, then entered the open door dressing room to retrieve my drum case. Honey, Ginger and Roxie were busily applying their several base coats, having already put on their requisite, meager, three-piece ensembles.

"Morning, ladies," I greeted the trio pleasantly.

Honey and Roxie nodded and grunted, Ginger got up and walked over to where I was taking the drum case from under the counter.

"We gonna' talk some more today?" she asked.

"Plan on it. We can get together between shows. In fact, I need you to do me a favor after one of the shows, before my friend Will gets here."

"Sure, honey," she replied, and while I knew the affectionate comment was standard generic language for these show business

260

girls, nonetheless it was unnerving.

Eddie politely made a few suggestions for improving some of my drum work, and generally gave me the impression that I had picked up on the routine well and was performing satisfactorily. High praise indeed from the impresario himself.

I didn't know when to expect Will, but given the lascivious look in his eyes the day before it wouldn't have surprised me if he walked in at any minute. Fortunately, he didn't.

After the first show when I came backstage Ginger was waiting and asked what the favor was that I needed from her.

"Get your clothes on and come with me. I'll buy you a burger and then tell you about a little purchase I want you to make."

In five minutes she was ready in yellow pedal pushers, a cut-off lavender tee shirt and sandals. I quickly noticed she had not bothered with any undergarments other than those used in her performance. No chance she would be mistaken for a local girl.

We did the café burger and then I said, "There's a department store down the street, Rose's. I'll give you some money and I want you to go in and buy a pair of ladies' panties, pink, lacy, and a very large size. Okay?"

"What for?" she inquired.

"When I finish with them they're gonna' be a surprise gift for Will, or his girl friend, whichever one opens his glove compartment first."

In ten minutes she was out of Rose's with a pair of pink undies, size 22. We returned to the Princess and went to her dressing room. Roxie was napping on a blanket on the floor, snoring rather loudly.

"Okay, I need a tube of lipstick and an eyebrow pencil." She got them for me as I spread the panties out on the counter. With the lipstick somewhat sharpened on the end I printed neatly in the crotch of the panties, SAT DAY. Then, with the eyebrow pencil I wrote across the upper part of the drawers, "Will...You know what's missing?" Lastly, under the question I signed the name Doris in a very realistic feminine cursive.

"That'll do it. Thanks."

"What's that mean? What's the SAT DAY about? Who's Doris," she wanted to know.

"Okay, but you have to keep it to yourself. No mention of anything to Will. Now, have you seen those women's panties that have the days of the week on them?" She nodded, "Well, think of Saturday, but spelled SAT DAY. Okay? Now, what's the question? What's missing?"

"Oh, wait…U R is missing. Like, You Are. That's funny. Who's Doris?"

"I don't know. No one. Want me to change it to Ginger?"

"Oh no. What are you going to do with them now?"

"Tonight when I get the keys to Will's car to put my gym bag in while he's back here , I'm gonna' stuff these in his glove compartment like I said. Sooner or later he, or Ellen, his girlfriend, will open it up and, surprise!"

"That's mean. It's funny, though. Hey, I'll see you after the next show."

After the next two shows we chatted backstage, mostly about the towns she had been to, her life back home, the guys who had abused her and how she might get off the circuit, get a job and finish school. Some heavy, serious discussions that I believed could bear positive fruit and, at some point, actually get her on a solid path to be some farmer's wife.

Ginger was not a bad kid and I got the impression she wasn't generally loose with her considerable female attributes either. She had common sense but had had no guidance, no direction, and certainly not much genuine affection at home growing up. It was obvious she had not had a serious, meaningful, mature conversation with anyone in a very long time, if ever, and she was beginning to come to the realization, in her final teen year, that her current lifestyle couldn't go on forever. In many ways she was wise beyond her years, but she needed some counsel and encouragement and a massive dose of self-respect.

Although I was no psychologist by any stretch of the imagination and had just managed to get B's in my Philosophy and Psychology courses, I really felt as if our backstage conversations had helped her see some better things ahead, if she would just take the bull by the horns. I imagined that Professors A.C. Reid and Bobby Helms would have thought this episode with Ginger would be pretty heavy case history material. Maybe give me an A?

Will showed up for the four-thirty show and, obviously, the duration. He had convinced Ellen he couldn't date her that night because he had to come get me. I let him know straight off that Gloria belonged to Angelo and Carmen was married to Daryl Danziger. Ginger was off limits strictly "because", and I knew so little about Roxie or Honey that I could not counsel him one way or the other.

At seven o'clock, after the fourth show, I suggested to Will that we find a barbecue restaurant in the area and invite Ginger, Honey and Roxie. It would probably cost us an extra three dollars each but he agreed.

The idea of eating something other than a hot dog or a burger for supper, and in an actual sit-down establishment, appealed to Ginger, and to Roxie, but Honey begged off, thanking us profusely for "being so nice." It occurred to me that perhaps she had been given a reprieve of some sort and Roxie would have to take the full brunt of Will's focus.

Buster's BBQ on the outskirts of town proved to be just what we were looking for. It was enjoying a big Saturday night business but when the manager saw the two obvious showgirls and we told him we were between shows down at the Princess, he worked us in.

For obvious reasons our table was the talk of the restaurant. The center of attention.

The way the two females attacked their dinners was nothing short of unbelievable. The ribs didn't have a chance. Hush puppies disappeared like snowballs in a heat wave. The cole slaw went faster than a rabbit running from a huntin' dog. Had there been a brunswick-stew-eatin', sweet-ice-tea-drinkin' competition, Ginger and Roxie would have taken home the blue ribbons.

"Where y'all putting all that food?" Will asked wide-eyed just before the peach cobbler was delivered, and subsequently devoured.

"First time we've sat down to a real decent meal in days," Roxie responded with a final, fatal bite of a hush puppy. "This sure is nice of you boys."

On the way back to the Princess, Roxie, who appeared to be about twenty-six or so with a tape-measure-defying chest and black roots that badly needed hair-coloring attention, sat in front with Will, literally up against his right side. As we got out of the Woodie, Will leaned over to Roxie and whispered something into her ear. She giggled. I didn't need an Ouija Board to figure out what was going on. Will had correctly assumed Roxie wanted to repay him in some way for his dinner-buying generosity. Ginger had kissed me on the cheek when we left Buster's, obviously my reward for buying her dinner.

With only two shows remaining, I could see the light at the end of the tunnel, or at least the $36 at the end of two days' steady work. After the 10:30-11:00 p.m. show, I would have worked a total of 12 out of the past 37 hours and made the same amount I would have brought in for three four- hour dance jobs. But three dances take a couple of weekends and I made it all in two days, plus getting something of an education that was missing from the Wake Forest curriculum.

After the nine o'clock show Ginger asked if I had 'planted' the panties in Will's car yet and when I shook my head that I had not, she suggested we sneak out and do the job. I got the sack with the undies, put it in my gym bag, and went looking for Will to get the key. He was nowhere to be found backstage. Nor was Roxie. Instead of stating the obvious to Ginger, I told her Will must be out and we'd have to try it later. I didn't need to explain. She got it.

The final Salute to America was a stem-winder and a major crowd pleaser. Since it was the final show of the run in Henderson, the fifteen beautiful showgirls had given their all, and certainly shown most of it, and the house was in a frenzy. Four of Vance County's finest were stationed between the audience and the pit and were prepared to thwart any real storming of the lady performers, each of whom was giving bows and throwing kisses. The female anatomy being what it is, the gyrating gestures of gratitude by the girls were being enthusiastically received. God Bless America! By 11:50 p.m., the theatre had emptied and the house lights in the theatre turned on. Will helped me pack my drums as I bade goodbye to Horst, Reggie, and Eddie who had become soul mates of a sort over the past day and a half. Angelo appeared and called me over to the side.

"You did a fine job, son, and I 'preciate it. Here's your money. I put a little extra with it 'cause you bailed us out of a real jam and you had to pay for your room last night. And you didn't cause no trouble with the girls like some fill-ins do. Give me your phone number. Maybe I can use you again sometime."

"Thanks, Angelo. I'm glad it worked out. It was a real experience and I had a great time. I sure do appreciate the extra money, too. I can use it."

He had put fifty dollars in my hand.

As I was carrying the bass drum and my gym bag out the stage door exit to the Woodie in the parking lot, Ginger ran up and asked about the panties. She was bound and determined to be a party to the prank. Having fun, even stupid, corny fun, was apparently something she hadn't done in a long time.

Will had unlocked the car door and gone back inside to bring the tom toms out.

"Got 'em right here," I said as I held the canvas bag out to her.

She unzipped the bag, reached in and found the Rose's bag with the size 22s. When we reached the Woodie, I put the bass drum in the back while she giggled and stealthily placed the panties from 'Doris' in the glove compartment. I went back in so I could get the drum case with the cymbals, pedals, sticks and stuff. Will passed me coming out with the tom toms.

"Be right there soon as I get the case," I announced. "And you might want to burn that shirt. I doubt if a laundry can get all that make-up crap off it. Or maybe Ellen can."

"Funny. Real funny," Will answered, turning to chat with Ginger in her robe, askew as usual, abundant flesh showing in the light over the stage door.

Stashing the case in the rear of the station wagon, I went to get in on the passenger side. Ginger was holding the door open.

"I want to thank you for being so nice to me and for talking to me and all," she said, looking me straight in the eyes. And for not trying to get fresh or anything. I remember all the stuff you said 'bout going back to school and I know that's what I need to do, and I'm gonna' do that just as soon as I can get the chance."

"Well, Ginger, I really enjoyed knowing you. I know you can do what you want to do if you just make up your mind and get on with it. There isn't going to be a perfect time. You're just going to have to take the chance, make the decision and do it. Soon. I believe you can. Remember, the longer you put it off the tougher it will be."

Just then, Will started the car and revved the engine. Ginger gave me a major kiss of sincere gratitude mixed with a touch of actual affection I thought. She turned and walked back to the stage door. It looked to me as if she were wiping a tear from her eye.

"Well, this has been two days I won't soon forget," I remarked to Will on the drive back to Wake Forest. "And you listen....in case any of this ever comes up in conversation, don't you dare get Ginny mixed up with Ginger!"

"Don't worry, I won't," he assured me. "And believe me, I sure won't forget these two days either," Will concurred, but for a very different reason.

"Yep," I mused out loud, "playing drums in a burlesque show with half-naked girls and trying to convince one of 'em to give up show biz and go back to school. My Mother would be so proud."

Chapter Thirty-Four

William and Pab had an aunt in Thomasville whose family, the Lamberts, was one of the furniture giants in the area. They were very generous with their wealth from a civic standpoint and when Thomasville's Centennial festivities were being programmed, Aunt Virginia and husband Charles, decided to throw a major lawn party at their Tara-like home outside of town for the community's better-heeled citizens and most powerful politicians.

Obviously, they booked their nephews' band, The Southerners, to play for the event.

In June Randy had married Jean and informed us that he would not likely be playing many, if any, jobs with the band since he had to find a job and go to school as well.

This was not good news for several reasons. First, Randy was a very good trumpet player who played the notes as they were printed on the arrangements. He could sing. He was always on time. He never complained. He was our conscience, our "Chaplin," our Father Confessor. He was a good guy, a solid guy. A friend. We would surely miss The Rev.

To replace him Will had enlisted Sammy Workman, a sophomore in the marching band who had indicated interest in joining The Southerners as third trumpet. This would be a good trial job for Sammy to determine if he fit in and if he wanted to commit to the band going forward.

The gala was on Saturday, September 13, starting at six o'clock in the evening and running until ten. We decided to bring the entire band and initially considered renting a bus like the touring bands had, for effect, but opted out for the Woodie, the Chevy, Pab's convertible and Ted's sedan, due to cost.

Most of us had never been to Thomasville, near High Point, so seeing the thirty-foot high cement Duncan Phyfe chair in the middle of downtown was a unique reminder that furniture was indeed king in this part of North Carolina.

The Lambert's home was, obviously, a furniture exposition in and of itself, with every room a showcase. Mrs. Lambert had spared no expense to decorate the expansive lawn with tents, massive floral arrangements, strings of white lights, tables with linen cloths, several bars , two lengthy buffet tables and, of course a portable dance floor. The bandstand was created out of two flatbed trailers side by side with a tier for the brass and drums. An array of tall potted palms on the grass in front of the bandstand hid the underside of the flatbeds. Steps had been positioned at one end of our flatbed bandstand.

We arrived in caravan-style at 4:00 p.m., immediately unloaded and set up. The weather was absolutely perfect, clear and calling for a slight dip in temperature during the early fall evening. As I set up, I noted the tier the trumpets, trombones, and I were to play on literally came within a foot of the back of the truck stage. Somehow we had to figure out how to get onto our positions from a side approach and make sure every time we got up we didn't take a step back and fall five feet or so. Occupational hazard.

Aunt Virgie, as we were instructed to call her, made sure we were fed before the soiree began, allowing us to 'dine' on card tables set up on the lawn off the kitchen entrance and out of sight of any early guests. While our fare was ample and tasty, we noted it did not include several items available to the non-hired attendees. Like caviar, pates, stuffed celery sticks and a variety of delectable fruit tarts. The bar was not available as well, thanks to Will's advance notice to Aunt Virgie.

The red ball sun began setting over tall pines and maple trees, bringing darkness quickly. The many strands of little white lights blinked like stars that had dropped in for the evening and an almost full moon filled the lawn with light. It was truly a spectacular display of class, dignity, good taste and money.

Guests dressed to the nines arrived early to avail themselves of the open bar and do what society folks, and publicly-elected officials, do so well, mingle and flit. Our early sets were calm, smooth, easy listening numbers and few took to the dance floor, preferring to chat and visit over our background sound and multiple cocktails.

Just before the 7:30 p.m. buffet we took a ten-minute break and returned to play an hour straight during dinner. The guest number now swelled to at least 200 well fed and well imbibed who were starting to get into the celebration mood. A goodly number of those present were directly descended from the folks who arrived in the area in 1852 and built the community, and the dynamic economy. Wealth was most everyone's middle name.

At 9:30 p.m., a half hour from "quitting time", the action was just beginning to heat up. The dance floor was filled, as were the glasses of most of the remaining guests, who still numbered well over a hundred.

Aunt Virgie called Will down from the bandstand for a brief conversation as to whether the band could keep playing for an additional hour. Naturally, she would pay us. Will quickly polled the band and all of us agreed to go one additional hour, until eleven, and three more dollars each.

Coincidentally, a black waiter, Roland, who was a sax player, had personally lifted the ban denying our access to the bar. He risked discovery, and likely dismissal, on behalf of his fellow musicians by bringing to the bandstand whatever libations we ordered. He was a busy young man from ten to eleven, for which we chipped in and created a sizeable gratuity.

It was a good thing the Lambert estate was some distance out of town because the partying was producing higher decibels on a continuing basis. There were no close neighbors and even so, the Sheriff was a guest at the soiree and, from his actions, enjoying himself immensely.

At eleven there did not seem to be any indication this party was close to being over. There were many people left, some finger food scattered about on the buffet tables, a few of those tarts, and the bar was still operating. For The Lamberts' sake, I hoped their furniture lines were selling well and the profit margins were sizeable.

Virgie...the Aunt part seemed to have been forgotten now... asked if we could play one more hour, until midnight. Another poll of the band indicated Randy, Mack, Rick, Lenny, Ronnie, and Pat needed to get home, reducing our number by two saxes, a trumpet, trombone, vibes and a vocalist. We still had plenty of musical power left. Ted stepped up and gave Randy his car keys, realizing the group would have to go to Raleigh and drop Pat off before they could swing back to Wake Forest. Hopefully, they would get to bed by 3:00 a.m.

For the remainder of the band it was as if we were there partly to play music and partly to join the party. Don, or Donnie, had an impulsive urge to forsake his sax, take to the mike and sing. Will, by this time not caring what took place, insisted he do so. Don was a very good saxophone player. He was not a very good singer, an obvious situation that didn't seem to bother anyone. In fact, when one lone person applauded his rendition of *My Happiness*, it only served to spur him to do an encore of *Little White Lies*. No improvement.

One of Virgie's dearest and closest friends, a divorcee in her mid-Fifties named Laura Jean who was deeply into her cups, concluded that she and Hank should spend some quality time together. Standing at the foot of the bandstand, staring at Hank, she yelled out most clearly, "Hey, pretty boy, why don't you come on down here and put them trumpet-puckering lips right here," pointing to her over-lipsticked mouth. I swear I saw Hank shiver. Further coaxing on her part gave Hank more reason to stay riveted to his trumpet position. When he did take a break, he jumped the five feet to the ground behind the stand rather than risk taking the side steps.

270

Since this was Pab's hometown and many of his relatives and neighbors were in the audience, I intentionally asked him to take over the drums off and on all evening, but especially as the night wore on. There were several thirty-something ladies in the crowd and their husbands or dates had either fallen by the wayside or gone home. These women were in a dancing mood. I felt it was my obligation to oblige them, singly or in groups. No matter.

A lovely older lady with blue hair had positioned herself on the piano bench, pushing right up against Moe who was puffing on a cigarette and banging away on the keys in his inimitable holy-roller tent-meeting style. The very busty lady was adamantly suggesting they do a duet while trying to convince him she was an outstanding pianist, having actually played with the all-girl symphonic group at Salem College about fifty years earlier.

In order to placate her after lengthy and irritating prodding, Moe simply got up and walked over to the bar, leaving the elated elderly prodigy to do whatever she wanted to in his absence. She did. It was terrible. And funny. While she was playing a song we didn't recognize, we continued to play our numbers without a piano. No one seemed to notice.

Finally, just after midnight when even the Sheriff had called it quits, Virgie gave up the ghost, shut down the bar and told us to stop playing. We had been on the stand for most of six hours. We advised Will he had better come up with considerably more than the basic twelve bucks plus six for the extra two hours. This was a $25 job if ever there was one.

Truth be known, none of the remaining Southerners was in any condition or frame of mind to make any attempt to drive over two hours to Wake Forest, assuming we would make it. Pab said he could put two of us up at his house. Will said he could take two at his parents' home. The remaining five of us were accommodated by Virgie who found cots, blankets, sleeping bags and space in her game room. I recall sleeping under the pool table. She had strictly forbidden our sleeping on it.

On the trip home in the Woodie on Sunday afternoon, Will allowed as to how he had a check from Uncle Charlie that would ensure that those of us who had braved the entire ordeal would each get $30.

Most of us were not in a mood to talk a great deal after the physically demanding night before, but for some reason Chip asked Moe why he had a pronounced limp.

"I grew up on a farm outside Lumberton. When I was five years old, I was riding on a tractor my dad was driving. He had been clearing some land and used the tractor to pull stumps out of the ground. Well, he hit a hole where a stump had been and the front wheel dropped into a hole, then bounced out. When it did, I fell off and hit the ground. A back tire rolled over my left leg. The ground was hard and the tire did some damage to the muscles in my leg. So my leg never developed like it should have from then on."

"Oh, jeez, I'm sorry," Chip said apologetically.

"Well, truth be known it was bad and good that it happened. Bad because my leg was hurt permanently and I wouldn't be able to play sports at all. And I'd have a limp. But good because I got out of school for three months, I got out of a lot of hard chores on the farm for awhile, it'll keep me out of the Army and because of it I learned to play the piano."

"How so?" Don asked, obviously interested.

"We had an old upright piano in the house and when my leg was healing and I wasn't walking around, my mother helped me get on the piano bench where I'd start picking out songs. Didn't have anything else to do and it took up time. I really got into it. Took some lessons after I started back to school and got into band music. Kept up with the lessons and that's it."

"Well, I'm sorry you had the accident but glad you became a piano player, for our sake," Chip added candidly.

"How'd you get into music, Don?"

"Girls. What else? I had a crush on this cute little girl in the seventh grade. She was in the band. I believe her name was Grace. Anyhow, I figured the best way to get to know her was to join the band. So I signed up. I didn't care what instrument so long as I got near the girl, and got a uniform. She played clarinet. They had enough of them so I took up the sax. Did okay with the sax but never made it with the girl. I think she took up with the drummer. No class."

"What's your story, Chip?"

"My mom played the piano. She got me, and my two brothers interested, or at least pushed the issue. I first started with the clarinet, one brother played trumpet and the other sax. In the ninth grade the band director, who was a real jerk, got upset at me for some reason and threw his baton at me. It really made me mad. I had a few adult-type choice words for him and was sent to the Principal's office. For some reason, maybe to spite the band director, I quit the clarinet and the marching band and started talking private sax lessons. Don't know how my quitting would get to the band director but that's what happened. I've played both instruments ever since."

Will joined in with his introduction to music by saying in grammar school the music teacher was putting together a little band and needed a flute player. She convinced him to take the position.

"Seemed to me after a few days that flutes were for girls, so I asked to play the saxophone," Will continued. "'Played it in the high school concert band, and was the marching band drum major. My parents somehow got me an appointment to Annapolis but I needed some courses I hadn't had in high school so they sent me to Staunton Military Academy in Virginia for a year. Played the sax there and was the drum major. Didn't take long to figure out that military life was not for me. Better to play a sax than march with a rifle, so I backed out of the Annapolis thing and came to Wake Forest. Still playing sax and still the drum major.

"What about you, Red?"

"Not very exciting. My mother wanted me to play the piano so I took lessons for seven months. Learned how to play *The Marines Hymn* with both hands, and quit. Hated to practice. When I was fourteen, I bought a used set of drums and would play along with big band records. I got to where I could play well enough that four other guys in high school and I formed a little group. Never got beyond just doing our thing, but it was sure was fun."

"You didn't mention you got the most crap to haul around and you make the most noise."

Moe was most supportive.

Chapter Thirty-Five

Will asked me one Saturday morning if Ginny and I would like to go to Mann's that night with Ellen and him. Always up for such an outing, we joined them in the Woodie after an early supper. On the way, Ellen turned to the two of us in the back seat and dangled a pair of very large pink panties in front of us.

Ginny was taken aback, then started laughing. "What on earth? Whose are they?"

Ellen, straight-faced, said very matter-of-factly but with a definite bit of sarcasm in her voice, "They belong to Doris...a friend of Red's."

Obviously, Will, or Ellen, had found the planted undies earlier and he, under severe duress, had figured out where they came from, and how and when they were put into his glove compartment. Now their idea was to put my neck in the noose. A little payback.

Ginny took hold of the size 22s, obviously not knowing what to think. Then, stretching them out, she saw the hand-written message on the panties, and in the crotch when Ellen turned on the overhead light in the wagon. "Wait," Ginny blurted out, "the inscription says 'Will'....not Red."

Will started laughing and Ellen, having put Will through the wringer several weeks earlier when she found them, joined in. "We just thought you should know who Red is running around with," Ellen commented.

I admitted to the prank but went into no details as to my accomplice. I imagined that Will had already gone over the Ginger business with ample embellishments with Ellen, leaving out any

275

particulars about himself or anyone named Roxie.

Ginny spoke up, "You know, I've seen that UR missing saying before somewhere. Oh yes, I remember. It was on a card my dad's church would send out to people in hopes they would come to services. But the line was 'CH CH .What's missing? 'I think I know where Doris got the idea. Shame on you, Red."

"Hey, look, there's a parking spot," I interrupted, hoping to get the subject changed as we approached Mann's, but without any luck. "Okay, when I was in Henderson I was killing some time and went into Rose's department store and got all that stuff. I though it would be funny. I put them in the glove compartment on Saturday night when you were backstage talking to one of the musicians, Eddie I believe it was. Remember, Will? Remember talking to Eddie?"

"Yeah, yeah, I remember. I wondered why you wanted the car keys. That Eddie, the piano player, was a real character. Yessir, a real character."

Subject ended.

• • • • •

Fall could hold its own at Wake Forest.

All around the little town leaves turned to golds and reds and yellows and oranges, creating a colorful patchwork tapestry across the campus. Townsfolk, many of them Wake Forest professors and Saturday Only gardeners, called out to each other as they raked pine needles in their front yards and placed them around the bases of bushes and shrubs as mulch. In a state where there were four distinct seasons, fall was a particularly beautiful and energizing time of the year.

Sitting in Groves Stadium on October 25, singing the fight song: "Rah, Rah, Wake Forest, Rah, Old Alma Mater sons we are…," and watching the Deacons beat Carolina for the third year in a row, everyone dressed for the game in their collegiate best, the thought came to mind that living this life forever would be just fine. Perhaps a change in major to Education and ultimately a faculty position, or a job in Administration. Whatever it took. But would it be the same as the years piled up, on another campus, away from the familiar buildings and surroundings and faces, a hundred and twenty miles to the west? Maybe. Maybe not.

Just about everyone walked the half mile from the campus to the stadium. There was often the unmistakable smell of burning leaves so associated with the fall season. On game days alumni wandered the campus re-living their past good times, looking for former classmates and professors, revisiting familiar haunts, re-kindling their old gold and black spirit.

Fraternities competed for a Best Homecoming Decorations trophy with the central themes usually focused on "whipping up on" the opposing team. Although the production quality was usually minimal at best, creativity was evident and enthusiasm obvious. Butcher paper, paint and crepe paper sold well in the local stores that week.

All the fraternities catered to their returning brothers who anxiously commandeered anyone who would gather around in the Chapter Room and listen to their tales of how great "it" used to be. They were assured "it" still was.

On non-local-football weekends, The Southerners were busy enough playing several high school homecoming events and in the Wake Forest Community Building for a Monogram Club return engagement. We had a repeat performance at WC, playing for one of the literary society's events; however, now that many of us were mature seniors and juniors, and sophisticated, seasoned musicians, we were less inclined to seek out old flames or show off musically on the bandstand as we had the year before.

The great Ralph Flanagan Orchestra played for the formal Homecoming Dance in Raleigh on November 1. Flanagan was known as the man whose arrangements re-popularized the Glenn Miller sound in the Fifties, a widely recognized style that prompted Will to consider doing a special Miller Salute set in most future engagements.

As anxious as we were to hang around the bandstand and drink in the music, dancing to Flanagan's *Rag Mop* and *Hot Toddy*, *Penthouse Serenade*, *Tippn' In*, *Save The Last Dance For Me* and *Just One More Chance* was a rare opportunity for guys who are usually playing, not dancing. The togetherness of fraternal circles, the glamour of gorgeous long evening dresses and solid black tuxedos, holding your date tightly and swaying to the sounds from that great sax section suggested we seek out a wishing well somewhere and deposit a few coins so this memory would never fade.

Just as Flanagan's music created something of an atmosphere bordering on rapture, I thought to myself, this is what The Southerners are all about. This is how all the high school kids, the college men and coeds, all the servicemen and women, all the folks who dance to our music in gyms and auditoriums and hotels, rec centers and drill halls, officers' clubs and warehouses, on concrete and slick wood planks, beach strands and temporary dance floors laid on lawns ought to feel when we play.

We should create the aura. We should make every dance we play a special time of unforgettable memories.

• • • • •

Back to reality a few days later, we were witness to the fact more people liked Ike than Adlai in the 1952 national elections, for 55% of the popular vote and 442 electoral votes went to elect Dwight David Eisenhower the nation's 34th president. A California senator, Richard Nixon, was elected Vice President after defending his acceptance, following his nomination, of a black and white 'gift', a dog his daughters named 'Checkers.'

• • • • •

A few weeks later, the annual Sadie Hawkins Day dance, as in square dancing and don't-get-too-close- to-your-partner dancing, was held in Gore Gym. This event gave the many non-fraternity folks and the more creative and enterprising students an opportunity to be Li'l Abner, Daisy Mae, Lonesome Polecat, Hairless Joe, Pappy and Mammy Yokum or other Dogpatch residents from Al Capp's imagination. A live fiddle band performed. A sort of apple cider was enjoyed by all. Or most.

• • • • •

The employee organization of Carolina Power & Light Company in Raleigh, The Triangle Club, was having its annual fall social at The Shrine Club on November 14 and wanted a live band. Their budget would not permit a full orchestra but was more suited for a small combo. A young lady on the arrangements committee worked for my dad in the CP&L Advertising Department and contacted me to see if I would put together a small group to play the job.

With Moe at the piano, Lenny on sax, vibes and guitar, Hank on trumpet, fill-in Jack Terrell on bass, I on drums, and Pat Carson singing, we created a solid sound and played mostly the old standards over three hours for the mixed-age audience. Lenny acted as leader and, as usual, won the oohs and aahs of everyone with his virtuoso vibraphone performances. To add a bit of spice to our offerings, Hank sang several duets with Pat. Apparently they had been rehearsing, among other things, on their own, alone, for some time.

The job paid $250 which would cover our union scale and gas money but that was about it. Our group arrived to set up about 7:30 p.m., a half hour before dancing was to begin. My dad was in attendance (my mother couldn't make it) and brought over to the bandstand many of his executive associates I had come to know over my growing-up years. It occurred to me that our little mini-Southerners aggregation had best not screw up since it was now well publicized who I was and who had put the combo together.

When the dancing began and couples took to the floor, I spotted one person I had forgotten worked for CP&L: Sarah, the girl who had become engaged the year before, as I was so informed when I had called her last Christmas. She was now married to a fellow power company employee, a NC State engineering grad, whose nickname was Ziggy or Biggy or Higgy or some such. They were very cheek-to-cheek on the floor and, naturally, when she spotted me on the bandstand she had to come up at the first break so I could meet Whatshisname. I wanted to ask her if she recalled the Nash and that white angora sweater back in 1949, but given the size of her husband, I decided against it.

• • • • •

On December 13, The Southerners once again took to the Raleigh Memorial Auditorium stage to play for the IFC Christmas Dance. This semi-formal event closed the year's social season at the College and, for many who would graduate in January, it was their collegiate social swansong.

Will smartly put together sets of the most popular songs of the 1948-52 years for nostalgic purposes and announced each as we played it, drawing applause every time and a few tears now and then.

Unfortunately, it was the last job for Mack.

He had decided to finish college in the summer session of 1953 which would require he take a full load of courses for the spring semester and through two sessions of summer school, plus he had secured a job in the cafeteria to help meet expenses. He simply, sadly would not have time for the band. Mack was one of the "original eleven." He was a steady, committed player who was a first class musician. Principled, straight-laced with strong character, he provided a bit of sanity and foundation to our crew. However, he had a definite sense of humor and was always among the first to laugh. He and I had been close. Tough loss.

Joseph (Jinx) Miller entered Wake Forest in the fall, bringing with him several years of playing tenor sax in a Hugh Morson high school combo and with local bands around his home town of Raleigh. A twin, he was a character, a fun and funny person with dance music in his blood. He liked the camaraderie, he liked the energy, the adventure, the nonsense and all that went with the band. He had sat in with us on several occasions and now joined the front line fulltime.

Now, not one of the sax section was an 'original', but The Southerners never lost a beat. If anything, the new blood brought more experience and considerable new enthusiasm to the band. In Don and Jinx it added a couple of characters as well.

• • • • •

Just before Christmas I drove the Nash to New Bern to spend a day or so with Ginny, and to give her a gift. Actually, two gifts.

I suggested that she open the package when we were alone, which gave her a moment's concern that I may have done something in the lingerie line which would be very difficult to explain to her folks. She took the gift with us as we went out for a few hours, ultimately locating a preferred location in a remote area of the Trent River Yacht Club parking lot.

When she unwrapped the package and pulled back the tissue paper she found a white cashmere sweater, bathed in moonlight through the windshield. That was the first gift.

Attached to the sweater, over the left breast area, was my Kappa Alpha fraternity pin. Gold shield with alternating small red rubies and white pearls around the outside edge and a pearl *T* for Tau Chapter attached by a very thin gold chain.

In fraternity lingo, getting "pinned" was a very big deal, the unofficial prelude to being officially engaged. As in 'to be married.' A major step, albeit not as binding as an engagement ring. I had obviously put a lot of thought into this major move. Ginny was the one.

Putting the pin on the sweater and placing it in a box, to be discovered, was not the normal 'pinning' procedure. The preferred approach for most males was to attach the pin to their lady's sweater, blouse, or whatever, while she was actually wearing it, whatever 'it' was. Indeed, there were certain sensual advantages to that process, but for some reason I chose what I thought would be a surprisingly romantic, albeit not an anatomically based, method.

The pin was her second gift. Thankfully, it was a major hit, as evidenced by her lengthy, genuine verbal and physical signs of appreciation, and apparent happiness. Then, to my surprise, she pulled the sweater she had on over her head and donned the new sweater with the jeweled emblem.

Amazingly, it was perfectly positioned.

Chapter Thirty-Six

Cognizant of the financial bonanza we enjoyed by playing on New Year's Eve at the Cherry Point Marine Air Station the year before, in September Will had been in touch with the Pumphrey-Allsbrook people about another military opportunity at year-end 1952.

The first one that came up was at Camp Stewart, Georgia, forty miles from Savannah.

At a band rehearsal Will presented the opportunity, indicating it was a bit early, and something bigger, and much closer, could well come up over the ensuing weeks. On the other hand," a bird in hand...," as the adage goes. It would be a long haul, and all of us had planned to be home throughout the holidays, but if it was anything like the Cherry Point experience in excitement, satisfaction, and money, then it could make for another fun job.

When Will told us the job paid $1000, suggesting each of us might earn as much as sixty dollars, there were fourteen fast 'aye' votes. Ted would get an extra $10 for gas and Pab would be paid $20 dollars for gas and equipment assistance. Pumphrey-Allsbrook would get their hundred-dollar cut, Will would make an extra fifty as leader and for gas and there would still be a few bucks profit.

Chick would not make it back from New Jersey, suggesting that Ted give up not knowing how to play the guitar for not knowing how to play bass. He had several months to learn some basic fingering which Chick provided during, and after, rehearsals. Lenny could play guitar as well as vibes to add to the rhythm section. Will asked Randy if he wanted to play this one job for the money, but he had a wife and a job and couldn't play although he wanted to, so we decided to go with two trumpets instead of three. Rick would not be able to get away either, so we enlisted Frank to play baritone sax.

Organizing for the trip was a challenge in and of itself since it was the holidays and we were widespread.

The plan was to drive caravan-style the 350 miles for eight hours or so down to Savannah, leaving Raleigh by 9:00.a.m. on Wednesday, December 31, hopefully arriving at Camp Stewart by 6:00 p.m. at the latest. That would give us time to set up, dress and be ready for a 9:00 p.m. dance start. The evening was to end at 1:00 a.m. Pumphrey-Allsbrook had included in the contract that Bachelor Officers Quarters billet for the band members would be available on New Year's Eve for two dollars a person. We would drive all the way back to Raleigh and Wake Forest on New Year's Day.

The logistics in arranging everyone's transportation to Savannah were formidable.

Will would pull the trailer and Lenny, Hank, Ray and I would go with him in the Woodie. Hank had returned to Wake Forest from West Virginia, staying in the Colonial Club and he would get to Raleigh on his own. Ray would need to get to Raleigh from Rocky Mount. Ronnie and Jud would go from Asheville and Forest City the day before to meet Ted in Statesville at his grandparents' home and drive to Raleigh that night. Larry would come to Raleigh from New Bern the day before as well, and he and Frank would ride to Georgia with Ted. Pab was to drive from Thomasville to Greensboro and pick up Chip, then pick up Jinx in Raleigh. When the caravan got to Lumberton on US 301, Pab would pick up Moe and Don, who was to get from Charlotte to Lumberton somehow.

It looked good on paper.

Miraculously, everyone who was supposed to get to Raleigh made it. We rendezvoused at our favorite spot, The Toddle House, where Glenwood Avenue ran into Hillsborough Street. Each guy had a small overnight bag of some description and his instrument case. Lenny and I had already loaded his vibes and my drums into the trailer the day before and Will had picked up a bass from Lupton's.

Unfortunately, the weather was not good. Dark, overcast, rainy, and cold. A major front was moving through much of the South, stretching from the NC-Georgia mountains west of South Carolina to the Carolina-Virginia border to the northeast. It would slow our drive but we had plenty of time.

When we arrived in Lumberton, the rain was coming down hard. We met Moe at the bus station, but Don had not arrived from Charlotte. Will found a pay phone and got him at home.

"Man, I tried to get out there early this morning and thumb a ride to Lumberton, but there's not much traffic. I've checked the bus schedule and nothing's heading that way anytime soon." Don was frustrated. "I should've gone over yesterday."

"Can you get a plane from Charlotte to Savannah?" Will asked. "We can pick you up there later today on our way to Camp Stewart."

"Man, I've never flown on an airplane," Don confessed, "but I'll see what I can do. You call me back in an hour."

Moe was battling a head cold that threatened to move into his chest and asking medical advice from one and all.

"Let's see if we can stop at a drugstore somewhere and maybe you can find a bottle of Hadacol," I suggested, "you know, it's good for moles, colds, sore holes, aching backs, windy cracks and makes childbirth a pleasure. Bound to be good for what ails you."

"Yeah," added Hank", and its only got twelve percent alcohol in it, as a preservative it says on the label."

"I'll get two bottles and really get preserved," Moe responded.

"Pickled would be a better term," I said to Moe who, despite the nasal and throat challenges, didn't let up on the Camel cigarettes. "Maybe you should switch to L&Ms 'cause I saw one of their ads that said they were just what the doctor ordered."

"Nope, "Moe insisted, "I'll stick with these smokes. Why, I'd even walk a mile for a Camel."

Switching back to the main subject, Moe continued, "I heard

285

that song about Hadacol on the radio. You know, *'Who Put The Pep In Gran'ma?'* It's a humdinger."

Hank agreed and added, "One of the radio commercials I heard was about a lady in her eighties. She said she had suffered from a bad stomach for twenty years, but after taking five bottles of Hadacol, now she'd put her stomach up against any man's!"

"Ah, the power of advertising," I commented, "that's the career path for me."

In half an hour we had arrived in Dillon at Pedro's South of the Border to top off the gas tanks, buy some fireworks and fill up on Pedro's wide offerings of Mexican cuisine. This was a decision that would come back to haunt us over the next several hours in closed cars since tamales can produce a sort of gastronomic fireworks on their own. Pedro's sold a wide variety of wine and beer, but no Hadacol.

When we got to Florence, Will called Don in Charlotte.

"They've cancelled the flights going out of Charlotte," Don reported. "Don't know if they'll start again. I'll keep trying. Call me later."

Stopping at a gas station in Manning, SC, Will called Don once more and it was now obvious the sax player would not make it. Frustrated, he had even tried to find a Carolina Trailways or Greyhound bus that would get him to Savannah, but no luck. Disappointed he hung up and Will knew he would have to play tonight and not just front the band.

Moe sought out a local drugstore that had either Dixie Dew cough syrup or Hadacol in stock. He opted for the latter, having bought in to the radio promotions for the product by a variety of show business notables. He purchased an eight ounce bottle for $1.25, took the cap off and took a swig of the brownish, foul-smelling liquid right there in the store, unaware the medicine should be mixed with water.

"This stuff costs more than booze, and it don't taste nearly as good."

"Mix it with water like the directions say and it probably won't taste much better," Jinx advised. "But let me know if it does 'cause I feel a cough coming on."

Although the rain stopped and the skies cleared, the last four hours to Savannah were boring and tiring. On the outskirts of town, we stopped at a diner for supper, then drove the 39 miles to the military base.

Camp Stewart was located west of Savannah near the little town of Hinesville, Georgia. First begun in 1940 on some 5000 acres as an anti-aircraft artillery training center, it was named for a native of the area, General Daniel Stewart, who had fought with Francis Marion during the American Revolution. Initially, training was spasmodic and low-key, but with the bombing of Pearl Harbor on December 7, 1941, training intensified. A detachment of WASPs (Women's Air Service Pilots) was brought in to fly planes towing targets for live-fire exercises.

By late 1943, in addition to its anti-aircraft and now tank and armor artillery focus, Camp Stewart was housing captured German and Italian solders in two separate POW facilities. It also became the site for an Army Cooks and Bakers school. At one time prior to the Normandy invasion on June 6, 1944 there were some 55,000 soldiers based there. In September, 1945 the camp was inactivated, used only by the Georgia National Guard in the summers.

When the Korean Conflict came about in June 1950, the camp was reopened as a permanent facility on August 9 and redesignated as the 3rd Army Artillery Training Center, growing to some 280,000 acres in five counties, thirty-nine miles wide, and the largest military base in the Eastern United States.

Arriving after dark we had no idea what the scope of the post was, or its mission, but it was obvious this was the center of considerable activity under wartime conditions. Even on New Year's Eve there were military vehicles moving continually, soldiers scampering about and all the elements of security in place.

Encountering armed MPs at the Main gate upon arrival, we were waved in after Will presented the appropriate credentials.

Two of the MPs lead our caravan in a jeep to the Officers' Club where we were to play and waited while we unhooked the trailer, backed it up to a rear service door, unloaded our equipment and quickly set up our stands. Several floor mikes were already in place. The MPs then escorted us to the BOQ where we showered, donned the blue blazers and walked the two hundred yards back to the one-story wood building that housed the Officers' Club.

We quickly ran through a dozen bars of five or six numbers. The two enlisted men assigned by Special Services told us that a number of the officers who would be in attendance that evening had served in Korea, but most were in training capacities and had not seen overseas duty during this military action but had served in World War Two. They quickly pointed out that virtually all these men have been working night and day for over a year to make sure our artillery forces were well prepared.

"I'm curious," Hank asked of one of our assigned privates, "but isn't there an Army band on this post? And wouldn't they normally have a dance band that would play for the officers?" Hank recalled our experience a year earlier at Cherry Point.

"Yes sir, we have a large marching band, and several music units come from there, including a dance band, a concert orchestra and a Dixieland group. But many months ago they accepted an invitation to march in some big parade tomorrow and play a concert in Atlanta tonight. They were bussed over yesterday." Now we knew how we got this job.

It was approaching nine p.m. and we already had had a long day but the thought of playing for these people, on this special night, invigorated us.

The dance floor was spacious, with tables arranged five or six deep around it on three sides. The ballroom, as it were, was adjoining the main dining room and was apparently used for large meetings, entertainment, shows and such as well as for dancing. A small but adequate stage with deep blue velvet curtains gave us an elevated position.

Some twenty-five couples were already seated, awaiting the

dance music and beginning their own three-hour countdown. All
the accoutrements for a New Year's Eve party were in evidence,
including the requisite crepe paper, hats, noisemakers, balloons,
and refreshments. The main dining room where most of the officers, dressed in their formal military attire, and their wives had
been enjoying a sumptuous repast, was alive with conversation
and laughter.

Moe had long finished his Hadacol and had found another liquid medicinal beverage more to his liking, thanks to one of our
'aides', Private Enrique Ortiz. It seems Enrique was a budding
piano player himself and had positioned his chair near, but a bit
behind, the piano to observe Moe's technique closely and to provide him with necessary potions from the bar.

For three hours the event went smoothly as over three hundred
military men and their wives, or friends, made the most of the
celebration. With the exception of the fancy uniforms, and the fact
we were on a military base, it could have been a typical upscale
country club affair. Lots of food, lots of booze, lots of camaraderie, lots of dancing, and lots of excitement in the air.

Will recalled that the old Army song was *"The Caissons Go Rolling Along,"* which certainly fit our location inasmuch as caissons
pulled by men, horses or vehicles of some sort had been hauling
artillery ammunition for centuries. We assumed the song was still
in vogue. The music was in our "Handy Tunes For All Occasions"
booklets, so we played it several times to raucous cheering by proud
members of the 3rd Army Artillery Military Training Center.

Entry into 1953 from 1952 by our audience was a non-stop
horn blowing, balloon dropping and balloon-popping, confetti-
throwing, and noisemaker-twirling five minutes in duration. It
was also a time for toasting and kissing while we played *Auld
Lang Syne* three times to underscore the merriment.

We took a fifteen-minute break just after the midnight doings
to get our breath, hit the latrine and enjoy the sandwiches and
refreshments Enrique and his associate, Private Walter Gilooley,
had arranged for us backstage. To suggest we were physically beat

would be an understatement, but we did the remaining forty-five minutes energetically somehow, and to the applause of our gracious hosts.

After being paid by the manager of the Officers' Club, we had to break down and pack the trailer before calling it a night. The temperature had dropped into the high thirties and the walk back to the BOQ seemed considerably further than the earlier walk over. There was some imbibing as we toasted each other to health and happiness, and peace, in the year ahead. We were counting on Ike to get this Korean mess over with.

Moe's head cold seemed to be considerably better, suggesting sufficient doses of twelve percent alcohol or better apparently will kill a lot of germs.

Chapter Thirty-Seven

The New Year showed up bright, clear and crisp. Knowing we had another long day ahead of us, our caravan left the BOQ and the Camp Stewart Main Gate at 9:00 a.m. By 10:30 o'clock, we had eaten breakfast at a roadside diner on the way to Savannah. There was little traffic on New Year's Day.

As the trip down had done, getting everyone back to NC presented challenges as well.

Ted was heading back towards Charlotte and on to Huntersville before returning to Wake Forest for classes, which began on Monday, January 5. His plan was to go back by way of Augusta and on north with Jud and Ronnie who were going to their homes in Western NC... Pab was going to go back to Lumberton, drop Moe off, proceed on to Raleigh where he would drop off Frank and Larry, then to Greensboro for Chip and on home to Thomasville. Will thought it would be better to go through Savannah, hit Highway 17 north to Summerville, S.C., then on 301 up to Fayetteville and into Raleigh on NC 50.

With Ted already gone one way and Pab another, the Woodie with Will, Hank, Jinx, Lenny, Ray and me would be on its own. No caravan.

To get to 17 we needed to go into Savannah proper. Entering the city on West Gwinnett Street, we got to Whitaker Street at Forsyth Park and took a left towards the north and US 17.

Suddenly the Woodie bucked, sputtered, sputtered again, and died. No noises coming from under the Woodie's hood. No smoke. No steam. No fire.

Will eased the wagon over to the right curb, adjacent to the park, cut the ignition and we all got out, quickly, to check on the problem. Will raised the hood. Nothing obvious.

Over the next several minutes, it became most apparent that none of us had a clue about automobile engines. We could change tires, add water to the radiator, inflate tires, add oil, pump gas, wash windshields, hook up trailers and drive. That was the sum total of our knowledge.

"Check the carburetor," Jinx said very matter-of-factly, as if an authority.

"For what?" Lenny asked.

"Maybe it's clogged. You know the air filter thing."

Will removed the carburetor, banged it against the radiator a few times, blew into it, ostensibly to remove debris, and uttered, "Nope, that can't be it."

"Check out all the wires and stuff, "I suggested. "Like the wires to the battery. Wait…the battery can't be dead 'cause the lights come on."

"Don't go pulling on all the wires or you'll do more damage," Will cautioned. "What about the spark plugs?"

"Could we be out of gas? Maybe there's an oil leak." Ray put his two cents worth in.

'We have plenty of gas," Will announced as he got on his knees to look under the wagon for oil leaks. "No oil coming out."

At this point, we were all well aware we didn't know what the problem was. We did know there was virtually no traffic on Whitaker Street. There was a multi-block, forested park to our right and rows of single-family houses lining the opposite side of the street, but no service station in sight and no people.

"Okay, I know its New Year's Day and most places are closed but let's see if we can find a gas station open somewhere. Hank you head back down that way, Jinx, you go back on Gwinnett Street, Red you go up ahead. Lenny, check out the park and see if there's anyone there or maybe a pay phone. Ray and I'll stay here and try to flag somebody down." Will was assuming command of his crippled ship.

"Fifteen minutes. Everybody be back in fifteen minutes."

Each of us headed in the appointed directions. The noon hour was approaching and traffic seemed to be picking up.

Jinx returned first, stating there was no gas station or anything else for blocks to the west.

Hank was back next and reported virtually the same information about his trek to the south. Lenny excitedly ran up saying he had found a pay phone but no phone book and since the receiver was hanging down, off the hook, and there was no dial tone, he doubted the thing worked anyhow. I had come across several retail shops, all closed, a laundromat, closed, a florist, closed and a funeral home. Open, I assumed, but did not check by going in.

"I imagine we could use the funeral home phone to call a garage somewhere if we have to. I didn't see anybody around but you know somebody's on duty." If the call was to be made my vote was for Will to do it.

Will and Ray had flagged down four cars but no one seemed knowledgeable about cars, or interested in helping, but assured him they would send someone down "if we come across a station that's open...and Happy New Year!"

The sun had come out brightly and taken the morning chill away, which helped as we stood around discussing our plight. We felt the best thing to do was continue flagging cars and hope to find someone who could take Will to an open gas station. While he and Ray stood on opposite sides of the street flailing their arms, Jinx suggested we relieve the boredom and attract some attention from folks in the nearby houses and in passing vehicles by jamming some, right there on the street.

We agreed that should certainly get some attention, it would kill time and be fun. 'What the heck' was the prevailing attitude. We opened the trailer doors and took our instruments out. .I set up my bass drum, snare and high hat. Lenny got his guitar, Jinx his saxophone, Ray came over and unpacked the trombone while Hank grabbed the trumpet.

In about ten minutes we had a session going, mostly Dixieland. All upbeat numbers we knew by heart. No music for this gig. Now, every car that came by would honk its horn and folks would wave but our performance was not getting any auto assistance, even with the hood up.

In fifteen minutes or so, several black kids wandered up to check out the music. They had come from the houses across the street. They never asked why we were there, or playing, but just began to clap and dance around and laugh. One had brought a tambourine. Before long, we had a dozen kids ranging in age from about five to maybe twelve doing their thing, having a ball.

When we finished playing *Won't You Come Home, Bill Bailey?* Will told the kids we were part of a band and had played the previous night at Camp Stewart. They all knew about the camp. He then asked one of the older boys if there were any grown-ups around, maybe somebody who knew something about cars. He explained our station wagon had stopped and we needed to get it repaired today.

"His Daddy know 'bout cars," the boy said, pointing to another in the group.

Turning to the identified boy, Will asked, "Is your Daddy home?"

While the youngster pondered whether he should get involved or not, Will pulled a half dollar from his pocket and handed it over. The pondering was over. The boy took the money, smiled very broadly, uttered a polite "thank you, mister" and scampered across the street, disappearing into a house several doors down the block.

We struck up another number, *"Rose Room,"* to keep up momentum, or lack thereof.

In ten minutes, the youngster returned with his dad, a very large, muscular black man who was obviously a little skeptical, and concerned, about what was going on.

"Sir," Will spoke up as soon as the man was within earshot, "we've had some car trouble and don't know what the problem is. We sure do need to get it fixed so we can back to school in North Carolina." He explained our being in a dance band and playing at

Chapter Thirty-Seven

Camp Stewart. "We'll be happy to pay you if you can help us out."
Noting we were all young, and not appearing to be the types to
create trouble, the man introduced himself as the Reverend James
Henry Bowers, fulltime dock worker on the Savannah docks and
part-time minister. We shook and introduced ourselves in turn.

"Les' see what we can find here," James Henry said as he stared
down on the engine. "Ummm, you say you got gas, and the oil
ain't leaking. You checked the carburetor. Nothin's smoking and I
don't smell nothin' burning. Hummmm."

Our impromptu concert was over, for now, and we all gathered
around as if to lend moral support to James Henry. One of the
youngsters was more intent on playing the drums than our car
problems. He was about nine or ten, a little kid, and he asked me;
"Mister, you think I might play them drums a minute or two?"

"What's your name? You ever played drums before?" I questioned.

"Lester. Naw sir, not all of 'em, but I play one right much, in
the school band."

"Okay, get up on the seat there....I don't believe your feet can
reach the foot pedal...but that's okay. Just play the snare and the
cymbals. You know how to hold the sticks?"

He nodded, took the sticks and placed each correctly in his
small hands. Then, with a snaggle-tooth smile seemingly as big
as a hubcap he turned and began to do a steady paradiddle on the
snare. Now and then he'd break into a rhythmic beat, hit a cymbal,
and get right back on his beat. I wished he could operate the bass
drum and the high-hat cymbals because he had it going.

Several of his buddies gathered around and clapped and shouted and danced and beat on the tambourine while Lester did his
thing. All this musical activity was attracting more attention, for
now others were coming out of their houses and crossing over to
see what the racket was about.

"Okay," James Henry spoke up," I don' b'lieve it's the spark
plugs 'cause they ain't likely to all cut out at the same time.
What I think is the coil wire to the distributor come loose. If I

got your pu'mission I can shove the wire back on and we can see if that works."

"You got it, Reverend," Will said quickly, anxiously.

James Henry felt around and took hold of the coil wire and shoved it firmly to the distributor.

"Okay, les' see if this gonna' work. Go ahead 'n start the engine."

Will jumped into the driver's seat, turned the key and pushed the ignition button.

Shazam! The Woodie came to life.

"Awwwriiiight!" everyone exclaimed. Everyone but Lester who did not want to see the Woodie start up and leave because that meant my drums would be gone as well.

"Great job, Reverend Bowers!" Will exclaimed. "We really appreciate it."

"Glad I could help, son."

Will took his wallet out of his right rear pants pocket and pulled a twenty out, handing it to J. Henry, who kept his hands by his side and shook his head.

"You don' owe me nothing, son. Glad I could he'p."

"Reverend, you really bailed us out of a big problem, and we appreciate it. I would've had to pay some mechanic a lot more than this, so please take the money. We'd all feel better if you would. You can contribute it to your church if you like, but I want you to take it."

"Well, tha's mighty kind o' you, son. Reckon I could use it awright. Yessir, I do 'preciate it. But I was only too glad to help."

By now the rest of us were packing our instruments in the trailer with the motor still running. The crowd began to disperse, except for Lester. He was still holding the drumsticks.

"Lester," I said, "you keep those drumsticks. And you practice, and soon as you can, you get yourself a drum and practice some more. You know what you're doing, so keep working at it."

"Thank you, mister. I'm gonna' save up and git me a drum awright. I 'preciate you lettin' me play while y'all been broke down."

Lester came up to me and hugged me around the waist. I patted him on the head and got into the Woodie. The Reverend James Henry Bowers waved as we pulled away from the curb.

"You know," I said to no one in particular, "one of these days that Lester is going to be a terrific drummer. Remind me to check the musicians playing around Savannah in 1963."

Hank spoke up, "when we look back on this, I'll bet we remember Reverend J. Henry Bowers and Lester and breaking down in Savannah more than playing at Camp Stewart."

Chapter Thirty-One

The Dow opened at 293.79 in January 1953.

USC had beaten Wisconsin 7-0 in the Rose Bowl, Alabama won the Orange Bowl over Syracuse 61-6, and Georgia Tech took the Sugar Bowl over Ole Miss, 27-7. The 8th Gator Bowl was won by Florida over Tulsa, 14-13, which reminded us that the first Gator Bowl ever was won by Wake Forest, 26-14 over South Carolina.

Classes began on a very cold, brisk, overcast Monday.

Ginny was showing off the KA pin, politely, without too much fanfare. Her girl friends thought the idea of my pinning the gift sweater without the girl in the sweater was very romantic, novel and certainly non-invasive. Predictably, my fraternity brothers were incredulous. When opportunity knocks, they said...

Ellen was showing off the KA pin she had received from Will during the holidays. She did not elaborate on the pinning methodology. As expected, Will did. It was considerably closer to the norm. Perhaps embellished somewhat.

January being a rather slow time for dances, the band guys settled into the school routine and attempted to get some high early marks in the semester to average out the anticipated less high marks as the dance season blossomed. Rehearsals continued nonetheless, and new numbers were added.

Lenny was not returning to Wake Forest, or to The Southerners. His former high school band director had successfully arranged a music scholarship at his alma mater, Indiana University, for Lenny, so he jumped at the chance.

Although he had been with us for only six months, including

the two beach combo jobs, he had made a major impression on the band, and our audiences. The vibes were unique and he was a talented performer when playing them. He was a superb guitarist and, obviously, as the only arranger the band had, he had provided us with several classy originals. We never saw Lenny again after dropping him off at his home in Raleigh late on New Year's Day. He received his scholarship letter in the mail on January 2 and telephoned Will with the departure news.

Ted was going to have to get a lot better on guitar or stay pretty well hidden during jobs.

• • • • •

After we all limped back to Wake Forest from Savannah in the Woodie Will realized 'the old girl' needed considerable attention. A stem-to-stern, top-to-bottom check-up.

Steve Prince, known as Slim, was a freshman KA pledge from Forest City who was a "grease-soaked hot rodder" at heart, by his own admission. What none of us knew about cars, Slim knew, and then some. He had fixed them, built them, raced them on dirt tracks and was happiest with a rag and a wrench.

Will asked Slim to take a look at the Woodie and render an objective opinion as to her potential longevity. After several hours over several days, Slim said he believed the Woodie still had some life left, but she'd need major work. Points, plugs and a variety of other new and/or useful parts. New retreads. Touch-up painting where the rust had taken hold. The trailer had about pulled the rear bumper off. There was a sizeable crack in the windshield, made by a rock thrown by a semi hauling gravel. The list went on.

"If I were you," Slim suggested, "I'd make the basic necessary repairs and keep driving the Woodie on short trips, but I wouldn't put a ton of money in her. I'd get a second vehicle that has lots of room and a sturdy frame. Something reliable. If you want we can go to the auction and take a look."

In addition to being part musician, part lover, part student, Will was part horse trader. "Deal" was his middle name, especially if the deal was in his favor. With Slim's help, maybe they could pick up something cheap. Maybe a used hearse. That would look great with the band name painted on the side.

Will wasn't accustomed to going to Mann's Auto Auction in the daytime, just the roadhouse at night, but he and Slim made the short trip one afternoon after classes. Slim quickly started nosing around the back lot for some of the better non-performers. When they saw an old black Dutch Darrin-designed Packard with its owner proclaiming it to be a real "diamond in the rough," Slim looked it over for a while, kicked the tires, studied whatever there was under the hood and realized why "black beauty" wouldn't fire up.

Acting as if he wasn't interested, he motioned Will to follow him around the corner behind a small delivery van up on blocks. "This may be a wild shot, and you'll need a good mechanic in Wake Forest to really test it and tune it up, but if you want to invest seventy-five bucks in it, I believe I can get that Packard to run back to Wake Forest. But offer the guy fifty and see what happens."

Like a shot, Will was back at the Packard, informing the owner he'd give him $75 for the car. Stunned with delight, the seller couldn't wait to sign an oil-spotted title transfer in record time, take Will's cash, hop in a friend's car and scratch off. Slim just sighed over the non-negotiation, took his pocketknife, loosened the distributor, and retarded the timing to the point the old heap could hardly get out of its own way. She started up with smoke pouring out the tailpipe and, with Slim at the wheel, the old Packard churned up US 1 with a new lease on life.

The local mechanic made some adjustments, added a few parts to both the Packard and the Woodie and now The Southerners had a second, albeit ancient, pair of band cars. Band folk simply tolerated the rattles and knocks, cracked windshields, windows that wouldn't roll down, faulty heaters and musty, well-worn upholstery. Goes with the territory.

Drivers behind the Packard, however, had to use their headlights and windshield wipers to get through the dense black cloud created when the hulk pulled away from a stoplight carrying a full tank of gas and a load of crankcase oil. Will decreed that Slim would be an ongoing, paid non-musician member of the band for every out-of-town job he wanted to go on so he could keep the cars operative.

• • • • •

The Oxford, NC Veterans of Foreign Wars, mostly WWII types, booked The Southerners for their Valentines Dance on Saturday night, February 14. The main event, an apt pugilistic term applied to a social event, was held in the Granville County Armory, and a rip-roaring affair it was. The women's committee had done a stellar job of theming the armory with red and white crepe paper and paper hearts of all sizes placed about everywhere anyone could slap up a paper heart. Tables had red and white paper cloths and napkins, and scattered on the tables was a variety of little heart candies with clever, quasi-romantic sayings on them. As the evening progressed, it was obvious a good time was being had by all even though a shouting, pushing and shoving altercation would break out here and there. Just good fun between good friends.

Following the 8-12 p.m. affair many of the party people went back to the VFW hall on the outskirts of town for a few parting libations. They invited the band to drop by. Those of us still riding the Woodie, Will, Hank, Moe, Ray, Don and I, accepted the invitation.

The typical cinder block one-story no-nonsense building fronted the highway. There were large dirt parking lots on each side and both virtually filled. A neon sign with lighted red letters V F W hung loosely over the entry double doors. The six of us, still wearing the blue blazers but now tie-less, walked in and were immediately enclosed in a fog of cigarette smoke punctuated by the unmistakable smell of liquor.

The man who had invited us to drop by the club greeted us as we entered, thanked us again for the music and escorted us to the very elaborate and extremely busy bar.

"Give 'em whatever they want," he ordered the bartender at

our end of the counter. "Or one round anyway." He laughed, told us to enjoy ourselves and moved on to join a group at his table.

The room was dimly lit. A colorful Wurtlizer jukebox up against a side wall was playing loudly and quite a few couples were dancing. As we stood watching the patriots party, Moe took off for the the restroom.

Ten minutes later he was back, eyes wide open.

"You know what's back of that door with the sign that says Janitorial Closet? A casino! I mean crap tables, a roulette wheel, poker, blackjack. It looks like Las Vegas in there!"

"No surprise there," Will observed calmly, "I've been in a dozen of these places, VFW, Elks, American Legion, some Shrine Clubs, and a lot of 'em have gambling…and wide open bars. Best if we all stay out of there."

As we remained glued to our positions, taking in the obvious violations of a handful of laws, a very attractive, very put-together dark-haired lady in her late thirties came up to the bar, presumably to get a drink. We were lined up, more or less, backs to the bar and facing the activity, with Will in the middle, Hank and I on his left and Moe, Ray and Don on his right.

She was not coming to get a drink. She was coming to ask Ray to dance.

She grabbed his arm and began to pull him out to the dance floor. Ray was caught by surprise and immediately began thanking the lady but opting out very vociferously. Having had more than her share of booze all evening, and apparently abandoned by her male partner, she was in no mood to be rejected. She turned in to Ray, putting her arm on his shoulder, shoved her body tightly up against his, and started to sway even before they got away from the bar. Ray continued to protest as vigorously, but politely, as he could, to no avail.

Like a flash out of nowhere a mountain of a man ran up, grabbed Ray and wheeled him around, drawing back a big fist, connected to a massive tattooed sledge hammer of an arm.

"Boy, whatta' you think you're doing? That's my wife you got ahold of there. I'm gonna' bust you up good!"

Ray quickly tried to tell the irate husband that he had not asked the lady to dance, that she had come on to him, that he had tried to resist, all the while trying to put his arms and hands up in front of his face, the assumed principal target of hostile hubby's ham hock fist.

"Don't lie to me, boy! I go to play one hand o' poker and you think you can put moves on my wife. Boy, you must be crazy." With that, he took a swing. Ray adroitly moved as he saw the punch coming. It landed squarely on his right shoulder, with a very loud thud. There would be a bruise there tomorrow, for sure.

By now several of the VFW members who had been standing at the bar as well and knew what had really taken place, jumped in and pulled the man back, pinning his arms down. The bartender emerged with a Louisville Slugger baseball bat he fully intended to use if necessary. Moe and Will grabbed Ray and pulled him back to the relative safety of the bar.

It took a couple of minutes, but calm finally was restored. GI Joe was convinced by his associates that Ray had never made any advances, and, indeed. was an innocent victim. Meanwhile, the attractive dark-haired thirties-something female had left the building, most likely scratching off in the family pickup. If that was indeed the case, then my guess was the truck had mud flaps, a whip antenna, a gun rack, an American flag window decal and an "America. Love It or Leave it!" bumper strip.

As quickly as it began, it was all over. Everyone returned to where he, or she, had come from except the angered husband. He walked over and apologized to Ray and offered to buy him a drink. To his credit Ray, still shaken and rubbing his shoulder, declined.

No vote was taken as to our next move, but at that point all six of us headed for the parking lot. We didn't stick around to thank our host.

Happy Valentine's, y'all.

Chapter Thirty-Nine

Hemric, DePorter, DeVos, Lyles, Lipstas, George, Davis, Preston, Williams, Phillips, McCrae, Alheim. Coaches Maury Gleeson and "Bones" McMillian.

The unheralded Wake Forest basketball squad rose to virtually every occasion and swept a three-game tournament at William Neal Reynolds Coliseum in Raleigh to win their first Southern Conference basketball championship. They beat the University of Pennsylvania and Holy Cross in the Dixie Classic, losing a close, tough battle to BYU for the title. Season record: Won twenty-one, lost six. Great year on the hardwoods.

• • • • •

Will learned through a union newsletter that the American Federation of Musicians would pay scale to members who performed concerts or played for dances in rural areas that normally did not have the opportunity, or the money, to hear live music. He jumped all over that income stream quickly.

Almost immediately he had booked concerts in high school auditoriums in Pilot, Mapleville and Hester, all within an hour of Wake Forest. He somehow arranged for each to be late in the school day so most of us could get to classes, grab lunch and then motor to the site. He put together a one-hour set of mostly the latest popular numbers in our repertoire, and encouraged the youngsters to sing along, which made for a lively, entertaining and certainly satisfying event all around. We were paid five dollars per person per concert job, and while this was not much money, we all definitely had the "feel goods" for playing them.

We played two of these 'special' events as three-hour Friday night proms, one in Ingleside and the other in Justice. We had never heard of either of these very small rural communities but found audiences that were appreciative and made the most of the opportunities. Each of us received nine dollars per job but would have probably played for nothing.

It is one thing to watch kids who have access to live music now and then enjoy themselves, but it is a much greater feeling to see youngsters who don't have that privilege dancing and laughing, all dressed up, under the crepe paper and balloons in their small gyms.

Two occurrences nearly short-changed us for one concert and one dance, however.

Don almost missed the Mapleville afternoon concert due to a difference of interpretation over the answer to a pop quiz question in a literature course taught by Dr. Jonah Broadus. According to Don, who usually was very smart in lit classes, the question was, "What is the difference between realism and naturalism?" Whether he did not know the answer or was in one of his 'creative' moods, he wrote, "In naturalism, you call a spade a spade. In realism, you refer to it as a damn spade."

Apparently Don thought it was a brilliant answer, but Dr. Broadus did not share the view, or the levity, or the use of profanity, although "Out damned spot, out I say" in Act V, Scene I in Shakespeare's Macbeth was highly acceptable. He demanded that Don return for a meaningful discussion in his office after lunch, a one-sided conversation that lasted far too long and almost caused Don to miss the Woodie's departure.

Several days before the Ingleside prom Moe came down with what we agreed was the flu. Against his loud protestations, we took him to the Infirmary where our very good nurse friends immediately confirmed our diagnosis and ordered him to bed. Cecile gave him a shot of penicillin over his suggestion that he'd prefer a shot of Jack Daniels instead. He did not balk, however, when she asked him to drop his drawers for the buttocks injection. Applying the serum she smiled broadly, winked at us and cautioned, "Don't get excited, Moe. I'm on duty."

Chip decided Moe's medical attention needed pharmaceutical variety, so five of us walked down to Holding's Drugstore and each bought a small six-eight ounce glass bottle of a patent medicine off the shelf. Five different potions. None Hadacol. Returning to the frat house, we emptied the contents down the sink and re-filled the bottles with our own elixirs: six-eight ounces each of bourbon, scotch, brandy, gin and genuine Johnston County white light'nin'.

We visited our sick friend after supper that evening and placed the five bottles, with their original labels, on his bedside nightstand, with our warmest wishes for a speedy recovery.

When Hank went to accompany Moe to his frat house room upon his release on Friday afternoon two days later, nurses Cecile and Florence told him to drink plenty of liquids, stay warm, get plenty of rest, cut down on the smoking and, by the way, thanks for the party last night.

• • • • •

Will came bounding into the Chapter Room with a letter in his hand. "Hey, y'all," he was shouting out to all in the room, "listen to this. The Carolina Cotillion Committees invites The Southerners to play for the 1953 June Germans in Planters Warehouse, Rocky Mount, NC on June 19 from 9:00 p.m. until 1:00 am..... man, they are asking us back!"

Ray and I were both in the room and were obviously delighted for the band to get a repeat invitation to this high visibility event.

"That's great, man. Wish I could be there," I said with a tone of sincere sadness. Reality had been setting in for some weeks now. Reality that I would be graduating in a couple of months and not playing any more dance jobs with The Southerners.

"Whatta' you mean?" Ray asked. He had concluded several

306

months earlier that he was not likely to pass Accounting II, despite his best efforts to con Professor Hilton Delmar, so he would not graduate. Instead he decided to enlist in the Army, do his tour and come back to finish in two years. He was given four months before reporting, and he knew he'd be around for the Germans job at least.

"Well, if things go as planned, I'll graduate on June 1 and start work on June 8 in New York. That's a long commute to make a dance job."

• • • • •

The last high school prom I played with The Southerners took place, coincidentally, in Ginny's home town of New Bern. Her sister, Jeannette, was now a high school senior and had influenced the prom committee to hire the band. It was also Larry's home as well and the first time the band had played there.

Jeannette, and her younger brother by two years, Charlie, had heard enough of my band stories from Ginny and me that expectations were very high. Even the Reverend and Mrs. Barker indicated an interest in coming to hear The Southerners. After all, their eldest child was seriously involved with the drummer.

During some of my overnight visits I had remarked about all the wishing wells we seemed to encounter at high school dances, suggesting to the very energetic and creative Jeannette that her prom have a suitable, if not spectacular, well also. She was on the decorations committee, naturally.

On Saturday morning, after standing for a half hour on "Miss Jo's corner" in Wake Forest, I finally bummed a ride to Raleigh to pick up the Nash (when *will* he trade this car????). I got to my house by 10 a.m. and was back in Wake Forest by 11:30. Ginny had gotten permission to go home for the weekend and we'd make the trip ahead of the band. We invited Larry to ride with us and by noon we had left Wake Forest.

At three-thirty we arrived in New Bern. I dropped Larry at his house, and quickly drove to 304 Johnson Street, the parsonage. The two-story wood frame house stood on a corner lot with an iron fence and an authentic and very old hitching post. It was located in an historic neighborhood in this very historic town. As we drove up, the thought crossed my mind: when will I see this place again?

The rest of the band was to pull into town by seven for an eight p.m. start at the high school gym. They would likely get barbecue at King's in Kinston on the way down. And banana pudding. Or cobbler.

Mrs. Barker whipped up mashed potatoes to go with the home-cooked deep fried chicken, small sweet green peas, Waldorf salad, rolls and iced tea. Lemon meringue pie for dessert. Home made. After an early supper and helping with the dishes to make Brownie points, I took a quick shower and dressed in The Southerners' 'uniform'. Ginny drove me in the "gray goose" to the school gym and dropped me off at 7:00 p.m. She intended to return home to help Jeannette with last minute primping before her date arrived and come back to the dance later.

As I got out of the car, I looked over at her in the driver's seat. She was wearing a very feminine short-sleeve light blue blouse on which there was a small piece of jewelry attached. "That pin looks really good on you," I told her.

She smiled, blew me a kiss, mouthed the word "later" and drove off.

The others had already arrived and were unloading the trailer. Pab had the drums inside and I finished putting the set in order while he checked the mikes. Shortly, Jinx, Chip and I wandered around the gym, checking out the themed décor.

The previous year John Huston had produced a successful film about Toulouse-Lautrec entitled *Moulin Rouge*, starring Jose Ferrer and Zsa Zsa Gabor. The theme from that movie had been an enormous hit and Will had fortuitously put it into our repertoire. The haunting melody sounded best when performed by a full strings orchestra, but we managed to do it justice.

The high schoolers had done an outstanding decorating job, transforming the gym into streets of Paris in the late 19th century. Artistically painted flats depicted a street with various shops, including a fromagerie, boulangerie, boucher, fruits et legumes and 'un magasin de chapeaux pour les dames.' They had actually created and erected colorful striped awnings in front of the shops and the "windows" were decorated/painted with each store's goods.

Across the way was a large backdrop of the Eiffel Tower, and a short distance beyond, Notre Dame. An actual dessert and coffee café was open for business with wrought iron tables and chairs outside on the 'sidewalk.' Too bad none of us had a beret or could play the accordion.

In a central location stood a very old, very ornate, very real and fully functioning water fountain within a circular pool. The wishing well! A hand-painted sign was placed at the base of the pool, reading: "Si vous voulez que votre souhait se realising jeter une piece dans ici."

As we were admiring the elegant late 18th century fountain, and attempting to translate the sign, a teacher/chaperone walked up and informed us that this was actually a work of art. It had been imported from Pernes-les-Fontaines, Provence by a local antique dealer for a wealthy couple who planned to build a French-style chateau outside New Bern. He passed away, the widow moved back to Massachusetts, and the estate sold the land, leaving the antique dealer with a marvelous, albeit pricey artifact on his hands. Now he rented it out for social occasions in hopes of getting some of his investment back.

Jeannette had outdone herself when it came to wishing wells.

When the prom began at eight most of the kids were already milling about, admiring the handiwork of their decorating committee. A bit after eight Ginny, Rev. and Mrs. Barker and Charlie, entered quietly and walked over to a table out of the mainstream to observe. They were soon joined by the school principal and his wife, members of Grace Baptist. Charlie was dispatched to obtain punch all around.

After opening with *Tenderly* and following with *The Theme from Moulin Rouge,* which was more popularly known as *Where Is Your Heart?* we played three slow numbers before doing an up-tempo *A Kiss To Build A Dream On.* I asked Pab to take over for one or two numbers so I could visit with the Barkers.

Walking over to the table, I greeted them all, was introduced to the Principal and his wife, Dr. and Mrs. Randall, and took a chair beside Ginny.

"I thought maybe you and I would do a little jitter-bugging, Mrs. B, when this spectacular orchestra plays a really fast number," I suggested, knowing the very handsome woman had a good sense of humor. Then it occurred to me she might just accept!

"Well, if Mr. Randall were not here...he's on the Board of Deacons you know...then I'd accept, but for now I'll take a rain check. But thanks anyway."

Everyone complimented the band and I was convinced the Barkers were relieved to see for themselves that we were a legitimate, professional organization.

Then I spoke up, loudly enough for everyone at the table to hear, "Oh, Ginny, we're counting on you to sing *Summertime* during the next set...while your folks are here." We had told the story at the supper table earlier so everyone but the Randalls got it right away.

"Yes, Ginny, that would be a treat for us all," the Principal quickly said.

"Mr. Randall, I'm afraid I'm not going to sing tonight. The *Summertime* thing is an inside joke. Very inside. But maybe Red will sing his famous *Maharajah of Magador.* It won't take much urging. In fact, one request and he'll do it, but I suggest no one ask him"

With that she gave me a very solid smack on the back and stated firmly, "I think its time for you to go play the drums."

Before I could say the goodbyes and leave, Jeannette and her date, Eric something-or-other, walked up and spoke to Dr. and Mrs. Randall and nodded to the rest of us. Eric stood a step or two behind her with a forced half-grin. This was not fun territory.

"Got to congratulate you and the committee on the super decorations, Jeannie," I said sincerely, "the Parisian scene is outstanding, especially your wishing well, uh, fountain thingie. Good job."

"Thanks. I really wanted to divert the Trent River through the gym and call it the Seine but the committee balked."

"No class," I answered. "But your fountain ought to attract a few coins, if anyone can understand what the sign says."

"Someone said it means 'if you want to make a wish put a coin in here', but I don't have a clue. I'm taking Spanish."

The impish girl then leaned over to whisper in my ear: "I'll let you know how much my date throws in, but I guarantee you he isn't getting his wish."

I laughed out loud. Mrs. Barker blushed. Even though she had not heard a word of what her daughter had said, she knew her daughter. I glanced over at Ginny, gestured towards Jeannette, smiled, shrugged my shoulders and walked back to the bandstand. Middle child.

Ginny drove her parents and Charlie home about nine-thirty and returned at eleven to wait for the dance to end. When I saw her, I asked Pab to take over and Ginny and I danced to every number until ten until midnight when I reclaimed the drum throne for the last three numbers, *You'll Never Know,* a reprise of *The Theme from Moulin Rouge* and *Goodnight Sweetheart.*

When the gym lights came on and couples began to leave, Jeannette and Eric came to the bandstand. Pab and I were already breaking down the drums and the others were gathering music and stands.

"You guys were great," she exclaimed. "I'm coming to Wake Forest this fall so I'll be seeing more of you I hope." She was staring at Hank who, unfortunately for Jeanette, would not be there. I walked over to the front riser to chat with her a moment. Ginny joined us.

Breaking loose from the handholding grip of Eric, Jeanette moved up to me and whispered, "A quarter and a dime. How cheap can he get?"

"You're worth all thirty-five cents, kiddo."

As the gym emptied, and the band guys vacated the stand, it struck me then, as I'm sure it did Hank, that after more than two years of playing, this had been our last dance job. We knew it would happen one night, somewhere, sometime, but it really had not sunk in. It would in a few days.

Ginny and I waited until the trailer was loaded and all the guys had gotten into the Woodie, the Packard, Ted's sedan and Pab's convertible. We stood quietly and waved as they pulled out of the parking lot and headed back to Wake Forest, almost four hours away.

A speck of something got in my eye. Or the springtime allergies were making my eyes water a bit.

Chapter Forty

In mid-January, Will, Hank and I had quietly appeared before the Chapel Program Committee to present our case for their allowing The Southerners to play a concert for the student body in late spring as a Chapel program.

For support, we brought Julie Watkins, Sara Helen Franklin, and Bette McGhee, all members of Tassels, women's honorary society, Whitey Bright, a ministerial student and president of the Baptist Student Union and Vernon Moorehouse, debater and non-fraternity campus leader. All faculty favorites and all favoring our proposal.

Our case was based on the Louis Prima precedent and the fact we had been openly playing as a band for two years , including a half dozen major Inter-Fraternity Council events, three Monogram Club dances and five Women's Government socials. In addition, we had represented the school with dignity (for the most part) in three states, even been the reason several students had enrolled at Wake Forest, and over two years several of our players had depended on band income to help pay their college expenses. Finally, we suggested the concert be in May, prior to finals as a morale-lifter.

In spite of our pleas and solid case, we did not sense the Committee was leaning our way. It seemed they feared another Prima-type program with musical naughtiness although we had indicated our repertoire would be basic standards and no novelty stuff.

Finally, Dr. Roger Gaines, head of the Business Department, a Sunday School teacher and instructor of just about every one of us in the band at some point over our college years, spoke up.

"Initially, let me emphasize that a number of these young men have, indeed, counted on income from playing in the band to help defray the cost of going to school here. In fact, several of them have been ministerial students, and while I found it hard to believe, the band actually performed as the choir in a small church north of here when their musician brother, Randy Warren, was preaching there. I can attest to their being diligent to make their classes in the Business school, even in tuxedos on a Saturday morning (he looked at the three of us standing to the side and winked), and I believe they have been a credit to Wake Forest as they played in high schools across the state. In my judgment, they have earned the right to perform."

I wanted to applaud, whistle, stomp, hug Dr. Gaines, shake his hand and give him whatever cash I had on me. It was a very sincere, unexpected show of support and it did the job. The Committee voted to allow us to play on Friday, May 1.

When Will informed everyone, he asked that we not overdo our jubilation for fear of queering the deal somehow. "Let's just keep our heads and work towards making sure we play the best we've ever played." In spite of our best efforts, the word was out and the tension, for us, was building. We especially felt the pressure knowing this particular performance would be in the Wake Forest Chapel.

True to his word, Will selected a safe set of nine numbers to play over forty minutes, plus one additional number as an encore in case of wildly, enthusiastic popular demand.

What does a ball player feel as he, or she, goes into a very big game? What does a couple feel standing at the altar to be married? What is the pre-curtain sensation experienced by an actor performing for the first time on Broadway? A new surgeon before his first major operation?

In the slow-moving hour before the concert, we had the butterflies, the queasies, the doubts, the goose bumps, the shakes, and whatever other emotional and mental maladies could beset us. It wasn't that we were unsure of our abilities or didn't have a wealth of experience or had not played for many of the students before. It was a combination of where we were playing as the first college dance band ever to take this stage and our collective desire to make our student peers proud of us. And, of course, to prove something to the administration.

I didn't know if Hank would continue to play trumpet after graduation, or if Chick would play bass again after the June Germans. I had fleetingly considered trying to get into one of the bands that played onboard cruise ships out of New York, but abandoned the idea when I realized I was simply not good enough plus getting on with a serious advertising career would be the wiser move. At any rate, I figured this was probably going to be the last time I would ever play the drums, certainly in a dance band.

Will demanded we all have our slacks and blazers dry-cleaned for the concert even though we would be at least forty feet from the front row. He assumed the shirts would be laundered. He pointedly instructed Pab to open the curtain and not back into any equipment, chairs or other noise-making elements backstage.

Most of us cut whatever classes we had before the ten o'clock start time. After Pab had made sure the risers were positioned properly and the house sound system was working, he set up the stands and laid out the appropriate music on each stand. At 9:55 a.m. we took our places while listening to students file in and settle into their chairs on the other side of the stage curtain. They had read in the Old Gold & Black four days previously that The Southerners were the program for May 1 and they came ready to be entertained.

After several requisite announcements over the chapel sound system from backstage, Student Body president Charlie Parham said very Jimmy Capps-like: "And now, from the campus of Wake Forest College, The Southerners!"

Will gave me the signal and I began the familiar tympani roll on the floor tom-tom as Pab pulled the curtains apart ever so slowly. By the time, the beige curtains had parted ten feet Hank was on his feet hitting those first notes of *Tenderly* as the audience applauded enthusiastically.

In order we played *I'll Never Smile Again, String of Pearls, Once In Awhile, Dancing In The Dark, Lullaby of Broadway, Melancholy Rhapsody, Moonlight Serenade* and closed with *Satin Doll*. Twenty-nine minutes, twenty-seven seconds.

The students showed their appreciation loudly over several minutes as we all stood in our places and accepted the plaudits. We took their enthusiasm as a call for an encore so we went quickly into *Take The A Train* with Pab pulling the curtains slowly together about a minute into the number. We played the tune through, finishing behind closed curtains as the students filed out, continuing to clap in time to the music.

When the last notes were out and over, and the audience had pretty much left the building, we all let out a yell. We hugged each other. Mack and Norm and Augie, who had been sitting in the front row, came bounding backstage to join their former mates in the celebration. Ginny came back, and Ellen and Julie and Bette and Sara Ellen, even Whitey Bright and Vernon Moorehouse and Dr. Gaines, whom we thanked profusely.

The Chapel concert was everything we wanted it to be, and then some. A two-year mission accomplished.

Most of us who had no immediate class, or if we had a class cut to spare, walked over to the Bookstore en masse to drink in the afterglow.

Chip, however, had a class in Ancient Civilizations under Dr. Herbert Norfleet, a brilliant academic, a noted and respected historian, a Greek scholar. And a pompous, somewhat arrogant individual who had, unnoticed by us in the band, gotten up and walked out of the concert during Chip's solo on *Melancholy Rhapsody* from the movie, "Young Man With A Horn." Originally written to feature a trumpet, Chip performed it masterfully on sax with special phrasing and deep feeling.

When Chip entered the filled classroom and took his seat, Dr. Norfleet stared at him and boomed out in his distinctive, authoritative and demeaning bellow: "Mr. Mills, the saxophone is nothing more than the illegitimate offspring of the bassoon." Knowing he could take the final exam, regardless, and he had the grades to pass the course and could prove it, Chip calmly got up and walked out, joining us at the Bookstore, where he regained his composure and enthusiasm.

With Pepsi cups raised on high, we toasted each other, followed by Chip making his own toast in questionable Greek: "Επάνω σε δικούς σας, γιατρός!" to the eminent and world-renown Dr. Norfleet. While none of us understood Greek, we all got the message.

Chapter Forty-One

The IFC came through with a powerful one-two punch with the back-to-back Finals Dances in May, taking the place of the Mid-Winters usually held earlier in the year.

The swinging Tex Beneke Orchestra on Friday night, May 15, and the dynamic Harry James Orchestra on Saturday night, May 16, provided spectacular big band sounds in Raleigh's Memorial Auditorium. Friday night was semi-formal, Saturday night, formal.

This was a dream come true for musicians in two ways: we'd get to hear two of the best in the business and we'd have two nights to dance to music, not play it.

Since the dances would both be in Raleigh, I suggested to Ginny that she stay at my parents' house over the weekend. It would eliminate the back-and-forth transportation and the dorm curfews plus give us more time together with only two weeks left until graduation. The necessary parental invitation and requisite formal request to the school were expedited.

When I bummed a ride from Wake Forest to Raleigh to pick up the car and return to school to get Ginny, I was met with a shock. There, sitting in the driveway, was a new 1953 automobile! Two tone blue exterior, V8, 160 horsepower, eight cylinders, custom upholstery, electric clock, directional signals, white walls, overdrive, radio. The works!

A Chrysler DeSoto Fire Dome Deluxe! Retailing for $2740, my dad had gotten another 'deal' from his dealer-deacon friend, who promised it would get 20.92 miles to the gallon. Desoto or not, it was a step up from the grey beetle-shaped Nash and this time I did not feel as if I had to park a half block away from Johnson Dorm when I went to get Ginny. However, with all its bells and whistles it had no reclining front seat.

This was Ginny's first time staying at my house although she had been there on many occasions for meals and brief visits. My parents liked her, especially my dad who seemed to like every girl I ever brought to the house. My mother, however, was never quite sure this girl or that girl was "right" for me. I could have brought home Miss America with a Phi Beta Kappa key, double majoring in Home Economics and International Law and she would have a tough time getting a green light from my mother. Even a preacher's daughter.

And here Ginny would be, just across the hall, second floor, with my parents downstairs, for two nights. So close, but oh so far. I'm confident my mother didn't sleep a wink either night, listening for footsteps. Mine.

With only a couple of weeks left before the semester ended, for many students these would be our final college dances.

An outstanding tenor sax player and sometime vocalist, Tex Beneke had been featured on many of Glenn Miller's original numbers. His *Chattanooga Choo Choo* and *Kalamazoo* were classics. After World War II ended, Miller's widow asked Beneke to assume leadership of the old Glenn Miller band. For many years he directed the famous orchestra and kept Miller's style and arrangements. But, after he broke out on his own in the late Forties, he added some innovations, even some bebop arrangements, but continuing to play some "Miller style" music.

Although unofficially Hank, Chick and I were no longer "active" with The Southerners, we were among a half dozen who made our way to the backstage door at intermission, flashed our pale green union cards and were admitted in hopes of getting an autograph. Beneke was gracious and readily signed. After the dance, our sax man Don, who did not have a date, again went backstage and somehow wound up going with the band for some post-engagement partying.

The next night, the mustachioed trumpet virtuoso Harry James, husband of Betty Grable, brought a whole new musical meaning to *You Made Me Love You , Honeysuckle Rose, Its Been A Long, Long Time, Where or When* and *You'll Never Know* in addition to his theme song, *Ciribiribin.*

The first big band to employ vocalist Frank Sinatra, James had a long list of hits for many years, and his classic stage persona when he played solos was the stuff of greatness. Since Hank had heard James play the Beiderbecke solos for Kirk Douglas in the movie, "Young Man With A Horn," he had emulated that style. He even attempted the James back-bent, trumpet-held-high image for two years, with notable success. I wondered if he had brought his cloth trumpet case with the Charlie Spivak autograph for Harry to sign.

Again, as if on cue, at intermission several of us temporarily abandoned our dates and headed to the stage door for a one-on-one with the master bandleader, and an autograph. With a towel wrapped around his neck, the handsome James invited us into his dressing room where he signed our cards and showed genuine interest in our band. Fortunately, Hank did not have the cloth bag for James' autograph but brought the sheet music to *Ciribiribin.* Smart.

Ginny and I danced to almost every number. It appeared that all the dancers had developed a severe case of melancholy as the evening matured and wanted to savor each note. The fraternity circles took on added nostalgia as seniors in the various groups knew this was likely their final such gathering. This year I sang the words to *My Kappa Alpha Rose* with far more meaning as I held Ginny closely around the waist.

Without having to get Ginny back to Wake Forest for a curfew, and with the new DeSoto at my command, after the dance I was anxious to determine if some of my old high school parking spots were still available. That new car smell does foster romance.

On Sunday morning, Ginny joined my parents and me for church. Turn about fair play. I'm sure that night, after we had returned to school, my mother had a more restful sleep.

W ill and I had arranged a little "outing" for all the current and former members of The Southerners still at Wake Forest to celebrate two plus years of success and to salute and bid farewell to those who were leaving the band.

We decided to go to Mann's on Monday night, May 25. There would be almost no one there on a Monday night, we could push tables together and accommodate everyone, we were not likely to be thrown out if we made a little noise and it had the best big band records on the jukebox of any place around.

Hank and I were graduating in five days. Mack, an original sax player, would graduate in August. Chick, who had played bass from the get-go, was bowing out to focus on studies his final year. Ray, trombone player and one of the four who started the band with Will, Drew, and me had joined the Army and Jinx, who had spent a year with us, had enlisted in the Navy. Both planned to return to Wake Forest after serving in the military.

Chip, Don, Ted, Jud, Moe, Pab, Larry and Augie, our first piano player, and Norm, an original sax player still in school, joined us. Studying for major finals the next day kept Rick, Ronnie and Sammy from being there. Probably some of those who came should have stayed in to study, but this event was a priority. Steve, the non-musician auto expert came long as well, driving the resurrected Packard.

The only person in Mann's when we all arrived at seven thirty was a waiter. We pushed three tables together at the edge of the dance floor with seven guys seated on each side, Will and me on the ends. In a major flamboyant gesture, Will took a twenty out of his wallet and put it in the middle of the table as the waiter came to take our orders.

"These guys have made me rich and famous," he falsely boasted, "so use the twenty until it runs out. After that we'll have to go to Plan B, whatever that is, and, oh, would you bring us four dollars in quarters, please."

At three plays for a quarter, we had 16 quarters and 48 songs coming. "Each one of us gets one quarter and three selections. "About two and a half hours of non-stop music. That ought to do it."

All of us voiced our appreciation for his generosity but figured he could pay for three rounds of drinks, all that juke box action, tip the waiter and still have a buck or two left over from the twenty. We knew he had figured as much already.

When the waiter brought the four Cokes and twelve beers to the table and they had been appropriately distributed, Will stood, raised his bottle, and spoke: "Before we start telling lies about the past two years, let's toast SaraWinberg, Drew Pearsall, Hal Dewey, and Randy Warren. True pioneers, good players and great guys."

"Hear, Hear", "To Dr. Drew", "Sara was some sweetheart, for sure", "ole' Hal, whatta' great guy," "To the Rev, awwwwright!" resounded around the table, bottles clinked and first swallows were enjoyed with gusto and flourish.

Will quickly rose, walked to the Wurlitzer, dropped in a quarter and pushed Ray Anthony's recording of *Tenderly, Sentimental Me* by the Ames Brothers and *Blue Light Boogie* by Louis Jordan and his Tympany Five. Quite an eclectic combination.

Ray picked up a quarter from the table and followed quickly, selecting Louis Jordan's *Ain't Nobody Here But Us Chickens, Harbor Lights* by Sammy Kaye and Nat King Cole's *Unforgettable*. Talk about a cross-section.

"So, Hank," Chip inquired, "you and Red aren't going to play the Germans?"

"I report to the Air Force on July 6, and want to spend the four weeks after school with the family, sleeping, fishing, sleeping some more, doing nothing mostly," Hank replied.

"I take a train on Friday night, June 5, to New York. Go to work for an ad agency on the 8th. Don't think they'll let me off a week later. But," I said sincerely," if any of you guys get to New York, look me up and we'll hit Basin Street and the Metropole, Birdland, Eddie Condon's. Check out some great music."

"What about Ginny?" Jud asked.

"She's taken a teaching job in Arlington, Virginia. Gonna' get an apartment with Julie Watkins and Alice Marie Arnold in Washington. She and I and three other couples are getting together next week at Topsail Beach for four days. One last fling...for awhile anyway."

"Wait a minute," Moe broke in, "if Ginny's in Virginia, who's gonna' sing *Summertime* for us? Twice a night. "

Everybody roared, including me.

"She sure bailed our butts out of a jam, old buddy," I said in Ginny's defense. "Come to think of it, maybe I'll just fly down for the June Germans and sing *The Maharajah of Magador!*"

Before all the groans and wails died down, Mack asked Ray and Jinx when they were reporting for duty.

"They gave me until the first of July, "Ray said. 'Then Fort Jackson."

"I'm to report to the Raleigh Recruiting Office on August third and then to San Diego I hear. Maybe they'll need a sax player in the Navy band at Pearl Harbor."

"More like you and a tuba player on a tug boat in the Aleutians," Chip countered.

"Beats hauling jet fuel to Korea on a tanker." Jinx nodded and clinked bottles with his saxophone partner.

"Talking 'bout jet fuel, will you guys ever forget New Year's Eve two years ago at Cherry Point Marine Air Station? That was some night." Mack had opened the door to the "do you remembers."

"That was special, once in a lifetime," Moe agreed, "but some of you guys missed a really wild night when we marched out into the ocean at the Surf Club in Virginia Beach last summer, playing *Saints.* "

"Shoulda' kept right on marching, "Ted interjected, "and joined a bagpipe band. You'd fit right in."

"Yeah." Moe responded, "There's something about Scotch... uh, I mean *the Scots.*"

I cut him off with "How 'bout the week before at Atlantic Beach when that fight broke out? Some drunk threw a beer bottle right through the front of my bass drum!"

"What a waste of beer," Moe observed predictably.

"You all remember Lenny Joles? He played the beach jobs and several dances last fall. That guy could flat play the vibes...and the guitar," Ray added, "and he was a fantastic arranger. Guess he'll turn out to be a world class musician one of these days."

Will jumped in, "Hey, I'll bet you remember Rosalie at Wake Forest High. All those pins in her dress. Loved the way she stuck 'em right back in those dumb guys' butts. They got what they deserved. That was a funny sight."

"I'll tell you what was funny," Chip said quickly, "that's the Shriners racing those little cars all around Josh Turnage's barbecue place. That was nuts. Place full of smoke. Josh yelling and waving his towel. Those fez guys were something else!"

"I'll bet you won't forget falling out of the Woodie when we were coming back to Wake Forest one night, Moe", Don was saying across the table to his favorite piano player. "The back door somehow flew open and you just eased right on out on the asphalt when we turned on College Street. We just got you up and brushed you off. You seemed okay. You were so limp we could hardly haul you back in"

"I fell out of the Woodie?" Moe asked, surprised. "Don't remember that."

"Waiter," Will called out. "Another round please, sir."

"I tell you what was a kick, "Hank replied quickly, "was when Will, Red, and I wore tuxes to Dr. Gentry's Advertising class after the Germans last year. Eight o'clock in the morning. We'd been up all night. Smelled very fragrant. Gentry took pity on us and sent us home. Some of you should do that this year. 'Course, you have to be stupid enough to stay up all night like we did."

Chapter Forty-Two

"Who's the big band that'll play after us at the Germans this
year?" Jud inquired

"Flanagan, I believe," Will responded.

I took a quarter out of the cash pot on the table, and studied
the many musical options. For my three selections I pushed Pee
Wee King's *Slow Poke*, *Night Train* by Buddy Morrow and Duke
Ellington's *Satin Doll.*

Round two was placed in the middle of one of the tables and
everyone reached in and seized his preferred beverage. I got up,
went over to the waiter, and ordered four bags of pork rinds. "Just
take it out of the pot."

By now, the pot was a glob of wet dollar bills and loose change,
drowning in melted ice water and condensation from the drink
bottles.

"I guarantee you, breaking down in Savannah last New Year's
Day was something to remember," Jinx brought up. "And that
preacher who fixed the Woodie. What was his name?"

"Reverend J. Henry Bowers", Hank, Will, Chip and I all shouted out in unison.

Will stood up, raised his Blue Ribbon and offered: "Another
toast to Drew and Hal and Sara and Randy. And the Reverend J.
Henry Bowers."

"To Drew and Hal and Randy and Sara and our good buddy, the
Reverend J. Henry," we responded.

"And to Steve, here, for keeping us running," Ray added, acknowledging our mechanic-in-residence." Wish you'd been with
us in Savannah."

"Hey, when you talk about Reverends, I think one of the best
memories for all of us was singing in the choir, and Moe, Chip
and Hank playing for Reverend Randy at that little church near
Franklinton," I proclaimed seriously. "That was truly inspired, un-
selfish participation by one and all."

Ray rose to his feet, raised his bottle: "To the Right Reverend
Randy. I don't know where he is but I guarantee you he's gonna'
make history, and save a bunch of souls."

"I bet he winds up with one of those TV evangelist shows like that new guy from Montreat, NC who's coming on strong...Billy Graham," I proposed.

"Or that Norman Vincent Peale guy who wrote that best seller, "The Power of Positive Thinking," Mack added.

"Don't forget my man Bishop Fulton Sheen. He's on TV every week, you know." Chick scored a point for his Catholic brethren.

We all rose and toasted Reverend Randy, and Graham, and Sheen and Peale.

"Shoulda' used grape juice for that toast," I suggested after the fact." Like at Communion."

Pab quickly interjected, "my church uses white grape juice for Communion, not red."

"White? Blood is red."

"Well, when they first started our church, the services were held in a real estate office. Had off-white carpet. They knew if anybody spilled red grape juice on that carpet the church couldn't afford to replace it, so they just went with white grape juice. Its all symbolic anyhow."

No one spoke for several minutes, pondering the rationale Pab had provided.

"Makes sense to me, "I said. Others nodded in agreement and the matter was settled.

Chick reminded us that the Turlington's Crossroads activity was his initial venture into a Baptist church, or any other non-Catholic church, and the priest who heard confessions at St. Catherine's the following week broke out laughing when Chick confessed his sin.

"You were very pious and sanctimonious in the choir loft, Chick, "Mack reminded him, "but I believe you let the plate go by without contributing."

"Had every intention to, but didn't have change for a half dollar."

Norm spoke up, "Am I the only one who remembers Ray taking off with the school teacher in Burlington? You never did fill us in on that."

"Just use your imagination. Your wildest imagination." Ray gave a Thumbs Up! salute to Norm for bringing the matter up. "Hey, I'll never forget how I almost got the crap beat out of me at that VFW club outside Oxford!"

Don spoke up, "if you hadn't put the moves on that guy's wife there would have been no trouble."

Ray sputtered, looked at Don innocently, "Man, I didn't put any moves on anybody's wife. He just thought I did. Maybe if he had stayed in the backroom gambling I might have though. She was a looker."

Larry, who had less than a year under his belt with The Southerners, but was obviously intrigued by the funny events of the past he was hearing, spoke out over the growing conversation volume, "Well, I hope we keep getting lots of work and that we have as much fun as you guys did."

"To lots of jobs and lots of fun and lots of money!" Pab was energized.

Everyone stood and toasted fun, jobs and money.

"There are a lot of things I'll remember, "Mack contributed, "like the Woodie, and the trailer about to pull the rear bumper off. I remember those bad blue cardboard stands we first had, and how none of you imbeciles knew what a Grand March was on our first job in Red Oak. And all the women's underwear Will stuck in the seat cushions for us to find. How we froze to death riding in Ray's Chevy. All those prom wishing wells. 'Course, there are some thing I'm trying to forget, too."

"Like what?" Ray wanted to know.

"Well, the hats and earrings and eye patches we had to wear. And one of you guys told that Lessie girl at Dick Frye's that I was someone she ought to hook up with. She tried to get me to go to the Hut with her after a rehearsal one night. Said she'd been there before."

Hank laughed. "That, my friend, is the solid truth. I can vouch for her being there alright, but I think it was Drew who suggested she take a crack at you. Told her you were a sexual deviate of some sort."

Mack broke back in. "Oh, that's good. Really nice. And what about that night we were coming back from a job in Raleigh and it was one o'clock in the morning and Will decides to go to this bootlegger's house over in the "Harrakin." Pitch black dark. Dirt road. Dogs started barking. Will drives up to the back door of this shack and somebody hands a paper bag out to Will. I thought I heard sirens and a shotgun firing off as we left the place. Scared me to death."

"Ahhh, such fond memories." Will was laughing and wiping his mouth on his sleeve." I'll wager there was a pint of Early Times in that bag." He paused a moment and continued, "The Hut will always have a place close to my heart. Cold, damp, smoky, convenient...and cheap."

"Let's hear it for The Hut," someone shouted out. We all rose and toasted The Hut.

"I still feel those tux pants I wore at St. Mary's riding up my rear end," Norm recalled with an agonizing look. "Indian style."

"Mine, too," Ray agreed. "And, Red, I finally figured out that country hotel riddle. No ballroom."

Chick recalled, "My pants legs came up to my ankles. Waist four sizes too big. Tough to play when you're holding your pants up with one hand and trying to hit the bass strings with the other hand, all at the same time."

"You coulda' just dropped your pants and hidden behind the bass, "Hank commented." "I believe the bass is wider than your butt. Or is it?"

Chick faked throwing his almost empty bottle at Hank, then took his pocketknife from his pants pocket and made a clanging sound on the bottle. "Time for round three, waiter, and some more of those redneck rinds. Hate to admit it, but I love rebel food. Even grits. And cornbread. Love barbecue. That's the only reason I kept playing in the band. We found the best barbecue joints."

Hank took his turn with the quarter at the jukebox, punching in three trumpeters' songs, *Harlem Nocturne* by Randy Brooks, *I Can't Get Started* by Bunny Berrigan and *Star Dreams* by Charlie Spivak.

"I hate to break the news to you, Hank," Moe shouted when he heard the Brooks trumpet being featured, "but there are other instruments in a band, you know."

"Not as far as I'm concerned," Hank yelled back candidly.

"Remember the old gal who wanted to play piano up in Thomasville, at Will's aunt's party?" Moe was laughing so hard he could hardly get a word out. "Almost pushed me off the bench until I just got up and left. When I came back, she asked me to go home with her. Said we could play some duets. Should'a gone."

"She was certainly good-looking, and built, "I reminded everyone, "especially for a 70-year- old. Just your speed, Morris. The blue hair was a nice touch."

"Still think I shoulda' gone with her. Love playing duets."

Will, laughing out loud, shouted over the din," Sometime you guys remind me to tell you about Red's playing in the pit band at this very classy, cultural event in Henderson."

"Be sure you tell the whole story, like you and the Roxie part," I reminded him.

Then, in a quick reversal, Will spoke in a hushed, almost reverent tone." You know, I don't believe anything will top our chapel concert last month. It was like we had finally been accepted. Finally been recognized by the school. I think it was a tribute to all of us for sticking together and working to make this band thing really happen. I'm really proud to be a part of The Southerners. It has been one helluva' ride. And I forgot to tell you, thanks to some help from Dr. Gaines, we can rehearse in the chapel now!"

Shouts of joy over having the chapel for rehearsals.

Once again, we all rose and this time we toasted the chapel, Dr, Gaines, and the Hut.

"To cinder blocks, mold, oil fumes, red clay mud, and the American Legion."

"And don't forget Lessie!" Hank added. Remaining on his feet, he spoke in a solemn, sincere tone. "Will, Red and I wanted to get you a parting gift. Something to show our appreciation to you for all your hard work and leadership. Something you would cherish, and would be useful..."

"...however," I chimed in, continuing the thought as Hank and I had planned, "the guy at the Texaco station wouldn't let us take the machine off the bathroom wall and have it bronzed for you..."

"So," Hank concluded, "we are giving you a one year subscription to that new magazine that's coming out this year called *Playboy.* Some 27-year-old guy named Hefner from Chicago is putting it out. They say a photo of Marilyn Monroe in the buff is going to be the centerspread! So, we figured if it will help you become the playboy you want to be, then the five bucks we blew was well-spent."

All the guys at the table jumped up, applauded and raised their bottles in a salute to Will. To Marilyn Monroe. And to her boy friend Joe DiMaggio. And to that Hefner guy.

"Long may he wave." Moe bellowed over the din.

Then Chip stood, raised his bottle of warm suds with his right hand and with his left appealed to the crowd to settle down. Then, in a most serious and sincere voice he intoned: "To Hank and Red and Mack and Ray and Chick...five great guys who have been with The Southerners from the beginning. Thanks for the music. Thanks for the friendships. You'll be missed. Good luck!"

Before everyone could join in the toast, Chip added quickly, "And to Jinx, who is about to bring havoc to the entire U.S. Navy!"

"Hear, Hear!" The cheers resounded around the room for several minutes as everyone toasted and yelled and toasted the six of us again.

For almost fifty more minutes, or five quarters' worth of jukebox time, and one more round, we joked and remembered the good times, which were getting better by the minute.

About nine thirty the money pile was exhausted. Everyone, without exception, had given his personal testimonies about being a member of the dance band from Deacon Town, the dance band from the 119-year-old college that didn't allow dancing.

I put one last quarter in the jukebox and pushed C 6 three times. *Tenderly.* Then I raised my near-empty bottle and said, "Here's to The Southerners. For the good times. The good friends. The great memories." Everyone stood and said, solemnly, "To The Southerners."

For about two or three minutes we all just stood silently, finished off our beverages and drank in that very familiar melody we had played so many times in so many places.

Finally, as he had often done before, Will tossed the Woodie keys to Mack. Ray gave his keys to Norm, Pab handed his to Augie and we all started to leave.

"Wait a minute," I shouted. "All of you line up beside me. Right here. In a straight line out to the side." Not knowing what I was up to, they all did as I asked, eight on one side, seven on the other. We were spread across the dance floor in front of the jukebox.

"Okay, on three, follow me ..."

On the count of three I started singing the notes to Les Marseilles as loudly as I could: DA DA DA DAAAA DA DAAAA DA DAAAA DA DAAAAAA...and marching across the dance floor. Like toy soldiers in a royal tattoo, marching up and back, arms entwined, then up again and back again, and again and again. The others joined in, their vocal flats and sharps blending in, and we did a Grand March, right then and there.

I lead them out of the front door into the parking lot, still singing at the top of our voices, all holding on to one another, laughing our butts off, and heading back to the familiarity of the beloved old Wake Forest campus as we had so many nights before.

"You know," I said to Will and Hank as I walked between them to the Woodie, "I don't know what the future will bring, but it just can't be any better than this."

• • • • • • • • • • •

Epilogue

During the researching and writing of this book I located and communicated with the seventeen other surviving members of The Southerners who played at some time between the spring of 1951 and May, 1953. Here is what happened to them after they left Wake Forest and where they are today (assuming they have been truthful!):

Bill Tomlinson, owner/leader/alto sax player, entered Wake Forest in 1949 after attending high school in Thomasville, NC and Staunton Military Academy. He graduated from Wake Forest in 1954 and served in the U.S. Army, including two years in Germany. Before going overseas he became the Drum Major for his military unit band at Ft. Jackson, S.C. Bill located in Raleigh, NC after the service and joined Marchant Calculator Company in sales. Three years later he entered the real estate field for several years before establishing his own auto leasing firm, one of the first in the country, which he operated for ten years. Following that he became a contractor, building spec homes and constructing interiors of commercial buildings. Ultimately he joined his wife, Addie, in representing people with disability claims berfore the Social Security Administration.

Bill retired in 1997. He and Addie relocated to Wilmington, NC in 2005. At age 78 he is Master of a 52-foot Hatteras 'convertible' boat, the Miss Addie.

It was Bill's vision and dedication that kept The Southerners alive and brought the band recognition and respect as a professional, popular, in-demand dance orchestra. He found the talent, lead rehearsals, bought the music and equipment, booked the jobs, was our traveling manager and chief promoter, paid the bills (and us!)

and is principally responsible for making it all happen.

• • • • •

Al Dew was the band's 'senior citizen.' After three years in the Navy and a year at High Point College, he came to Wake Forest in 1949. A native of Fayetteville, NC, Al played trombone in both the high school's marching band and its dance band, the Blue Knights. He was a member of the Wake Forest marching band throughout his college days and one of the two original trombonists in The Southerners, continuing until his graduation in 1952. After a short stint with an oil company in his home town he relocated to Greensboro, NC where he joined the former Jefferson Standard Life Insurance Co., spending thirty-nine years with the company in Home Office administrarive and claims areas. He retired in 1991.

Al played trombone for several years with a church orchestra in Greensboro and was an avid two-three-times-a-week tennis player until a shoulder replacement required that he retire from the game in 2007. Al's first wife passed away in 1981. He remarried and he and Jerry have celebrated 25 years together. They have a combined seven children and four grandchildren. He's 80.

• • • • •

Elias "Mack" Matthews, alto saxophone, was a quiet, dependable, conscientious and very focused native of Laurinburg, NC with a dry, understated sense of humor. Following graduation from Wake Forest in the summer session of 1953 he entered the Army and after two years mustered out of the service in Honolulu, Hawaii. He remained in the islands, working for over forty years in the auditing and accounting divisions for the State of Hawaii. He and his wife, Ruth, had two daughters. Mack did not play sax after college.

Note: Regretfully, as I was researching material for this book, Mack passed away unexpectedly of double pneumonia on April 21, 2008 at age 75. From 1992-1997 when I was working in Honolulu, he and I would "do lunch' every other month and recall many great times we had with The Southerners. He often encouraged me to write the story and prior to his passing I had one phone conversation and a follow-up letter in which he recounted several memorable incidents, which I have incorporated in the book. He was a good friend and I know he would have thoroughly enjoyed reading this story and gleefully pointing out my errors.

• • • • •

Vander Warner, Jr. of Wadesboro, NC was a high school band trumpeter who came to Wake Forest after a year at Pfeiffer College. He was president of the Wake Forest marching band and played with The Southerners from the fall of 1951 until the fall of 1952. He married in 1952 and was studying for the Baptist ministry; however, he ran low on funds and left school in early 1953. After working for a church organization in Maryland, he accepted an offer to pastor the small First Baptist Church in Pocomoke, Md. which he lead for four and a half years. Called to the Oak Grove Baptist Church in Bel Air, Md., he built it into the largest Baptist church in the state over seven and a half years.

In 1965 he became minister of Grove Avenue Baptist Church in Richmond, VA. and spent twenty-six years leading that congregation. During this time he received his degree from Virginia Commonwealth University while building the church's membership from 800 to almost 2000. He also developed and was principal speaker on "The Victory Hour", the oldest sustained television ministry in America. He was honored with a Doctor of Divinity degree by Brown Theological Seminary.

Vander assisted in starting a new church with thirteen members in 1996, helping it reach a membership of 367 in six years. One of his members was a professional musician who started a church orchestra. After more than 40 years, Vander revived his trumpet-playing, joining the group for six years. His first wife, Jane, whom he met and married while at Wake Forest, passed away in 1992. They had two daughters. He remarried (Winifred) in 1993. He has written two books, spoken across the U.S. and in many foreign countries, continues to do "fill in" preaching and operates a pastoral coaching firm called Home Before Dark. The Warners live in Chesterfield, VA. Vander is 78.

• • • • •

Richard "Dick" Beach, baritone sax and clarinet, grew up in Raleigh, NC and was in the Broughton High School marching band. After attending NC State for three years, he abandoned a mechanical engineering degree for one in mathematics, enrolling in Wake Forest in 1952. He graduated in 1954. For eight years he was band director for three rural high schools in Johnston County, NC (Smithfield, Clayton and Pine Level). Concluding he was "making far too little money" and with a wife and child, he took a sales job with National Gypsum in Durham, NC, remaining with the company for thirty years.

Dick played with the 30th Division National Guard Band for some 42 years, retiring in 1990. He and his brother, Joe, had an eight-twelve-piece band for fifteen years that went by the name The Southerners after our original band faded away in the late 1950's. Dick, 77, continues to play week-end jobs with The Continentals, a big band out of Raleigh. He and his wife, Pat, have three children and one grandchild.

• • • • •

James E. "Tiny" Mims grew up in Greensboro, NC where he played saxophone in his high school's marching band and in a four-piece combo. He was given the nickname by an older brother when an infant and the name stuck. His mother was a musician who encouraged her three sons to take up musical instruments. "Tiny" initially selected the clarinet and later mastered the alto saxophone. He came to Wake Forest in 1951, transferring to Guilford College in 1954 where he finished his degree.

Professionally known as Jim Mims, for five years after college he was in the real estate business, then joined a chemical company in credit administration. In 1967, Jim joined North Carolina National Bank and served in Greensboro, Eden, Charlotte, Raleigh and Tampa, FL., rising to Senior Vice President and Regional Executive. He became president of the banking division of First Home Federal in Greensboro in 1986 and in 1992 was named Chairman and CEO of Triad Bank, where he remained for five years until retirement.

He and his wife of 53 years, Katherine, recently relocated to High Point, NC from Greensboro. They have a son, a daughter and one grandchild. Now 75, Jim has a tree-farming business as a side venture and continues to play baritone and tenor sax several times a month with the Burt Massengale Orchestra.

• • • • •

Gilbert H. "Bud" Hames is a Forest City, NC native who played trumpet in his high school marching band and, upon entering Wake Forest in 1951, joined the college band and The Southerners immediately. He played four years with both in addition to the ROTC Band. He graduated in 1955. Following college "Bud" entered the Army and continued in the Reserves, retiring after active duty as a Lt. Colonel. Moving to Charleston, SC in 1957 he became Director of the Retail Merchants Association for four years before obtaining a franchise for International House of Pancakes (IHOP) which he operated, with his oldest son, for almost forty years.

He and his wife, Doris, have four children and "a bunch" of grandchildren. They retired to Lake Lure, NC in 2001. "Bud" is 75.

• • • • •

Hugh O. Pearson, Jr. grew up in Pinetops, NC. He entered Wake Forest in 1949 and was one of the original four founders of The Southerners. He played tenor saxaphone and clarinet with the band until entering Duke Med School in the fall of 1952. Hugh did his residency at Grady Memorial Hospital in Atlanta where he met, and married, Nancy, a volunteer "candy striper." Preferring to live in a "middle-size community", he established his General Practice of Medicine in Beaufort, SC, continuing to serve there for over forty years. His youthful appearance earned him the title of "the boy doctor behind the Piggly Wiggly," indicating his office was near the well-known grocery store.

Hugh and Nancy have three sons and four grandchildren. Nancy's health prompted the couple to move to a suburb outside Cleveland, Ohio in 2001 to be near one of his sons. Early on in his residency Hugh played the sax and clarinet "just for fun" with a group of music-minded doctors but he hasn't played in the past forty years. He is 77.

• • • • •

Agamemnon "Aggie" Hanzas, from Asheville, NC, entered Wake Forest in 1950 and graduated with a B.S. Degree in Chemistry/Biology in 1954. He was the original piano player for The Southerners and played from the onset in 1951 until early 1952. Following college he served in the military, after which he began a career in the pharmaceutical industry which ultimately spanned more than five decades. He began with Lederle Labs as a chemist and later moved into product service management in New Jersey in 1956. In 1967 he entered into regulatory affairs management with Geigy, and over the ensuing years continued in a similar capacity with four other pharmaceutical companies. He finished his career with Italian-based Sigma Tau Pharmaceuticals as Senior Regulatory Director.

Aggie was principally engaged in presenting new drugs for approval by the FDA. One of his most significant professional achievements was securing FDA approval of a break-through cardiovascular product, a calcium blocker type, anti-hypertensive drug. He retired in July, 2008 at age 75. Married in 1962, he and his wife Tina live in Potomac, Md. They have a son and a daughter. He performed in piano concerts in the late '50's and early '60's in New York and continues to play classical piano, often for private events in the D.C. area.

• • • • •

Phil Cook is a West Belmar, NJ native who came to Wake Forest in 1951 and was an original alto sax player with The Southerners. He played one semester with the band, opting to concentrate on studies and student activities "since the money was not that great and I was a Northern boy trying to acclimate." Graduating in 1955, the first WF class to graduate ROTC commissioned officers, he was assigned to Ft. McCelland, AL, then spent eighteen months in France. Lacking Officers Quarters he was "forced to rent a twenty-two room chateau for sixty dollars a month!"

During this time he met Rosemary, an English girl, and they were married in 1959. That same year he joined Motorola where he remained in various sales and sales management positions for thirty years. Upon retirement he opened a two-way radio business with his son. Now74, he continues to work in the business his son now manages. Rosemary passed away several years ago. He has three children and two grandkids and lives in Wall Township, NJ. Phil says one reason he needed to leave the band was that he didn't own a dark blue jacket and was afraid he would be caught "borrowing" his Sigma Pi brother's (Bill Johnson) jacket over and over from the closet. While he no longer plays sax he is an accomplished organist. The sax lives on as his son played the same instrument through eight years of high school and college.

• • • • •

Mary Finberg, the first vocalist for The Southerners, came to Wake Forest in 1949 from Wilmington. NC where she had sung "pop" songs on a teenage radio show. She immediately became involved in all the school's musical programs and was soloist for the Wake Forest orchestra. She left school in 1952 for employment in Raleigh but continued to go with Larry Spencer, a noted Deacon student-athlete. They were married in 1953. Following his graduation in 1954 and duty in the miliary they lived in Watertown and Syracuse, N.Y. and Toledo, Ohio where he was with the YMCA and she did substitute teaching.

Mary received her B.A. degree from the Universty of Toledo and was employed there for 23 years. She also became very involved in Christian Education and served in a variety of official church capacities. Living in Toledo, and retired, the Spencers celebrated their fifty-fifth wedding anniversary in August, 2008. They have four married sons and ten grandchildren.

• • • • •

Norwood W "Red" Pope of Raleigh, NC got the nickname from his carrot-colored hair as a kid. He entered Wake Forest in 1949 and graduated in 1953 with a B.A. Degree, English major. The drummer, he was one of the original members of The Southerners and played from 1951 until May, 1953. After college he worked for a national advertising and public relations agency in New York City for four plus years, principally in client PR and commercial broadcast management. For two years he was assistant to the Advertising Manager of R.J. Reynolds Tobacco Co. prior to entering banking in 1959. Over the next thirty-seven years he was senior marketing executive for First-Citizens Bank in North Carolina, Sun Banks of Florida in Orlando, Valley National Bank in Phoenix, AZ and First Hawaiian Bank in Honolulu. Red was a marketing columnist over thirteen years for *The American Banker* newspaper and lectured in five banking schools. He was selected one of six original members of the Bank Marketing Hall of Fame in 1995.

As a civic undertaking, in 1965 he initiated and was the driving force behind the creation of the North Carolina Zoological Park, the nation's first state-owned/operated zoo and was appointed chairman of the first NC Zoo Authority by Gov. Dan Moore. He held the post until 1972 when he relocated to Florida. Retiring in 1997 from the daily banking scene, he consulted to community banks for eight years. In 2007 he authored and published Travel*Speak,* a humorous spoof on what travels writers say about places to go, see, stay and dine. He and his wife, Linda, have been married for twenty-three years and have a combined three children and four grandchildren. They live in Scottsdale, AZ. He hasn't played the drums since 1953 but plays a mean homemade "gut bucket". He's 77 and while he has hair, it is no longer red.

• • • • •

John Brock, a Charlotte, NC native, transferred to Wake Forest from Mars Hill in 1952 and played alto sax with The Southerners until he went into the Army in 1954. Following the service, he became a newspaper reporter and at age 24 became editor and ultimately publisher of six newspapers in the Charlotte/Shelby/ Gastonia area. He was reported to be the youngest newspaper publisher in America. Ever the entrepreneur, he dabbled in real estate, headed one of the largest mechanical contracting firms in the state and manufactured antique lighting fixtures. He returned to get his degree from Mars Hill University, then a Masters in History from UNC-Charlotte, attending at night. Lured back to academia, John taught Communications, Fine Arts, English and History at Gardner-Webb University for ten years before being named a Vice President in the school's administration. Later he produced five feature-length 3-D movies and TV commercials for several years and was spokesman for The Freedom Foundation at Valley Forge on ABC TV network.

He and his wife, Barbara, an accomplished artist he met at Wake Forest, have three sons and two grandsons. They live near Pawley's Island, SC from where John continues to write weekly columns for several newspapers under the *Southern Observer* title. He has written and edited a number of books and in 2007 published a collection of many of his columns, *Southern Breezes Whistle Dixie*. He hasn't played the sax since leaving The Southerners.

• • • • •

Joe Mims, from Raleigh, came to Wake Forest in the fall of 1952 and immediately joined The Southerners as a tenor sax player. Graduating from Hugh Morson High where he was in the band, Joe also played for many years in the 30th Division National Guard Band. In addition to commuting to and from Wake Forest to classes and playing in The Southerners, Joe carried a daily morning newspaper route. The load was too much to juggle so he enlisted in the Navy in December, 1953. After his service hitch in 1957 he re-enrolled at Wake Forest and played in two small dance bands until his graduation in 1960. He was a member of the first Deacon Pep Band. Following graduation he was in a sales position with several Raleigh area companies before joining his twin brother in the beer and wine distribution business, which has operated successfully for over forty years.

Joe, 74, hasn't played sax since his college days. He has four sons, four grandsons and four granddaughters. He and his wife, Linda, live in Raleigh.

• • • • •

Kenny Jolls of Raleigh was perhaps the most accomplished musician to play with The Southerners. In addition to being featured on the vibraphone, he played guitar, piano and sax and was an arranger. A Broughon High graduate, he spent one year at NC State and transferred to Wake Forest in the fall of 1952 after playing several jobs with a combo made up of musicians from The Southerners the previous summer. He played one semester with the band before receiving a music scholarship to Indiana University in January, 1953.

Kenny would have completed his degree at IU but in 1954 he contracted polio and was hospitalized in Raleigh for a lengthy period. Recovered, he entered Duke University and completed his music degree in 1958. Having developed an interest in chemistry, he went back to NC State and earned a BS Degree in Chemical Engineering in 1961, after which he earned a Masters and PhD from the University of Illinois. In 1965 he became an assistant professor at Polytechnic Institute of Brooklyn, serving for five years. He then located to Ames, Iowa where he became a professor in Iowa State University's Department of Chemical Engineering and remains in that post today at age 74. He is divorced, and has one married son with a family.

While his focus has been on academics, his musical interests remain. He conducted a 25-piece pit orchestra at ISU for performances of *Hair, Jesus Christ Superstar* and *Bye Bye Birdie*. Ken continues to play the piano for his own enjoyment, and every Saturday afternoon he plays in an upscale candy store in Ames. He also plays vibes periodically, including on the Oveido, Spain jazz scene in the summers.

• • • • •

Barry Eubanks came to Wake Forest in1952 from New Bern, NC where he had played tenor sax in the high school band and during the summers in a small combo at the New Bern Yacht Club. In addition to his musical talents he performed as a water ski clown. He joined the sax section of The Southerners immediately and played both tenor and alto. He recalls the first notes of his first solo were played at an Inter-Fraertnity Council dance in Raleigh's Memorial Auditorium and they came out "squeaks", much to his embarrassment.

Barry left Wake Forest in the fall of 1953 to serve in the 82nd Airborne Medical Battalion as an instructor while jumping out of C 119s. Following military service he was married in 1955. He and his first wife had four daughters. He now has eleven grandchildren and one great grandchild. Barry guaduated with a BS Degree in Advertising from Richmond Polytechnic Institute, now Virginia Commonwealth University, and subsequently spent three decades in the packaging business, including opening his own packaging brokerage firm. In 2007, he married Carmen Murphy and the couple lives in Fresno, CA. Barry is 74 and while he no longer plays sax, it is sitting in a closet, just in case.

• • • • •

Fred Hastings, bass, from Huntersville, NC graduated from Wake Forest in January, 1956. Commissioned a Second Lieutenant by the ROTC he served three years in the Army and seven years in the Reserves. Following military service he joined CIGNA Corp., remaining for thirty-five years and working in Charlotte, Atlanta, Philadelphia and Orlando. After being retired from the insurance business for five years, he became a manufacturers' rep for twelve years before finally retiring in Orlando.

Fred was married in 1959 (Peggy) and they had two sons. She passed away in 1988. He remarried (Betty) in 1995, gaining another son and a daughter and now has eight grandchildren. He has served as Deacon, Elder, Trustee and lay reader in his church and been very involved for thirty-five years with Boy Scouts programs. Fred has served WFU on the Alumni Council, Alumni in Admissions program and on the major gifts leadership council. He's been on the Board of Visitors and Board of Trustees of Oak Ridge Military Academy. A traveler and sometimes golfer, he hasn't played the bass since 1955. He says he "was not very good" but had great fun being with the band guys.

• • • • •

John (Johnny) Carr, trumpet, of Goldsboro, NC, did not attend Wake Forest but played a number of jobs with The Southerners when a student at East Carolina College (University) in Greenville, NC. Prior to college he served in the military, playing trumpet in the U.S. Air Force Far East band. After receiving his business degree, majoring in accounting, he spent a year with a studio band at New York's Radio City Music Hall and most of the next year was traveling the East Coast with a large band, doing one nighters, which he terms "the worst job in the world,"

John then worked as a regional auditor with American Motors in North Carolina, followed by seventeen years in credit and bank card management with First Citizens Bank in Raleigh. He continued his career in executive credit management with the premier major appliance distributor, Warren Distributors in Raleigh. He retired to Emerald Isle near Morehead City and remained there for some 20 years until two years ago when he settled in Raleigh. He is divorced, has two grown sons, five grandchildren and one great grandchild. He continues to shoot golf in the seventies but hasn't played the trumpet in 25 years. He is Red's first cousin.

• • • • •

Of the original eleven members of The Southerners, four have passed away:

Roy Lee Fulcher, trombone, was killed in an automobile accident in Rocky Mount, NC, his home town, on October 30, 1963. He was married, had a son and operated a real estate firm which did site acquisition work for Hardee's Restaurants. He was 43.

Jack Lynn Rogers, trumpet, from Hinton, WVA, retired to Weaverville, NC, near Asheville, after a career in the Air Force. He was married. He died February 5, 2001 at age 70.

Joseph Anthony (Chuck) Lucarella, bass, native of Trenton, NJ, died on March 4, 1988 at age 56. He was living in Bucks County, PA.

Elias 'Mack' Matthews, tenor saxophone, of Laurinburg, NC, died unexpectedly of double pneumonia in Honolulu, HI, his home, on Apri 21, 2008. He was married and had two daughters. See **Epilog** above.

Also deceased:
Joseph Conrad Taylor, piano, of Lumberton, NC, was married and living in Kinston, NC when he died at age 47 on June 12, 1977.

Patsy (Pat) Carter Caveness, vocalist, of Raleigh, NC, passed away in Jacksonville, FL of cancer on January 7, 2004. She was married to a Navy pilot, Pat Caveness, who was also a NBHS graduate. They had a son and a daughter.

Paul Alvah "Al" Boyles, equipment manager/drums, a Thomasville, NC native, finished Wake Forest in 1955 and married Wake Forest May Court beauty Jean Sink. They had two children. Al had a successful real estate business in Southern California and was a parttime studio musician in Los Angeles before his death.

Joe Neil Ward, trumpet, Raleigh, NC, graduated from Duke Medical School.

Jack Upchurch, saxophone, Raleigh, NC, graduated from UNC Dental School and practiced in Raleigh.

Tommy Huff, trombone/vocals, Asheville, NC, graduated from Wake Forest in 1956. Died in Asheville.

Cary Holliday, saxophone, Raleigh, NC.

Special Note: For those who read the book, Will did not marry Ellen and Red did not marry Ginny. Both did get their fraternity pins back, however.

Some of the numbers in
The Southerners' Library

Tenderly	Mexican Hat Dance
String of Pearls	Begin The Beguine
Dancing In The Dark	The Bunny Hop
Wang Wang Blues	Amapola
Too Young	Harbor Lights
September Song	Moonlight Serenade
Night and Day	It's All In The Game
The Gypsy	I'll Be Seeing You
Stardust	It Had To Be You
Oh What It Seemed To Be	Smoke Gets In Your Eyes
White Christmas	Mona Lisa
Because of You	Mam'selle
Blue Christmas	There's A Small Hotel
I'll Never Smile Again	Unforgettable
For Sentimental Reasons	It Isn't Fair
Mood Indigo	Deep Purple
Sentimental Journey	Where Is Your Heart?
As Time Goes By	Undecided
Tuxedo Junction	I'm Confessing That I Love You
With My Eyes Wide Open	A Pretty Girl Is Like A Melody
Take The A Train	Golden Earrings
Stompin' At The Savoy	Goodnight Sweetheart
Satin Doll	Always
Flyin' Home	Winter Wonderland
Maria Elena	A Kiss To Build A Dream On
There's A Tree in the Meadow	How High The Moon
Siboney	At Last
Dream	Embraceable You
Frenesi	When The Saints Go Marching In
Serenade in Blue	Nevertheless

Laura
Someday
Fools Rush In
JaDa
Dance Ballerina Dance
Imagination
Sweet Georgia Brown
Maybe
Body and Soul
Once In Awhile
Moonlight in Vermont
Lullaby of Broadway
The Hucklebuck
Melancholy Rhapsody
Half As Much
Perfidia
High Noon (Do Not Forsake Me)
Little White Lies
Again
Green Eyes
I'll Walk Alone
Time After Time
I'v Got The Sun in the Morning
   and the Moon at Night

"Playing with The Southerners gave me an appreciation for big band music which endures to this day. There's no other sound comparable to a good five-man sax section getting with it!"
Jim "Tiny" Mims, Alto Sax, The Southerners

"When it comes to love affairs and experiences to remember, being a member of The Southerners qualifies in both instances."
Barry Eubanks, tenor saxophone, The Southerners

"Making music is a lifetime fascination. My lifetime started in college with The Southerners."
Phil Cook, alto saxophone, The Southerners

Playing with The Southerners was a dream come true. Being in that big band with good guys who were outstanding musicians made it all the more special."
Rev. Vander Warner, Jr, trumpet, The Southerners

"Certainly one very memorable "sentimental journey' about Wake Forest is to recall dancing to the wonderful music of The Southerners, from the Community Building to Raleigh's Memorial Auditorium."
Clara Ellen Francis Peeler and J.L. Peeler, Jr. WFC '53